LUCID

Crippled Dream Warrior

Brett B Jacobs

'Just a Dude'

Copyright © 2024 Brett B Jacobs

All rights reserved

The characters and events portrayed in this book are fictitious. Any similarity to real persons, living or dead, is coincidental and not intended by the author.

No part of this book may be reproduced, or stored in a retrieval system, or transmitted in any form or by any means, electronic, mechanical, photocopying, recording, or otherwise, without express written permission of the publisher.

ISBN-13: 9798326502940
ISBN-10:

Cover design by: Art Painter
Library of Congress Control Number: 2018675309
Printed in the United States of America

CONTENTS

Title Page
Copyright
Introduction
Lucid   1
Chapter 1   2
Chapter 2   11
Chapter 3   26
Chapter 4   42
Chapter 5   59
Chapter 6   76
Chapter 7   92
Chapter 8   110
Chapter 9   125
Chapter 10   143
Chapter 11   163
Chapter 12   178
Chapter 13   194
Chapter 14   209
Chapter 15   225
Chapter 16   240

Chapter 17	256
Chapter 18	276
Chapter 19	293
Chapter 20	307

INTRODUCTION

A wise man once said...

"We all face challenges from time to time in life dude. For some people, the challenges that we face never end until we close our eyes. In our dreams we can see the good and evil that every waking decision throughout our lives
created. It's there that we decide which path to take forward".

-The drunk guy eating a double cheeseburger on a park bench at 2:30am last saturday night...

LUCID

CHAPTER 1

I was six years old when my life transformed from a pretty typical existence, into a strange one. Before that day I was a normal kid trying to make friends during the second week of first grade. The private school my parents chose for me was close to home, and had the one and only thing I had demanded. Monkey bars!

I remember swinging back and forth during morning recess every chance I got. I was strong for a first grader, and all the other boys took turns trying to outlast me in various games of "Chicken." A tall boy named Billy Foster challenged me to a battle royale on one particular day, and as always I accepted.

Both of us started on opposite sides of the horizontal ladder until a little girl in our class shouted "GO." We both charged at each other swinging from bar to bar before meeting in the middle. I rocked my feet up and clashed with his shins while trying to wrap my legs around his waist. I eventually won the battle for position and clasped my ankles around his hips. That's when I began to feel it.

A cold tingle began running from the tip of my toes all the way up to the top of my head. My hands went numb, and I could feel all of my muscles beginning to cramp at the same time. Billy noticed something was wrong, but couldn't catch me in time.

I fell onto the woodchip covered ground and convulsed for a few moments before the recess lady arrived to help. She called for an ambulance just as I passed out.

The next thing I remember from that fateful day is waking up in a hospital bed, staring up at concerned faces. Both of my parents were whispering in hushed tones by the door. My arms and legs felt weird, and my fingers had a strange curled look to them.

The Doctors ran tests for days before they were able to figure out what was wrong with me. Apparently I was the lucky owner of a really rare disease. Worse yet the doctors said that there wasn't even a name for what I had. They were going to name the damn thing after me. Not even the specialist could fully explain to me or my parents exactly what was happening to me. The closest he could come was educating us on some sort of fast onset muscular dystrophy.

I remember the look on my mother's face when the prognosis sunk in. She was devastated. Her hands gently cradled the growing baby inside of her. My father tried to hold it together, but like my mother he asked the question that they both were thinking at the same time.

"Is it genetic?"

The doctor tested the fetus and was happy to report that my little brother was negative for the crippling disease that was raging through my body.

It didn't take long for the full force of my affliction to make its mark. Two months later I was relegated to a wheelchair. I couldn't use my hands, and my toes and fingers were curled up in a very unnatural way. Eating was almost impossible. My mother had to make special milkshakes so that I didn't choke to death during every meal.

After my little brother was born, things got really hard. As part of my therapy I was forced to see a psychologist once a week to keep track of my shifting depression. It was right around that time if I remember correctly that I started having extremely vivid dreams. The dreams weren't like the ones that I experienced before my disease. In these dreams I was in a place that felt just as real as the world where my body was stuck in a wheelchair.

I made the fatal mistake of telling my psychologist about how real my dreams felt. I told her all about the friends that I made there, and all the things that I could do. I told her that I believed the place I went in my dreams was a real place, not a delusion.

It never occurred to me that she would betray my trust. Two days later my mother started asking me weird questions about where I went when I dreamed. At first I think she just thought that I was being a kid with a healthy imagination. After weeks of questioning me about various things, she scheduled an appointment with a Psychiatrist.

The night before the appointment I overheard my parents arguing about something in the kitchen. I heard my father say...

"It's the best facility in the state, he'll get the specialized care he needs there! We can't keep living like this Charlotte!"

I was more stressed than normal the next morning. I didn't know the difference between Dr. Fields my Psychotherapist, and her friend Dr. Shade. My mind was focused on other things when the appointment began. Dr. Fields got my attention and pointed at a tall man with kind eyes entering the room.

She introduced the man as her friend, and told me that I could trust him. That's the only part of the ensuing conversation I can remember. He asked me questions that no one else had asked before. I liked him from the start. He seemed trustworthy, and didn't stare down at his notepad the whole time I spoke to him, like some of my other doctors were prone to do.

I told him that I was sad during the day, but at night when I sleep I'm happy again. He took in everything I had to say before excusing himself to speak with my mom and dad in the hallway. I could see that my father was nodding up and down the whole time as the doctor spoke to them. My mom came into the room and gave me a big hug.

She told me that her and my father had decided that I was going to be staying here at the Institute for a while. I didn't understand. My father then entered the room and explained that I was going to need all kinds of treatment that him and mom just couldn't give me at home. I can still remember that feeling. One of abandonment and betrayal. It was crushing, and still is when I think about it to this day.

I stuttered as I made my feelings of anger known. I told them I hated them, and that I never wanted to see either one of them again. I refused to look my mother in the eyes when she tried to give me a kiss goodbye. She told me that she would visit every chance she got, but I didn't believe her.

She was crying when dad shut her car door and walked around to the driver's side of the SUV. She waved the whole time as the car pulled around the circular drive of the building before merging onto the main road.

The sound of truck horns still set my teeth on edge to this day. I watched in slow motion as a giant semi-truck smashed through my parent's car like it was made of paper. I was frozen in fear as flames engulfed the pile of wreckage holding the only two people in this world that I knew for sure loved me. The last thing I ever saw on my mother's face was the look of utter sadness.

There's nothing quite as strong as regret. I carry as much as any person could ever handle.

My thoughts got real dark after my parents were laid to rest. My little brother Abel was taken in by mom's sister, Aunt Jodie. *At least he didn't have to see them die. He's the lucky one. He was too young when they died to know what he was truly missing.*

My disease continued to progress after the loss of my parents. Two months after losing the ability to speak, I suddenly went into remission or something. Just like before, the doctors couldn't explain it.

My dreams continued to be the only place that I felt any sort of joy. It didn't help that the doctors at the institute loaded me up with a small handful of pills three times a day. They said that they were worried that I might try and hurt myself. They acted as if I magically could stand up whenever I wanted to and jump off the roof or something! *My damn hands and feet didn't freaking work for heaven's sake!*

I did my best to communicate through the eye tracking software connected to a voice modulator on the side of my power chair. Let's just say that Stephen Hawking made it look way easier than it really is to operate. It took months for me to become efficient enough to explain how I felt to the doctors during our weekly "Wellness" meetings. The only thing that took place in those visits was the addition of some sort of new sedative to help me sleep.

Somewhere around my seventh birthday some idiot doctor new to the Institute decided to put me on a new medication. Something that he said would control my delusions about the dream world. Instead, the medication had a different side effect entirely. I started seeing shadow people. They would speak to me in languages that I seemed to barely understand, but I was afraid of them all the same.

Eventually I got used to all the dark faceless figures following me around, and convinced the doctors to take me off most of the daily anti-psychotic drug regimen. I had hoped at the time that the Shadows would go away if I stopped taking the drugs, but whatever those damn pills had set into motion was now permanent.

Fast forward eight years. I spend most of my time in a twenty by twenty room painted bright white. If I'm lucky I get about two or three hours a day of free time to motor around the gardens, or watch TV in the Rec Room. Most of the orderly's and nurses don't pay me much attention. Except Burt.

That dude is cool as hell! He takes time every shift to shoot the breeze with me. I tell him what I was up to the night before in my dream land, and he listens and takes notes. Burt's an aspiring animation artist. For Christmas last year he created an entire comic book detailing the stories I told him about my dream land. He never makes me feel like I'm crazy. Every time I finish telling him about a dream, he says, "our little secret."

Not everyone working at the Institute is nice. If Burt is on one end of the spectrum then Ms. Stella is on the other. I can't tell you how many times that angry woman has locked me in my room, or taken away my free time for no reason at all. She hates me for some reason. I always try to avoid her when she's on shift, but for some reason she always seems to seek me out. Her beady little eyes are always watching me.

Today has been a pretty good day. Burt sat beside me during lunch and helped me slurp down my daily banana flavored smoothie. I didn't even choke once this time. After lunch I drove my power chair around the garden and listened to the frogs and birds hanging out around the pond in unison with the sweet sounds of Nirvana coming through my headphones. I would probably think that this place was really pretty if I wasn't forced to live every moment here.

My afternoon appointment with Dr. Shade is productive. I convince him that he should adjust my medication schedule so that I can take my sleeping pills an hour earlier every night this week as a trial period. I try and hide the obvious nature of my ulterior motives, but the doctor see's right through them. He doesn't mind though. Over the years I've convinced him that there isn't much harm in my belief that the dream world is real.

I'm really excited to have one more hour every day in the world that feels like my real home. I try and drive around the Shadow Man waiting for me outside of the doctor's office. He's persistent though.

"Not now man!"

The Shadow blocks my path, so I drive right through him. I

don't want to swerve around a non-existent obstacle and draw the suspicion of any of the medical staff. Worse yet they might try to take away my driving privileges if I seem like a safety threat to others.

"I can't believe you just ran right through me!"

The voices that I began hearing when I was younger have never gone away. The people in the dream world speak the same language of the Shadow People in reality. It was a tough language to learn, but eventually I trained my mind to adapt to the challenge.

"I got some good news from the other side!"

I'm curious what Shadow John is about to tell me, but I don't want to let anyone see me carrying on a conversation with thin air. It's impossible to have a discreet conversation when your voice sounds like an expressionless robot.

I do my best to shake my head sideways, but it looks more like I'm having a seizure. One of the nurses on duty sees me.

"You okay Cameron?"

I shift my focus and spell out a response with my eyes. I hate the voice setting on this translator. They got me the cheap version. Maybe I'll ask for a software update for Christmas. I think it would be cool to change my modulator setting to Darth Vader's voice, or maybe Samuel L Jackson.

"I'm okay Nurse Bridget."

My robot voice sets her mind at ease, and I see her smile before bending over to read the magazine article that my little seizure had drawn her attention away from. Speaking of distracting. I can't take my eyes off the third button down on her blouse. It's rare these days that I get to see a nice set of knockers like that up close.

My wheelchair bumps into something as I stare down the unbuttoned shirt of Nurse Bridget. The object in front of me is none other than crazy Kevin. He too is staring at the boob show at the nursing station. Other than Burt, Kevin is the only other person in this place that I like to talk to. We're about the same age from what I can guess.

Kevin isn't very forthcoming. All I know about his story is that he got committed to this place after stabbing a couple of people to death when he was twelve years old.

Bridget must have felt our eyes glued onto her figure. She cocks her head to the side before calling out our poor behavior and shooing us away with a limp wrist.

"Get out of here you little perverts!"

Kevin laughs while slapping my shoulder on his way to his appointment with Dr. Shade. He's always scheduled in the time slot right after me for some reason. At least we get to say hello in passing before and after our appointments!

My heart is still racing from staring at Bridget's chest. If I could get erections I'd most likely be pitching a tent right now. From what Burt tells me, puberty is one hell of a time for a boy my age. My heart rate has been relatively calm for the last few months. A development that I have been working hard on achieving. Hopefully, I can keep it this way, and convince the doctors to take me off some of the anti-anxiety meds that make my brain feel dull and slow. It should be easier to keep a steady blood pressure now.

Thanks to Kevin and his search history, the staff finally figured out that we had bypassed the "safe search" function on the common room computer. No more looking at half-naked Instagram models for me or my fellow "Crazies" I guess. That's what some of us who live in the Institute call ourselves when none of the doctors are around.

I angle my chair down the hallway. I can see that the sun is going down over the tops of a field full of birch trees at the edge of the hospital grounds. Only a couple more hours of immobility until medication call. I can't wait to go to sleep. There are apparently big things waiting for me when I close my eyes tonight.

The night nurse helps me get into bed before tucking in the sides of my sheets and fluffing my pillow. Luckily, it's Nurse Bridget's turn to put me to bed tonight. She gives me a wink as she stuffs the edges of a black microfiber blanket under the mattress.

"You want me to put on another blanket Cameron? It might get kind of chilly tonight…"

I politely refuse and watch as she shuts the door to my room. I hear the distinct click of the lock engaging and the small blue light of the monitoring camera appear above the door. I'm all alone now. I close my eyes. Soon I won't be laying in this bed in New York. I'll be living my other life in the dream world, also known as Cyadonia.

CHAPTER 2

Before I can even open my eyes, I feel a rush of energy course through my body. Each one of my three protectors hover over my resting place in "Stone Sentinel" form.

I rise from a bed of yellow rose pedals to set them free. My hands pulse with a power that can only be described in terms of magic. I touch the three stone statues. The outer stone layer melts away at my touch.

Each one shakes off the hours of inaction and retreats from the dark place of my slumber and into the light of Cyadonia. I can see their skin soaking in the radiant glow of the violet sky, and I rush to stand beside them at the precipice of a stone staircase leading down.

John stretches out one of his six arms while yawning deeply and taking in the fresh air of the temple peak. His thin bird beak twitches slightly as a tiny breeze enters his nostrils. Beside him stands his life partner Ruth. In the dream world she takes the shape of a human. Unlike her husband and son, she prefers to maintain one form in both worlds.

Her son Fred follows in his father's footsteps. He stands beside his parents in his Guardian form. Two stubby horns protrude from his lion shaped head. His wings extend the length of his body on either side. The fluffy puff of fur on his tail flips around to ward off the flying insects attracted to his smell. I'm sure that to the normal person we look like quite a crazy little family!

The temple that protects me in my absence is situated in the heart of the "City of Light." The people who live here call it

Immaru. I just call it home. Small groups of blue birds chirp and flutter from tree branch to tree branch feeding their newly hatched nestlings as we all stare out at the morning light.

Since I was a boy this place has been my only refuge from my pain and suffering in the real world.

A tiny man slowly walks up the stone stairs leading toward me and my Guardians. He holds in his hand a curved staff made from the heart of a sacred oak tree. I am intimately familiar with this wooden staff. It has been the bane of my existence here since we were first introduced to one another. Many a bruise has been formed on my body with that damn piece of wood.

His name is Thoth, but he prefers if I just call him "Wise Teacher." For some reason he doesn't think I have earned the right to use his real name yet.

The Wise Teacher has been training me in the use of magic and sorcery since I was a little boy. He has been training the protectors of Immaru for countless generations. I just so happen to be his latest pupil. I often think that he might be disappointed with my progress. He keeps saying that I'm not ready.

Little does he know that I've been sneaking away with my trio of Guardians for the better part of two years to fight in battles that he doesn't even know about. Or does he? I can't be sure if he is just faking ignorance. I wouldn't put it past him.

The battles that I speak of are becoming more frequent during my time spent in this realm. This world consists of five large civilizations. Immaru is home to the people of the light, or what I call "Littles." They are a people small in stature, but big in love and empathy for others. What they lack in physical traits they more than make up for with their magical talents. They very rarely make war, and for the most part try and stay out of the politics of the rest of the realm.

I look out past the Wise Teacher climbing the stone stairs and see the unpassable mountains to the west of the city walls. The magical peaks of the Breathing Mountain range denies access to the territory of Immaru from the western approaches. Old magic exists there. Magic that not even the Wise Teacher will tell me about.

Immaru is ruled by the beautiful Queen of Rain. She is really freaking hot. Like super model hot, but also, like, approachable. I have a major crush on her. Unfortunately for me the Wise Teacher says that she doesn't go for guys younger than her. I'd say that's a problem for me considering that she's at least a thousand years old or something. She looks good for her age though!

To the north of the city lies the Kingdom of Plenty. The people there are pretty much like the humans of the middle ages. They make war on horseback, and wear suits of armor. They're the closest thing to an ally that Immaru can speak of. As I say that, I think I should amend my statement. They are more like neutral partners in not dying.

A great King named Nero rules over the Kingdom of Plenty. His people worship him as a god, and his reputation for protecting the common folk from the forces of evil surrounding their Kingdom has kept him in power for generations. Most of the common folk living in the Kingdom are simple farmers, and most have no ability to wield the magic of the realm in their own defense. They have always been flanked to the north and west by an undying evil.

I speak of the lands of Gomorrah. These lands are surrounded by borders of thick black fog, and contain a magic that is truly evil. Some people in the realm call the Lands of Gomorrah the land of darkness, or the Demon lands. I get the references. The armies of darkness in those lands are made up of ferocious beasts, and actual Demons.

I have fought these beasts now on many occasions. They are

large disfigured creatures who wield a magic that attacks not just in a physical manner, but also exploits your own fears. Those are just the Demon's though. Often I'm forced to fight off small incursions of disfigured beasts that have wandered across the border and into the Kingdom of Plenty.

The land of Gomorrah is ruled by a Demon named Gallus. I don't know much about him. The Wise Teacher won't tell me anything about him, and none of the citizens of Immaru will utter his name. It's like the guy is freaking Lord Voldemort or something.

To the east are the lands of the Sky Gods. A vast wall of shimmering magic protects the borders of this region. No form of evil creature or Demon can penetrate the ancient magic of the Wall Of Judgment. I went there one time to see the wall for myself. I couldn't resist after hearing the Wise Teacher tell me of the two tribes that are protected by the wall.

I remember him telling me that only the purest of heart can penetrate the wall. Those with ill intentions will be denied passage through the magic barrier, and punished according to each shortcoming the magic incantations identify. Lucky for me I only got a quick jolt of electricity when I touched it. *Too much lustful Instagram scrolling apparently!*

Behind the Wall of Judgement, the Gods of the sky realm make their home among the tallest mountain fortresses. Very few people have ever seen the Sky Gods, none the less been fortunate enough to speak with them. As a "Centurian" I have always hoped to meet them one day, and if everything goes to plan be given a heroic task to complete.

I very much wish to earn their favor. My Wise Teacher says that If the Sky Gods are impressed enough with me, they might use their magic to let me live in this realm for the rest of my mortal life. That would be quite an upgrade, considering that creatures in this realm can live for hundreds if not thousands of years.

I hear the sound of a deep breath before I feel the sting of wood on my shin. I had totally zoned out and forgot to bow in greeting to the Wise Teacher. This mistake was a great disrespect, and was punished swiftly.

I hop up and down on my good leg while grasping at a swelling section of shin bone.

"Dang, take it easy man!"

I watch closely as the Wise Teacher grips his staff firmly in hand.

"I didn't mean it Wise Teacher… Please forgive me?"

He raises the curved staff and examines the sincerity of my apology before slapping the stone stair next to my foot. John, Ruth, and Fred all watch quietly, afraid to draw the ire of my teacher. I can see that they're all just as afraid of his punishment as I am. These three Guardians are responsible for my safety and security at all times, and in both realms.

Every time I leave this realm and return to my crippled body, their bodies in his realm turn to stone until I return. In this way we are all vulnerable to attack when I'm gone. I'm not fully sure how it all works, but somehow this realm and the world where I am crippled are connected somehow. In the real world my Guardians only have the ability to exist as shadows. Kind of like ghosts, that only I can see.

I'm not the only one like me. There are others. Most of whom I have never met, and will never meet in this lifetime. The Sky Gods are responsible for our creation, but they do not dictate the peoples that we serve. That alone is our choice. The only other Centurian I have been able to meet is a Goddess named Beth. We aren't supposed to tell one another where we exist in the real world, but just knowing that I am not alone is comforting beyond words. I wish that we could meet in real life, but I'm not exactly capable of traveling.

The Wise Teacher interrupts my thoughts again.

"You have been summoned by the Sky Gods! I must take you to the Celestial door in the Rain Palace!"

I get excited at the prospect that I might get to see the Queen again. The Wise Teacher points down the winding stone stairs leading to the city below my pyramid shrine. We all descend as quickly as possible. Thoth glides down the path using his magic to levitate over each step effortlessly. I try to emulate him, but trip and fall hard enough to decide to just climb down the old fashion way.

My three Guardians keep a close eye on me during the journey through the bustling city. Each citizen we pass is much smaller than me. I tower over them like a giant. Most smile and bow when I pass by, and some I recognize from the lunar festival the people throw once every few months. That's my favorite time to be here by far.

There's dancing, and drinking, and sky shows like you can't even imagine. You think that the good old United States of America knows how to put on a good fireworks display? Forget about it! These guys know how to literally light the sky on fire. Good thing we have the Queen of Rain to keep the city from burning down.

We weave through streets made of green glass. The busy road separates massive hollow step pyramids on either side. Each structure is covered in smooth white stone. At the top of each pyramid is a giant diamond that emits a light that shines down on everything below it. From each diamond a stream of invisible energy powers every machine and light within the city and beyond.

We pass over a gentle stream atop a glass bridge. Small roaming groups of dragonfly's fill the voids between ornate gardens filled with flowers of every imaginable color. This part of the city reminds me a little bit of the gardens outside of the Institute. The one that my body is currently locked up inside. *In more than one way if you get my drift?*

I get excited and feel my heart start to race when I see a glowing orb connected to a black rope. The Orb pulses in white light as the Wise Teacher places his hand on the surface. He is levitated into the air and carried alongside the black rope towards a massive structure at the top of a hill. I watch as he zooms away before I can place my own hand on the glowing orb.

My feet leave the ground after I feel a pulse of electricity flow through my chest. I'm flung forward as if I've been shot out of a cannon. The black rope guides my journey to the top of the hill that the Wise Teacher was whisked away towards.

On top of the hill is a massive castle decorated in green vines flowering with white blooms. The stone walls are made of perfectly fitted gargantuan stones, and have a quality that suggests that they have been melted to fit together tightly.

The castle is shaped like a six pointed star. In the center of the stone fortress are four towers made out of a material that looks like green sea glass. Rising above and out of the center of those towers is an octagonal tower that emits a storm like quality. It looks as if the stone itself is made of the most violent thunderstorm. I can see what looks like dark clouds and lightning inside the outer surface of the stones.

We walk past the main gate and greet the two stone statues guarding the castle. They look like formidable warriors. I wouldn't even know how to fight a giant made of stone. While daydreaming about that unlikely scenario, I can feel electricity and fire pulse in my palms.

One of my gifts in this realm is my ability to control certain elements. Mainly Lightning, but I can also summon up a pretty potent fireball when the need arises. I'm also pretty proficient with a blade. A skill that has been drilled into me by Thoth since I arrived here as a child. The thought makes me realize that I didn't bring any weapons with me on this visit. I feel a little naked without at least having a sword strapped to my hip.

I guess my lightning hands will have to do the trick if anything goes down.

We enter the main tower and approach a circular pattern in the middle of the floor. Thoth points into the circle and shoves me forward.

"You must meet with the Sky Gods alone! The Queen of Rain will help you navigate the "Celestial Door" at the top of the tower."

I'm confused. I've never been to the top of the tower before. I don't know how to get there, or what to expect. The last time I met with the Queen of Rain we just chatted in one of the smaller towers nearer to the ground.

Thoth points again at the circle on the floor before shoving the blunt end of his staff into the small of my back. I lunge forward and stand atop a small pool of glimmering water. I place my hands out to my side.

"What now?"

As I say the sarcastic words, I feel the first drop of rain hit the top of my head. A wall of white smoke surrounds my body collecting the water falling from above. My feet stay firmly affixed to the top of the water pool forming underneath me. *I didn't know I could walk on water!* This is a new sensation entirely!

The rain from above gets more intense, and I realize that as the area below me fills with water, I am quickly rising up into the air. I must be at least five hundred feet in the air when I see a hole open up in the ceiling. I burst through the hole, and the rain stops falling.

The floor beneath my feet is now solid. I glance to my right and see the Queen of Rain grinning from ear to ear. Her long black hair is woven together with sprigs of golden leaves. Her gown is made from a silken material that glows with an intense light. She wears a necklace of bright blue stones, and her fingers are adorned by raindrop shaped diamonds.

I bow politely before engaging in the playful banter that she has come to expect from me. I'm soaked to the bone from her little rain shower.

"Your Highness! I appreciate the lift…"

I pause and wait for her to respond to my sarcastic statement. I'm dripping from head to toe, and the miserable look on my face must be sticking out.

I watch as her lips curl into a mischievous smile. She has a pretty dirty mind for a goddess, and loves it when I make inappropriate, or sarcastic jokes. It's one of the things that I like most about her. She has a strangely human feel about her.

"I apologize that you had to get a little wet to get up here!"

She reaches forward with both hands and twists her fingers in my direction. I feel the moisture leave my body and clothes before materializing in the air around me. I then watch as the rain drops produced from my body evaporate into thin air.

"That's a pretty neat trick…"

She plays along.

"I do know how to turn a good trick you know!"

I look at her sideways before seeing the grin appear on her face.

She points at a small pile of items resting on the floor.

Sitting there is my favorite blue steel sword, and a set of light armor covered in diamond dust.

"Thanks! I forgot my stuff down at the shrine."

She turns her back as I strip off my shirt and trousers and put on the set of armor. I'm pretty sure she might have peeked a couple times when my shirt was off. No way of telling for sure though. Probably wishful thinking!

After I'm fully clothed she turns back around.

"Thanks again!"

"No problem young Centurian! I knew that you couldn't 'Get Up' without my help…"

This time I'm not sure if she's aware of the inuendo in the statement. I'm pretty sure she is.

The Queen of Rain points towards a rectangular stone cutout along the far wall of the chamber we are standing in. Surrounding the angular alcove are inscriptions written in glyphs and symbols that I can't recognize.

She places her hand against the stone glyphs and begins to sing a melody that puts me into a trance like state. The stone glyphs illuminate in a fire like color and begin to dance and vibrate to the melody of her words. She stops singing and claps her hands together one time before extending her fingers to the center of the cutout.

A bright blue light replaces the stone surface that I was looking at only seconds before.

She points into the center of the magical doorway.

"God speed young Centurian. Be wise, and speak only the truth. And be wary of the Gods of the Sky. They speak riddles that very few can solve. Though they might be representatives of the Creator, I sometimes feel that their power and control over the people of this realm are more important to them than the 'Will' of the Creator they serve!"

I turn and bow in respect before entering the doorway.

This magical door isn't like any of the ones I've seen in the movies. I'm not whisked away anywhere. Instead I'm walking under my own power on a road made of stars. I can't stop looking down. The road itself is more beautiful than anything I have ever laid eyes on.

Ahead I can see seven magical doors. All of the doors are

covered in a thick layer of ice, illuminated by a red glow, except one. The second door to the right I can see is pulsating in a color that I could only describe as yellow fire. I poke the surface of the door beside the one I know I should be going through. A cold feeling shocks my finger.

I flex my hand into a fist trying to regain feeling in it after my stupid decision to touch the other door has backfired. I walk a few more paces before reaching a flat palm against the door that I instinctually feel I'm allowed to travel. I can't help but wonder where the other doors lead to.

I feel a warmth rush through my body. I close my eyes before walking through the glowing stone door in front of me.

After passing through the stone surface, I decide to open my eyes again. Sitting in front of me on three stone thrones are massive humanlike shapes surrounded by impenetrable light. I shield my eyes with my hand and bow in reverence as Thoth has taught me to do.

A booming voice echoes in the Throne Room of the Sky Gods. My eyes can't handle the light coming off of my hosts, and I decide to keep my eyes on the floor until they can adjust. I can see out of my peripheral vision that the room is decorated in fine metals and polished stone. I see white marble statues on the outer edge of the room depicting familiar gods that I recognize from ancient temples in the real world.

"Welcome young Centurian! We are most pleased that you have accepted our invitation."

My mind races. *I wasn't aware that I had a choice in the matter. Thoth sure didn't mention anything about a choice.*

"I was honored to be invited."

I can almost tolerate the angelic light coming from the three gods sitting before me when I decide to lift my head up.

I still can't make out their faces very well, but at least I can tolerate looking in their general direction with a heavy squint.

"I would have brought my sunglasses if I knew it was gonna be so bright?"

I don't get the reaction I was expecting after trying to make a joke.

"I apologize, I was just trying to lighten the mood!"

Apparently the Sky Gods don't appreciate a good pun. The Queen of Rain would be rolling with laughter if she could see me now.

"We did not ask you here to entertain us with your ill-gotten humor Centurian!"

Somehow I've already managed to piss off the three most powerful beings in all of Cyadonia. *Nice work man!* My confidence is shot now.

"We have asked you to come in order to warn you of a great danger that is coming. A danger that could affect you both here in Cyadonia, and in the place you refer to as "The Real World"!"

I'm confused as to how they know what I call the place I go when I'm taken away from this realm. The only person in Cyadonia that I have ever told that information is Thoth. I didn't think that he would sell me out like this.

"Fear not young Centurian. We know more than you could possibly imagine. Turn your eyes to the sky."

I look up and watch as the stone roof disappears and is replaced by a sky filled with small clumps of white clouds. The Sky God sitting atop the center throne reaches his hand up and swipes it to the side in a brisk motion. All of the clouds clear out of the way revealing a large blue crack in the atmosphere.

"What the hell is that?"

The ceiling turns back into stone as my words echo in the hall.

"That is a rip in the fabric that separates this world from the world where your broken body slumbers!"

"The Demon lord of Gomorrah has discovered a weakness in the protective magics that we have used to keep our worlds apart. We fear that he has sent his dark minions into your world to hunt down and destroy any Centurian that threatens his dominance in this world."

"And I'm guessing that I would probably fit into that category… Right?"

I feel a deep seeded fear begin to bubble up in my stomach. A fear that is normally reserved for the crippled body I inhabit in the Real World.

"Can't you just close the blue hole thingy? You do know that I can't exactly defend myself back there… Right?"

"We are well aware of your limitations in the human realm."

Three black stones appear next to my foot as if arriving out of thin air.

"Take the Stones of Arafat and give them to your Guardians. The magic contained within the stones will allow them to interact with the realm of man. Go now before it is too late!"

I feel an insane rush of adrenaline fill my blood. The stone door that I came through begins pulsating in fire colored light. I walk through with more confidence this time. The star filled floor glimmers with a cosmic significance. I wish that I had more time to admire its majesty. Instead my feet break into a run towards the glowing blue door in the distance. Before I jump through it, I glance back and take one more look at the seven ice covered cosmic doors.

The Queen of Rain is waiting for me when I arrive. She's surprised that I am back so quickly. I try to explain as quickly as I can and describe the blue rip in the sky. She waves her arms in the air and disappears on top of a wave of water through one of the tower windows.

I'm worried that she has just accidentally killed herself. My worry dissipates when she comes back through the same window surfing the same wave.

"What you say is true young Centurian! It is not only you who is in danger. We must protect the Kingdoms of man and beast. We have no idea what this evil omen could bring. Your world is no longer safe! Go now and save yourself!"

"How the hell am I supposed to save myself? I'm a damn cripple in a wheelchair!"

I hold out my hand with the three black stones given to me by the Sky Gods.

"You hold the Stones of Arafat! Go quickly and give them to your Guardians! They are the only ones who can save you now!"

The Queen of Rain begins surrounding me with a whirlpool of water. I'm violently thrown out the window. I fall for a brief moment before my rear end touches down on a surface of water flowing quickly at a steep angle towards the front gate of the castle. It's the coolest water slide in the history of water slides.

I hit the ground running. Thoth is waiting for me, and he seems more alarmed than usual.

"We must get you back to your shrine!"

My Guardians look equally concerned as I look around for comfort and reassurance. We all run tirelessly up the long stone staircase leading to my shrine. I enter the shrine and turn to face my three Guardians.

"It's up to you guys to save me in the Human world! Here!"

They look confused before I open my fist and reveal the three stones in hand. All three look at one another as if they have won the lottery. I hand a black stone to each one of them.

Ruth places the stone into her mouth and swallows hard. I watch as John and Fred follow her lead.

I lay down on the bed of flower pedals on top of my stone

shrine and close my eyes. Normally I'm here a few more hours, but time seems to be against us all this night. I can feel my strength waning until it is gone entirely.

CHAPTER 3

I wake up and see that the clock reads 3:33 in the morning. I can feel the deep fear bubbling up inside of me getting stronger. *Of course it had to be the exact same time that all those damn Demon possession movies take place*! I make a mental note to stop watching scary movies so often.

Outside of my tiny window the trees are swaying in a heavy wind. The clouds look dark as though a strong thunderstorm is brewing in the distance. A crack of lightning on the other side of a thin glass window sends my nerves on edge.

I don't feel very safe laying in this bed. Every instinct I possess is telling me that I'm in imminent danger. I hear the lock to my door turn and click open. I tilt my eyeballs as best as I can towards the door. A tall man enters the room wearing a long white doctors coat. I can't make out his face in the shadows. He approaches my bed. I can see that the name badge says Dr. Shade, but I know that this face does not belong to my doctor.

The man lifts my body out of bed as if I'm as light as a feather.

"We got to get you out of here! They're coming!"

I immediately recognize the voice. Normally this voice comes from a useless shadow figure. This time it belongs to a tall muscular man. I've never seen John in this human form before.

In the 'Dream land' he's a six armed blue birdlike creature. This form fits him better though. I never liked the look of his thin little beak in Cyadonia.

He places me in my wheelchair and grabs the voice modulator from my power chair. His fingers work quick and install the device to the smaller chair he intends to whisk me away in. The only downside is that I won't be able to control the chair myself. I will be completely reliant on someone else to move me around.

Not that my power chair is fast or anything. I would probably be better off trying to run away in one of those battery operated Fisher Price Jeeps that they make for toddlers.

I hear the uncanny buzzing sound that signals the unlocking of every door in my section of the facility. There are loud clicking sounds followed by the inevitable creaking of opening doors.

"What's the plan John?" John wheels my chair towards the door and positions me outside of the view of the tiny round window. He peers through while looking for something or someone.

We're both startled when a flat hand hits the glass. John jumps backwards and raises his hand like he's going to cast a spell of protection. He relaxes after seeing the grinning face of Fred. Fred smashes his cheek against the window and slowly melts downward causing his lips to quiver.

"Quit monkeying around and help me with him!"

The door swings open and Fred steps behind my chair. I think that out of all three of my Guardians he's my favorite. He has a knack for finding the bright side of every situation. I can't imagine living the rest of my life sitting in this chair without his dumb motivational speeches.

John peers out the door like he's looking for something.

"Where is she at Fred. I gave her one job to do!"

We all hear the sound of breaking glass, followed by a familiar roar coming from somewhere inside of the facility. I watch as half-dressed psychiatric patients run down the hallway towards the security door at the end of the wing. I can't handle the suspense anymore.

"What's happening guys?"

The sound of my robotic voice always makes Fred crack a smile.

"Ruth is out there seeing what we're up against!"

I feel a bit of drool slide out of my mouth. Fred pulls down his sleeve and wipes my mouth before making a sarcastic comment about my drooling over the coming fight. He can be a real insensitive guy sometimes. I hate that I'm pretty much useless right now.

The sound of squeaking sneakers on the hallway floor snaps me out of the depressing thought.

Ruth slides to a stop after passing right by my door. She turns back around and shoves a small girl away from the side of my door where she had been leaning against the wall making whimpering sounds.

"We need to get moving! There are six of them out there! Four of the small ones, and two of the big guys!"

Ruth reaches forward and hands both John and Fred the sharpened kitchen utensils that she had gathered from the mess hall. John looks down at the pronged meat fork clutched in his right hand.

"This is all you could get?"

She shakes her head incredulously.

"It's a mental hospital for crazy people John! They don't exactly have a wide selection of items that can be used to stab someone!"

Fred cackle laughs while holding the tiny kitchen knife that Ruth has just handed him.

"I can work with this. If we win this fight with kitchen tools…"

He pauses and looks at his two fellow Guardians like he wants them to finish his statement.

"We will be freaking legends back home!"

John peers around the door frame before turning back to respond to Fred's ludicrous comment.

"That's a pretty big "IF" son!"

I guess that now would be a good time to explain the dynamic between my three Guardians. The people of Cyadonia Call them the Trinity. John and Ruth are life partners, and Fred is their son. He's very close to my age in appearance, but due to a difference in the way time flows in the dream land, he's much closer to thirty years old here in the human realm.

I think that the Trinity reference is a myth to some of the Christian teachings here on earth. John is the Father, Fred is the Son, and Ruth is the Holy Spirit. It has always made sense to me. Of the three, Ruth has always been the most powerful of them. She has a rare talent to be able to manipulate matter using her magic.

None of that matters here in the human world though. Magic doesn't exist here!

Fred pushes my wheelchair out of the bedroom before hanging a quick right leading toward the interior of the facility. I protest at first.

"But the outer door is that way!"

If I could point back in the other direction of the hallway I would! John shakes his head at me and then puts his finger up to his lips.

"Shhhhhh. Keep your damn robot voice down!"

I can't help that the volume settings are set too high on my voice speaker. I decide that it's better if I just let them do their jobs to keep me safe in silence.

Ruth opens the door to the recreation room and enters with a large butcher knife in hand. She has obviously kept the best kitchen weapon for her own use. I'm not opposed to it though.

I breathe in the air wafting through the hallway. I feel a slight shiver run down my spine as soon as I identify the smell of freshly mown grass and rotten eggs.

John must smell it too. He looks at me with wide eyes and snaps his finger to get Fred's attention. I feel Fred grab the back of my chair and turn me around to face the opposite direction. I hate the fact that he has now faced me away from the coming action.

Behind me I hear a large window shatter. There is a Demonic scream that makes me wish with every fiber of my body that I could stand up and run away.

I hear yelling from Ruth and John as they battle the creature in the Recreation Room behind me. I feel a massive burst of energy hit me in the back of my head. The sound of hand to hand fighting is over. I can almost feel the nervous energy coming off of Fred as he looks behind me at the battle results.

He cracks a smile, and I know that John and Ruth must have won the fight. They both appear by the side of my chair. John had traded in his meat fork for a small knife made from black and green obsidian. He looks like he's about to say something when the door down the hallway is kicked off of the hinges, and slides to a rest at the foot of my chair.

Three small Demon Warriors enter the hallway followed by a large horned beast. Each one looks as if they have been dipped in black tar. The smaller warriors look more like standing goats than human. They stand on their hind hoofs holding long spears tipped with stone points.

The larger beast looks like what would happen if a snake had a baby with a minotaur. Its skin is covered in scales reminiscent of a beast that should slither instead of walk. In its hand is a knife similar to the one John is now holding in his own hand.

All three of my Guardians rush forward to attack. I'm fearful that they might not be able to prevail in the coming fight. My eyes ache while following the action without blinking.

John tackles two of the smaller Demon Warriors after sliding between their thrusting spears. Fred is close behind and dislodges one of the spears from his enemy. He wields the spear as if he has been training with it his entire life. Ruth wastes no time and slashes back and forth at the largest Demon. He counters while avoiding her knife thrusts and kicks her in the chest. I can't help but imagine the Demon screaming "This is Sparta!" *I probably watch too many movies!*

Her body slides to a stop right at my feet.

"Well, that wasn't how I saw that going in my head!"

She gets back to her feet and rushes back towards the ensuing battle. Fred is pinned against the wall by two of the smaller Demons when a knife thrust from his passing mother evens the odds for him. The wounded Demon falls to the ground while clutching for the knife slash at the back of its neck. As it falls to the floor, a bright blue light engulfs its body and collapses its corpse into a ball of lightless energy that disappears.

Fred gains the upper hand on his foe before thrusting the spear that he has stolen through the belly of the horned beast. He places the heel of his boot against the creatures chest as it falls to its knees. With a quick kick the dying Demon dislodges from the spear tip, and skids across the hallway floor hitting the side of my chair. I'm turned slightly sideways as a ball of light engulfs the dying Demon and takes it back to the dream land.

I struggle to watch the rest of the fight taking place down the hallway. My chair is now perpendicular in the secure corridor, and I can only use my peripheral vision to keep track of things. I hear a loud scream of pain. It sounded like Ruth's voice. I hate not being able to see what's happening. I can feel a wave of energy hitting the side of my chair. It rotates my chair even further away from the battle.

I'm now staring at the door leading to the Recreation Room. I hear John yell out in pain this time. There is a loud thump followed by a Demonic scream. I hope that the scream is one of pain, not victory. A burst of light brighter than the first two fills the hallway behind me.

I breathe in deeply hoping that the battle is over. Instead of safety, I smell the distinct odor of mowed grass again. My worst fear is now standing in the doorway to the Recreation Room looking down at me. Thick black tar covers every inch of the scaled skin that my eyes paint over. Its eyes look like glowing embers from a dying campfire. Its breath is rhythmic, and smells of rotten eggs and sulfur.

My eyes shift down and I can see that the Demon is holding the handle of a long obsidian blade. I'm defenseless. The sounds of battle are still echoing down the hallway from behind me. I make every attempt to move. Every attempt I can muster to summon my power in defense. If this battle was taking place in the dream land I would have already melted this Demon with bolts of lightning, or chopped it in half with my sword.

Alas I am not in Cyadonia. Here, in this world, I am just a crippled boy with twisted fingers and broken legs.

I can hear the sounds of Demonic chanting coming from the approaching creature. It raises its blade while standing over me. I close my eyes and wait for death to take me.

Instead I hear the distinct sound of a deep inhale, preceded by two gentle squishing sounds. My cheek is covered in a splash of fluid. I open my eyes and see the two broken ends of a pool stick protruding from the chest of the Demon standing over me with blade raised overhead. A bright ball of light blocks my vision of which one of my Guardians has saved me this time. When the light disappears I'm shocked to see who's holding the makeshift wooden spears.

Crazy Kevin looks down at me in disbelief while holding either end of the broken pool cue. There's a sharp pop of light behind me before my three Guardians return and stand beside me gasping for air.

"Holy crap, Did you see that? Crazy Kevin just killed that Demon!"

Fred approaches and reaches his hand out to shake Kevin's hand. He is met with a firm refusal before Kevin speaks.

"I'm sorry that you guys had to experience all this."

I'm shocked to hear Kevin speaking in this way. It isn't clear to me why he thinks that this whole thing is his fault. I can tell that Ruth and John are confused as well. John steps forward.

"You don't need to be sorry Kevin... It's not your fault this happened."

He lowers the ends of the broken pool cue and makes eye contact with my Guardians.

"You don't know what you're talking about. They came here to get me! I've been waiting for them to find me for years now. You guys should get out of here before more show up."

None of us can figure out what the heck Crazy Kevin is talking about. Ruth tries her hand at talking with the crazy eyed boy.

"They weren't after YOU Kevin! They were trying to kill Cameron!"

I can see the confusion on Kevin's face. He pauses for a moment before looking at me with his patented crazy eyes.

"You can see the Demons too?"

I aim my eyes toward the computer tablet that tracks my movement as it formulates my voice commands.

"Of course I can see them... So can my Guardians here! Are you telling me that you've seen these creatures before tonight? Is that what you're trying to tell me Kevin?"

I can see that Kevin is still confused. He looks to be trying to decide how much of his life story he wants to reveal to us.

Almost like he doesn't trust me for some reason.

"Those Demon things are the reason they locked me up in this place in the first place! I thought that I was the only one who could see them. These ones are different though. Usually they don't look like this. Except the eyes, the eyes are always the same!"

John snaps his fingers to get everyone's attention back.

"As much as we're all curious, we should probably get out of here Cameron!"

I agree. I'm not sure how the Demons knew where I was hiding in the human world. It's not like I have a homing beacon or anything. I can see that John is wondering the same thing. He also seems to be looking at Kevin like he's searching for something else. Some reason to believe his story.

"Ruth has a van waiting in the back. We should head that way and get as far away from here as possible!"

Fred pushes my chair as my other two Guardians scout ahead for danger. Kevin is trotting beside my chair still holding the two sides of a broken pool cue. He slides around me before every corner. His feet are covered by fluffy bunny slippers. I can tell that this whole thing is exciting him. This is the first time I've ever seen him smile so big.

When we all get outside I can tell that my Guardians don't understand the full concept of blending in. Ruth pulls up in a bright green windowless van. On the driver's side panel a large artful mural is painted in wildly vivid colors. My eyes are plastered to the side of the van. I'm actually pretty impressed with how lifelike the pink unicorn looks. I am, however, a little less pleased when I see that there's also a mural of the lands of Cyadonia underlaying the mythical scene on top of it.

"Where the hell did you get this thing?"

I pan my eyes to look at my three Guardians. Ruth glances back at the van and shrugs her shoulders.

"What? I grabbed it from the employee parking lot! What's the matter with it?"

John and Fred both point at the vibrant mural painted on the side of the van. Ruth had missed it at first, but then recognized the city names painted in red glossy paint overtop clearly defined magical borders.

"Aww man! I had no idea!"

I can see that John is worried. Before he can suggest that we get a different vehicle, we all hear a loud commotion in the birch trees surrounding the property.

"I think It's pretty Bitchin!"

Kevin breaks the tension before sliding open the side door of the van.

"What do you say Veggie Boy? In or out?"

I feel John and Fred each grab a side of my chair and lift me inside the van. It smells like every memory I have of McDonalds as a young child. I glance down and see about twenty crumpled up cheeseburger wrappers and decide that my nose was accurate with my first assumption. Fred jumps up into the back of the van before Kevin jumps inside and slams the door. I can tell that he's having the time of his life right now.

Ruth takes the wheel and twists the car keys. Beneath the dangling pile of keys hangs a replica Lightsaber. Specifically the lightsaber carried by Luke Skywalker in Return of the Jedi. I have seen this exact set of keys on many occasions.

"What did you do to Burt?"

John spins around from his position riding shotgun.

"What's the matter?"

"I recognize those keys. They belong to a friend of mine!"

Ruth reaches onto the dash and tosses back the remainder of a small amount of energy drink from a squished aluminum can.

"Chill out dude! I didn't hurt him! I just bopped him on the head and covered his body with a blanket behind the reception desk. He will be just fine!"

I breathe a sigh of internal relief. Of all the people in that damn place, Burt was most definitely my favorite. I would even go so far as to call him a friend.

The van tires screech as Ruth slams her foot down onto the accelerator. I start rolling backwards toward the back door before Fred is able to stuff his toes under one of my wheels. I feel Kevin slap down the small rubber handle that engages the brakes of my chair on the other side. I stop rolling and rock back slightly before coming to a rest facing backwards.

"Nice one guys! I thought I was going to smash against the back doors for sure!"

I feel Fred's hand grab the arm rest of my chair and swivel me back to face forward. He then activates the brake on the second rubber wheel.

"Where are we headed Ruth?"

"West... Just as far as we can go to the west!"

**

We have been driving now for the better part of six hours. I hear Ruth cuss under her breath.

"We need to stop and get some gas!"

The van veers off the next exit. I can see the yellow lights of a large Shell station approaching at the end of the offramp.

"Thank god! I need to take a piss!"

Kevin's comment reminds me of an unfortunate side effect of my condition. I watch as Fred pulls up my right pant leg and inspects the small plastic bag filled almost to the brim with urine.

"Yeah, Cameron needs a dump as well!"

I watch as John rummages through the glove compartment looking for a way to pay for the purchases ahead of us. Ruth wiggles a brown leather wallet in his face. I watch a rolled up comic book fall to the floorboard before I call out in my robotic voice.

"Fred, grab that rolled up comic, and help me read it."

I recognize certain familiar features about the graphic novel and its stylish art. It's very similar to the one that Burt made me for Christmas. But this one has a different title, and the color is different too.

As Fred flips page after page I realize that this comic is telling my life's story. There are details in this book that I have only ever told to one person. I immediately decide to give Burt the benefit of the doubt, and decide that he was probably just making me another gift or something. That's when I'm distracted by movement beside my feet.

Kevin begins opening a large cardboard box that he had pulled out from underneath the driver's side seat. He unfolds the top of the cardboard box before pulling out one of a hundred copies of a comic book titled "The Crippled Dream Warrior."

"Um, I think that Burt is some sort of comic salesman or something. I always knew that guy must have a side hustle. He was always wearing a new set of sneakers every shift."

Kevin's finger points to a small white label on the corner of the comic book cover. $7.99. I don't believe it at first. *Was Burt just using me all these years so that he could sell comic books? Was he really even my friend?*

Kevin must have sensed the thoughts of betrayal running through my head. He reaches into the middle console separating the driver's seat from the passenger side. His hands rattle around before finding what he's looking for.

I watch nervously as Kevin powers up the small iPad that he is gently clutching in hand.

"That thing is gonna be useless without the password!"

Kevin smirks in my direction.

"You're not the only one who struck up a friendship with Burt. He used to let me log onto his iPad from time to time when no one was looking, this iPad, to look at girls on Instagram. He let me make my own profile and everything!"

I watch as Kevin types in the password "Yoda.padawan3!".

"Dang! There's no internet! That just figures!"

The windowless van pulls into the gas station before stopping at a pump next to a nice black Mercedes. The woman holding the gas pump handle is wearing a tight black mini skirt and a white spaghetti strap tank top. Kevin Stares out the side door without moving. He seems to be mesmerized by her.

"Snap out of it Kevin!"

I watch as a film lifts from Kevin's eyes. He shakes his head as if trying to rid himself of the images that his puberty filled brain had just conjured to life.

Ruth pulls a credit card from Burt's stolen wallet and swipes it at the gas pump. I hear the flow of gas running into the tank situated below the spot where I'm sitting. Kevin jumps out of the van and stares at the woman in the tank top the entire walk towards the mini mart. He finally catches her attention after tripping over the curb leading to the front door of the station. She smirks and replaces the gas handle back into the pump station before placing a hand to her mouth and blowing him a kiss.

The black Mercedes drives away as my thoughts are drawn to the events of this morning. I hear the bell attached to the mini mart door ring, and glance over to see Kevin holding a white bag of candy and snacks in one hand, and the iPad in the other.

"The lady at the counter let me use her WIFI for a second to do a google search. I downloaded a few articles relating to that comic book series."

The word "Series" hits me like a ton of bricks.

"Can you read it to me please?"

Kevin nods his head before biting off a piece of red licorice. I would normally be annoyed with someone reading me a story with a mouth full of sticky candy, but desperate times call for desperate measures.

"The Crippled Dream Warrior has racked up awards for its gritty tales of magic and melancholy…"

He pauses.

"Dang… This literary critic is really freaking dramatic!"

If I could operate my hands I would snatch the iPad out of his fingers and read the article myself.

"Just read it please!"

"Fine! Where was I? Melancholy… Its Author and artist Burt Shill is a newly born rockstar in the comic book industry. His meteoric rise to fame and fortune is spurred on by his retelling of fantastical magical battles against the forces of Cyadonia's Demon Hordes. But behind the magic and realism in his storytelling, he has also developed a character that makes everyone who reads his comic books actually feel something. The real magic in his stories are not the characters in the dream land, but the struggle of an orphaned boy living most of his life from a wheelchair. This publication awards "The Crippled Dream Warrior" all five daggers on our scale of readability. If I could give it a sixth dagger I would. You can pick up your own copy of any one of Burt Shill's twenty volumes at a bookstore near you!"

"That Dickhead! He was just using me to make money?"

Kevin can't help but snicker after hearing my robotic voice say the words.

"He really screwed you over huh? Did he ever tell you about all this...? The dude wrote over twenty volumes. He's a freaking millionaire now. It says here that he claims to have come up with the stories in his own dreams. Kind of ironic wouldn't you say?"

If I could nod my head, I would.

"He never said a thing. I should've known he was up to something when he started taking notes with that damn audio recorder!"

My mind clicks away from Burt's deception and exploitation for the briefest of moments.

"I guess we know how the Demon warriors were able to locate me. This damn comic book pointed them strait to me! And Burt..."

I feel myself getting angry.

We keep driving for so long that I lose track of time. It's almost my bedtime, and I realize that the person driving this van is going to disappear and go back to Cyadonia when I close my eyes.

"Listen closely Kevin. Pretty soon I will need to go to sleep. When that happens Ruth, John, and Fred will all turn into black smoke and disappear."

Kevin scrunches his eyes together in a look of disbelief.

"Don't look at me like that dude. I'm telling you the truth. When I go to sleep I won't wake up until something in this world wakes me. Try not to let anything like that happen, alright?"

Kevin shakes his head.

"I'll make sure that the Demons don't get us Cameron!"

I'm strangely comfortable with the idea of Kevin watching over me while I sleep. He has proven himself capable so far. And I really don't have much of a choice anyways.

He crawls up to his knees and eats the last of his licorice vines before tapping Ruth on the shoulder.

"We should switch places, and I should drive! I hear you're all gonna turn into a black cloud or something soon. I don't think it would be a good idea to crash the van."

I can't quite hear everything that's being said, but I can tell that John and Ruth are giving Kevin a strict set of rules to follow. I feel Fred twist the knob on the back of my chair before I slowly recline backwards. He snaps a leather seatbelt over my lap. I can feel my eyes getting heavy. They are too heavy to keep open any longer.

CHAPTER 4

"I thought you guys were supposed to disappear or something!"

Kevin glances into the back of the van to witness the mouth that long drawn out snoring sounds are currently emanating from.

"I only mention it, because Cameron is snoring away back there, but I'm still sitting on your lap."

Ruth shoots a look of annoyance over at the smiling face of her partner in the passenger seat of the van. She only caught a small glimpse of his wide mouthed grin, but his obvious appreciation at her uncomfortable predicament was just enough to piss her off.

"I'm starting to think that the 'Stones of Arafat' might cause a permanent adjustment in our normal routine John!"

"I got a feeling you're probably right Ruth, Like always!"

Kevin shifts his boney butt atop the lap of Ruth. His sharp teenage hips have been digging into her waist for some time now. She also can't shake the smell of baby powder coming off his shoulders while she peers past his neck and into the flow of oncoming headlights.

"Get off me kid! I think it's safe to assume that we won't be needing you to take the wheel after all!"

Kevin slides his slender body below the steering wheel before climbing back into his place between the driver and passenger seats.

"You don't have to ask me twice! I don't even know how to drive for the record!"

Fred nudges his elbow into Kevin's back while repositioning himself to check on Cameron's breathing.

"He's definitely asleep! Does this mean that we're all stuck in the human world now?"

John turns his shoulders while staring back at Cameron. His hand instinctively reaches out to feel the wrist pulse of his ward.

"We shouldn't jump to any conclusions! Who knows how these magic rocks work? But you should be ready to grab that steering wheel at all times just in case we disappear!"

John points a firm finger at the teenage boy kneeling beside him. Kevin nods his head from the position he has occupied on his knees.

"Hand me that small plastic chair Fred!"

John's order causes his son to search with his eyes for the object that his father has just asked for. In the back of the van sits a blue plastic chair. The type that was made for children and toddlers. Fred hands the item to his father, who in turn places the plastic chair in between the driver's seat and himself.

"Sit here Kevin! And make sure that you can reach the steering wheel at all times when Cameron is snoring. Got it? You're the backup. It's a big responsibility!"

Kevin crawls forward and carefully places his bottom on the plastic chair. After sitting down, his knees are bent awkwardly, nearly touching his chest. He quickly decides that the small chair is better than the stained carpet he has been kneeling on, and makes himself comfortable. He softly rubs the developing rug burns taking shape on both of his knees.

"What's the plan guys? If you guys are sticking around... Maybe I won't need to hide in an alley with Cameron until he wakes up?"

John begins rummaging through the glove box before pulling out a small stack of napkins.

"Here, wipe his face with these!"

Fred reaches forward and grabs a stack of brown fast food napkins from his father's hand. He then turns while peeling off the top napkin and wiping a healthy amount of drool from Cameron's chin.

"He's definitely out cold! Should I give him the injection so that he doesn't wake up?"

John looks intently at his son before shaking his head in the negative.

"Not until we know that we're clear, and no one is following us! We got lucky that they only sent a scouting party to the Institute. If they'd sent a sizable force we would all be dead right now!"

**

The smell that greets my arrival in Cyadonia seems somewhat different this trip. Before my eyes open I sense the aroma of burnt wood in the air. Beside me stands the three normal stone statues of my Guardians slumbering in 'Stone Sentinel' form. Their hardened rock faces dawn a look of boredom. As I reach out to wake them, I can sense that something is different.

The stone statues remain cold to the touch as my fingers and palm make gentle contact. I try over and over again, but they refuse to wake from the human world.

"They will not be joining us Centurian!"

The voice of Thoth startles me out of the melancholy that I have begun to feel captured by.

"Why can't I wake them up? Are they okay?"

"They are chained to the human world until you remove the

'Stones of Arafat' from their bodies."

"How the hell am I supposed to do that? You don't want me to reach up their butt's or something right?"

Thoth slaps the end of his wooden walking stick down onto my big toe. I jump up into the air and grasp at the throbbing toe that has just been wounded.

"What was that for?"

"You inject smart ass comments where none are needed Centurian."

"I didn't think it was that far off of a question Wise Teacher! They swallowed the Stones! How am I supposed to get them out of their granite bodies now?"

Thoth approaches his young apprentice wearing a glimmering wardrobe of battle dress. His chest armor reflects the light of the sky, adorned by the crest of the Queen of Rain.

"Why are you all dressed up for battle? No one can get to me in the city! Right?"

Thoth points a firm finger towards the wall opposite of his gaze. Sitting against the wall is a pile of armor and weapons that look familiar to me.

"Put on your armor Centurian. Not even the City of Light can protect you from what hunts us now!"

I gently slide past the three stone statues of my Guardians on the way to get my gear. The armor sitting in a neat pile fits my body tightly. After dawning my battle gear, I holster a long sword into its sheath along my left hip.

"Where to now Wise Teacher?"

Thoth points down the long stone pathway leading to the city below.

"We must leave the city at once. The people must not be harmed. The Queen of Rain has gathered a small force to escort us to safety up in the mountains. Only there can the magic that tracks you be shrouded and removed."

I watch as the long fingers of my teacher wrap gently around a thin sword attached to his hip. This is the first time that I have ever seen Thoth carry a weapon outside of the training arena. My stomach tightens, and I can feel a small growing heat building in my palms.

"Follow me Centurian! For now I must act as Guardian and Protector. A job that I have not fulfilled in generations! Stay close, and ready your hands to fight!"

We descend the stairs quickly and jog down empty streets that are usually filled with a mass of activity. The markets seemed to be closed, and the taverns and eateries are all shut up tightly.

"Where is everyone?"

Thoth refuses to slow his pace of travel while responding to my questions.

"Hiding at the Queen's orders! Gallus has sent his assassins to hunt down every Centurian all across Cyadonia! They do not spare the innocent in search of their prey!"

"I get that part, but why do we need to hide? I've fought the evil creatures and Demons from Gomorrah many times before... What makes these 'Assassins" so dangerous to me?"

Thoth enters a large empty courtyard. At the far end of my vision I can see ten small men dressed for battle and holding glowing spears in hand. Gripped tightly in the other hand of each of the warriors is a kite shaped shield with a long spike protruding from the bottom of each defensive weapon. Some sort of protective magic radiates from each shield.

"These are the ones assigned by the Queen to escort us into the 'Breathing Mountains'... We must protect them at all costs. Without their guidance we will be unable to navigate the magical barriers surrounding the mountain passes!"

I look over at the ten warriors as they bow in respect before forming two five man columns on either side of us. Their Commander raises his hand to his mouth before blowing into a small silver horn. The sound that comes out of the horn is deep. Small stones on the ground shake and shiver as the main gates to the City of Light opens to the world existing beyond it.

We move quickly to exit the city. I glance back one last time as the city gates close behind us. There's a single warrior atop the gate walls that raises his hand to bid us farewell.

As we walk quickly alongside the wall of the city, I feel a small jolt in my chest. Thoth must sense something is wrong. He reaches out with his hands to catch my falling body with his magic. Everything goes black for a moment. Then I wake in the real world.

**

"Just run them off the road Ruth!"

The frantic tone in John's words send a shiver down my spine. The van is bouncing and rocking back and forth as Ruth drives in an erratic fashion.

"What the crap guys! There's some serious drama going down in Cyadonia right now. I need to get back there quick!"

The van tilts to the side as a solid impact hits it in the rear corner panel. Ruth cranks on the steering wheel and regains the road.

"Sorry Cam! Somehow we were followed by someone! Spotted them about a mile back before they sped up and rear ended us! Now this damn chick keeps pulling up beside us and trying to run us off the road!"

Fred gently grasps my arm and keeps my body from hitting the wall as his mother overcorrects the vans path of travel.

"Now this crazy chick keeps flashing her brights and trying to get beside us!"

Kevin is huddled behind the driver's seat holding onto the back of the chair for dear life.

"To be fair Ruth, you did brake check her pretty hard! She might not have rear ended us on purpose!"

Ruth scowls into the tortured gaze of her husband.

"Fine! You want to take over mister perfect? So be it!"

Ruth removes her hands from the steering wheel as John tries to make his case for deescalating the situation. He lunges sideways and grabs the wheel with one hand before the car behind us bumps into the rear corner panel.

The van slides sideways and comes to a stop alongside the dusty road of the interstate. Kevin runs toward the back of the van to open the back doors. We all watch as a tall brunette climbs gracefully out of the driver's seat of the truck that has just forced us off the road. John and Ruth stand side by side ready to defend me from the person that has been following us all the way from the Institute.

"Don't come any closer girl!"

The words only seem to spur the mystery girl closer to the van.

"Keep your mouth shut Grandma!"

The insult hits Ruth like a ton of bricks.

"Do I look that old John?"

She turns with a wounded look and waits for her husband's response. John stands there looking like a deer in the headlights. A slight pause lingers in the air before he blurts out an answer in haste.

"Of course not Hunny!"

He does his very best not to crack a smile at the ongoing war of words being exchanged between his wife and the mystery girl.

"If you don't get back right now I'll be forced to hurt you!"

Ruth points the tip of a Demon dagger as the mystery girl

stares past her as if she isn't even there. The girl makes deep eye contact with me. Almost to the point where I can feel our souls intertwining. *Like in the comic books that Burt reads to me on Thursdays.*

"Call off your dog's Centurian! I mean you no harm! I was sent to protect you in case these Guardians weren't up to the task!"

Fred has been so busy activating my speech device that he has forgotten to arm himself. I angle my eyes in a particular pattern. The robot voice engages and speaks the words that I have formulated only moments before with my eyes.

"Who are you, and who sent you?"

The girl places both of her palms into the air before slowly walking in front of John and Ruth. Each of my Guardians wait on edge for something to go down.

"I too am protector of the City of Light! The Queen of Rain has asked that I do what I can to protect you in the human world. I was confused at first with her request. I see now why a Centurian of her realm would need my protection."

The girl runs her eyes over my disfigured body before giving a curtsy of sorts and smiling at Ruth and John.

"I too am a Centurian of Cyadonia. I was lucky to finally find you. If that Comic Book didn't exist I would have never been able to follow nurse Burt. He's the only reason I was able to track you down in this world! You didn't kill him when you escaped did you? He seemed like a pretty nice dude!"

Ruth scoffs at the suggestion that she would kill a helpless human.

"He slumbers beneath a blanket back at the Institute. No doubt he will wake with a headache though!"

The mystery girl nervously nods her head in my protectors' direction.

"What are we waiting for then? Let's get going. We need to keep moving if we're going to have any chance at those Demons losing your scent!"

Everyone hesitantly climbs into the van. John has decided to take a turn driving while the mystery girl climbs into the back of the windowless vehicle with me and Fred. Ruth seems to watch her every move, ready to strike if the need arises.

"I know that we aren't really supposed to meet each other in the human world. But the Queen decided that old traditions must not risk the lives of her Centurians when mitigating circumstances are at play."

I rotate my eyes to formulate a response. The robot voice makes the girl smile. She is mind boggling pretty. Her green eyes and thin upper lip make for a sultry appearance. I can't help but stare for a moment while trying to come up with the perfect line.

"I can fix your voice If you want?"

Her hands are warm to the touch. As her fingers wrap around my throat I feel the familiar vibrations of magic at work. There's a short but sharp pain in the front of my neck before it disappears. I clear my throat. Something that I have been unable to do for years.

"How are you using magic here? Magic doesn't exist in the human realms!"

I watch as Ruth's facial features shift from a defensive posture to pure admiration. The girl reaches down and pulls out a small silver pendant adorned with a bright green gemstone. After showing me the necklace, she gently tucks it back beneath her shirt. Giving it one gentle pat to make sure it's secure.

"Magic used to live here too in the days of old. This pendant collects the remaining wisps of magic in the sunlight, and allows me to use that magic however I want."

"Can you heal my whole body then?"

"I'm afraid that would require way too much magic. I can only capture small amounts. Returning your voice is probably all that I can do for you in this world. But I'm sure that the Sky Gods have a way to heal you. Maybe they can use the portal between the two worlds to send more magic?"

I instantly feel a lingering sense of hope that has been missing from my life in this realm since that fateful day on the monkey bars.

"What should I call you?'

The sound of my own human voice is startling. I almost forget for a moment that I am not in Cyadonia. The thought reminds me of what was happening there before I woke up.

"Holy crap. You need to dose me Fred! I need to get back to Cyadonia. I'm being hunted!"

I watch as the mystery girl grabs a small backpack laying on the floor that Ruth is pointing her finger at. The bag lands in my Guardian's hand before she rummages through various items looking for something.

"You better give me something too! If he's in danger, that means I'm in danger there too. Where are you at in Cyadonia Centurian? I will come find you!"

"Thoth is taking me to the Breathing Mountains in the West! We're traveling with ten men of the Queen's army."

"I know the place. I'll see you on the other side."

Ruth slides the tip of a long needle into my arm. I feel the lids of my eyes get heavy before the ceiling of the van goes dark.

**

I open my eyes and watch as white fluffy clouds shake in the sky. My body bounces along as four men below me support my weight and carry me down a tree lined path leading towards the mountains in the west. I wiggle my fingers in front of one of the little men carrying me.

"I'm back guys. Put me down if you will!"

I watch as Thoth turns his head away from the trail ahead to check on me.

"What happened Centurian. You collapsed!"

"No kidding dude! Did you notice that?"

I've had enough of his "Wise Teacher" condescension for one day. He stops walking before staring into the tree line ahead with sword in hand. He slowly draws a blade from its sheath and whistles to our escort.

"Prepare yourselves warriors!"

I grab hold of the purple cape I'm wearing and give it a good shake to get rid of the dust that clung to it after my fall. As a small cloud of dust surrounds my body, the air is split in two by a bright blue streak of light. I've seen this magic many times. I use it myself.

In the palm of my hands I can feel the building power of my lightning bolts forming. Thoth must have seen the confused look on my face after witnessing the magical attack.

"You have never faced anything like this before young Centurian! Fight, like your life depends on it. Because it surely does!"

Two more streaks of light shoot out from the bushes thirty yards to the front of our protective detail. The Queen's men rally together into a line and raise their shields into a wall before plunging the spikes at the bottom of each shield into the ground. Thoth moves behind the shield wall and squats down to wait for the coming attack.

In one hand I focus all the magic needed to unleash a lightning bolt big enough to kill anything that I have ever faced before. In my right hand I grasp across my body and pull out my long sword.

Three small groups of longhorn sheep crash through the

bushes in front of us. Each one has been touched by an evil that has distorted their shape. They are followed closely behind by ten large Demon warriors, and what appears to be a human. The man waits patiently as his allies charge forward. Even from this distance I can see the red glow of his ember eyes staring at me.

"Who the hell is that?"

Thoth lifts his head into the sky and whispers into the wind. From behind the charging beasts a dozen branches from the trees of the forest break away and impale the enemy from behind. Their bodies crash to the ground and slide to a stop in front of the shield wall. I unleash my bolt of lightning into the closest charging Demon warrior.

The concussion of the impact upon the Demon's scaled skin splinters the electricity of my attack into three fingers of blue light. Each finger of death strikes the charging beasts around my original target. There is a loud sound of collapsing metal as the armored Demons fall to the ground in a pile before exploding into black clouds of dust. The armor that they had worn falls to the ground in big piles.

The enemy man wearing a red cloak by the tree line releases a devastating attack on the shield wall. I watch as men and shields are thrown into the air and onto the ground beside me. Even Thoth is unable to deflect the incoming attack with his protective magic. What's left of our escort engages the remaining Demon warriors and the foul beasts who survived our initial assaults.

Thoth draws his sword and joins the ongoing battle ensuing in front of him. I have never seen him fight like this before. He has always been reserved and controlled in our sparing sessions. He now looks like a hurricane of death. Spinning and striking with such precision that I make a mental note to try harder during our training sessions.

He stops fighting for a moment and looks at me.

"What are you waiting for Centurian? Get into the fight. The one by the tree line is yours. Prove yourself young warrior!"

I step forward and point the tip of my sword towards the enemy still standing by the trees. He raises his palm and sends a bolt of lightning directly at me. By sheer instinct I raise my hand to block the incoming bolt. I feel the impact, but instead of pain I feel a rush of energy fill my left palm. Somehow I have absorbed his attack. I send the bolt right back at him.

Before the attack lands a small green bubble appears around my enemy. The lightning bolt bounces off of the defensive bubble. This is a magic that I have never seen before. I have never seen anyone resist my lightning bolts during past engagements.

I notice that Thoth is engaged in sword play with two large Demon warriors, and most of the men in our Queen's Army escort are either wounded or are trying to fall back and form a new defensive line. I approach the man standing by the tree line with both fists pointing at me. When I get to within twenty paces he reaches to his hip and pulls out a long edged weapon.

On either end of the handle portion are two curved blades with small sharpened teeth pointing in opposite directions. I charge a strong magic in one hand and ready my sword in the other. His words catch me off guard.

"At long last we meet Guardian of the City of Light! I have met many like you before, but none have been so young and weak!"

I can hear Thoth exerting himself behind me, and the smells of freshly cut grass and rotten eggs are getting stronger. *He must be doing okay back there, I think to myself.*

"And who are you to attack a Centurian and hope to survive?"

The man gently reveals a mouth full of blackened teeth while displaying the evilest of grins. His face bares a long vertical scar running from the edge of his mouth up to the corner of his right eye. His red cloak is decorated with small black writing. The words are unreadable from this far away. Not to mention I can't even understand the Shadow language.

"I am the collector of souls young Centurian. Before my time serving the Master, I was called 'Cain,' but you will never have reason to call me by this name! I shall send your soul to my master now!"

I can hear a small chorus of whispers coming from the man's lips as he takes two steps to the side and brings his blade down upon my head. His spoken incantations fill each of his arms with strength. I narrowly deflect the incoming attack and release a burst of lightning into the chest of my attacker. He's faster than I could anticipate. He dodges my magic with a quick spin followed by a stabbing attack that glances off the armor covering my right shoulder.

I take a step back and grasp my sword with both hands. The enemy is fast, and I will surely need all of my strength to parry his attacks. Clash after clash echoes through the countryside as we battle back and forth. After mistiming a defensive parry, I feel a sharp sting in my right armpit. I glance down and see that his blade has sawed open a small gash between my arm and ribs. The exact place where my armor doesn't protect the flesh below it.

I grab the wound with my left hand while taking two big steps backwards to gather myself. The assassin wastes no time. He doesn't want me to regain my balance. His zealous attack works out in my favor. As the man raises his weapon overhead I charge my lightning and send a small charge into his planted foot. The bolt strikes home.

The charging assassin loses his balance and falls forward right into the swing path of the sword clutched in my right hand. I feel the blade cut deeply after momentarily glancing off of some sort of armor underneath his red cloak.

The man stumbles forward grasping at his belly. The red color of his cloak begins to darken underneath the spot that I have struck. Without pausing, the assassin raises both hands into the sky. His weapon falls to the ground as his entire body is surrounded in a bright blast of green light. He disappears without warning.

I reach down to pick up the enemy's weapon as Thoth limps up behind me. I could feel his eyes watching me closely the entire duration of the battle. Like this was some sort of big test or something.

"You have done better than I expected young Centurian! You have survived your first encounter with a 'Dark Priest' of Gomorrah. I must admit that I was unsure if you could be victorious."

I stand beside him out of breath and stare at the Wise Teacher with a look of pure disbelief on my face.

"Then why the hell did we come out here in the first place if you thought I would die?"

"I told you! We must not put innocent people at risk to protect you. You must learn to stand on your own if we are to change this realm for the better. For far too long you have relied upon your Guardians and sheer luck when confronting the evil that lives in these lands. Now you must take your training seriously, Alas if you don't, you will not survive."

I look back towards the group of wounded men that had accompanied us from the City of Light.

"What about them? They're innocent too aren't they?"

"They are innocent, but they have also sworn to fulfill the wishes of their Queen. And she seems to like you for some odd reason I will never understand!"

I start the short walk back to the Queen's soldiers to render aid. My hands begin to go cold as I gather the magic necessary to heal their wounds. I work fast covering each wounded man with a white mist of healing. All but three recover and are on their feet before the healing mist has dissipated. Two will not wake, and one man is strangely immune to my healing magic.

Thoth gives instructions for two of the healthy soldiers to get the rest of the wounded men back to the City of Light. The remaining five soldiers form a protective detail around me like they originally did when we left the city gates.

We walk through tree covered paths until I begin to see small patches of snow in the distance. Thoth puts his hand in the air to stop the column before having a quiet conversation with the leader of my protective detail. The bearded man tells us all to stay put.

He walks ten paces forward and places his hand on a grey stone beside the animal worn path. Black birds the size of refrigerators appear in the sky overhead. I am startled slightly by a nudge from one of the Queen's soldiers.

"They're watching us! Gallus knows that the only safe place to hide from his assassins is in these mountains. Or in the realm of the Sky Gods behind their walls of magic! But the Gods rarely open their gates to strangers."

The man beside me points his spear up into the sky to point out the birds.

"What's so special about these mountains? Why doesn't Gallus just send his men to kill me there?"

The soldier shakes his head at me as if he is disgusted with my lack of understanding.

"You are more foolish than I thought young Centurian. These mountains are protected by a fierce magic that is far more powerful than the magic that you or Gallus can wield. The peaks of these mountains have long been a refuge for those that hide from the reign of terror that comes from the North. A terror that has come in waves from the beginning of recorded history. This wave feels stronger than those of the past though!"

I watch as a small glimmer of light fills the path ahead. Thoth pokes his walking stick through what looks like a wall of plastic wrap before waving us forward. After we pass through the protective barrier I see a look of relief wash over the faces of Thoth and our escort soldiers.

"We should be safe now. No evil beast or Demon may pass through this barrier. The Gods of the past saw to that."

I look up and watch as one of the massive black birds following us slams into the side of the invisible barrier. It plumets to the ground and hits the rock beside the path. Blood and feathers cover the rock. The rest of the birds overhead watch as their companion expires in the dirt below them. Each one glides away from the magical barrier and begins circling a safe distance away.

Thoth snaps his fingers in front of my face to get my attention.

"Hurry up. We don't have much time, and we have a long distance to cover to find shelter. We may be safe from Gallus and his minions up here, but the cold will kill us all the same."

CHAPTER 5

The cold air of the mountain is beginning to get to me. Each exhale that leaves my mouth forms a cloud of white smoke that trails my face through the unknown mountain pass. The small puffs of smoke from my escorts are beginning to form a visual at my hip that suggests that I am floating on air.

I look at the back of Thoth's head as we climb yet another in an endless series of sloping hills. Each time we traverse a mountain pass we take time to navigate through a maze of magical barriers. Each one requiring a special incantation to be spoken.

"Seriously, I can't feel my fingers anymore Thoth! And I have been charging my palms with fire magic for the last three hours. If I'm this cold I can't imagine how cold the rest of these guys must be!"

I look down and catch the look of thanks coming from the small soldier marching beside me. His lips are a shade of blue that I have never seen on the face of a 'Little.'

"No joke man! This one is actually turning blue! I have an idea!"

Thoth slows his pace before turning to face me.

"And what is this idea of yours Centurian. Are you to raise the sun back into the sky to fight off the chill of night?"

I glance over the nearest snow covered mountain peak to contemplate the possibility that has been presented.

"Not exactly! Wait... Can I do that?"

"No! You cannot do that Young Warrior! No one can control the celestial realm... Not even the Sky Gods!"

I squint my eyes while staring at the dying light of day over the peak in front of us.

"I was thinking that you could raise a protective bubble around us... Then I could charge up my fire balls and hover one for a while to heat up the air surrounding us?"

I can see that Thoth is contemplating my suggestion while pretending to look in the opposite direction.

"We shall do as you say Centurian! Although, I am unsure of the use of magic in this way."

One of the soldiers elbows my thigh as Thoth creates a magical bubble to surround us. I charge a fireball in my right hand and use the fingers of my other hand to contain its flight. The ball of fire hovers slightly above the soldiers walking all around me.

I hear a small moan of relief from the soldier to my right. His lips are still quivering and blue, but they are now spread wide in a big smile. I too can feel the heat of the fireball. As we continue forward I concentrate on maintaining our heat source. A few times the ball of fire gets really close to touching the helmet of my soldier friends beside me.

We march forward like this for the better part of three hours. I'm starting to worry that the injection that I received in the back of a windowless van might wear off soon. The thought of me dropping the fireball on the heads of my own men scares me enough to extinguish it.

Thoth too seems relieved by my realization. He lowers the magical shield bubble. A rush of cold air enters each of our lungs as the Wise Teacher points at something on the side of the mountain.

I squint hard through a flurry of small snowflakes that have just begun to fall from the night sky. A small dot of light sticks out from the snowy background of the mountainside.

"What is it?"

"That's our destination Centurian! We have made it at last!"

"I can see that Wise Teacher! But made it Where?"

"We have found the 'Cave of Lost Travelers.' Here we will find shelter and safety from the night air. I must warn you though, do not speak to the ones from the shadow realm who rest within. Their words are filled with lies and dark omens."

We all walk about another half mile through ankle deep snow. If by any chance someone was trying to follow us, they surely would have an easy time of it.

The cave entrance is flanked on either side by statues hewn from the mountain itself. Each statue is shaped like a warrior from the City of Light. The stone spears in the hands of the statues match the ones in the hands of each of the "Littles" in our company.

I glance down at the blue lipped soldier to my right. He seems to understand my question without words being exchanged.

"The City of Light was built by the people that once inhabited the Breathing Mountains. It is here that we were created. It was here that we thrived while the evil in the north ravaged the land that we once called home."

I feel a weird tingling sensation on the back of my neck before a tightly packed ball of snow hits me in the head. Spears lower as I form a lightning bolt in my palm and turn to strike back at my attacker.

I unclench my fist as the person standing in front of me is familiar to my eyes. *She actually came!*

"You better not hit me with a bolt of lightning kid! I'll kick your ass!"

She looks even more radiant here in Cyadonia. Her face is the same, but her hair is the color of the sun, and her eyes the shade of the most beautiful purple sapphire I have ever seen.

Her armor reflects the light of the dancing flames lighting the entrance to the 'Cave of Lost Travelers.'

I look down at my own armor and realize that mine is nowhere near as glamourous as hers. Each plate of protection covering her body glimmers in the colored light of a rainbow from certain angles. At the center of her breast plate between the curves of her body sits the crest of the Queen of Rain. I point down at my own chest Sigil.

"Looks like we're a matching set!"

"Not likely kid. I've been serving the Queen of Rain since before you were born!"

I do some quick math in my head before realizing the exaggeration in the statement. Our conversation is interrupted by the Wise Teacher who is now bowing beside me in the direction of the approaching girl.

"I am most pleased to meet you Centurian! Who do you count as Wise Teacher in the City of Light?"

The girl tosses her hair in a way that makes my blood pressure rise. I just can't stop staring at her lips. This is going to become a problem at some point.

"I was trained by the great Muson of the Serpent Temple. Her soul moved on when I was just a small girl though. I completed my training with a master of swordplay at the temple of steel."

"Ah, You must know Wise Teacher Kingsley then?"

"Yeah, I know that old fart. He's like a grandfather to me!"

I interrupt knowing full well that my interjection will anger Thoth.

"Maybe we can get inside before we finish the interrogation Wise Teacher?"

I instantly feel the sting of his walking stick on my shins. The girl erupts into laughter upon witnessing my punishment. As we all enter the cave I feel a hand slip over my neck and rest on my shoulder.

"I remember when my Wise Teacher used to slap my knuckles with a palm branch. These times don't last forever kid. Enjoy them, cause soon enough you'll be on your own."

As we descend down a set of stone stairs carved into the floor of the cave, the light from ahead begins to grow brighter. Instead of firelight, the cavern in front of me is filled with white light from tiny gems imbedded in the ceiling of the cave.

"They're called "Seeing Stars." The 'Littles' create them by embedding magic in small diamonds."

I stop staring at the roof, slightly embarrassed by my lingering gaze and childlike wonder on display.

"You never did tell me your name back in the van!"

She brushes aside a flowing piece of hair with her fingers while simultaneously pursing her lips and blowing another chunk of hair out of her sightline.

"In Cyadonia I am called "Centurian of Mercy," but you can call me Estee."

"The Queen hasn't named me yet... But you can call me Cam. Short for Cameron."

I see a look in the eyes of my new friend that I also feel in my own body. We both sit down quickly before laying back onto the ground. The meds have worn off. We are waking up!

**

"They're both waking up!"

I can hear the sound of John and Fred's excited voices. I open my eyes to see the bright reflection of sunlight coming off of the windshield. It must be close to midday at this point. Kevin is fast asleep in the van, curled up in a ball at my feet.

Estee rubs the sleep from the corners of her eyes before moving forward to speak with Ruth and John in the front of the van. I can barely make out the details of their conversation. The only thing I heard for sure is the word "hungry."

The van takes a slight turn to exit the highway. Before we stop I notice that we are pulling into a small diner. The thought of food excites my stomach. It has been years since I've been able to work my own mouth and throat. The thought of swallowing a mouthful of breakfast food makes my mouth begin to water out of control.

The van stops abruptly after bumping into a curb, waking Kevin from his nap. He shakes off the cobwebs of an interrupted sleep cycle before moving to the side of the van and helping Estee jiggle the door handle open. They both grab hold of a rubber wheel and lower my wheelchair to the asphalt. I watch as Kevin brushes off Estee's attempt to push my chair from behind. For some reason he has claimed the sole right to push me around.

He rolls me up a small wooden ramp and through the front doors of a well maintained Denny's. John leads the way followed by Ruth and Fred. They all seem a bit on edge. I'm sure that everyone is starving by now. Countless hours riding in a windowless van couldn't have helped anyone's mood.

A woman wearing a bright green button on her apron points us towards an empty table in the center of the dining room. John slides away one of the chairs making room for my wheelchair to roll into place. Kevin takes a seat on my left, and Estee dawns a big smile while sitting in the chair to the right of me. Fred hasn't taken his eyes off of her since sitting down.

She lifts up a menu and holds it in front of me before John clears his throat to get her attention.

"He only eats banana shakes! Otherwise he might choke. His muscles that control swallowing don't work anymore!"

Estee scoffs at the idea.

"Yeah, that was probably true. But I fixed his throat with magic dude! He can probably eat whatever he wants now!"

I realize that what she's saying will change my whole life in this realm. I can't even describe the feeling of hunger that I live with every waking moment. John shrugs his shoulders while looking at me.

"It's your choice Cameron! But you better be ready to reach down his damn throat if he starts choking!"

He points at Estee, who returns his gesture with her own middle finger.

"He'll be fine!"

She lifts the menu back up in front of my face. I read through the options before landing on a plate of eggs, bacon, and buttermilk pancakes.

The waitress takes our order before marching back towards the kitchen to alert the cooks. This time I get a good look at the button on her apron. "Just the tip." I can see that Estee and Kevin saw the button too. Each one was now wearing a small grin after reading the old waitress's sarcastic slogan.

"It's ironic cause she works for tips!"

Estee chuckles for a quick second before unfolding a napkin and placing it under the table on my lap. She seems far too comfortable with the process of helping me do everything.

"How do you know how to do all this? It's like you've cared for a 'Vegetable' like me before."

She grins at my comment while placing a straw into my water cup. I can tell that my Guardians are also perplexed by her natural ability to take care of me.

"This isn't my first rodeo kid."

All of us remain silent while waiting for her to tell us more. She remains silent while lifting the straw up to my lips. I take a small sip and swallow. I can feel a new sensation as the cold water runs through my throat and into my belly. There's a sense of control that has been missing within me for a long time.

The waitress saunters over to our table and deposits two baskets full of jelly pouches before reaching onto her tray and placing a big jug of maple syrup into the center of the table. Estee reaches into the basket closest to us before stopping.

"You want grape, or strawberry? We need to make sure you can swallow."

I choose the grape. She rips off the corner of the jelly pouch before placing it to the end of my lips. I open my mouth as she squeezes a healthy amount of jelly onto my tongue. The taste is unlike anything I can remember. I let the Jelly coat my tongue before taking a big gulp. I brace myself for the inevitable cough to come. Nothing happens.

"Nailed it! Looks like I repaired your throat enough for you to eat solid foods again!"

Estee stands from her chair and sarcastically bows in victory while twirling her hand in the air.

"I think I love you!"

The words blurt out in less of a sarcastic tone than I was going for. Estee squints at me and brushes away my comment with a smile.

"I don't date younger men Cameron. As cute as you are!"

She reaches forward with her finger and wipes away a small drop of grape jelly clinging to the corner of my mouth. I'm fully mesmerized by everything she does. I can tell that Fred and Kevin are also finding it hard not to stare at her.

Our collective adoration is interrupted by the waitress returning to the table carrying a large tray balanced in hand. She quickly distributes our food. The plate in front of me slides to the side. Whisked away by Estee's hand. She points at the maple syrup as everyone else at the table begins eating.

"You want butter and syrup?"

I nod my head as well as I can manage. She grabs a dull silver knife and scoops out a healthy slab of soft butter from one of the baskets in the center of the table. Next she grabs the syrup dispenser and pours a healthy amount all over the stack of pancakes I ordered. The first forkful to enter my mouth tastes like heaven. I chew slowly before taking one fateful gulp.

The mouthful of food slides harmlessly down my throat without issue. I devour every bite, including both pieces of bacon before exhaling loudly.

"You should eat before your omelet gets too cold."

"That's mighty kind of you Cam."

Kevin reaches past me and grabs the edge of the plate containing the small amount of food I have left. He makes a show of taking a turn feeding me. I can tell that he's trying to impress the girl sitting to my right.

"Smooth dude! Real smooth!"

I whisper the words so that Estee can't hear. Kevin grins before forking a sizeable chunk of yolk covered egg into my mouth.

We all finish eating before the waitress returns to check on us.

"Golly, y'all must have been starving! Is there anything else I can bring ya?"

We all remain silent except for Estee. She politely thanks the waitress before asking for the check. I watch as Ruth reaches into her pocket and pulls out a credit card belonging to Burt. My mind wanders back to the Institute. Even though I'm still mad at him for the whole comic book exploitation, I still hope he's okay.

"Alright Y'all, I'll be back in a jiffy with your check…"

As the waitress walked away I glance out the window and notice something odd. Two large shadows streak across the parking lot before disappearing.

"Did you see that?"

I glance at Estee with a look of concern. She doesn't question me at all. She's already on her feet and crawling across a booth to peer out the window before any of my Guardians have moved.

"I don't see anything Cam… Are you sure you saw something?"

"I'm sure! Two big shadows flew by. I saw them on the concrete."

The waitress returns with the check and places a small tray with six mints onto the table.

"Safe travels friends!"

Estee returns to the table as Ruth attaches the credit card to the check tray. Our waitress smiles before returning to the bar to run the card. She comes back shortly after with a weird look on her face.

"Which one of you is Burt?"

John raises his hand in order to normalize the interaction.

"I'm sorry sir, but your card has been declined. Do you have another card you want me to run?"

Estee reaches into her pocket and pulls out a folded clump of hundred dollar bills. She hands one to the waitress and smiles wide.

"You can keep the change… Just the tip!"

She points at the button which brings a big smile to the waitress's face.

"Well aren't you a dear! God bless you Sweetheart!"

Kevin is quick to stand up and grab both handles of my wheelchair. As the double doors to the restaurant open we all feel a sense of danger ahead. I watch as Estee's nostrils flare and her face twists into a look of discomfort.

"I smell it too."

The distinct odor of rotten eggs fills the windless air. We decide to make a break for the van parked thirty feet away in the handicap parking spot. John runs forward towards the van. When he's three steps away from the safety of the restaurant overhang, his arm is suddenly clutched in the talon of a flying beast.

The winged creature looks as though it has just been extinguished. Its feathers resemble snake scales more than feathers, and its beak is dripping with a black ooze reminiscent of tar. Ember eyes stare down at us from the roofline.

John is thrown against the side of the van. He doesn't move. Ruth makes a break for it, but is gobbled up by the second evil beast waiting for her. She too is thrown to the ground beside her husband. We all watch as she crawls helplessly towards her injured partner. I feel fear like I've never known.

I'm surprised to see Kevin grab the lid of a garbage can and wield it like a shield. Fred holds a black knife in hand while trying to decide on a course of action. We're all startled when the bell attached to the door above our head rings. Someone opens the diner door from behind.

Marching with the resolve of a seasoned war veteran is the waitress who served us breakfast. The scowl on her face and the shotgun in her hand would normally be a funny thing to witness. In the current circumstances I can't even bring myself to crack a smile.

We all hear the distinct sound of a shotgun slug racking into the chamber of the weapon. I glance up and read the writing on her shiny nametag. "Tilly."

The old woman strides forward while raising the butt of her rifle to her shoulder. She seems perfectly comfortable with the action. One loud concussion followed by another creates a puff of black smoke in the sky overhead. There is a loud squeal of pain before Tilly pumps the handle of her shotgun and aims at the second beast in the sky.

She unloads three more shells into the flying beast before it falls to the ground and crawls in our direction. Fred marches forward with his knife. The edge of his blade opens the throat of the expiring beast floundering on the asphalt. All that remains of the two evil creatures are small piles of sticky black tar underneath the places that they have expired.

Tilly tosses the empty shotgun into Kevin's hands before checking on John and Ruth beside the van. Both of my Guardians get back to their feet and express their gratitude to our elderly savior.

"I've seen a lot of birds in my day... Shot plenty of em too. But them damn creatures were something else. I hope y'all don't judge our lovely state of West Virginia too harshly y'all. I can't even say how embarrassed I feel right now."

We all stare at Tilly as though she's crazy. For some odd reason she seems perfectly okay taking responsibility for the odd scene that has just transpired.

"My Grand Pappy told me stories about Thunderbirds snatchin folks up, but I never thought he was tellin me the truth! Hot damn was that a fun time! Y'all better be gettin on your way now, I'll let the sheriff know what happened when he gets here."

We all walk like dazed zombies to the van. To be more specific I roll like a dazed zombie. There is something in the odd smile that Tilly gives us when we are pulling out of the parking lot that makes me extra thankful for her help. I can't put my finger on it though. Estee seems perplexed as well.

"What the holy hell was that all about? I'm not the only one who's baffled by what just happened, am I?"

John and Ruth both begin shaking their heads.

"You're not crazy Estee! That was other worldly crazy! Do humans really think that what just happened is normal?"

I shake my head while blinking rapidly.

"I guess they do in West Virginia. If we survive this adventure... I'm moving in next door to Tilly!"

We all collectively laugh and breathe in a deep sigh of relief as the rumble of the engine gets louder. Ruth rolls down the window of the van as we merge onto an empty highway. She gently flicks Burt's useless wallet into the grass filled center of the road.

"Looks like we need to find another way to fund this adventure now."

Estee reaches into her back pocket and pulls out the folded pile of hundred dollar bills.

"I got like a couple of grand here. Should be enough to get us back to my hometown!" Just keep heading west. I live in Texas."

John reaches forward and turns on the radio. I'm mildly annoyed that the music has ended the conversation. There is so much more that I want to know about Estee. Where she lives, what she does to make money, how old she is, and everything about her alter ego in Cyadonia. The one thing that we for sure have in common. There's really no telling how much she can teach me.

We drive the speed limit for hours on end stopping only for gas and what Kevin refers to as "Piss Breaks." Each time we stop Estee checks on me and makes sure that the urine bag attached to my leg is emptied. I can't help but be a little embarrassed that she is the one dumping out my pee bag.

The sun is beginning to set when ruth pulls off of a highway exit and drives along a small country road for a few miles. She turns the wheel and steers us into a motel whose vacancy sign is only half lit.

"At least they have free HBO!"

Kevin's comment breaks the tension that I'm feeling about sleeping in a strange place. Estee hands John her wad of money before opening the side door of the van. As the rest of my

Guardians get me to the ground and gather the two backpacks we are traveling with, John makes arrangements at the front desk.

He returns to the van and hands the remaining wad of bills back to Estee.

"I got us two rooms. Ruth and I will stay in one room with Kevin. Fred will watch over you two while you sleep. Silently!"

John shoves his finger into Fred's chest as he says the word "Silently." His son nods his head and reaches out to grab a hotel key from an outstretched arm. Attached to the key is a squishy floatation device. The key chain seems strange until we enter the motel room and see a large pond filled with fishing boats lining a wooden dock. If the room didn't smell like popcorn, I might consider leaving a good Yelp review online.

The room is small but clean. A flat screen tv is attached to the wall over top of a small dresser. Two twin beds fill the space opposite the tv. The bathroom is wheelchair accessible. I can't even describe how good a shower would feel right now. The thought of Estee seeing my crippled body naked sends a shiver of fear down my body.

I glance up at Fred after he exits the bathroom. It's as though he can read my mind. His eyes shift in the direction of our new companion.

"Ladies first in the facilities. After you're done, I will try and give Cam here a good scrub down."

I'm relieved that Estee doesn't try and volunteer for the job of helping me shower. Fred gives me a wink before sliding open the curtains covering a small back porch. He slides open the door and rolls me out into the fresh air. Behind us he closes a mangled screen door. There is the slight sound of buzzing in the air.

I stare out onto the lake and watch as small fish jump up out of the water to devour hovering bugs. There's a small rowboat in the center of the pond harboring a man with a large straw hat on. His torn overalls and greasy face make me guess that he is just unwinding from a long day of work. This is the first time I have thought back about the events that have transpired over the last few hours.

Fred turns his head as we both hear the sound of the shower in our room squeak to life.

"What I'd give to be in there right now!"

I'm slightly caught off guard by Fred's comment. He grins while I widen my eyes and nod in agreement.

"You and me both buddy! Just not at the same time!"

Fred laughs out loud at my joke as Kevin emerges on the porch next to ours.

"I can't believe I'm stuck in this room with your parents. They haven't stopped sucking face since we opened the door. It's freaking unsettling. Can I come hang out with you guys?"

"Sure thing Kevin."

The teenage boy grabs hold of a plastic lawn chair and sets it down on the porch surface beside me.

"Never thought we would make it this far did you... Veggie boy?"

I grin and spit out a bug that has unfortunately made its way onto my lips.

"I thought that we would make it this far. But I figured you would have run off somewhere along the journey. Why are you sticking around? I'm the one being hunted!"

I watch as Kevin shifts his gaze to the pond in front of us. The fisherman in the rowboat is tugging on his rod and twisting his hand against the reel. Kevin turns to look back at me with a sincere gaze.

"You're the first person I've ever known that doesn't think I'm crazy! Where else am I supposed to go? For the first time in my life things actually make sense! They will have to pry my dead hands off the handles of your wheelchair before I leave you behind."

I can't quite understand the feelings that rush into my heart after hearing Kevin's words. I know exactly how he feels. My mind wanders to the memories of what having a family felt like. I replay the feeling of warmth that I can remember when my mother hugged me. I decide that Kevin is the closest thing other than Fred that I have ever had to a brother.

The feelings coming to life inside of me spark a reminder that I still have a "Real Brother" in this world. A brother that I have not seen since the fateful day that my parents disappeared from this world.

The wind picks up slightly, shifting small puffs of cottonwood, and with it comes a slight chill in the air.

"We better get inside and get you cleaned up for bed!"

Kevin watches as Fred wheels me inside of the room.

"I'm just gonna relax out here for a while still. God only knows what's happening in my room right now. There are just some things in life that you can't unsee!"

The sliding glass door shuts behind us as Estee walks out of the bathroom door, with a towel covering her wet body stretching from her chest to her upper thighs.

"Your turn kid! Scrub him down good Fred. My gut tells me that we will work up quite a sweat tonight."

I glance behind us and see Kevin's lustful eyes peeking through the glass door. He averts his gaze like nothing happened when Estee turns and flips her hair toward the floor.

The door to the bathroom shuts leaving a half-naked beauty in the room behind us. I can't help but see her perfect figure every time I close my eyes. Fred does a better job at bathing me than I expected. He carefully puts my clothes back on before sniffing the pajamas I have been wearing since escaping the Institute.

"We really need to get you some fresh clothes buddy!"

"Look who's talking!"

Fred glances down before dusting off the front of a band t-shirt he's wearing. The second half of 'Nirvana' is almost unreadable through the sweat stains and dust covering it. The armpits of his shirt are also stained a darker color than the rest of the fabric.

"Good point. I'll try and get us something in the morning!"

When the bathroom door opens, Estee is laying in one of the beds wearing a tight black tank top. Fred places me carefully into my own bed before reaching onto the lamp table beside the bed and grabbing the remote control.

"Don't worry, I'll put on the subtitles and mute it!"

His body rests comfortably beside mine on the bed. A large pillow is wedged against the wall propping up his neck. I lay facing the ceiling before hearing two distinct claps. The lights go out at the sound.

"I can't believe they have the freaking clapper here! Epic!"

I see the dancing light of the television on the back of my eyelids. Fortunately enough my room in the institute faced some sort of blinking light in the distance. One of those lights that is used to warn aircraft about objects to avoid flying into.

The last thing I hear before the darkness takes me is the soft humming of a nursery rhyme that I have never heard before. The soft cadence of the noises coming from my fellow Centurian comfort me. I can't wait to wake up in Cyadonia.

CHAPTER 6

"You have failed me Cain! Of all those who serve me, it is you who I trust most! And you failed me!"

The wounded priest bowed deeply while holding the bleeding wound below his stomach.

"Forgive me master. The young Centurian is far more powerful than our spies had suspected! And he was not alone! Thoth served as protector, and the Queen's Army marched with the target as well!"

Gallus leaned forward in his large stone throne from its position towering over the assembly hall. His shadow danced over the bowing priest, cast down by massive fire braziers hanging from the ceiling.

"The Queen sent her Army to protect her young Centurian? So she is no longer protected by her legions of Shield Bearers?"

Cain instantly regretted his embellishment of the forces that had defeated him. He now needed to explain that only a handful of Immaru soldiers had helped defend the Centurian from his assassination attempt.

"Not exactly master... I may have unintentionally misled you when I said that the Queen's Army was present! Only a handful of her warriors accompanied the target."

Gallus let a growl come out of his mouth from between a clenched jaw. It was one thing for his priest to have failed the mission. It was an entirely different thing for one of his subjects to lie to him.

"Be careful Cain! This is the only time I will warn you to speak only the truth in my presence! Lest your tongue be removed as my Jailor finds the darkest cell for you to occupy."

"Forgive me 'Oh Deepest of Darkness.' No light shines while your presence is near!"

"Dispense with the flattery priest! What do you know of the other Centurians of Immaru? Have our spies located them yet? I hope that I do not need to remind you of the importance of this task."

Cain snapped his fingers at a cloaked man standing behind him in the doorway to the Great Hall.

"Tell the master what you have learned Thadius!"

A man covered in a dark cloak approached the throne before kneeling and looking up at his master. Gallus reached forward with his palm up and signaled for his messenger to rise. After getting back to his feet the man pulled out a small yellow piece of parchment covered in blood splatter.

"We intercepted this message from the Queen of Rain's personal messenger. The message was meant for King Nero in the Kingdom of Plenty!"

Gallus tilted his head and rocked his chin from side to side to rid himself of a small cramp forming at the nape of his spine. Attached to his shoulders were two mangled stumps of flesh and bone where once lived a set of celestial wings. Wings that were taken when he was cast down from the realm of the Sky Gods.

"Do not dither with your words Thadius! What does the Queen's message say?"

Thadius unrolled a long piece of yellow parchment before starting at the top of the letter.

"I write to you Mighty King with heavy words. Our scouts report a massive force of Demon soldiers gathering on your northwestern border. The force seems to have plans on crossing the Tigris river by your fortress of Knifespike. I write to you in order to offer assistance in the defense of both of our realms. As you read this letter I have dispatched two of my Centurians to Knifespike in order to help you keep the enemy on their side of the river. Should they be allowed to cross, there will be much death and dying not just in your territory, but also in mine. I have barred the gates to the City of Light for the time being. We both know that Gallus relies heavily on spies and saboteurs during his times of onslaught. Be well great King. I eagerly await your response."

Gallus chuckled for all in the Great Hall to hear. He rose from the precipice of his throne and descended the steps leading to his lordly perch. When he arrived in front of his servants, his shadow engulfed them. His shoulders sat a good four feet above those of the tall priests in front of him and the blackened veins pulsing on his arms displayed his heightened mood.

"Go forth Thadius, and tell my commander's to make haste to the river crossing. Make them aware that they will face two Immaru Centurians when they arrive. I wish for the Queen's warriors to be captured. Bring them before me so that I may twist their souls and bring them under my spell. I have need of more 'Priests'!"

Both cloaked priests bowed one last time before scurrying out of the Great Hall. When the doors of the hall closed Thadius placed his hand on the shoulder of his wounded ally.

"Stay still for a moment brother. I shall attempt to lessen the pain in your wound."

Cain shook his head from side to side.

"It's of no use Thadius. The wound was made not with magic, but with the blade of the Centurian I battled. Its nature is protected by a deep magic that not even our magical skills can disarm. I shall just need to heal this wound the old fashioned way!"

A small wince crossed the priest's face as he made way past his brother and in the direction of the castle entrance.

"Follow me Thadius, I will need your help cleaning my afflicted flesh. I do not know if I can do it on my own."

The two priests walked side by side out of the castle in the center of the fortress complex. Tall towers jutted out from the ground in every direction. The sides of each tower were pockmarked with sharp stone edges and a black gooey residue.

Each man gave a sullen head nod to the Demon warrior guarding the main castle entrance.

"Go forth and be shrouded with darkness Priests!"

The Demon's words were received as the two cloaked men walked through a small crack between two massive stone doors. Below the fortress complex sat a sprawling city. The City was bustling with drug and alcohol fueled fight pits. Every possible combination of foul beast roamed the streets looking to distract themselves from the coming war.

The Priests walked side by side until coming to the end of a wide alley. In front of them rose the outer walls of the "Church of Devouring." Living inside was the rest of the Priests of the "Order of Gallus." A brotherhood consisting of fallen Centurians, recruited and corrupted by the Dark Master of Gomorrah.

The doors to the Priestly Palace opened with the flick of Thadius's magical finger. Inside the main sanctuary the red painted walls were lined with worshipers of the dark arts. The air filled with the chants of dark magic and shadow realm prayers.

"Take my arm brother. I shall see you to the healing chamber!"

**

"Can we talk about what happened during that battle? Who the hell was that dude wielding magic against us?"

Thoth sipped at the edge of a small cup of hot tea. His slurping caused the soldiers from Immaru to glance at him in annoyance.

"He was once a young Centurian just like you... But he gave into the desire for power and prosperity, and chose to follow the teachings of Gallus. We all choose the master's that we serve. Let this be a lesson to you young Centurian. Where there is good, there is always an evil. The Creator has seen to this."

I turn my head and watch as Estee rolls a small stick between her thumb and forefinger. Her eyes haven't stopped watching the flames of the campfire that we awoke next to. She hasn't spoken a word in the five minutes that we have been awake in Cyadonia.

"You're really deep in thought over there?"

I watch as her eyes come to life. The fog covering her eyes lifts as she cracks a smile and tosses the stick into the coals of the campfire.

"Sorry, what were you saying?"

"I was asking Thoth about that dude that I had to fight. The one who could wield magic like we can!"

Estee glances at Thoth before speaking.

"You haven't told him about the 'Fallen Priests?' That's kind of information that he should know about!"

I shift my gaze to Thoth's face while waiting for him to answer her statement.

"He was too young and inexperienced for me to inform him. But you're right Centurian. He should know of the danger that he will face. And the choices that he will be forced to make."

I shake my head and look back and forth between my Wise Teacher and my fellow Centurian.

"Somebody needs to say something that makes sense now! Quit beating around the bush and just tell me everything! I can handle it!"

I see Thoth nod his head towards Estee.

"Here's the truth Cam. Before you and me, there have been many Centurians that chose to serve The City of Light or one of the other realms. There are also those that choose to serve the darkness. Many Centurians have been lured by Gallus into his service by promising riches and power. Even I have been tempted in the past to give in to his lies and luring, but I will never serve the Master of Darkness. He is the rot that destroys the hearts of men."

I listen carefully as Estee tells me all about the other Centurians that have fallen. She was once friend and ally to the man named Cain that I was forced to fight. They once fought the forces of darkness side by side, until Cain made the fateful decision to serve Gallus. Estee refuses to expand on her former ally's reasons for joining the enemy.

"For as strong as we are, they too are formidable. The dark magic is just as strong as the magic we wield against it. Take warning Cam, the whispers of temptation will one day find you. He will know your deepest desires, and he will offer you something that will be hard to reject. This is how he turns the forces of good to his cause."

I can see that her mood has changed. Her tone is somber and hints at a hidden pain that I can't put my finger on. Thoth interrupts story time by standing up and pointing his cane towards the back of the cave.

There are two sets of ember eyes watching us. Each set of eyes hovers inside of the faceless shape of a Shadow Person.

"Remember what I told you about the Shadow people Young Centurian!"

I stand up and put on my armor as one of the Shadow People begins whispering into my ear.

"You are truly powerful young warrior! We possess the power

to help you. If only you would serve our Dark Master. We could give you anything you desire. Even the healing of your body in the human realm. Think carefully about our Master's divine offer."

I squint my eyes as the words echo in my ears. Thoth waves his walking stick, and Estee places her palm in the air pointing towards the two Shadow People whispering into my ears. There's a bright burst of light before the two sets of Ember eyes are flung away from me and explode into puffs of black smoke.

Estee stares at me without breaking eye contact. I can see that she wants something.

"What did they offer you Cam? Did Gallus offer to fix your body in the Human realm? That's what I would tempt you with if I was trying to shift your allegiance!"

I shake my head up and down. The thought that I could be whole in the real world is tempting to say the least, but there is a strong feeling in my heart telling me to serve the light.

"Yeah, that's exactly what they offered. What did they offer you Estee?"

"Something similar…"

Her response is vague and shrouded in secrecy. I realize that I really don't know anything about her. She's a mystery, and that seems to be the way she wants to keep it.

Her shoulders twist towards the cave entrance in an obvious attempt to shift the conversation away from her own story. I decide to play it cool.

"Fine! I don't need to know everything about you… You barely know anything about me. Fair is fair."

I grin at the beautiful face that seems to be returning from a place of great sorrow. She squints one eye while staring at me. The old Estee is back. Her emerald eyes capture the small amount of light coming from the magic gems overhead. Her attention is again captured by something at the front of the cave. I can't help but think that maybe I was wrong about her intentions during our conversation.

Against the backdrop of the cloudy sky outside the cave, an imposing figure stands with sword in hand. Estee grabs hold of her own sword and unsheathes it before I can even get to my feet. Her and Thoth are already approaching the stranger as I gain my balance and charge a lightning bolt in my hand.

Both of my companions stop before reaching the stranger. The remaining Queen's soldiers form a small shield wall behind us. The man holding his ground in front of us stands with a slight lean in his posture. I notice a rather large clay jug in one of his hands before Estee calls out to him.

"Show yourself! Remove your hood so that we may look on your face at once Stranger!"

I always find it funny that people talk like that in Cyadonia. It's even funnier to me because I know how Estee talks in the real world. Her cadence and word choice while speaking in Cyadonia is almost poetic. I chuckle for a second, an act that receives a swift rebuke from Thoth's walking stick.

The man staggers two steps sideways before catching his balance against the wall of the cave. He seems to be drunk.

"Calm your pretty little self Centurian! I come baring friendly tidings, and other things."

The man reveals a large sack that he has been hiding during the conversation.

"King Nero sends his regards! He has sent me to protect the young Centurian that the Queen of Rain has sent to shelter from the coming storm."

The man raises his hand in the air with the intention to point out the fact that we seem not to need his protection.

"Not that you need any help from a drunk like me! That's

probably why the King sent me instead of one of his other Centurians. Figures as much! I never get sent on the cool missions!"

His speech tone and words remind me of the New Yorkers that I'm used to speaking with at the Institute. The man stumbles again before catching his balance. The bag that he had slung across his shoulder slides off and comes to a crashing stop on the floor. Whatever was inside of the bag begins leaking onto the stone floor from whatever vessel has just broken.

The Centurian from The Kingdom of Plenty realizes his mistake. He quickly drops to one knee and begins rummaging through the bag of booze filled containers.

"A lot of help he's gonna be. Dude brought enough booze to drown himself for the better part of the month."

I watch as Thoth approaches the man and lifts his hood up using his walking stick. The man's face is partially covered by lengths of black hair. His chin and cheeks are painted with a thick stubble, and his eyes are watery and bloodshot.

"Help me get him to the campfire. He could use a good long nap to sober up."

Estee and I both grab an arm and slowly drag our fellow Centurian towards the campfire behind us. I hear the distinct sound of clay cracking, and some sort of fluid running down the stone stairs we have just traveled.

Behind us Thoth is emptying the jars of booze that our ally has brought along on his journey.

"How pissed do you think he's gonna be when he wakes up and finds out that Thoth poured out all of his Honey Wine!"

I see Estee calculate her response. She has a mischievous way about her.

"At least you might get to see someone beat Thoth up for you. Cause when this guy sobers up, I have a feeling that he is gonna be pretty formidable."

I glance down and give the man's arm that I'm grasping onto a quick squeeze. She's probably right! He has big muscles, not just big, they're tightly packed to the touch as well. *Dude must get to the gym like twice a day or something.*

"You've never met this guy? I figured that you 'older' Centurians might have a secret club or something. I was starting to feel a little bit left out that my invitation must have gotten lost in the mail or something?"

"No kid! There's no secret club or anything. We Centurians normally don't interact with the other Guardians from the realm we serve. The only reason we met is because the Queen decided that we should. I've only ever met one other Centurian from the City of Light. I'm not even sure how many of us there are. My Wise Teacher once mentioned the rule of seven. 'Seven torches light the fires of the halls of glory'… Or something like that. I was young, and my listening skills back then were definitely not top notch!"

I feel the familiar sting of Thoth's walking stick in the small of my back. The impact of his correctional strike is light this time.

"Take my Centurian to the place we talked about earlier Estee. It is more appropriate that he learns the history of this world in the very place it began. Go!"

I feel Estee grab my arm and tug me in the direction of the cave entrance. She walks at a brisk pace. We walk mostly in silence through paths flanked on either side by leafless trees and bushes. The tops of the mountains we travel are covered in snow and ice. The wind is biting. I charge my fire magic in each hand and direct the heat towards my face and neck from time to time to thaw my skin.

After cresting the top of a hill I feel the temperature rise a bit. Estee stands at the ridgeline looking down into a large valley covered in yellow and purple flowers. She bumps her shoulder into mine and grins.

"We're here!"

We both trot down a steep mountain trail until my guide stops beside a large boulder. When I look closer I can see that the boulder has been carved into the likeness of an angelic warrior. Much like the statues that I saw in the Throne Room of the Sky gods, but these statues have wings, and the faces of men.

"Who came all the way out here to carve these stones?"

Estee exhales and points out to a field of boulders much like the one we are standing beside.

"No one carved them Cam. These are the hero's that saved the Realms of man and beast from 'The Fall.' It was a great battle waged between the warriors of the Sky God's, and those who had betrayed their maker. Gallus was the first of the Sky God's servants to betray them. He desired power over the other creations that the Sky Gods had begun to favor. Mankind to be more specific."

I run my hand along the stone sword blade of the frozen warrior. I almost feel as though there is still life within the casing of the rock surface. Much like the feeling I used to get when waking my Guardians after arriving in Cyadonia. I concentrate hard and try and wake the stone warrior beside me.

There's a slight tremble in the ground as I spread my magic over the stone soldier. I feel a swift tug on my arms. The look on Estee's face suggests that I have made a huge error.

"What, I was just trying to see if I could wake this one up!"

We both take a small step back as the stone covering the frozen Warrior begins to melt. I'm surprised when Estee unsheathes her sword and charges some sort of spell in her hand.

"I thought you said that these guys fought for the Sky Gods! What's the big deal?"

I pull my own sword just in case while Estee steps in between me and the waking being.

"Get behind me you fool. There's no way to tell which side this warrior fought for. You might have just woken an ancient enemy."

The stone surrounding the Sky Warrior crumbles to the ground. Its wings extend over a human body almost double the size of a fully grown man. His eyes are the brightest color of blue that I have ever seen. Estee digs her back foot into the ground and prepares for battle. I feel a rush of guilt wash over me.

"Stay your hand human! You stand no chance to defeat one such as me! Who has woken me from the deep slumber cast upon me by my Creator?"

I can see that Estee is still ready to strike. She places one hand behind her back, trying to signal for me to remain quiet. It's not in me to remain silent. There's something about this warrior's bright blue eyes that calm my spirit.

"I woke you up!"

"Shut up Cam, Stay behind me!"

I push past Estee's sword hand and watch as the Sky Warrior unsheathes a massive sword covered in a thin layer of shifting flames. He runs his fingers along the blade in adoration before stretching both of his wings out to the side and fluttering them quickly.

"You're lucky that I once served the Creator in this battle young man. I have lingered in this place for many generations. Captured by the dark spaces that imprisoned my mind. It was many a time that I contemplated my decision to remain loyal to the Creator."

The Sky Warrior sheaths his sword and packs his wings behind his back. I can feel the tension in the situation growing less and less with every moment.

"Why have you come to this place?"

This time Estee gives me a look that I dare not disobey.

"I have brought this young Centurian to this place to tell him the stories of the past. But then he..."

She pauses before continuing.

"Then he 'Woke' you somehow. How do we know that you did not serve Gallus during the battle? He and the ones who serve him are the purveyors of lies and trickery!"

The Sky Warrior places one hand against the ground before lowering himself into a sitting position. He seems far less intimidating in this posture. A development that I'm sure is on purpose, if only to stay the hand of the girl standing next to me ready to strike.

"If I had served Gallus, you surely would already be dead young woman! The forces of the 'Fallen' do not value human life. They only seek to twist and occupy your hearts. I can sense that this place is still protected by the magic that the maker bestowed upon it! It's good that Gallus has not been able to wake his minions contained within the stone in this valley. Should they ever awake, this world, and many more would suffer greatly."

I see Estee's shoulders relax a bit. She seems to believe the words that are being spoken.

"I am the one called Fendril. My creator named me such in the ancient times. You may call me by this name as well humans. I must warn you not to wake anymore of the stone warriors in this valley. The Creator cast a powerful spell when the battle seemed to be going poorly. A spell that was encouraged by those of us fighting in his name. We sacrificed our lives so that Gallus would not be able to take over the realms of man. He was the lone coward among us that retreated as the spell was being cast from the heavens."

I look down at formations of stone warriors engaged in battle.

It's as if I can see the fight taking place hundreds if not thousands of years ago. I squint my eyes as the sun pops through the clouds overhead. It seems that the main battle had taken place in the center of the valley where a thick layer of flowers covered the ground.

"Why were you so far from the main battle Fendril?"

I see ghosts of the past fill his blue eyes. He looks at me and points at the ridgeline that we descended from only minutes before.

"I was chasing Gallus when the spell took effect. I can still see the wry smile on that bastard's face as I and every other Sky Warrior, both 'Fallen' and 'Loyal' were turned to stone. He ran away like the coward he is! Now that I am free of the Creator's slumber, I shall chase him to the ends of this realm and any other he exists."

Our conversation is cut short as Thoth appears on the hillside. He limps down the mountain path until he comes to a stop and bows deeply in respect.

"You wear the crest of the Creator! Are you 'Loyal" or 'Fallen'?"

"I am and will always remain 'Loyal' little man!"

I can see that Thoth is unsure if he should believe Fendril's words."

"Show me your wrist Sky Warrior, and prove your loyalty before I strike you down!"

I watch as Fendril smiles wide. He reaches out his wrist. At the edge of his hand a thick golden tattoo is visible. It looks as if the colors of his tattoo itself contains the sun in the sky overhead!

"Here is the tree of life!"

I see lines of gold ink forming the image of a tree with long thin root lines. Below the roots are two symbols that I don't recognize. "☐".

I watch as Thoth bends down so low to the ground that his

forehead rests on the dirt.

"Forgive me! Forgive my reluctance to believe your words!"

Fendril nods his head towards the Wise Teacher before smiling.

"There is nothing to forgive. I too would be cautious old man. Tell me, How long have I slumbered in this valley?"

I can see that Thoth is confused.

"It must be a hundred generations or more! There is no way for me to tell you truly. The ancient writings were lost five hundred years past when Gallus razed the City of Light and the library of Enlightenment."

"So he's still alive? Point me in his direction old man. I shall smite him in the name of the Creator!"

I can see that Thoth is hesitant to answer Fendril's question.

"Please have patience Sky Warrior, his fortress of darkness is far too well protected for you to defeat him alone. I shall take you to the Realm of the Sky Gods and ask them for an audience. But first we must get you somewhere out of sight. Even here in the valley, Gallus has Shadow People that report what their eyes and ears discover."

We arrive back at the cave entrance after a long and boring journey. Before entering Thoth casts a powerful spell.

"The Shadow People will not be able to see in this cave anymore."

I glance at Estee to get her reaction to the spell that my Wise Teacher has just cast.

"Why didn't he do that from the start?"

She shrugs her shoulders before entering the cave.

"Cause it's important that you understand the forces that we are up against. It's important that you overcome your own temptations. Only then will you wield a power that can defeat

Gallus himself!"

The day is almost over. I sit by the man that showed up drunk hours before. He's struggling with the news that his Wine reserve is gone, but his attention seems to be firmly attached to the Sky Warrior that has now joined us.

"This day just keeps getting weirder doesn't it!"

His voice is raspy, and its cadence suggests that he is still feeling the lingering effects of the booze that he consumed on his journey to the cave.

"Yeah man. You should probably just sleep it off a bit more. We'll all be here when you wake up!"

CHAPTER 7

"Welcome back to the real world."

I lift my head up from a surprisingly comfortable motel pillow. This is the first time in a long time that I am able to move my head so freely. Thanks to Estee's magic necklace. Fred is still lying next to me watching some sort of reality television show with the subtitles on and the volume muted. I can hear the rustling of sheets coming from Estee's bed as she wakes from the dream realm.

"I don't feel as well rested as I normally do when returning from Cyadonia. How do you feel Cam?"

I swallow a small clump of saliva that appeared on my tongue after smelling the odor of burning bacon from somewhere nearby.

"I feel a bit drowsy. Why do we feel different this time?'

"I don't know, but it better not be permanent. I need my beauty sleep!"

She climbs on her hands and knees to the end of the bed before reaching up with both hands to stretch. I can see Fred's eyes wander momentarily away from the TV show that he has been binging all night long on the discovery channel.

His eyes dart back to the TV for a moment before looking over at me and realizing that he has been caught peeking.

"Nice man! Real nice!"

He grins before pushing the top button on the television remote. I feel his hands grasp onto either one of my shoulders before propping me up against the headboard. It feels good to be sitting up.

Estee finishes her morning stretches before reaching into her backpack and grabbing a pair of running shoes. Before I have a chance to alter my gaze, she's bending over in front of my bed tying the laces to a bright yellow pair of running shoes.

"I'm gonna have a quick jog! Be back in fifteen!"

She literally runs out the door at a pace that makes me laugh out loud. She's a strange girl sometimes. It's a good thing she's so pretty, or people might think she's a bit weird. I'm not sure if other people in this world would enjoy her quirks as much as I do. And the more time we spend together the more quirks I discover.

The door closes behind her as a gust of wind comes through the sliding glass door that Fred has just opened. The morning air is brisk and cold, but the smell of bacon coming from a small stove by the lake is a welcome treat.

"Let's get you out of bed and see what they have to eat around here."

Fred lifts my broken body from the bed and places it into the wheelchair sitting in front of the TV. He's pretty strong, and the look on his face suggests that I don't weigh enough to be a burden to lift.

"You been hitting the gym when no one is looking Fred?"

"No time for that Cam. This body is all natural dude. You're just not used to seeing me in it yet! Hell, I'm not even used to being in this body yet!"

He rolls me out onto the back porch where Kevin is sitting with his knees bent and feet placed by his butt on the plastic chair. He's holding a white ceramic mug that sends small puffs of white mist into the air every time he blows on the surface.

"I grabbed some coffee from the front desk. It's not bad."

He gently sips at the rim of the mug before his tongue is burned by the hot liquid inside.

"Not quite ready yet!"

He squeezes his eyes shut and then back open again as the pain of his burnt tongue sends a shockwave through his body. I look out over the small lake in front of us and notice that there are far more fisherman out on the water than there were the night before.

The man in the overalls and straw hat is once again sitting inside of a rowboat while bobbing the end of his fishing rod up and down in a rhythmic fashion.

"What do you think they're fishing for out there?"

Kevin's reply is short and blunt.

"Fish!"

I glance at Kevin's smart ass face.

"I know that retard! I mean what kind of fish!"

"Who knows! Probably some type of trout or something! Not my area of expertise. I didn't exactly take a lot of fishing trips with my dad!"

It is the first time I can remember Kevin even mentioning that he had parents. For all the time we have lived together in the Institute, we both know pretty much nothing about each other.

"Me either! Boats aren't exactly wheelchair friendly!"

I see a small grin appear on Kevin's face. He turns toward me and reaches out the coffee mug in his hand.

"You want some?"

I shake my head in the negative.

"No thanks. Coffee gives me the runs. Like explosive diarrhea! I'm pretty sure nobody wants that to happen when we're all stuck in that van."

He withdraws the mug while shaking his head up and down.

"Good looking out bro!"

Fred reappears on the porch and takes a seat on the stairs leading to the wooden deck. He grabs a handful of small stones and begins throwing them one at a time towards a small tree stump. Inside the middle of the stump is a small pool of water left over from the rain that fell overnight. Each time he hits the mark a small splash of dirty water covers the edges of the dead tree.

All three of us turn our heads as we notice movement coming from the tree line. Estee bursts out of the bushes running at a full blown sprint. I feel my chest tighten and my jaw clench in worry. Kevin and Fred must also be worried by the frantic pace of our friend's exercise.

She puts all our minds to ease as she sprints past us with a smile. Before disappearing she leaps up on top of a picnic table and flips forward before vanishing again around the far end of the motel.

"That chick is crazy! She should have been the one locked up in the Looney Bin!"

Me and Fred both agree with Kevin's statement. The wild nature of her exercise routine and frantic pace was strange to witness at best.

"Somebody needs to tell her that she needs to try and blend in a little better!"

Kevin points out at the lake. Every person floating on the surface has diverted their eyes in the direction that Estee disappeared. Instead of reappearing outside, we all hear the front door of the motel room open and slam shut.

"I'm back! Gonna take a quick shower, then we should get some food and try and find somewhere to buy some new clothes. You boys stink!"

All three of our eyes are spread wide before a cascade of laughter fills the morning air. The shower in the room activates and I can tell that all three of us are visualizing what is happening inside the confines of those shower tiles.

"Snap out of it Kevin."

I can't stand to stare at the perverted grin displayed openly on his face.

We all start laughing again as John and Ruth appear on the porch next to us.

"What's so funny boys?"

We all look at each other and make a silent pact to hide the truth of our laughter.

"Nothing at all Mother! How did you sleep?"

We watch as John slaps his wife on the rear end and whispers something in her ear. Her giggle suggests that whatever he told her would be kept in confidence.

"Gross! You two need to chill out!"

Kevin glares at my two married Guardians as they climb the steps onto our deck.

"Next time I'm not sharing a room with those two. There's only so much sound a pillow can keep out. There are not enough pillows in the world to forget some of the noises those two were making last night!"

Fred shook his head in disgust while staring at his parents.

"Gross you guys! You guys are too old to be doing that stuff!"

I watch a grin forming on John's face.

"How do you think you got here Fred? You should be thankful that your parents still love each other!"

"EW! That's enough guys, let's keep it professional!"

I can't help but smile a bit as the awkward energy that

surrounds us disappears slowly. We all decide on a plan for the day before breaking up and going to our separate rooms.

After packing what little belongings we brought along, Fred exits the room tossing two backpacks into the van. Kevin pushes my wheelchair towards the main office of the Motel complex. Inside is a table covered in bagels and breakfast foods. After eating, we all pile into the van and start driving towards the nearest Walmart.

We roll through the doors and are greeted by an old man wearing dark glasses who can barely stand upright without the help of his walker. His yellow and green vest hang loosely from his body. His voice is shaky when he greets us and asks if there is anything in particular we might need help finding.

John says "no" as we all pass by. Only Kevin gives the man one last defensive look while pushing my chair past the checkout lines.

"We better keep our eyes on that guy. Something about him gives me the 'Willies' Cam!"

I turn my head and see that the old man is still staring at us as we disappear down a grocery aisle and out of his range of vision.

"Seemed pretty harmless to me man!"

"Maybe, but thought I smelled something funny when we passed him…"

"He's like ninety years old Kevin! He's probably wearing a diaper. Poor guy probably can't retire. I feel bad for him!"

I watch ahead as John and Ruth both cruise down the clothing racks looking for items to purchase. Estee returns to me and Kevin and lays a black t-shirt over my chest to make sure it will fit.

John does the same with a Hawaiian button up shirt. The look on Estee's face is one of disgust as she rips the colorful shirt out of John's hands and tosses it onto the nearest clothing rack.

"You just focus on yourself John! I'll take care of Cam!"

She glances over at Fred who has just snatched the Hawaiian "Bird" themed shirt from the rack where she had just deposited it. As he holds it up to make sure it will fit, Estee's quick hand reaches out and reclaims it.

"Looks like I need to find suitable clothing for you too Fred!"

She glances down at me and leaves me with the image of her grinning face. We shop quickly, filling a cart with two or three outfits for each of us. Estee has taken great care in constructing my new wardrobe. To her undying pleasure.

We stop by the sporting goods section of the store to gather a few supplies that my Guardians are pretty sure we should have. I see John's eyes locked onto a black shotgun attached to the wall behind the gun counter. Estee calmly approaches him and whispers into his ear.

I can't make out what my fellow Centurian tells the leader of my Guardians, but whatever it was, causes a small smirk to appear on John's face before he slaps Estee on the back in celebration.

After gathering a couple sleeping bags, and a few other items that Fred needs to create a survival kit, we approach the self-checkout line and begin scanning our items. Everything seems normal until I feel Kevin's hand grasp my shoulder.

The old man from the front door is now flanked on either side by two elderly women wearing the same yellow and green vests as he is. Estee seems to sense something similar to what Kevin does.

We finish checking out and move towards the sliding doors at the front of the store. To our surprise the old man stops us and asks for our receipt. John hands the man the receipt as the two woman move to either side of us. We are now surrounded.

"Nothing to be worried about, but we need you to follow us to the security station for a routine inspection please!"

The old man points towards a door labeled "Security." I can sense something is wrong now.

"What's the problem Sir? We paid for everything, you can see on that receipt!"

"Nothing to worry about Son… This is just standard procedure."

I hear a deep inhale from Kevin's mouth. From the sideways angle we're now looking at the old man, we can both see around the frames of his black glasses. His eyes are the color of ember!

Kevin claps his hands before wheeling my chair around and pushing me as fast as he can. He yells back to the rest of our friends.

"They aren't human!"

I can't see how the fight begins, but I hear loud shrieking, like the sounds that come from the Demons of Gomorrah. There's a commotion from behind that sends plastic shopping baskets flying overhead as I speed away from the ongoing conflict.

Kevin keeps pushing me in one direction as Estee catches up to us and begins jogging backwards looking for a weapon. As we enter the sports section her eyes fixate on a long curved wooden hockey stick.

"This will do fine!"

She grabs the stick and a long aluminum baseball bat from beside it and sprints back towards the ongoing fight. Fred appears next holding a long machete that he has scavenged from the gun counter. I'm surprised that he isn't holding a gun, but he's used to fighting with a sword, so it makes sense the more I think about it. Kevin has grabbed hold of a compound bow and is struggling to open a package of blunt tipped arrows when the entire shopping rack leans over and crashes down on top of us.

My chair is tossed away as I slide out of it and am pinned to the floor by the massive metal framing of the shelving unit. Kevin carefully crawls under the shelving structure and begins pulling me out. There's a dull pain coming from my right thigh. I look down and see that there's a small piece of the metal shelving unit that has punctured my leg.

Kevin's eyes get big once he sees the protruding piece of metal.

"That's not good man! We need to get you to the hospital or something!"

I reach down and touch the piece of metal running from the front of my shriveled quadricep muscle and out the side of my leg. The metal lodged itself at an angle, probably missing my main artery. As weird as it sounds, I feel a profound sense of luck wash over me.

"Should I pull it out or something?"

I shake my head at Kevin. He has a panicked look in his eyes. That look turns to fear as I watch his gaze shift from my leg, towards the toppled sport's section in front of us. His hands grab the bow that he was holding before the current events had transpired.

There's a small Demon dressed in the skin of an elderly woman limping toward us. In her hand is a blade made from some type of shiny stone. Behind her are the sounds of hand to hand combat. There must have been more of the Demons hiding than just the three elderly greeters at the front door.

The Demon woman limps forward on a broken ankle probably suffered during the ensuing moments of the fight. I hear a 'Thump" as the string of Kevins bow releases an arrow towards our approaching enemy. I'm defenseless, and the realization of that particular piece of information causes a sweat bead to form on my forehead.

The poorly aimed arrow zips well above the Demon, lodging in the side of a cardboard box containing a baby stroller within. I glance at Kevin who is attaching the split end of another arrow to the bow string.

"That wasn't even close dude!"

"What the heck do you want from me? I've never shot a bow dude. Closest thing I've ever come to this is watching robin hood in the rec room!"

"Well… Aim lower!"

The next arrow Kevin fires strikes the approaching Demon in the stomach. The ember eyed Demon grasps hold of the arrow shaft and pulls swiftly. A small squirt of black sludge spills out onto the floor as the arrow is tossed into a pile of stuffed animals beside her path of travel.

I see Estee leap over a falling rack of flip flops while trying to evade two of the bigger Demon warriors like the ones we faced at the Institute. She has her hands full. I can pretty much only hope that Kevin can pull himself together and defend me.

"Last arrow Cam!"

"Make it count buddy!"

I watch as Kevin's hand strategically pulls back the bowstring while shaking almost uncontrollably. His eye is fixated down the shaft of the arrow. He whispers something akin to a prayer while releasing the string. The black sunglasses that the elderly Demon is wearing shatter as the rounded tip of the arrow breaks through, penetrating her eye socket.

There's a guttural scream before the frail body of the old woman hits the floor. Black ooze pours from the Demon's mouth as Kevin stands up and thrusts both fists into the air in celebration.

"That's my third if you count the two that got me condemned to the "Looney Bin." And you sure as hell know that I most certainly count those "Dickheads"! You just got 'Hunger Gamed' bitch!"

His celebration is cut short as Estee appears holding a tar covered hockey stick in hand. The tip of the blade has been fractured forming a jagged curved edge. From the look of it the makeshift weapon has been used to great success.

She snatches my wheelchair from the next aisle and helps Kevin get me back up before noticing the metal piece sticking out of my leg. Her hands gently wrap around the end of the metal piece.

"No! I saw on a TV show that you're supposed to leave it in!"

She shakes her head and pulls out the pendant from beneath her shirt. The pain is sudden and intense. Before I even realize what has transpired, there's a blood soaked metal piece sitting on my lap. I then feel an intense cold feeling at the wound site. I look down and see that there's still a pretty big wound on my leg.

The look on Estee's face is one of partial embarrassment.

"I didn't have enough magic to fix your leg completely! But I stopped the bleeding at least, and reanimated most of the muscle. Not that your skinny little bird legs have much of that!"

I feel Kevin push me forward at the behest of my fellow Centurian. We run down aisle after aisle until we finally reach the front of the store. The fight is over. The old man from the front door is headless, and there are at least five large piles of Demon residue left behind by dispatched Demon warriors from Cyadonia.

My smile dissipates as I notice that John and Ruth are kneeling down in conversation with someone on the ground. That someone is Fred. He grasps tightly onto a large gash running from his shoulder down to his hip. The floor is covered in blood coming from his wound. I hear a pained sound come from my own mouth.

John and Ruth rise to their feet as a bright light erupts from their son's chest. Both of my remaining Guardians have tears in their eyes. John points at the door.

"We need to get moving! He sacrificed himself so that all of us could live! Let's use his sacrifice wisely! There will be time to mourn later!"

I look back the entire time that Kevin is pushing me out towards the parking lot. I feel my eyes welling up as John and Kevin place me into the back of the van. After everyone is inside, the doors close and the engine starts. We speed away from the last place that we will ever see Fred.

My memory engages and I replay the first time that I ever saw Fred. It was he who greeted me when I awoke in Cyadonia for the first time as a young boy. *Fred was my oldest friend, and now he's gone!*

I see John's hand reach sideways from the driver's seat and rest on his wife's leg. She seems more angry than sad. A feeling that I'm starting to understand.

"How the hell did they find us again?"

I can see that Kevin is trying just as hard as I am to figure out how the Demons were still tracking us. Then I see his eyes light up.

Kevin reaches into the back pocket of the driver's seat and pulls out the iPad that belongs to Burt.

"You guys think that this thing could be tracking us?"

I nod my head and look over at Estee.

"Only one way to know for sure!"

Estee and Kevin decide to formulate a plan to figure out how the enemy is tracking our movement.

**

We park the van in the empty lot of a "Park and Ride." Ruth stays behind and hides in the tree line to watch the van. Kevin and Estee take the iPad after stealing a car and drive it two miles to the south. There they place the device under a wooden bench beside a greyhound bus stop.

We communicate using the kids radios that we snatched from Walmart before escaping. The range is limited, but we should be able to figure out if the Demons are following the iPad, or worse, if they have a way of tracking the van we stole while escaping the Institute.

Three hours go by. I'm nervous that the enemy will show up after I fall asleep. My worry is relieved when a call comes over the radio from Estee and Kevin.

"A big U-Haul truck just showed up. Like twenty human Demon hybrids jumped out and surrounded the bus station! I think we can be pretty sure that they were tracking the iPad!"

I can see that John is relieved that we have figured out how the enemy is tracking our movement. Before we can celebrate too much, I notice movement entering the abandoned "Park and Ride" station.

A large black truck pulling a big luxury trailer pulls up next to the van. I watch the look on John's face darken as a man gets out of the driver's side of the truck, and begins to inspect the van. There's something familiar about the walk of the man in the parking lot.

"Is that who I think it is?'

I nod my head in John's direction.

"Looks that way John! It also looks like he's alone… You think he might be working with the Demons?"

I can see that John is taking my question seriously.

"I don't know. But I can guarantee we are about to find out!"

I radio for the rest of the group to sneak back to the van

location. John parks my chair behind some thin bushes. The leaves are just thin enough for me to make out what happens next. I hear a girlish scream as a portly body is grabbed from behind and tossed down onto the pavement.

Estee and Kevin arrive and stand beside me and Ruth. The radio in Kevin's hand receives a message from John who has detained the man inspecting our van.

"You guys won't believe this. It's safe. Come check this out!"

Kevin off-road's my wheelchair over tree roots and fallen branches before arriving on the dilapidated concrete of the abandoned parking lot. He pushes me quickly while maintaining a jog.

As we arrive back at the van I can see that John has pinned a man to the concrete face down, and has his knee in the small of the man's back. I immediately recognize the man.

"What the heck are you doing here Burt?"

I try hard to contain my rage. Burt's eyes light up when he hears my voice. He doesn't seem to act like someone who wants to harm me.

"Holy crap Cam! You can talk now? That's awesome man!"

He lays face down in discomfort on the concrete as we all gauge his surprising reaction to hearing me speak.

"What are you doing here Burt? Are you tracking us? Are you working with the Demons?"

I see a look of confusion enter his face.

"Those asshats were Demons? Like from Cyadonia? Holy crap... I just thought they were from the FBI or something, with those black glasses and crappy attitudes!"

John lift's his knee and lets Burt crawl up from his belly and roll over onto his butt.

"I reported my van got stolen to the police, then these weird

FBI dudes showed up and started asking all kinds of questions about you and my comic books!"

He pauses while retelling the story of the recent events that happened to him. His eyes meet mine and I can tell that he feels some sort of guilt. Either for using me, or for getting caught using me to make money.

"I'm sorry I didn't tell you about the comic series Cam! I was going to tell you! But then I thought I'd surprise you. The timing just never felt right."

Kevin interrupts the conversation in his typical sarcastic tone.

"I'm sure the money had nothing to do with the timing never feeling 'right'?"

"You have to believe me Cam! I never meant to exploit you or anything! I was planning on sharing all of the profits from your stories Fifty-Fifty! I swear, I even set up a separate savings account and everything! My lawyer said the money transfer was tricky because you were a committed minor without a parent Guardian! But the money is still yours!"

Estee steps forward and raises her hands into the air in a questioning fashion.

"What the hell is this guy talking about, and who is he?"

We all remember at the same time that she joined our little adventure party after the revelations about Burt's betrayal presented themselves.

Kevin takes the chance to explain everything to Estee in as few words as necessary.

"This guy was a nurse at the Institute. He tricked Cam into telling him stories about Cyadonia. Then he made a boat load of money off of a comic book series he published about Cam's dreams. We stole his van when we escaped, and now he tracked us down. Does that sum it up enough?"

Estee purses her lips and nods her head up and down.

"Strait to the point. I like your style Kevin."

Kevin's cheeks began to turn bright red as the words spoken by Estee sink in. She notices almost immediately, and responds.

"For the last time. I don't date younger men! Is everyone clear on that now? Can't even give one of you a freaking compliment without complications!"

My thoughts drift back to Fred. I'm startled back to reality by the slamming of the van door.

"Here! I put one of these 'trackers' on the van a long time ago. I tried to get the cops to get it back, but they told me that they don't do vehicle recovery, and that I would need to hire a private company to get my stolen van back! That's why I came here in the first place!"

"Figures that your reason for being here would be selfish!"

The cutting rebuke in Kevin's words make Burt lower his head in shame. He lifted his chin slightly to make his case.

"I didn't tell the FBI guys about the van tracker. Something inside me told me to keep that to myself. And the cops that I did tell didn't even take a report or anything!"

Burt's eyes made eye contact with my own as he spoke the next sentence.

"I never wanted to hurt you Cam... And now that I've witnessed the reality of the stories you have been telling me for years... I only want to help protect you!"

Burt points towards his truck and trailer.

"That's why I brought my trailer. I figured that if my hunch that it was you who stole my van panned out, that you might need somewhere to hide out. It's yours! And yours too!"

He looks around at the group for sympathetic eyes. I decide that Burt has suffered enough for one day.

"So you're coming with us then?"

His eyes light up after hearing my probing question.

"I'm not sure where you're going Cam, but I'll go anywhere at this point. Those FBI guys kept calling and showing up every day asking about you! I had to go full blown "spy mode" to get my trailer from storage and escape those guys that were following me!"

I can see that John is worried after learning that Burt was being followed.

"How do you know you got away clean. Could you have been followed here?"

"No way. I snuck out in the middle of the night and rode my electric bicycle to the storage facility that I keep in my mother's maiden name. It's a secure facility just outside of the city. I drove strait here, following the tracker on the van. I was careful to double back from time to time and check my mirrors to make sure I wasn't being followed."

We are all a little impressed with Burt's ability to escape the Demon entities back in New York. He points to the truck.

"We should get moving though. We can leave the van here. Hopefully, she'll be okay. I hope nobody tries to steal her...It took weeks to get the paint job done right!"

Burt and John climb into the truck pulling the trailer, while ruth helps Estee and Kevin get me up the stairs of the towed section. Once inside I realize that the inside of the tow behind trailer is really nice. The seats are leather and there is a full kitchen and bathroom. At the front of the trailer is a large queen size bed. I notice that Estee too see's the bedroom.

"That looks like me and you Cam!"

I nod my head as Ruth locks down both stoppers on my wheels to hold me in place. The trailer begins to roll forward. Before long we are on the main road again heading south. John keeps in radio contact from the pull vehicle with the radio.

Estee gives him general directions to get to her place in Texas. John seems hell bent on getting there as quickly as possible.

Kevin turns on a TV attached to the wall above the kitchen sink. To our surprise the channels are being fed into it by satellite or something. *Burt must have spent a pretty penny on this trailer.* My mind once again shifts back to the last images of Fred that I can remember before he disappeared into a ball of light. I can tell that Ruth is thinking about the same thing.

"We won't let his death be in vain Ruth! If it's my last act, I'll kill Gallus and everyone who chooses to follow him!"

The truck and trailer bounce down the road while Ruth and Kevin whip up a small snack of cheese and crackers. Hours go by as I look out the trailer window and watch the forests and fields disappear into the distance. It's almost time to sleep now. I can see that Estee is thinking the same thing. We have lots to do when we wake up on the other side!

CHAPTER 8

When I wake up in Cyadonia I can feel a heavy amount of crusted tears filling the corner of each eye. I carefully wipe away the pain that my body experienced in the dream world, while I experienced it in the real world. The pain of losing Fred makes me want to lay here in front of this small campfire and not move for hours.

The continual pokes from Estee's toes as she tries to wake me eliminates the possibility of mourning in peace.

"What is it already?"

My tone is angrier than I'd intended. I watch as a confused look dawns on my companion's face.

"I've been talking to the Drunk Centurian… He mentioned that Gallus' war Commander plans on bypassing the Kingdom of Plenty, and laying siege to the City of Light once his army crosses the bridge at Knifespike."

I sit up slowly and glance across the firelight at the hungover Centurian. His eyes are no longer glazed over, and the small red veins that once covered the whites of his eyes are gone as well. He does however still have the look of a man that is sickly and frail. Estee's voice interrupts my judgmental gaze as my eyes clear up from the tears that have filled them throughout the long sleep.

"What about the Sky Warrior? Did he leave?"

"Yeah, he took flight this morning after having a slight argument with Thoth. He said that he needed to speak to the Sky Gods. We tried to tell him that he would be unable to break through the magic barrier that guards their realm! But he didn't seem too concerned and just flew off."

I stand up and readjust the sword sheath that has twisted into an uncomfortable position on my hip.

"He did ask me to thank you for accidentally waking him. And he said to give you this."

Estee tosses a small gold coin into my palm. I rotate the coin to look at the finely decorated scenes on each side. On one side is the golden tree of life. The symbol of our "Creator" according to Fendril. On the other side is the image of a broken triangle. Inside of the triangle is a coiled snake with ember eyes made with two small gems.

"What am I supposed to do with this?"

Estee shrugs, and I notice the other Centurian take notice of the coin in my hand.

"He was cryptic about it. Just said to make sure you got it. Then he muttered something about the coin holding the key to the Creator Realm!"

I tuck the coin in my pocket for safe keeping and place a spell of containment over it. That way it can't be jostled free without my knowing. I gently push past Estee and stand in front of Thoth. He is deep in conversation with the recovering Centurian. My ears pick out a few words.

"I too think we must go there!"

I catch the last bit of the conversation before interrupting their quiet strategy planning session.

"What's the plan Thoth? I'm in no mood to hide out in this dank cave for the next month or so while the realm gets thrust into chaos."

"I'm glad to hear it young Centurian. That's no longer an option! We must make haste down the mountain to protect the Queen!"

I'm mildly confused by the strategy my Wise Teacher is presenting.

"But didn't she send us up here to protect me? As much as I want to protect her, this plan seems to go against her wishes... doesn't it?"

"You're right Cam!"

It's the first time that the Wise Teacher has used my real name in the eight or so years that he's been teaching me. I'm shocked to hear the name come out of his mouth. I pretend like everything is normal, but inside I feel a wave of happiness wash over me.

"The Queen did not know of Gallus' plan to besiege the City of Light when she sent her Centurians away to protect them from assassins. I'm afraid that Centurian Yakuza has brought us information about the enemy's plan that is quite alarming. The Queen of Rain is the main target of this invasion! They wish to capture her, or kill her if she is unwilling to surrender."

I feel a sense of protective instinct fill my belly. I can see that Estee too feels a rush of adrenaline after the Wise Teacher tells us that the Queen is in danger.

"What are we waiting for then? We need to get back to the City before the armies of Demons can form a perimeter around the city walls!"

"We will go at once then! I will ask Yakuza to relay our plans to King Nero in the north. He has chosen to wait out the coming conflict with his army at the mountain stronghold of 'Stonepass.' There he will be able to resist any Demon armies that attack. The narrow paths leading to the city are easily defended!"

Thoth looks back at Yakuza and bows in respect before pointing towards the cave entrance.

"Good luck to you my friends! I shall pass on to the King the message you have given me."

I glance at Thoth as we all leave the cave and are coated in warm sunlight. He seems to be reluctant to reveal what the message was.

"It's not like we'll tell anyone! Just tell us what the dang message is."

We are halfway down the mountain pass leading away from the cave before Thoth decides to tell us what the message meant for King Nero was. The Leader of the Immaru warriors reaches behind his armor and pulls out a small piece of parchment. He hands me the scroll and I slowly unroll it and begin to read it out loud.

"My dearest Thoth, I shall remain here in the City of Light as is my place. The people must be defended, and I have made arrangements for my Army to assemble on the city walls to protect this realm from the coming storm. You must guide and protect my youngest Centurian. He is more important than you can know. I have sent another of his kind to aid in his defense in this realm and the waking world. She is kind in spirit, and can lead our Young Cameron down the winding path to his full potential. If you have the opportunity, please relay a message to King Nero of the Kingdom of Plenty. Although he may feel honor bound to help in the defense of the City of Light, he must not leave his stronghold in the north. My spies report that there is an army even greater and more powerful than the one that marches against me as we speak. Gallus plans on using the siege of this city to draw out the forces of King Nero, and destroy them on an open field of battle. It is of the utmost importance that he remains in his mountain fortress. Without his warriors to repel the coming onslaught of evil from the north, I fear that only the realm of the Sky Gods will remain unconquered. Go with haste my friend! – Queen of Rain"

I roll up the scroll and hand it back to the Immaru shield soldier that had handed it to me.

"Two armies? How the hell are we going to fight two armies? How many men does the Queen command?"

"She has two thousand shield warriors to defend the walls of the city. But she's also surrounded the city with magical spells to defend against the coming assault. As long as those spells remain in place, the city will be safe."

The journey down the mountain is much quicker than the one that led us to safety only days before. When we reach the last protective barrier, I feel my body pass through what feels like a pane of cold water. My hands instinctively reach up to wipe away the water on my face, but there is nothing other than a thin layer of sweat when my fingers arrive to accomplish the task.

"That was weird! I didn't feel that when we entered the protection barrier."

Thoth points his walking stick towards the silhouette of the city walls jutting a hundred feet in the air. From the center of the city, the tops of several massive pyramids poke their diamond covered heads from the safety of the wall surrounding them. To the north, I can see a rolling wave of black figures cresting the hills. Like ants from a hill, the hordes of the Demon army has arrived quicker than Thoth expected.

"I hadn't thought that the forces of evil could travel so quickly! They must have travelled day and night without slowing. Or the spies from which the Queen receives her updates were sorely mistaken on the enemy's progress."

There are tens of thousands of Demon warriors forming defensive lines opposite from the main city gate. Below them are groups of humans digging trenches and forming piles of dirt and stone to protect the Demon forces from the defensive attacks of the city. Each human digging is put to the whip by the Demon overseers directing the construction of the siege defenses.

"There's no way we can get through their lines unseen!"

The look on Estee's face suggests that she agrees with my rather dire analysis.

"Yeah, I'm with Cam. No way we can fight through that to get to the city!"

Thoth points down to the river that runs through the city walls on the west side and exits the walls over the edge of a steep cliff facing the southern wall. We call that place the "Falls of Fortune."

"We are not going to go through the Demon lines! We need to find a way to sneak around them!"

Ahead I can see small groups of Demon warriors roaming the flanks of the main line of siege. Above them are black clumps of flying beasts and ember eyed birds patrolling the perimeter of the City of Light. There is a newly forming bright blue light emanating from the Storm Tower atop the Queen's castle.

The sky fills with rain clouds before releasing a deluge of fist sized hail stones. Thoth forms a protective shield overhead, but I can see some of the human slaves digging ditches falling to the ground in pain. The beasts in the sky retreat to the edges of the localized storm before landing on the ground and hiding beneath large oak trees.

"We must not be seen! This is our chance to move!"

"No matter what... Cameron must not be taken! Swear it to me!"

The Wise Teacher stares at Estee for reply.

"I swear it! I shall keep him away from the honey tongue of Gallus and his fallen brethren!"

For the first time in my life I sense fear in the words being spoken by the Wise Teacher. We sprint through the hailstorm as balls of ice bounce off of the protective bubble that Thoth has created around us. He squints his eyes in concentration the whole way to the riverside. When we reach the edge of the river the hail falling from above ceases.

The storm clouds dissipate quickly and are replaced by the cover of a thick fog.

"The Queen aids our travel! Take a deep breath and let the current take you to the city gates."

I take a deep breath and jump into the water. Estee is close behind, and I feel her grasp onto my arm as the current sweeps us away from the shore. There is a scream overhead as one of the flying Demon beasts grasps Thoth. He draws his sword and chops off the talon adorned limb dragging him into the air.

My head is thrust under water while watching him fall. I pop back up above the rapids of the river to see my Wise Teacher crash down onto a rounded boulder. I cry out for him!

"We have to go back Estee! We can't leave him behind!"

Estee wraps both arms around my chest and rolls onto her back. I can feel her legs kicking and her momentum dragging me further into the current.

"I made him a promise Cam!"

She lets go of my chest with one hand and points up to the sky. More foul beasts are circling overhead. I begin to charge my lightning bolt before I feel the energy from my hands leaching out into the water all around us. The pain is sharp. There is nothing to do but cease my actions.

"But he's still alive! Look!"

We both watch as the figure on top of the rounded stone slashes wildly with his sword at the flying beast trying to grab him.

"There's nothing we can do Cam!"

I charge a fireball and throw it into the air at the circling creatures overhead. My attack lands home and sends one of the winged beasts falling into the river. The rest are too far away, and getting further with every moment the current drags us toward the city walls.

I hear a voice in my head as clear as day.

"Dive deep, and go under the metal bars of the city wall young Centurian. May the Sky Gods smile upon your journey."

The voice is that of my Wise Teacher. I can tell that Estee heard the voice as well. The city wall is fast approaching. As we approach I can see that thick metal bars block the path forward for anything larger than a sword handle.

"Take a deep one Cam!"

I feel Estee's chest rise against my back as she breathes in deeply. I do the same as I feel her arms flex and watch the sky disappear under white capped waves. I don't struggle at first, but soon I feel my shoulder hit the metal bars that extend from above.

I open my eyes and see blurry dots of air bubbling up from mine and Estee's mouth. The current is strong, and I can barely fight through the pressure of the water pushing me into the bars. Instinctively I grasp onto the bars and begin pulling myself up towards the surface. Estee grabs my hand as I try and ascend and pulls me in the opposite direction.

Hand after hand I pull my body deeper. Each time I slide my hands down the vertical bars I hope that they will end. My wish is granted. Estee tugs my body through a small gap in the metal screen protecting the city from water infiltration. We both swim frantically towards the daylight above the surface.

I feel a desperation unlike anything I have ever felt when my head breaks the surface. The air that fills my lungs is the most welcome gift that I have ever received. Estee smiles at me while shaking her head to get the hair unstuck from her face. I too feel a deep sense of relief that we are now safe behind the city walls.

We swim slowly towards a small fishing dock. Two Immaru

citizens drop the baskets of bread they carry in hand and help us climb up out of the water. I notice that the older of the two men has recognized me. I too know the face looking up at us. It's the fish vendor that makes the best fish stew in the city. Many a time Thoth would take me and my Guardians to the Fish Market to eat this man's stews.

"Is it truly you?"

The man seems surprised to see me in particular.

"Sure is! Why do you seem so surprised?"

The man smiles widely and nudges who I assume is his son standing beside him.

"I knew that the rumors from the North could not be true! There was word that two Centurians of Immaru had been captured during a great battle!"

I look at Estee who seems worried by the story the fisherman is telling us.

"Nope. Not us! If you will excuse me fine sir... We need to talk to the Queen!"

"Yes, of course Centurians! Do not let me waste another moment of your time!"

The man bows deeply and encourages his young son to do the same. We return the gesture before moving in the direction of the Storm Tower."

I can tell that Estee is still concerned about something.

"What was that all about...do you think?"

She picks up the pace while pointing towards the Queen's castle.

"I'm not sure, but I think that fisherman might have been mistaken. It's possible that there were other Centurians that were defeated... We need to get to the Queen!"

After arriving at the castle gates, two stone Queen's Guards open the doors for us.

"She is waiting for you in the Storm Tower!"

Estee runs forward into the castle and stands in the center of the room. She has definitely been to the top of the tower before. I stand next to her as a white mist surrounds us.

When we reach the top of the tower I can smell the lingering scent of something burning.

The Queen is staring out of the window of her Throne Room to the north. Her arm is dangling at an unnatural angle held tightly by her other hand. The sleeve of her gown is black from the flames that have melted away some of her skin.

"Are you okay my Queen?"

Estee rushes forward and grabs hold of the Queen's arm.

"I do not know how, but the enemy used the Celestial Door to infiltrate my tower."

The Queen's finger points down at three distinct pools of black tar covered by the armor and weapons carried by Demon warriors. Beside the piles of tar is a dead man clothed in a black cloak. Upon his cloak is the same image that I have recently seen on the back side of a gold coin.

As if she can read my mind the Queen explains what we are all looking at.

"He was once my chosen defender. His name was Cassiel when he served me. I had thought him killed by Gallus in the war that preceded this one. Alas he chose to serve the forces of darkness. He was quite formidable as a 'Fallen Priest'!"

"Get over here and help me heal her Cam!"

Estee's plea for help draws my attention away from the look of pain stamped on the dead priest's face. I step over the piles of dead Demon and began chanting the healing incantations that Thoth taught me as a child. I can feel the tendrils of flesh covering the Queen's burnt arm weaving themselves back together as a bolt of lightning hits me in the side!

From the Celestial Door, two more Demon warriors appear beside a man wearing a bright red cloak. This man wears a different symbol than the one adorning the chest of the priest killed by the Queen.

Estee is already engaged in swordplay with the two Demons before I regain my feet and focus my attention on the enemy priest. The Queen too is fighting. Her hands swirl in the air moving small splashes of water into the path of the incoming fire balls emanating from the enemy priest's hands.

I charge my lightning. Estee is knocked to the ground by the war axe held in hand by one of the Demon warriors. Her foot had slipped on one of the piles of tar on the floor. I spring my fingers forward and capture the falling axe head meant for her exposed skull. The charge of my lightning attack swims down the metal axe handle and sends the Demon crumbling to the floor in convulsions.

Estee is quick to get back up to her feet and engage the remaining enemy Demon. I refocus on the man casting magic towards my Queen. I pull my sword from its sheath and charge forward as a wall of water lifts me up off the floor and towards the enemy. The Queen has seen fit to let me fight the coming battle.

I hear a grunt, followed by the distinct smell of rotten eggs. There is a large thump followed by two bright lights. Estee has finished off the Demon Warriors. All that is left is the 'Fallen Priest.'

I step over two piles of tar covered armor after arriving in front of the enemy with a splash. Both literally and figuratively. Estee circles to the side of the enemy, but remains at a distance. The Queen is hovering a small cyclone of water overhead.

I engage the enemy with my sword. He is fast and strong like the other 'Fallen Priest' I fought below the mountain passes.

His blade finds its mark atop my armor many times before I feel the sting of its attack. I hack up and down with a precision that I have never felt before. It's as if I can see the moves the enemy will make before he makes them.

I hear the familiar laughter of the Queen from behind me as I duck under a killing blow that my enemy has levied against me. I see the slightest look of fear wash over his face. His chest is beginning to heave up and down with each breath, and I can see beads of sweat rolling down his brow.

I gain confidence with every strike that I deflect with both my sword edge and the armor plating of my forearm Vambraces. I dodge a sweeping attack and place my back against the Celestial Door that the enemy has infiltrated the castle through.

"What do you say my Queen? Should we ask this one a few questions?"

The man is caught off guard as his body is engulfed in a wave of water. His legs kick back and forth as his body floats in the Queen's water spell. The sword falls from his hand as his eyes roll backwards into darkness.

The drowning man crashes to the ground as the water bubble surrounding him explodes. Estee and I both grab one of the man's arms. We hold him down to the floor atop his knees and wait for the Queen's orders.

"Just hold him! Contain the magic in his hands while I ask him a few questions."

The Queen walks over to her throne and grasps her crown in hand. She balances the head piece on her brow while standing over the priest. Small flows of water pour from the captive's mouth as he begins to cough out the water that has almost drowned him.

I feel a weird sensation surround my body as the Queen of Rain approaches us. There is a strange and powerful magic coming from the crown she's now wearing. I feel as though I would tell her anything she would want to know.

"How have you come to use the Celestial Door Priest?"

The man spits out a mouthful of water before lifting his chin to answer.

"Gallus sent us through the passage with his dark magic."

The Queen nods her head.

"And should we be expecting more company anytime soon?"

"No my Queen! The magic needed to open the Celestial Door was most taxing on the strength of my master. He will need much time to recuperate from this task."

"And why did Gallus send you forth priest?"

"I was sent to aid the ones who traveled before me in capturing you and returning you to Gomorrah to be placed on your knee's before the Dark Master!"

"I see, And how does your master plan on bypassing my defense of this city?"

The man makes a pained look on his face before shaking in a seizure like quality.

"He knows nothing more of use!"

The Queen snaps her fingers twice. In the corner of the room a small cage made of light appears next to the Celestial Door. Estee and I drag the exhausted man towards the cage and deposit him inside. When the magic door to the cage closes, a bright light blinds my vision. When I reopen my eyes the prisoner and the cage are gone.

"Where did you send him?"

The Queen removes the crown from her head and places it atop her throne where it rested before the interrogation.

"He shall keep the other 'Fallen Priests' that I have captured company in my dungeon! It is the safest place for them. I do so much hate ending their lives!"

The Queen glances down at the piles of dead Demon remains, and the fallen priest for which she has killed. A stream of water rushes from her hands and sweeps away the remnants of death from the Throne Room.

"It's most alarming that Gallus was able to access the Celestial Door. There are very few of us with the power or knowledge to use the pathways contained within it. For now I shall need to lock my door in the proverbial sense!"

I squeeze my hand and realize that I'm still holding my sword with a tight grip. I sheath my weapon and look over just in time to see Estee do the same.

We all look out over the vast hillside in front of the City. Black figures move in every direction preparing for the siege to come. I can't help but feel a tightness in my throat. It almost seems as if we are trapped. It's as if the Queen can read the thoughts going through my head.

"Don't fear Centurian! I have a plan in mind to destroy the army of evil you see in front of you! And I will need both of your help to make it happen!"

The Queen sends us forth from her tower after sharing her plans to defend the city from the army preparing outside the gates. She winks at me once before I leave. A wink that I don't quite get the meaning of. Estee follows along behind me after deciding that she would be joining me for the coming slumber. While climbing the steps of my Pyramid Shrine, large explosions begin erupting against the magical barrier that the Queen has surrounded the city with.

Each fiery impact sends a shockwave of sound and vibration onto the roofs of the civilian dormitories. The shimmering light from enemy fire attacks glimmers off of thousands of spear points poking above the castle wall parapets. Knowing that the Queen's army is standing guard on the wall makes me feel a little more confident that me and Estee will be safe when we wake in Cyadonia on the morrow.

We reach the top of my pyramid and walk through the stone doorway of my shrine. Estee jumps back and grasps the hilt of her sword as a familiar voice startles us both.

"What took you so long! I've been so lonely sitting up here by myself!"

CHAPTER 9

My eyes open before glossing over the drooling mouth of the crippled boy lying next to me. I roll onto my side and blow on his face as hard as I can muster. He wakes with a sour look on his face.

"Ew! Brush your teeth Estee!"

I giggle and kiss him on the cheek, filled with joy over the reunion that we have just been torn away from. I feel rested and full of energy this time after waking.

"We need to tell them!"

Cam nods his head in the direction of the back of the trailer. I roll off the bed and reach for his wheelchair before his excited voice changes my priorities.

"Go tell them first!"

I push the wheelchair to the side of the bed next to Cameron before sliding open the thin door separating the bedroom from the rest of the trailer. The kitchen table is gone, replaced by a pullout bed. Ruth and Kevin are spooning together when my voice wakes them up.

"He's alive!"

Ruth wakes up with a knife in hand and a scowl on her face. I take a step back, surprised by her defensive reaction upon waking.

"Easy Ruth! It's me Estee!"

Ruth lowers the knife point before scratching the top of her head with her free hand.

"You can't wake me up like that Centurian! I'm still not used to these things you call 'dreams.' I find it hard to differentiate from Cyadonia since I have been travelling between this world and that for eight years. Thank god the dreams that I just lived inside are not real!"

Kevin throws off a thin blanket that was previously covering his legs.

"Can I just wake up without chaos erupting one time this week!"

Ruth stands by the side of Kevin and zips up the black hoodie to her neckline.

"What's so important Estee?"

I begin jogging in place and waving my arms like a bird fluttering its wings. I'm filled with excitement, and ready to reveal the good news.

"Fred is alive!"

Ruth's eyes squint down in confusion.

"But we watched him disappear into a ball of light?"

"Cameron will tell you too! When we got back to his Pyramid Shrine, Fred was there in his Guardian form. He's alive!"

Ruth does a small happy dance before wrapping her arms around Kevin's thin waist and lifting him into the air. Even his tortured face can't help but transform into a wry smile of celebration. We haven't known each other long, but each one of us have fought together for survival. An action that forms bonds of loyalty and love quicker than any other.

I head back to the bedroom to gather Cameron. His body rolls neatly onto the chair that I placed by the bed. His body is frail and light from his immobility for the last eight years. His legs look like skin covered bones, and I can count his ribs with my eyes.

"I heard the commotion."

"She's excited as she should be! Why didn't you tell me to wake her up gently?'

"I don't know... I've never woke up one of my Guardians in this world. We are in totally new territory here. I'm not even sure how those stones work. For all I know they might get sucked away at any time!"

I hear Ruth activate the radio connecting the trailer to the truck cab. Her message is received. The sound of the road under tire begins to lessen. A small squeak of truck brakes fills the air as the truck and trailer pulls over into a rest stop along the highway.

The trailer door is flung open by John. He runs up the stairs and grabs his wife in a huge hug before twirling her in the air. Kevin jumps out of the way to avoid being knocked down. It's nice to be able to celebrate something. The death of Fred the day before had lowered all of our spirits. This news is most welcome.

Cameron clears his throat. I push his chair forward and place it next to the kitchen sink.

"Fred says hello! He scared the crap out of us when we showed up at my shrine. He was sitting in a dark corner acting all EMO!"

John smiles before placing his arm around Ruth's shoulder.

"He never was any good at being alone! He's always had you to keep him company when his mother and I are away on a mission for the Queen."

"Well, I set him straight. I told him no more moping around. It's actually a good thing that he's back in Cyadonia. We might need his protection in the shrine in the coming days while we are here in the real world. Gallus' forces have surrounded the City of Light and are laying siege!"

My story is interrupted by the sound of a small button being pressed down. Burt stands in the doorway to the trailer holding a vintage tape recorder in hand. We all look at him and stop talking. His face shows a sullen look of surprise.

"What? This is good stuff! Am I not supposed to record your stories anymore?"

I walk over to Burt and make a show of pressing the record button on the rectangular recorder. A small click and the rising of the button indicates that the device is no longer recording. Everyone is staring at Burt when he smiles and places the recorder on the counter beside the sink.

"Message received!"

I step back behind Cam's chair and rock him backwards a bit. He lays out the situation developing in Cyadonia. John and Ruth seem especially concerned with the safety of the Queen of Rain.

I add my own two cents into the mix.

"She is well protected, and the Celestial Door is no longer active in the Storm Tower. The Queen has a plan for when we get back there!"

I take the chance to move the conversation away from the dire situation in Cyadonia.

"Where are we at? Did we make it to Texas yet?"

Burt speaks up after looking at John to answer my question.

"Oh, is this the part where the human is supposed to speak up?"

There's a thick layer of sarcasm in Burt's voice. I can see Cam's lips lift into a small smirk.

"Are we in Texas yet or not?"

"We are still in Oklahoma. About twenty miles from the norther border of Texas!"

I close my eyes and do a quick calculation on how long it will take to get to my place.

"Okay, when you cross the border start heading southwest on highway 79! Let me know when we get close to Henrietta. I'll give you more directions from there!"

"Why don't you just ride in the truck with us for a while. We should only be a couple hours out."

I decide that Burt's suggestion is warranted.

"Yeah, alright. I'll navigate from the cab!"

Burt claps his hands twice and makes a dramatic show of ushering me out of the trailer with his hand. John decides to ride in the back until we get to where we are going. When the door to the trailer closes I can hear Cameron going into details about the plan that the Queen has concocted to defend the City of Light.

I climb into the passenger side of the truck. The seats are black leather with red stitching. I can tell that Burt is proud of his truck. The floors look freshly vacuumed, and the dash is spotless.

"I wouldn't have pegged you as a neat freak Burt. I saw all those McDonalds cheeseburger wrappers in the back of your van."

"You saw that huh? That's a little embarrassing! I only use the Van when I go on tour to promote my comic book series. There's not a lot of time to eat at those events."

I nod my head and begin to inquire more about the comic book series and Burt's intentions.

"It wasn't cool what you did to Cameron!"

Burt reaches to the cup holder of the center console and tilts back an aluminum can of Monster energy drink. His eyes dart away from my judgmental gaze in fear or shame, I can't tell which one.

"I'm ashamed of what I did! But I really did have good intentions!"

His hands reach back into the back seat and pull out a small present covered in silver wrapping paper and a bright red bow! He tosses it into my lap.

"Open it. I got this for Cam about a month ago. I didn't get to give it to him before this whole debacle happened."

I tear open the package. It's been years since my fingers have torn open the wrapping of a present, even though this one isn't for me!"

Inside is a flat box with a green sticky note attached to the surface. The note is a handwritten message from Burt to Cameron.

"We joked about this, but I decided to make it happen!"

I open the box and see a small thumb drive in the shape of a surfboard. I pick it up and rotate it in my fingers.

"What's on it?"

Burt stares out at the open road in front of us while switching lanes to avoid a tractor pulling a load of hay in the slow lane.

"It's a software update for his voice modulator. Well... For the voice modulator he used to need. I paid Samuel L Jackson like fifty grand to sit in a room for a week and read all the phrases necessary to replicate his voice. Then I paid a company to write a program to integrate the new sound repository into the existing program on his power chair."

I'm caught off guard by what Burt is saying. *Maybe we were all wrong about his intentions?*

"If you care so much about Cam, why did you hide your success from him?"

"Cam isn't the kind of person that likes a lot of attention! I thought that he might be embarrassed or something. And the longer I kept the secret, the harder it was to tell him the truth. I didn't want him to feel like I was using him! Even though I knew that there was no other way to see what I was doing."

I listen as Burt lays out his case. He sounds remorseful. I watch every facial feature as he talks. There's definitely a lingering look of regret in his eyes. I can feel my disdain for Burt's actions beginning to melt away.

"He's felt so much betrayal in his life, and he has so much built up anger inside of him! I guess I just didn't want to be responsible for adding to any of that. I've seen the good inside of that boy. He has a big heart, and what's happened to him in life is totally unfair. I just wanted something good to happen for him. But in the end I messed everything up!"

"You seem to think that Cam is a fragile little boy Burt! He is anything but that! If you just tell him the truth, the whole truth, he will probably forgive you. In any case, that's your only option if you truly care about him!"

A big green road sign catches my attention.

"Take this exit and go west!"

Burt steers the truck and trailer onto the exit before pointing at the golden arches at the precipice of the offramp.

"I could go for something to eat! I've been driving all night…"

I nod my head and press the button on the radio.

"You guys hungry? We're gonna make a McDonalds stop!"

I can hear a commotion coming through the radio. I hear Ruth's voice say yes. In the background I can also hear Kevin yelling out a laundry list of items that he wants to order.

"Copy that. Me and Burt will go in and order. You guys write down your orders on a list. It's probably better if you guys stay out of sight!"

"Copy that Estee!"

Burt pulls into the parking lot and blocks all ten parking spaces on one side of the lot. We jump out of the cab and collect a piece of paper dangling out one of the trailer windows from Kevin's hand. The list is long, and I feel my lips curl up into a smirk while imagining Kevin writing his long ass order on this piece of paper.

After splitting up the long list of items to appear more normal, we both approach separate kiosks and enter our orders. We wait together for ten minutes before two large bags of food are placed in front of each of us. Carrying a bag in each hand we walk outside and open the door to the trailer.

Kevin is waiting impatiently on the other side of the door. He grabs the bags out of our hands and pours out the contents on the table. Me and Burt grab a couple of sausage McMuffins and head back to the truck. After wolfing down a breakfast sandwich, Burt turns the truck keys and gets us back on the road.

I count the white mile markers all the way down highway 148. We pass the town of Henrietta before I point to the highway entrance leading further south. For five minutes we continue to travel on highway 148 before reaching a distinct clumping of trees that I recognize.

I tap Burt on the shoulder and point at a black asphalt driveway leading away from the highway. We travel down the driveway for a half mile through a thick forest of trees. Burt points out a small black post along the side of the driveway. Sitting on top of the post is a security camera.

"You got this place pretty well covered in camera's? I saw a few more of those in the tree line!"

"Yeah! The guy that I bought this place from is what you would probably consider a 'Prepper.' He only agreed to sell it to me when I offered him a ridiculous amount of money that he could use to build a new bunker in some old missile silo on the other side of the ridgeline! I still talk to Bernie! He's a pretty nice guy if you can get past the whole 'Apocalyptic Conspiracy Theory' side of his personality."

Burt pulls up in front of a small log cabin. He seems unimpressed.

"How much did you pay for this place?"

"About ten million dollars!"

I watch Burt's jaw drop and his eyes go wide!

"I think you might have gotten swindled!"

"Just wait till you see the inside!"

"How the heck did a girl like you afford to pay ten million dollars for a property?"

"None of your business how I afforded it!"

The truck engine turns off. John and Ruth lower Cameron's chair onto the black asphalt below the trailer steps. Kevin's feet hit the ground. He wanders twenty feet through short grass and stands under a low canopy of tree branches. His eyes stare at the small dilapidated cabin looking back at him.

"I'm getting a real 'Texas Chainsaw Massacre' vibe coming off your place Estee! I think I'll sleep in Burt's trailer tonight!"

I walk up the gravel path leading to the front porch of my cabin. My eyes search for a particular object. I find the fake stone I'm searching for that contains my hide-a-key. With a firm twist I shoulder through the door! A puff of rusty dust drops from the hinges.

John and Ruth follow close behind me. The floors and countertops are covered in an impressive amount of dust.

"When was the last time you were here Estee? This place seems abandoned!"

"That's the point guys! Wait for one second. Watch carefully!"

The rest of my companions enter the foyer of my cabin and look at me like I'm crazy. I've never shown anyone my secret space before, and I feel the excitement of the big reveal filling my chest.

I walk over to the kitchen sink and put my fingers down into the garbage disposal. I feel a shiver run down my spine every time I do this. Underneath the seized blades I feel the switch that I'm looking for. I slide it to the side.

There is a loud clanging sound that erupts from the floor in the hallway. I can see that my companions are surprised. They're all staring as the stained floor covering the hall slides under the wall and reveals a large titanium plate. A loud hissing sound startles them all. Air rushes out from the edges of the hidden hatch.

"You guys ready to see my 'Real" home now?"

I grab hold of a small round metal ring attached subsurface to the trap door before lifting. More air escapes from the opening hatch, and soft yellow light leaks out from the space below.

I look back and see a smile forming on Cameron's face. Even Kevin is now standing with his mouth wide open collecting dust.

"No freaking way! You have a 'Secret Bunker' Estee? Holy cow, you just massively leveled up on my 'Coolness' scale!"

"Thanks Kevin! I think?"

John and Ruth are the first to walk down the descending staircase. Each step is made of polished aluminum, and the walls are lined with smooth stones that appear to be some sort of sealed concrete. At the bottom of the stairs everyone gathers in front of a large steel door.

I walk forward after closing the trap door overhead. My fingers work the hidden mechanism to open the vault door. Along the side of the door are six sets of symbols with small notches carved into them.

I spin each symbol dial until the final one lets out the sound of snapping metal. A red light overhead begins to blink rapidly as the vault locking pins slide sideways and into the concrete and steel wall. I then spin the big wheel attached to the front of the door, disengaging the last latch keeping us from entering my home.

The door opens revealing the size and scope of its protective construction.

"Wow, that thing is like two feet thick!"

I flip the power switch by the door and watch as warm lighting fills the entryway. A small hallway leads to the entrance to the living spaces of my bunker.

I close the vault door behind us before looking at everyone in the group.

"Make yourselves at home everyone! Welcome to my humble home!"

John points at the end of the hall. I almost forgot that I still need to open one more door to let them all in. Beside the door is a small alcove concealing a camera behind bulletproof glass. The door opens revealing a large room filled with creature comforts.

John and Ruth walk inside and immediately try to get their bearings. Kevin pushes Cam's chair into the living room before testing out the couch and TV. Burt seems a little nervous, so I make sure to tell him a bit more about my place.

"There's a hidden well that provides filtered water for the whole place. I have a six hundred gallon holding tank, so nobody needs to worry about skipping showers! This place is powered by three overlapping systems. If the main power from the coal plant down the road goes out I have a backup generator. If that goes out, there are wind and solar collectors spread out around the hundred acres that surround this compound."

I grab John's arm and drag him past the kitchen and into a small hallway. At the end of the passage is a glass door leading to my pantry. He seems impressed while counting the shelves filled with canned goods and nonperishables.

"There's a couple thousand pounds of rice preserved in a temperature controlled dry room over there."

I point at a separate door beside the racks of canned foods and stacks of ramen noodles. Beside that door is an aluminum door leading to my walk in freezer.

"I got like twenty full cows packed and chilled in there, for those of us that like to eat meat! There's also a pile of frozen vegetables just in case we are stuck down here for some sort of Apocalypse!"

I point back out of my food storage area and to a door leading down an additional hallway. At the far end of this hall is another vault door.

"That's the room I told you about when we were in that Walmart!"

John stares at the door with a grin.

"Can I see it?"

I walk down the hallway and enter a five digit code onto a digital keypad. I make sure that John see's the number. Besides me, I figure that John is the one who might need to get into this room in a hurry if something happens.

"Tell Ruth the code too!"

I see a look of disappointment come across Burt's face. As much as I think his intentions are probably pure, I still don't trust him to have unfettered access to the arsenal on the other side of the door.

I walk in after opening the armory door. Each wall is lined with rifles and pistols perched on small metal pegs sticking out from the wall. Underneath each weapon is a rack filled with the correct ammo for the hardware above.

John walks to the wall and grabs hold of a black Benelli Shotgun. He flips the weapon over and looks at me for permission.

"Take your pick! Who knows when those Demons might show up again. Better to be ready at all times!"

I walk to a black cabinet and open the split front doors. Inside is my favorite set of leg holsters. Next I wrap each holster around my thigh on either leg before cinching the vertical straps to my belt. I reach up to the top shelf and grab two black M18 pistols.

Each one slides neatly into the holsters on the side of my legs. I grab hold of a small ammunition belt with four pouches for extra pistol magazines. After stuffing four extra magazines filled with 9mm ammo into my belt, I slam shut the door and face John.

He seems content with the shotgun. I show him how to load and operate the weapon. He stuffs a box of extra slugs into a fanny pack that he previously gathered from beside the shotgun rack.

I notice that Burt is still standing at the precipice of the doorway. It seems like he doesn't want to enter the armory.

"You okay Burt?"

He steps back after realizing how weird he must look to us.

"Yeah, I'm alright... I just don't like guns!"

As I close the armory door I make eye contact with Burt.

"I can respect the fact that you don't 'Like' guns... If you can respect the fact that they are necessary sometimes!"

I watch the wheels of logic turn in Burt's head. He seems disarmed by the smile I flash him after our interaction. His eyes linger for only a moment on the two pistols strapped to my body.

Two loud clicks signal that the armory is locked again. We all make our way back to the main hallway before re-entering the living room area. Cam and Kevin are scrolling through the camera feeds being fed live into the media center displayed on the TV.

I point behind the kitchen and make an announcement.

"There is a full bathroom down there! The shower is separate but located in the same hallway."

I point across the room towards a big fish tank filled with vegetation, but missing fish. I can see that Cameron is confused by the lack of fish in the tank.

"No fish?"

"They keep dying! Every time I leave for more than a few days... It's not like I can let someone come and feed the fish while I'm gone! That would ruin the whole point of this place!"

I stroll to the side of the brightly lit tank.

"Back here is the hallway to the dormitories. I got three king sized beds back there. So it looks like you and Kevin will have to share."

I grin towards Burt. He looks over at Kevin.

"You don't like to cuddle right?"

I hear Ruth laugh out loud. So far she is the only one who has shared a bed with Kevin.

"He likes to be the little spoon!"

Kevin objects to the comment.

"No I don't! It was just cold last night. You were the one cuddling with me from what I remember! Laying there crying into the back of my neck because Fred died!"

"Kevin!"

I lash out at the teenage boy's penchant for hurtful words. He recoils at my chastisement before returning fire.

"Oh take it easy Miss Sensitive! He isn't even dead anymore! So you're just whining about nothing!"

Even Ruth agrees with the logic the young boy is employing.

"I'm not offended Estee, Kevin can speak the truth! Even if it is a little insensitive!"

Ruth sends Kevin a sour look. We all spend the next few hours getting comfortable in our new hideout. We take turns getting cleaned up, and I go back up to the surface to collect the extra clothes we picked up that fateful day at Walmart. After resealing the vault door to the cabin, I walk back into the living room holding three bags of personal items from the trailer.

Cameron waves me over and yells at the rest of our party enjoying the comforts of my bunker.

"Everyone get over here! Is anyone else seeing this?"

I jump over the back of the couch and focus on the security footage coming from the live security feed displayed on the TV. I grab the remote control as John and Ruth sit beside me on the couch. Kevin leans forward behind me and breathes in my ear.

"One step back please!"

He snorts in disapproval before stepping back and pointing at the TV.

"Focus Estee! What is that?'

Scenes of two black SUV's traveling down the driveway appear in separate parts of the screen. I click the remote to display a singular camera that is hidden in the trees pointing down at the front of the cabin.

In the frame we can see that Burt's truck and trailer are present in the center of the space. The two SUV's stop about forty yards short of the cabin. Four men in black suits get out of each vehicle carrying machine guns. They open fire on the trailer and truck. I pan the camera slightly in one direction to get a better angle of the one sided battle overhead.

One of the men runs to the back of the lead vehicle and opens the rear hatch. He reappears with a grenade launcher in hand as the rest of his companions continue shooting at Burt's prized possessions.

"Oh man! They're killing my trailer dude! What the hell! Those look like the same type of guys that were watching my house!

How the hell did they find us?"

The man with the grenade launcher unloads the weapon into and underneath both empty targets. Large fireballs erupt all around the camera feeds. The truck and trailer are both engulfed in explosion and flame.

"Sons of bitches just killed my trailer!"

Burt collapses into the couch cushions holding the sides of his head in distress!

"Give me that gun!"

He reaches out to grab the shotgun resting between John's legs. I make a point to block Burt's path to the weapon.

"No way dude! This might be good for us. They might think they killed us and leave! Besides… I thought you didn't 'like' guns?"

Burt sits back down on the couch and lets out a long frustrated exhale.

"We'll see how you feel when they light that cabin up there on fire!"

I listen to the words coming from Burt's mouth before noticing a large shadow covering the cabin from above. The shadow sways back and forth in the wind suggesting that it is hovering in a stationary position over top of my cabin.

"They have a damn helicopter too?"

We all sit on the couch and watch as two missiles streak into the camera frame and explode after entering the cabin. Large flames erupt into the air causing the Helicopter to pull back a short distance. The water in the fish tank on the other side of the living room begins to shift into small waves after the explosion above.

"Is this place built to survive that explosion?"

I glance at John and shake my head.

"Yeah. We'll be just fine down here! Bernie built this place to withstand a nuclear apocalypse. Let's put a big tally mark on the scoreboard for paranoid people!"

The men on the ground begin high fiving each other before tactically circling the burning cabin. They seem happy with the outcome of the missile strike. The shifting shadow from the helicopter shifts back and forth between the burning cabin and Burt's burning property. The search for bodies is impossible through the flames of their handywork.

The men in black suits walk back toward their black SUV's and get back inside. Both vehicles pull around the burning wreckage in the driveway before speeding away in the direction they had come. The helicopter follows their path of travel. The entire attack team drives onto the highway and speeds away like nothing has happened.

"Who the hell are those guys? Is the government after us?"

I listen as Burt throws out a myriad of questions that I don't have the answers to.

"Who knows, but I didn't see any markings on those vehicles or the helicopter."

We all sit on the couch and go over the possible connections that the men in black suits might represent. An hour goes by before the camera's pick up movement coming from the highway. Two red fire trucks speed down the asphalt driveway and arrive at the cabin. The front truck attaches it's hoses to the water tender truck behind it before extinguishing the flames.

Ten men in yellow jackets and helmets circle the smoldering wreckage looking for bodies. They find nothing before running yellow caution tape around the perimeter of the smoldering piles of debris. Both trucks pull out of the driveway leaving behind a scorched scene.

I look over at the clock on the wall. It is only six thirty in the afternoon, but I'm anxious to get back to Cyadonia and fight for the Queen. I glance over at Ruth before shifting my gaze to Cameron.

"You got any more of that 'Sleepy Juice' you can inject us with? We could use some extra time in Cyadonia. And we're all as safe as we can be down here!"

Ruth reaches into her backpack and pulls out a clear vial filled halfway with medication.

"Sure do! I got enough left to keep you guys asleep till tomorrow morning if you want?"

Me and Cameron make eye contact before he nods his head.

"Let's do it then!"

CHAPTER 10

"Oh snap!"

Estee wakes up staring at the faces of my stone Guardians looking down at her. I wake beside her feeling the warmth of her body against mine.

"Doesn't that freak you out to wake up looking at those scary faces?"

I sit up and scratch the top of my head.

"Not really... Been waking up to those ugly mugs for years."

I look closer at the stone faces of John and Ruth in Guardian form. Estee might have a point. They both transitioned to the real world while scowling down at my shrine. Ruth isn't so scary looking in human female form, but the teeth that John is showing send a bit of a fear shiver down to my feet.

We both climb down from the temple shrine. Small clumps of yellow rose pedals fall to the ground as we slide our feet over the edge of the stone altar and onto the floor. The sun has still not risen in Cyadonia. This is only like the third or fourth time that I have ever looked down upon the City of light in total darkness.

The siege outside the city walls is in full tilt. The Demon hordes are bombarding the magical barrier protecting the city. I quickly dawn my armor for the events to come. Estee too puts on her full complement of armor. The dancing light of a small fire torch makes her shadow look long and mis figured.

We both skip every other stair on the way down to the city streets. The people of Immaru seem to be mostly inside of their homes, but two or three 'Little' people are still moving about the city gathering supplies for whatever they plan on eating during the siege. I stop by the fish market and say hi really quick. Mostly I wanted to stop in order to grab some breakfast.

"Welcome Centurian!"

I can never pronounce the cooks name properly, so me and Fred decided to give him a nick name.

"Hey Cyrano! Two bowls of pink fish stew please!"

The tiny man smiles and scoops a bowl full of meaty stew into two bowls. I hand one to Estee and grab the one closest for myself.

"You doing okay with the siege?"

"I do not fear the forces of darkness at our gates. But the fish seem to have been scared out of the city riverways. I have no more fish for tonight's stew."

I glance over at Estee who seems annoyed that we have been stopped on the way to the Storm Tower. She relents after seeing my puppy eyed gaze. After setting down her bowl of fish stew, she extends all of her fingers toward the river beside the "Stew Shack."

Estee closes her eyes and begins bending her fingers in and out in the direction of the river. Two large fish appear on the surface before jumping out of the water and landing on the wooden dock. Cyrano sprints wildly onto the dock and uses a wooden club to beat the fish lifeless. He returns holding the two fish at shoulder height. As he waddles in our direction back to his shack, the tail section of each fish drags behind him leaving a trail.

"You are most kind Centurian. I will make stew for the people with these fish, and give it away for free."

In times past I used to look forward to eating meals in Cyadonia. This was the only realm in which I could handle solid food. The fish bone broth and small chunks of pink fish flesh roll into my stomach. I slurp the last bit of juices from the bowl before placing it back down onto the Stew Shack's wooden counter. Estee too finishes her meal.

After expressing gratitude for the meal, we both make our way towards the Storm Tower. We reach the gates of the castle and notice that the drawbridge is up for the Queen's safety. Loud clicking fills the air as the chains lowering the bridge are stressed by the weight of the structure.

We run across the drawbridge and enter the castle. I get a small chill as the water elevator covers me in cool water. Without the heat of the sun, Cyadonia can get quite chilly during its seasonal cycles.

The Queen is excited to see us so early in the morning. She rises up from her throne and greets us, before walking over to the window facing the siege lines of Demon warriors.

"Should we get this show on the road?"

I nod my head and look at Estee to gauge her response to the Queen's question. She's smiling from ear to ear while grasping the handle of her sword.

"I am almost positive that there is a spy in our midst. I have not received word back from King Nero in the north. And I have sent three of my most trusted messengers to deliver three separate messages. I even sent one of Nero's own Centurians with a message. Be it true that he was drunk and had been that way for the better part of his life.

"I think we met him! Was his name... Wait.."

"It was Yakuza! The Centurian we met in the Breathing Mountains was named Yakuza!"

I look over at Estee while snapping my fingers and pointing at her mouth.

"Yeah, Yakuza, That's what his name was!"

The Queen nods her head slowly while looking out at the colorful show of fire striking the water spell of protection covering the city.

"My spies found him in a Sake bar by the river. He was drowning his sorrows in a lake of liquor when I summoned him. I was unsure if he was still in good standing with his King, but he still bore his Wrist Band from the Kingdom of Plenty."

I think back a few days and try and remember the details of his arrival.

"He showed up at the 'Cave of lost travelers' like a day after we did."

"So he disobeyed my orders? I sent him on a path directly to King Nero. The message I entrusted to him was most important to our plans here!"

"He showed up drunk as a skunk and told us that King Nero had sent him to protect me! I knew something was off about that dude! Why was he here in the City of Light anyways?"

The Queen begins to put together the pieces of the debacle playing out.

"It is possible that I have handed my battle plans and the requests that I would make to King Nero directly into the hands of the spy I have been searching for. How could I be so stupid?"

Estee points out at the field of battle. The sun is beginning to glow over the horizon, and something is causing the groupings of Demon warriors to move into lines. With the scant light of the coming day it is hard to make out what is going on.

I begin to see a gathering of movement on the hillside above the Demon siege line. Men in armor from head to toe sit atop large war horses with lances raised in the air. There must be five hundred mounted soldiers forming a line atop the ridge.

"King Nero has sent aid! He must not have gotten any of my messages!"

"What should we do my Queen?"

The Queen raises her hands while chanting magical spells into the dawn air. She pauses for a moment before looking to Estee.

"Go quickly down to the city walls! Tell my commanders to attack the Demon siege lines! Those riders are outnumbered. We need to draw the attention away from them! My men shall form a shield wall and allow our allies to ride behind them and into the city. Let Commander Minsk know that he should retreat back behind the safety of the city wall once all of the Knights of the North are safe!"

After doling out orders the Queen looks at me and gently grabs onto my shoulder as Estee runs off to fulfill the orders.

"Not you Cameron. I need you to do something else for me!"

"What is it my Queen?"

"You will go with your lone Guardian in this realm and deliver a message to King Nero!"

"But there is no way to get through the siege lines without being captured. I'm a pretty good fighter, but I don't think that me and Fred can fight hundreds of Demons by ourselves!"

The Queen points at the Celestial Door as Fred appears shaking off the water from the elevator he has just exited.

"Third door on the right if I remember correctly."

I follow the Queen to the magic passage before she begins chanting. The lighted runes and symbols surrounding the door light up and shift from one color to another. The Queen nods her head at me while pointing at the door.

"Go now Cameron. Tell the King that he should not send anymore of his soldiers to lift this siege. Tell him that the safest place for him and his people is to remain at Stonepass. I will destroy this army surrounding our gates on my own, and then join him at Knifespike to defend his lands from the army that Gallus has hidden from us!"

I slap Fred on the back below his wings. He seems happy to see me, if not a little nervous to walk through a wall of glowing stone.

"Don't worry pal! It feels like walking through a thin layer of morning mist!"

I extend my arms in front of me out of pure instinct before traversing through the Celestial Door. Once inside I wait for Fred to appear. His eyes suggest that he is just as impressed with the Celestial hallway as I was when I first saw it.

"Pretty cool huh?"

"It is the single most beautiful thing I have ever laid eyes upon!"

"Come on. The Queen said it's the third door on the right."

I look up at three doors on opposite sides of the path, and a larger door at the far end of the hallway. Unlike the last time I was here, every Celestial Door is covered in ice and a red glow.

"She did say the third one on the right...right?"

I look at Fred who is still enthralled with the picture perfect Starscape below our feet.

"You with me Fred?"

He shakes his head and looks at me as if I have just jostled him out of the perfect dream.

"Sorry, I wasn't listening. What did you say?"

I grin at my Guardian and point down the short hallway of doors.

"She said the third one on the right...right?"

"Yeah! That's what I heard."

I walk down the hallway and stop in front of the door indicated to be the correct one by the Queen of Rain. I reach forward and touch the ice covered surface of the magic passageway. A bolt of fire ripples through my insides. I fall back into the ice covered door behind me and receive an equally painful jolt of energy.

"What the hell! It's locked or something. Go see if we can get back through the door we came through to begin with!"

Fred takes five large paces backwards and touches the Doorway leading back to the Storm Tower with the tip of his finger. When his finger touches the door, his body goes into convulsions and drops to the floor. I rush over ignoring the pain of my own experience to make sure he's okay.

His eyes shine bright with fear.

"Thanks for that!"

I can tell that he's still in pain as he rolls onto his side and climbs back to his feet.

"I didn't know it'd be booby trapped! Besides, I just took two hits for the team! You don't hear me complaining do you?"

Fred points to the far end of the majestic hallway. My eyes too find the appearance of the larger door at the end of the walkway different in appearance somehow. There is a yellow glow emanating from the edges of the stone cutout door. The carved runes around it are rotating colors like the doorway in the Storm Tower did before we travelled here.

As if he can read my mind, Fred blurts out the only obvious thing in the hall.

"I think we should try that one!"

"Oh really genius? We should try the door that looks different from the others? Good idea!"

I glance back at my Guardian and send him a sarcastic smirk before walking forward to inspect the door at the end of the hall. I stop a few feet away and inspect the surface of the door. The stone is smooth except for a small indentation underneath a small carved rune. I recognize the symbol from somewhere.

My hand instinctively reaches into my pocket to gather the coin that Fendril gifted to me. I pull out the coin and place it between my face and the carved symbol on the stone surface. The two markings are identical.

"What are the odds?"

I whisper the words so quiet that Fred doesn't hear them. Nothing happens when I touch the surface of the coin into the cutout that it seems destined to fill.

"Flip it around!"

I'm almost angry at the simple nature of the comment coming from behind me. I look down at the orientation of the coin and see that the snake and triangle side of the coin is facing away from me. I flip the coin around and gaze upon the sigil of the Creator as I push it into the center of the door.

The coin glows for the briefest of seconds before returning to its original gold finish. A loud snapping sound echoes in the hallway, and the surface of the massive stone door glows blue instead of the yellow it glowed before.

"Well, I guess we don't really have a choice Fred."

I push forward through the Celestial Door. On the other side I'm greeted by a light that can only be described as blinding. Fred bounces off of my back after arriving behind me. He raises one of his wings in front of us to block the light coming from ahead. I notice movement. My hand grips the handle of my sword.

"Welcome young Centurian! I hadn't dreamed of seeing you again so soon!"

In front of us stands the Sky Warrior I know as Fendril.

"I'm sorry that the Creator has manipulated your visit here, but he has need of you. I have been sent to gather you for an audience."

"You do know that there are some pretty concerning things going on… right? The Queen sent me to deliver a message to King Nero. I need to get there fast!"

Fendril flaps his angelic wings in the air causing the light from overhead to dim to a level in which I can squint through the pain of seeing. We walk behind our guide passing by throngs of humans and magical creatures, each one going about their day as if everything was normal. I glance back every few moments to make sure that Fred hasn't gotten lost while traversing the small market we are passing through.

"We climb now young Centurian!"

Fendril points to a set of stairs that must rise a thousand feet into the air.

"You have to be kidding me dude?"

A smile appears on Fendril's face as he steps up onto the first stair of hundreds, if not thousands.

"Up we go to the Creator's Throne Room…"

By the time we get to the top of the winding staircase, I can barely breathe. Fred is also laboring. If we needed to defend ourselves anytime soon it would be an embarrassing effort to say the least.

I look forward through squinting eyes and see a bright light atop a white marble throne. Surrounding the throne are golden statues depicting the tree that decorates one side of my coin. *Or Key as I now understand.* A surprisingly gruff voice calls out my name. Fendril bows his head before kneeling and averting his eyes to the floor. I see that Fred has decided to do the same.

"Come forward Cameron. I have been watching you for a long time now."

I walk forward while trying to avoid looking directly at the blinding light coming from the man talking to me. From the look of his shape, he seems to be more human than creature.

"I apologize for my appearance, but for a human to look upon my face would surely cause him to die."

I close my eyes and try and picture the person that I'm speaking with.

"You are wise for one so young in years. I must first thank you for returning Fendril to me. He is one of my most loyal creations, and I now have need of all the allies and friends that I can find. I have need of you too son!"

I nod my head as respectfully as I know how to. There is a warm feeling that surrounds my body and penetrates my skin in his presence. I feel strong and at peace. The anxiety that normally flows inside of me is gone entirely.

"How may I be of service to you and the ones who represent you in the Sky Realm?"

There is a slight pause.

"The ones you call the Sky Gods do not represent me any longer. For many generations they have twisted the meaning of my words to create a place of power for themselves. They are no longer my servants. Neither do they serve my son Gallus. They live only to further their own power under the guise of representing my will."

I think back to the circumstances that existed when I was summoned to the Sky God's Throne Room. At the time nothing seemed out of place. There was no reason to question the teachings that I had received from Thoth describing them.

"If what you say is true... Why not remove them from power and assert your dominance over the realms of Cyadonia. You do know that things are getting pretty bad down there without you!"

"I am well aware of what goes on in Cyadonia and all the other realms for which I have created. You should also be aware that I have given every creation of mine free will. A decision that I did not come to without great contemplation."

I hear the words, but I can't understand how the all-powerful being in front of me won't just do something to help the people he created.

"But wouldn't it just be easier if you removed all the beings that choose to hurt everyone else? I think it would be better!"

"You are young still Cameron. You do not understand the meaning of the life I have given you. There is no other way to deem the character of a man so efficiently as to tempt him into doing wrong. I value right action and honesty above all things, and I gladly give forgiveness to all who would turn from their dark desires and choose the light."

I feel as though the words coming from the creator make sense, but I also can't help but feel conflicted over his ability to end the ongoing conflicts with a flick of his wrist.

"What is it that you ask of me?"

"You shall deliver a message to Gallus for me. He has blocked out my voice for far too long, and I offer him one last chance to repent and rejoin my flock."

"What?"

I feel a rush of anger fill my chest. The warm feeling of comfort filling my chest disappears entirely.

"You want to forgive that guy? Are you freaking crazy? He's the worst! Like seriously… He is worse than Hitler! And that's saying something!"

"Who do you think gave Hitler the ideas to do what he did? That's right! Gallus lives not only in this realm, but also in the human realm as well. Now maybe you can see the level of my capability for forgiveness?"

"Oh, I can see it! I just don't think it's a good idea!"

"Even so... Will you deliver my message when first you see him?"

I nod my head.

"Yeah, I'll deliver your message! But how do you know I'll see him?"

The light brightens on the back of my eyelids as I hear the final words of the Creator.

"Because I have seen it Young Centurian. Now go forth and fulfill the message that my loyal servant the Queen of Rain has given you! Waste not a moment!"

I bow in respect before turning away from the throne of light. I walk between Fred and Fendril and stop before looking down the massive stone staircase leading back down to the market.

"The Creator needs to build a freaking elevator or something!"

I feel Fendril's arm wrap around my waist and pull me tight to his side.

"I will fly you back to the Celestial Door my young friend!"

I feel the pit of my stomach twist as the overwhelming force of falling takes hold of my body. Fendril points his head towards the fast approaching ground before unfurling his wings and gliding us over the market. We land in front of the shrine dedicated to the Celestial Door.

Fred arrives behind us. He seems happy to have found a good reason to stretch his wings. There never seems to be a good time to use them these days. Especially because he isn't quite strong enough to carry both of our weight. If that wasn't the case we would pretty much fly everywhere I guess. *Walking is for the birds!* I contemplate the commonly used phrase in the human realm. *That makes no sense, birds can fly!*

I place the gold coin against the door and wait until it glows with the same hugh as before. After arriving inside the

Celestial Hallway, my eyes are drawn to the first door on my left.

"Look dude! It's green this time, and the ice has melted away!"

Fred shakes his head after appearing beside me.

"Do you get that pain in your head when you travel through the doors?"

"Yeah man, It's like that feeling you get when you eat your ice-cream too fast."

I stand in front of the door that the Queen of Rain wanted me to go through before being detoured by the Creator.

"You ready for this Fred?"

"Let's do it kid!"

**

I arrive inside of a dimly lit room. On either side of the Celestial Door are two metal bowls of fire hanging from the ceiling. I look around but don't see anyone else in the room. There is a short hallway in front of us that seems to break off in two different directions. I hear the sound of metal boots walking atop stone flooring echoing down the hallway in front of us.

Four men carrying shields and spears approach us. As they get closer the tips of their spears lower to form a wall. Each man is wearing a solid breastplate with the sigil of the Kingdom of Plenty. The sigil consists of two stallions standing on their back feet facing one another, with a strange symbol between them.

"Halt, stay where you are!"

I raise both of my hands into the air and stay as still as possible.

"I was sent by the Queen of Rain to speak with King Nero!"

"The King is on patrol. He rides the cliff edge to scout the forces surrounding us!"

"The Demon army has already crossed the river?"

"Indeed, They crossed during the night after slaughtering our soldiers inside the fort of Knifespike!"

"Crap, we are too late then!"

One of the soldiers raises his spear and walks forward to inspect our faces.

"You are Centurian to the Queen of Rain?"

I nod my head and point to Fred.

"Yes I am, and this is my Guardian. We were sent to deliver a message strait to King Nero from the Queen."

The man returns my bow and signals for the men standing behind him to lower their guard.

"I am called Julius. I am General of the King's armies and sit on his war council. Speak freely young Centurian."

I hesitate to give the Queen's message to anyone but the King himself. Julius notices my hesitancy. I can tell he feels slighted by my refusal to give him the message. We are interrupted by the sound of trumpets signaling the return of the King.

"I think I'll just tell the King!"

"As you wish Centurian, follow me, and I will take you too him."

We climb down two sets of spiral stairs before arriving in the Throne Room. Braziers are roaring with hot fires, and a table in the center of the room is filled with food and jugs of beer. The Kings throne is covered in the white and black pelts of slain animals and beasts.

Two massive doors swing open on the opposite end of the room. A man with flowing blonde hair enters swiftly flanked on either side by soldiers and hounds. He removes his helmet and places it on the table causing a bowl of bread to be dislodged. He seems angry.

"How the hell did they take Knifespike so quickly? I had five hundred men manning the fort and another two hundred patrolling the river edge to the north of the bridge."

"My Lord..."

Julius steps forward and stops the King from continuing his angry tirade.

"This Centurian has come with tidings from the Queen of Rain."

"I sure hope he has good news!"

King Nero waves me forward while taking a seat at the head of the table and telling his men to feast.

"Come Centurian! Sit beside me so that we can talk at a normal volume."

I walk forward and sit in a sturdy wooden chair next to the King.

"What word does the Queen of Rain send?"

I reach forward and grab a beer mug before taking a sip of the glorious liquid inside.

"It's not good news my Lord! She sends word to remain in your fortress of Stonepass, and send no armies to lift the siege of the City of Light."

The King scoffs at my words.

"A message received too late I'm afraid. I sent five hundred of my heavy cavalry under the command of my most trusted Commander to break the siege two days past. They should have arrived already. I gave orders to travel through the night!"

"They did arrive, just hours ago. And I'm sure the Queen will do everything she can to save as many of your men as possible... But I'm afraid that many will not return. The Queen sent a message meant for you days ago. Carried by one of your Centurians. Yakuza!"

The King begins laughing while stuffing a large turkey leg

between his teeth and ripping away a healthy chunk. He then picks up a large mug and washes the meat down his gullet with a big swig.

"That drunken fool? He has not been in my service for many years now! He was caught feeding information to a Fallen Priest along the rivers of the Tigris. I disavowed him and exiled him from the Kingdom of Plenty. He is lucky that I did not take his head."

A tense feeling arrives in my stomach as the King's words echo in the Throne Room.

"The Queen didn't know that when she gave him the message. Me and a small group of warriors left his company at the pass leading to the Breathing Mountains."

The King leans back in his chair and begins to talk to the hound sitting next to him.

"If only my hounds could deliver messages... I never question their loyalty!"

The dog looks up at its master and grinds its head into the palm of the King's hand. Nero pushes the rest of his turkey leg onto the floor for his companion to join in the feast.

"Is this all that the Queen has asked you to relay?"

I think about the contents of the full message that I'm supposed to relay to King Nero.

"No Sir... She says that she will destroy the army surrounding her city. Then she plans on marching north with her army and what remains of the men you have sent to aid her. She is to meet you at Knifespike, and with your combined armies defend the river crossing from an army that Gallus has constructed."

Nero reaches forward and tilts back the remaining beer in his mug. He swallows deeply before looking me in the eyes.

"A fine plan if it were still three days ago. I have seen this

Demon army with my own eyes. Many thousands of armored Warrior Demons accompanied by hundreds more foul war beasts. They even have a god damned company of flying beasts. You know, The ones with razor sharp claws and beaks filled with bone cracking teeth?"

"Yeah I know the ones you speak of. My Wise Teacher was snatched by one of those things only a day past! How long until they get here?"

The King places his mug back down onto the table before waving over a woman wearing a long gown made of embroidered silk. The hems of her dress are lined with golden flowers. Above her stomach is the sigil of the Kingdom of Plenty.

"Adrianna, come here daughter!"

The young woman approaches the King and kisses him on the cheek.

"What is it father?"

"Take this young Centurian to the highest tower and let him see the army that marches towards our stronghold! Go with my daughter and see for yourself! I have only three of my own Centurians to help me defend this place, and I will most likely need your fighting spirit to aid me in the defense of this fortress."

I stand up from the table and bow one last time before following a flowing white train of silk leading me to a passage behind the King's throne.

"Keep up Centurian. I must move quickly up the steps to avoid tripping on my gown."

I break into a trot after seeing the King's daughter glide gracefully up the spiral staircase. We pass by seven landings before arriving at the top level of the tower. The roof is lined with torches around the perimeter of the structure. The Princess startles me by gently grasping my hand and pulling me to the edge of the northern parapet.

"What should I call you Centurian?"

I look at the princess's mouth as she speaks. Her lips are covered in a shiny substance filled with sparkles.

"You can call me Cameron. And you are called Adrianna?"

"I am. It is a pleasure to meet you Cameron. Look out upon the coming storm."

I look past the pretty face of the Princess. The sun is now well above the mountains of the eastern kingdoms. I can see many stone towers lining the perimeter of the mountain fortress complex. Each tower is connected by a thick stone wall almost twenty feet thick. You could ride four horses abreast between the defensive parapets lining the walls.

Below the defensive walls are sheer cliff faces descending hundreds of feet towards open meadows and cleared land purposed for growing crops. I scan the fortress while walking around the tower edge. Cliffs on all sides except the one to the south. The southern approach consists of a winding path through fifty foot walls of carved stone. Three men standing abreast would have a hard time walking the path together.

Above the path leading through the southern approach, are curved bridges flanked on either side by tall towers. Atop each tower is a strange device that I don't recognize.

"What are those things atop the towers below?"

The princess leans slightly through the parapet and points at the towers flanking the southern approach.

"Those are war weapons that toss stones on top of anyone who tries to attack the fortress. Those little black dots beside them are filled with a sticky substance that we can heat up and shower down on any unwanted guests."

I continue looking over the layout of the only entrance to the fortress of Stonepass. A large steel gate blocks the entrance to the main castle housing the tower I am now standing on.

"Do you know how many men your father has to defend this place?"

"I do not know the exact number, but it is close to two thousand or so! The best warriors in all the land!"

My eyes are distracted by a small clump of dark clouds moving towards the fortress from the north. Upon further inspection I realize that the clouds are made up of the same flying beasts that captured Thoth. Below the clouds of foul beasts are tiny black lines stretching back miles towards the river. They look like the lines of ants that I have seen when watching the discovery channel in the real world.

I shake my head. Among the small lines of soldiers are war machines like nothing I have seen before.

"We need to get back down to the King."

I shoot a look of concern at Fred who is still staring out over the approaching army.

"Let's go Fred!"

He snaps out of his daze and races to catch up to me and the princess. We arrive at the bottom of the stairs. Adrianna bows in front of me before leading me back to her father, still sitting and drinking at the head of the table. I'm not one hundred percent positive, but I'm pretty sure she winked at me as well.

"Have you now witnessed with your own eyes the evil that comes hither?"

"I have your Highness! I shall report back to the Queen at once."

The King scoffs at my remark.

"I will send word back to the Queen of Rain. You and your Guardian shall stay here! I'm sure the Queen will not mind lending you to me for the defense of the Realm!"

I see a concerned look appear on Fred's face. I shake my head as covertly as possible to assuage his concern. His relaxing posture suggests that he has received my covert message.

"Very well King Nero! I will serve you as I would the Queen. What would you have me do?"

The King snaps his finger. A man wearing blue plated armor approaches and leans in to hear the King's command.

"At once my Lord!"

The man places his hand on the small of my back and guides me away from the King's table.

"Follow me young Centurian!"

I comply with the man's request and walk in the direction that he leads. We exit the Throne Room and travel down two sets of hallways before descending into a room filled with weapons and armor. Inside I can see soldiers preparing themselves for the battle to come. On the far end of the hall are two tall men dressed in the finest black armor I have ever seen.

The man leading me stops in front of the men and looks back at me.

"May I introduce the Queen of Rain's Centurian... The King wishes for him to aid us in the battle to come. These are the King's Centurians."

I look at the battle worn faces of the men in front of me. As I stare I can tell that they are also sizing me up. The uncomfortable stare down is interrupted when a woman wearing the same black armor as the men in front of me steps between us. Atop her head are braids of long black hair coiled up like a snake about to strike. She makes me feel nervous almost immediately. Her voice is calm and pleasant to the ear.

"Don't be rude boys! Introduce yourselves to our guest!"

CHAPTER 11

"Push forward men!"

Balls of fire explode overhead from the catapults being manned by Demons along the main line of siege. I keep my head down behind the wall of shields formed by the Queen's Army. The little men grunt loudly after every surge of Demon attack is pushed back in a collective effort. The line is holding in front of the city gates.

"Send word to the Knights on the ridge to ride around behind our lines and retreat behind the city walls."

My messenger rides away on the back of a black and white striped tiger. I blow away a chunk of my hair that has been burnt from the falling ashes of the enemy attacks.

I brace my hand against the back of the soldier protecting me from frontal attack. He grunts loudly and repositions his shield one step forward before sinking the short spike at the bottom of the shield into the ground.

A tiny man sitting in a saddle atop a lightly armored Jungle Cat appears behind me.

"My scout reports that the mounted knights from the Kingdom of Plenty are riding north to confuse the Demon army. They will then turn west and ride through the bushes lining the forest and appear again against the city walls. If we can hold the line for a few more minutes we should be able to save a significant amount of them."

I glance up to see a new volley of fire coated stones exploding against the protective barrier the Queen of Rain has erected to protect us from attack. Small chips of burning stone flutter down on top of us.

"Brace for impact!"

I yell out words of encouragement to the Queen's men bravely fighting to save the lives of their human allies from the Kingdom of Plenty. A wave of wild Demon soldiers crash into the line of shields. I hear the shrieks of death all around me. Small puffs of black powder denote every Demon who falls in battle.

I look around at the faces of the soldiers in the shield wall. Each one is covered in a layer of black soot. The whites of each soldiers eyes pierce through the layers of dead Demon residue clinging to sweaty skin.

There is a rumbling in the ground below my feet. I look to the west and see a long column of fast moving Knights riding behind the Shield Wall of city defenders. A man in black armor steers his horse towards my position. As his horse slides to a stop beside me, the rest of his men ride in two single file lines across the wooden drawbridge separating the city walls from the field of battle.

"You can begin collapsing your lines from the flanks Centurian."

I glance at the Queen's General sitting on top of a Jungle Cat next to me.

"You heard him General. Have your men begin peeling back from the flanks and into the city. Send word to the Queen that her orders have been fulfilled, and we await further instructions."

As waves of 'Little' soldiers begin retreating, a storm overhead releases a barrage of frozen icicles upon the Demon ranks regrouping to charge the retreating shield wall and push through into the city. The charging wave of armored Demon warriors is obliterated by the sharp chunks of ice falling from the sky. The closing wave of enemy attackers is slowed enough to allow the shield wall to fall back swiftly and orderly.

The moment of peace is only temporary. After recovering from the shock of the magical attacks hitting all around, the remaining Demons begin charging forward towards the convergence point of the shield wall at the main city gate.

As the shield wall retreats under cover from the Queen's magic, a small storm of arrows begins falling on the cowering Demons hiding in trenches. The Knights from the north have dismounted and are now raining down arrows using the weapons left behind by the Queen's Warriors.

The main Demon force falls back to the siege trenches to hide from the incoming steel rain. Each Knight releases arrow after arrow until the ammunition barrels lining the wall are empty.

I stay behind until the last of the shield wall has retreated to safety behind the drawbridge. The wooden bridge lifts up and comes to rest after being locked in place with two massive metal pins on either side of the gate. I run up the steep stone stairs and stand next to the Queen's General to assess the losses that we have just taken.

"I counted at least a hundred dead, and twice that wounded. A fair trade to save all but twelve of our allied riders sent by King Nero."

The man in black armor appears standing next to me. He removes his helmet revealing a weary face. His eyelids and forehead are coated in a thick black dust. His eyes are the deepest blue color that I have ever seen. His neck is bleeding from a thin cut running from the edge of his chin to the top of his Adam's Apple.

He reaches up and touches the wound while looking out over the field of battle.

"What was the Butcher's Bill?"

"About a hundred of the Queen's men dead, more wounded!"

The man nods his head as I relay the numbers from the Queen's General. He seems tired and worn from the battle.

"I thank you for coming to our aid! You could have stayed put and hid behind the Queen's magic and your thick stone walls. We surely would have been surrounded and defeated had you not attacked! For this act I am ever grateful Centurian!"

"You can thank the Queen Commander! It was she who ordered the attack! I just follow orders. Much like yourself I imagine?"

The man grins in my direction. His smile is disarming. I guess that he is probably in his mid-thirties by the look of it. He has obviously been in many battles. Part of his right ear is missing, and there is a small gouge in the bridge of his nose. Neither of his battle scars reduce the instant attraction I feel for him.

"It's true that I serve the King much like you serve your Queen. If only my King was as wise as the Queen of Rain... I would still have all of my men alive today. We had no idea of the size or scope of the Demon army surrounding your city!"

I watch as the Commander brushes away a thin layer of black dust covering the yellow sigil on his chest. He reaches out to the Queen's General. Both men shake hands and share a look of thankfulness that the battle went their way. The Queen's General points to three large Pyramids resting beside the river.

"You may take your men to those domiciles. There are shelters by the river where you can feed and water your horses. Your men will find food and drink there as well. I must ask you to come and speak with the Queen after you have gotten your men situated."

"It will be done General! I shall see you soon at the Castle. And I will see you there too?"

His eyes lock onto mine. I feel a rush of anxiety fill my stomach. His stare and friendly smirk are intoxicating. *Get it together Estee!* My inner voice is screaming at me.

"I will see you there..."

I can see that he is waiting for me to finish the sentence before he answers the question I desire to ask.

"Commander Brutus... Marcus Brutus!"

He smiles one more time as I bow to show respect. I can feel his eyes follow me as I walk behind the General in the direction of the Shadow Tower.

The Queen is waiting in the Throne Room when I arrive. The General explains to the Queen the full cost of the battle before leaving us alone in the room.

"A necessary sacrifice I must say my dearest Centurian. I watched you as you stood behind the Shield Wall. You are truly brave! What do you make of the Commander that King Nero has sent to 'Rescue' us from the forces of darkness?"

Her question catches me off guard for a quick second before I regain focus of my thoughts.

"He seems confident and competent. I don't really know much about him. Have you met him before? His name is Marcus Brutus..."

The Queen's smile widens while she probes my response for secret clues.

"Indeed I have had the pleasure of meeting Commander Brutus before. But when I met him back then he was just a lowly captain leading a small company of the King's Cavalry. I knew then that he would one day have a command of his own. There's something about his character that is very attractive... Is there not?"

I can tell the Queen is probing my response with her eyes. There's the smallest hint of a smirk being hidden by her firm upper lip.

"I don't deny it my Queen! He is a very attractive man! And you're right, there is definitely something that I can't put my finger on that makes me feel a certain way about him!"

The queen grabs both of my shoulders and shakes me out of my thoughts while laughing out loud in a giddy fashion.

"I knew as soon as I saw him up on that ridge, all 'Knightly' on his noble steed, with his black armor and disarming smile... I knew you would like him!"

The Queen gives me one last happy shake before pointing towards her chambers behind the Throne Room.

"You better go clean yourself up! We can't have the Commander seeing you again covered in Demon dust!"

The Queen claps her hands twice. A little woman rushes into the Throne Room holding a half mended dress in hand.

"How can I be of assistance my Queen?"

The woman curtsies after approaching the Queen. I see a judgmental look run across her face after seeing the status of my appearance.

"Take my Centurian to my chambers and help her become more presentable. Put her in that dress you made. The light blue one with the white lace overlay. And make sure she takes a bath as well!"

The little woman seems to be excited about the prospect of transforming me into a lady of the court. She gently pushes me into the Queen's chamber. A large feather bed in the shape of a five pointed star fills the center of the room. On the far side of the tower chamber is a large silver bathing tub with bent feet depicting the legs of a bird. The water inside is already warm, but I place my hand on the inside edge and power my fire magic.

The Queen's maid unstraps the leather latches holding all of the pieces of my armor in place. When I'm relieved of the protected layer, I slide off the tight leather underlayer covering my skin.

The water is the perfect temperature. I sink down under the

water while running both hands through my hair. The water fills with a cloudy mixture of Demon dust and dirt from the field of battle. I notice that there is also a red tinge in the water. My hands search my body for wounds. I find a small cut on the tip of my chin. I must have just avoided taking an arrow to the throat. A development that makes me feel grateful that I'm still alive.

The maid returns after placing my armor in a peculiar closet next to the tub. From the ceiling of the closet a small trickle of magical rain falls atop whatever is placed inside.

She reaches into the tub after looking at the cloudy nature of the water.

"Oh no! This will not do Centurian."

The little woman closes her eyes and starts waving her hand in a tight circle. The dirty water from the tub I'm sitting inside rises into the air like a water tornado and splashes out the closest window. I feel bad for anyone standing at the bottom of this tower.

The maid reaches into a small basket under the tub. Her fingers reappear holding a small blue gemstone. She places the stone beside my feet at the bottom of the tub before singing in a tone that makes me long for sleep. Clean water begins filling the tub. I power my fire magic and heat the water as it spills out of the gemstone.

When the tub is full, the woman smiles at me while removing the blue stone and placing it back into the basket below me.

"It is most convenient that you can heat the water yourself! You saved me a step! But we are still missing one thing."

Her hand reaches back into the wicker basket. She uncorks the top of a round glass bottle and pours out a small stream of yellow liquid into the water. Her hand swirls the oils to spread them around the tub. I'm surprised by the sweet smell of cupcakes infusing the bathwater.

Before long, the scent shifts tones and reminds me more of the smell of pepperoni pizza. The maid sees the shift on my face as my nostrils flare in and out.

"The scent will change based on what you desire most when being subjected to its spell!"

I know right away that she is telling the truth. I famished after the battle, and the last thing I ate today was a small bowl of fish stew. At the very thought of my last meal, I remember that the Queen has sent Cameron away on a mission of his own. I say a quick prayer to the Sky Gods to keep him safe.

My prayer is joined by the maid sitting beside the tub. She seems to be able to read my thoughts.

"I can read your thoughts!"

I'm startled out of my head by the admission of the Queen's maid.

"I have many gifts, but the ability to read minds and anticipate the needs of my Queen are most useful."

"I bet they are, but I'd prefer it if you would stay out of my head please? I'll tell you if I need anything."

The maid smiles and leaves the room for a short moment before walking back in holding a light blue dress. Delicate patterns of white silk weave in and out of the blue background forming small detailed storm clouds. In her other hand is a pair of glossy white heels with blue straps.

"These should fit you well Centurian! You and the Queen share a similar size and shape!"

I stand up and squeeze the water out of my hair before stepping out of the tub. The Queen's maid arrives by my side and drapes a thick robe over my wet body. I rub the towel fabric all over before removing the robe and putting on a set of light blue underwear matching the dress that I will be wearing.

"Sit here Centurian! I shall dry your hair and style it for you."

I feel a warm rush of air running all around the maids fingers as she runs both of her hands through my wet hair. Before long, the wetness is gone, and I can feel my hair being shaped into some sort of fancy hairdo. I hear a short sigh come from her lips as she smiles while inspecting her handywork. I glance over at a body length mirror to inspect the work that she has done.

"I don't think I have ever looked prettier madam. Thank you!"

"You may call me Celeste if you wish Centurian!"

"Thank you Celeste!"

The Queen's maid collects the dress hanging above the mirror. She pulls it off of a black velvet hanger and helps me climb inside. Her hands move the thin straps over my shoulders before zipping up the back.

"Don't tell the Queen, but you look better in this dress than she does!"

I look around the room to make sure the Queen can't see me before letting a big smile cross my face.

The Queen is sitting in a marble throne twirling her crown in hand when I reappear for the big reveal. Her mouth opens wide in total surprise at my appearance.

"You look breathtaking Centurian! I'll be surprised if Commander Brutus can take his eyes off of you for even a moment. Maybe I should keep you hidden away from his eyes while I speak to him about my plans. I don't want him to be distracted!"

The smile on the Queen's face suggests to me that she's joking. We make small talk while waiting for the guest of honor to arrive. I take the time to ask about Cameron. She tells me that King Nero has sent word that Cameron and Fred arrived safely at Stonepass.

I'm a little less thrilled when the Queen tells me that she

has allowed the King to borrow Cam and Fred to help defend Stonepass.

"There seems to be some sort of ulterior motive for keeping Cameron at Stonepass. I don't sense ill intent from the King, but he's up to something for sure. Fred will keep him safe either way. That winged idiot is one of my favorite Guardians!"

"I sure hope so! The kid has kind of grown on me."

I watch as a small puff of white mist arrives slightly before the Knight Commander of the Kingdom of Plenty appears. He has taken the time to clean his armor and wipe away the filth of battle from his face. I feel the warmth of his eyes wash over me. He nearly trips over his own feet while approaching the Queen.

The entire walk forward I can see his eyes darting between me and the Queen sitting in the throne on my left.

"Welcome Commander Brutus! I am most happy to see you in these halls once again!"

"Thank you your Highness! I fear that my arrival does not bring to memory the same happy circumstances of our last meeting!"

"Ah yes,"

The Queen turns to me while speaking.

"Commander Brutus was still a Captain when he last graced my Throne Room. I believe that he was tasked with escorting the Princess to the City of Light to entertain a proposal of marriage from a Nobleman in the Kingdom of Plenty."

"You are correct my Queen! King Nero had requested that you gauge the intentions of the suitor in regards to his daughter's hand. And a good thing that he did!"

I focus as the Queen looks at me and points at the crown in her hand. She leans over to me and whispers.

"Pretty handy having a crown that can force people to tell you the truth!"

I smile after putting the pieces together. The Queen returns her attention to the man standing in front of us.

"Alas it was not meant to be for that wicked Nobleman, but I see that you have found favor with King Nero!"

"I have indeed. He values my honesty when sharing plans he has concocted, in both battle and politics. There are far too many 'Honey Tongues" in the King's council. A reality that I plan on addressing when I return."

"The King is lucky to have you in his confidence Commander! Will you dine with us? I have need of your wisdom in the ways of war!"

"It would be my honor to counsel you my Queen! The King gave me leave to remain by your side until you feel that the threat is no longer."

I notice the Queen's eyes glimmer with mischief after the Commander expresses his ability to remain in the City of Light until she sees fit that he may leave.

"Careful Commander, I may never let you leave. Perhaps we can find something to keep you here for the time being?"

Her obvious intentions are becoming clear. The Queen stares over at me with the look of a seasoned matchmaker. I can see that the Commander is also catching on to the Queen's innuendo. My spirit lifts a bit when the Commander looks me in the eyes while responding to the Queen's comments.

"I would be truly blessed to remain in your presence for any length of time…"

He pauses for a long time while still looking at me. He then turns his head and looks at the Queen with a wry smile attached to his lips.

"My Queen!"

It's clear to me that the man standing in front of us can play the game. His deep eye contact, combined with the way his lips move while forming words, draws me into a lovesick trance. Secretly I wonder if he's wielding some sort of magic to make me fall for his charm. I make a mental note to inquire with the Queen if he has secret magical talents she's aware of.

The Queen points to a square table filled with food and drink. Below the table she has filled the space with a dense white fog. We sit at the table and begin filling our plates with the various items available. It feels as though we are sitting on a giant cloud.

"Tell me Centurian, do you have a name that I can call you by? I do not wish to address you as 'Centurian' for longer than I must."

I swallow a chunk of bread that I have just placed in my mouth. He notices that his question has interrupted my eating. His hand grasps the crystal glass filled with water from the table in front of him. He drinks deeply while giving me time to reply to his question at my own schedule.

"You should call me Estee."

"Estee? This is a name that I have never heard before. Is it common in the human realm?"

I shrug my shoulders and try to think about how many people I have ever known with the same name as me. I can't come up with even one.

"I guess it's pretty uncommon. I don't know anyone else with the same name!"

"My name is uncommon as well in Cyadonia. According to my teachers, my father shared this name with me and no other. I would very much like you to call me Marcus... If you so desire of course! I do not wish to make you feel uncomfortable!"

The Queen sits at the head of the table watching our conversation. Her head snaps back and forth between us. It seems that she is enjoying the words being shared. A small grin hasn't left her face since the dinner began.

Her voice breaks the back and forth.

"It seems that the two of you have much in common! We will have to see if the chemistry I feel at this table transfers to the battlefield tomorrow!"

I'm brought back to the harsh reality of war from the developing fairy tale being fostered around the Queen's table.

"Shall we discuss my plan for ridding the City from the army of foul beasts and Demons at the gates?"

Marcus nods his head before spearing a sausage with the two pronged fork in hand.

"We shall my Queen! What plans have you made? And how can me and my men assist you?"

The Queen leans back in her chair while swirling a healthy amount of red wine in her cup.

"They have the numbers. That much is easy to see. But they do not know the terrain like I do. We shall use that to our advantage."

"How shall we use the land against the enemy?"

The Commander's questioning tone catches me by surprise. So far he has shown every form of respect to the Queen. I decide to give him the benefit of the doubt.

"Forgive me my Queen. I do not know these lands like you do. From what I saw from the ridge above the enemy's siege trenches, they have complete control of who comes and goes from the city. I also would wager that the forests surrounding the city are also being watched. What advantage do you propose?"

"I propose we use ME... as bait!"

I look at the Queen and realize that she isn't joking.

"I am one of the most powerful entities in all of Cyadonia. You shall use me as bait to lure the enemy into a disadvantageous position where my Shield Bearers hold the enemy at arm's length. Once the enemy leaves the safety of their earth works they will be vulnerable to attack from your mounted Knights. We will lure the enemy into the open, and you will ride them down with hoof and spear while my men squeeze them from the sides!"

Marcus leans back in his chair while rubbing the stubble on his chin. He seems unable to find error in the Queen's plan.

"What makes you think that the enemy will abandon their defenses in pursuit of you?"

"Gallus has sent them specifically for this reason. My spy's have learned that Gallus sent this army to capture me. He thinks he can corrupt my mind in the dark cells beneath the city of Gomorrah."

I see a nervous look cross the face of the Commander as he ponders the Queen's plans further.

"It's not the worst plan I've ever heard, but we risk everything, including yourself, if the enemy does not pursue you with reckless abandon. Worst case scenario you catch an arrow or any of a hundred stray siege munitions before we are able to spring this trap. Are you willing to risk your own life? We could always hide behind the power of your magic and the stone of your thick walls! The enemy must surely run out of supply and willpower to continue this siege. The city has access to fresh water and abundant fish from the river."

The Queen stands from her chair at the table. She flips the bottom of her hem away from her feet while leaning forward and looking across the table at Marcus.

"I will not sit here trapped in my own Castle while the rest of Cyadonia burns. I will not be remembered as the Queen who watched the world burn from the Storm Tower. Whether he knows it or not, King Nero will need my assistance to turn back the forces of Gallus. We must destroy this army and come to the King's aid. There are things that even he doesn't know about the enemy at his gates!"

CHAPTER 12

"So all three of you live here in Cyadonia all the time?"

The King's Centurians look at me as if I'm stupid or something. The female Guardian puts down her mug of ale before explaining.

"You, and other 'Dream Walkers" like you, are really rare in Cyadonia. For the Queen to possess two of you as her Centurians is quite rare. Normally the lords of this realm search the countryside for small children with small amounts of magical ability to train as Centurian to the realm. I myself can only produce a small flame if I focus all of my strength, but I can wield a sword better than most!"

I accept the information while feeling a little bit of nervous energy leave my chest. The King's Centurians, although fierce to behold, treat me in a way that's quite gentle.

"I met the King's former Centurian named Yakuza! He was a 'Dream Walker' Right?"

I see the look on the faces of my hosts twist in the direction of discomfort. The two men in black armor stare at me while shaking their heads in disgust. Their female partner exhales long and slow before answering me.

"You are correct young Cameron... But Yakuza suffered from a break in reality. At some point in his lifetime he became a permanent citizen of Cyadonia. Something happened to him while occupying the human realm. From that day forward he never slept, and he became twitchy and unreliable."

"What happened to him in the real world?"

"He would tell none of us, but whatever it was, it started the cycle of perpetual drunkenness that led him to betray King Nero, and the rest of us. I sometimes feel deep sorrow for him. He's a deeply damaged man in more ways than one!"

I twirl the handle of my sword while leaning forward in the chair I'm sitting in. The blade tip spins easily atop the stone floor of the armory we are all sitting inside. I feel a big yawn come over me before glancing over at the occupied rocking chair by the fireplace. Fred has been napping for the better part of two hours now. I'm happy he's getting some rest. He'll need to watch over me extra careful while I slumber in this armory.

I can hear the beginning stages of battle begin outside as the sun goes down over the horizon. The enemy forces have begun constructing their siege engines and trebuchets. From time to time we all flinch as flung stones from below the cliffs hit the walls surrounding the fortress. My hosts inform me that the King has decided to wait out the night in defense only. He plans on striking back in the morning.

The development makes me happy. Whatever happens tomorrow, I really want to be a part of it.

"The King will parlay with the leader of the Demon Hordes. I heard whispers from some of the tower watchmen that the personal banner of Gallus himself was seen marching with the approaching formations."

I'm reminded of the message that I have been given to relay to Gallus when I first meet him. I'm worried what King Nero will think of me when he hears the Creator's message. Gallus and his minions have spread their evil and malice over the Kingdom of Plenty far more than any other place in Cyadonia. I fear that the King will think me weak for offering forgiveness to the entity that robbed him of his only legitimate son.

My thoughts are interrupted by a short nudge from behind. Fred has woken from the much needed nap he was engulfed in.

"You should lay down and try and sleep Cam. Your body here in Cyadonia will need all its strength when you return. I will watch you closely, none will disturb your sleep."

The female Centurian looks me in the eyes.

"I too will watch over your body while you slumber, but we are very safe in this place. Thousands of warriors patrol the stone walls surrounding the fortress, and we will seal the doors to this room to make sure that any winged intruders are unable to get to you."

The two male Centurians in black armor finish the beer in hand and stand to exit the room. They are both very quiet in nature. After they leave the room, I hear a loud crack as a metal bar falls behind the steel doors sealing the room.

"They like you very much Cameron! They will protect you against anything if it comes to it. I can sense that you are nervous around them."

"Hell yeah I'm nervous around them. Those dudes are exactly what I want to be when I grow up. Why didn't they even want to tell me their names though?"

"You can't take that personally Cameron. Armond and Josephus have lost many friends and brothers fighting the forces of darkness. We Centurians of the Kingdom of Plenty try not to get too familiar with one another, lest we feel the sting of mourning at all times. The King is often heavy handed in sending us with the Vanguard of his army to achieve victory. We are not treated as the Queen of Rain treats you. To the King we are tools to be used!"

I can understand the idea that getting close to people is dangerous. I too try to avoid close relationships with people in the human world. My experiences there have shifted somewhat recently though. I have great respect and loyalty for everyone inside that bunker.

"I get it... People die in war. They just see the young boy in front of them. But I'll tell you what Joan, they are gonna crap their pants when they see me in action. Those Demons out there have no idea the fate that I have planned for them!"

A small grin forms on the young woman's face. We are interrupted by a familiar person entering the armory from a passageway beside the fireplace. Adrianna, the Kings daughter, arrives at the bottom of a short staircase. Her dress hem is no longer as white as it was in the King's Throne Room. She reaches her hand out to me. I'm confused with what she wants me to do with it. I think back to every movie I've ever seen containing princesses.

I grasp her hand in mine and lean forward planting a kiss on the back of her hand. Both Joan and Adrianna begin laughing. I have no idea what's so funny.

"She offered you her hand to help you stand up young Cameron. Not to receive your 'favor'!"

I can feel my cheeks filling with blood. I just hope that the fear and embarrassment I'm feeling isn't too obvious. I decide to try and play off the misunderstanding as a planned joke.

"I knew that. I was just messing around!"

The Princess leads me and Fred up a short staircase and down a long hallway lined with thin windows looking out into the fortress. The section of Castle she's taking me into is in the middle of the fortress, and seems to be some sort of separate fortification. I glance up at the ceiling and notice that there are suspended metal bars hanging every ten feet.

I assume that the metal barriers are a defensive feature should this portion of the castle be overrun.

"Please follow me Centurian. My father has asked me to look after you during your absence from our realm."

I glance over at Fred who's marching beside me. He seems a little bit jealous that I will have multiple levels of protection this evening. I can tell he's feeling a bit overlooked and underestimated.

"Don't worry dude! I know you got it handled all by yourself! But look at the bright side! At least you will have a pretty girl to keep you company tonight."

Fred shrugs his shoulders while glancing over at me.

"I'm not the one she wants to spend time with. I think the Princess might have a slight crush on you Cam! I'll make sure she keeps her hands off you when you're sleeping though!"

His wide smile is disarming. It feels good to speak about something a little less serious than the battle on the horizon.

"You better not Fred! This is the only world where I might have a chance at getting the girl dude! Don't ruin it for me! If the Princess wants to snuggle up, you better let her!"

We both laugh out loud. The Princess turns around to see what we are laughing about. I elbow Fred in the ribs as we enter an elaborately decorated chamber. There is a large bed in one corner of the room, and a long wooden table filled with food. I can smell the funky smells of exotic cheeses. My favorite!

After spreading some soft cheese across a large piece of bread I gulp down my creation. I wash it down with a small glass of wine before removing my armor and laying down on the bed for the long sleep ahead.

**

I open my eyes. The spot on the bed next to me is empty. My first thought is of Estee. *Where is she?*

"Wake up Veggie Boy!"

I feel the mattress rumble as Kevin jumps on the edge of the bed I'm lying in. He helps me sit up before transferring my frail body back into the wheelchair by the bed.

"Where is Estee?"

"Take a chill pill dude! We're in a freaking doomsday bunker...

She woke up a few minutes ago! I think she's talking with John in the kitchen!"

"Take me out there! We got separated in Cyadonia!"

As Kevin wheels me out of the bedroom, I recognize the music coming from the kitchen.

"Country rooooooad... Take me hoooome... To the Plaaaaace... I beloooooong... West Virginiaaaaa. Mountain Mommaaaaaa! Take me hooooooome... Country road!"

I can't help thinking back to the sight of Tilly blowing away those flying monsters outside of that diner back in West Virginia. My lips spread wide while watching John dance around in the kitchen while learning the words to the song.

Kevin wheels me over to the breakfast counter before leaving me to join Burt on the couch.

"Where did you end up Cam?"

I watch as Estee fills her mouth with a handful of trail mix after asking the question.

"Oh man, I'm currently in the Princess's bed right now at Stonepass!"

I see John's head snap around after he hears my words.

"What? Is Fred watching over you?"

"Take it easy John... Fred is in the room too. The King wanted his daughter to watch over me while I sleep. Nothing weird going on!"

"The hell there's not! You do know that the King has always desired to marry his daughter off to a Centurian like you! He thinks that he can breed more Centurians, and as a member of his family, you would no longer be suitable to serve the Queen of Rain any longer!"

"You aren't the only one who's been getting set up!"

Estee leans on the counter in front of me while recounting the tale of her whirlwind romance being perpetrated in Cyadonia.

"The King sent a 'Dreamy' Commander to help break the siege, and the Queen had a nice dinner to discuss strategy with him, but I'm pretty sure she was just trying to play matchmaker!"

I try and imagine Estee sitting at a table in an evening gown. Kevin is obviously listening in on the conversation from the couch. He seems to be jealous that Estee is hanging out with another man. Even though he clearly has no shot.

"I met a few of the King's Centurians too. Two badass dudes in sleek black armor, and a chick that reminds me a lot of you Estee!"

I can tell that I've now secured her full attention.

"Did you tell them that we met their buddy Yakuza in the Breathing Mountains?"

"Yeah I did. I have bad news... That guy is a traitor! He abandoned his pledge to the King! He now feeds information to Gallus himself."

"Oh crap! The Queen said that she's been searching for a spy in the City of Light! He must be the spy! That's why her message to King Nero never showed up! Worked to my advantage though!"

I can tell that Estee is really excited about her new love interest in Cyadonia. Our conversation is interrupted by the excited voice of Burt from the couch.

"Um... Guys! There's some dude in a black FBI coat sifting through the rubble above us!"

Estee runs over to the security monitors and begins rotating through camera angles. The man on the surface is alone, and he seems intent on searching through the rubble of the cabin overhead.

"We should be fine... Even if he finds the hatch, the only switch to open it was in the kitchen sink! Only me and Bernie even know this place exists. He did all the building himself with his son!"

I glance over at Estee with a look of concern on my face.

"I mean, how well do you know this 'Bernie' guy? Can you trust him to keep your secret?"

"We don't need to worry about Bernie! He would never cooperate with the government! And he was an oncology patient of my dad's. He would never betray me!"

I point at the video screen as the man in the black FBI jacket sifts through the rubble. He moves a large section of fallen roof before rolling it away from the bunker hatch. He then begins fidgeting with something under the scorched floorboards.

"He sure looks like he knows what to look for Estee!"

Estee runs back into the hallway behind us. I hear a loud snapping sound. She reappears in the living room holding a desert colored assault rifle. She loads the rifle before telling John and Ruth to follow her to the security door underneath the bunker hatch.

"You guys stay here! If that dude comes inside we'll be able to stop him at the security door. That's if he somehow can bypass my bunker door, which is highly unlikely!"

As Estee and John disappear into the security hallway, Burt keeps them updated about the man's progress.

"He definitely sees the hatch now. He's fidgeting with something beside the staircase hatch."

Estee's voice has taken on a pitch that suggests that her heart is racing.

"Let us know if he gets it open!"

Burt leans forward from his place on the couch. Kevin has returned from a short disappearance holding a shotgun in his hand.

"What are you gonna do with that Kevin? Do you even know how to use that thing?"

I look at him in a questioning fashion.

"I might need this thing if that FBI dude gets past our friends!"

I nod my head with the intent not to downplay Kevin's suggestion that things could go bad really quickly. I know that he's right!

"Hatch just opened guys! How do I rotate to the interior camera's?"

Burt's voice reflects the ever increasing tension being felt by all of us. I hear Estee's voice echo down the hallway from the security door.

"Ctrl Alt I!" use the keyboard on the coffee table!"

Burt leans forward and grasps a small black keyboard before entering the command sequence that Estee yelled to him.

"It worked!"

"Of course it worked! I told you what to do!"

Burt rotates the camera mounted above the vault door leading to the interior of the bunker. The man wearing the FBI jacket is working the door lock sequence.

"He's entering a code Estee!"

We all hear the distinct sound of the Vault door pins retreating into the wall. The man spins the locking wheel on the outside of the bunker door before pulling it open. Burt changes camera angles by selecting the camera beside the security door.

"Vault door is open!"

There's no reply. Kevin begins to fidget with the shotgun he's holding. I look him in the eye before trying to calm his nerves.

"Take a deep breath dude! We still got a solid titanium door blocking the path leading to us!"

I watch as the man removes the black hood from his head. He's a balding man probably in his mid-fifties or so. He has a short beard and piercing eyes. The camera zooms in on the face of the man. His lips begin to start moving.

"I mean no harm Estee! Do you recognize me?"

The security door opens in the camera feed. Estee walks forward aiming her rifle at the stranger. After exchanging a few words she lowers the muzzle of her weapon and hugs the man.

We all watch along in total disbelief. After securing the bunker, Estee guides the man inside of the bunker and through the security door. Kevin and Burt both stand up from the couch.

"Everyone... This is Bernie! He came to make sure that I was okay! Bernie, This is everyone. That's Burt, and the kid next to him is Kevin. You already met John and Ruth in the hallway, but the kid in the wheelchair is Cameron!"

The man waves his hand awkwardly at the people in the bunker living room. It's obvious that he is uncomfortable meeting so many new people at the same time. He has a real 'Mountain Hermit' feel to him.

"It's nice to meet you all... My sensors picked up the explosions from my own bunker."

He turns and looks at Estee.

"Who did you piss off Estee. I saw black SUV's and an unmarked helicopter heading south after the explosions. They sure as hell were not official government. I looked up the radar tags of that chopper. It's registered to a private security company out of Fort Worth Texas. It was well hidden, but I had my son track down the controlling company."

I can see that the conspiracy wheels in Kevin's mind are spinning.

"Was it a company called 'Cinatas Solutions'? The priests I

killed when I was a kid... They both kept saying something about the 'Company' before attacking me! I overheard them say the name 'Cinatas Solutions'! I've always wondered about that conversation."

I see the look on Bernie's face change.

"How the hell did you know that kid? My son had to bribe a shady government official to find out that information! Who is this kid Estee?"

"He's just a friend of mine Bernie!"

Estee tries her best to turn Bernie's attention back to her questions.

"What are we up against here Bernie?"

"I'm not fully sure yet! Robbie is running down some leads from my bunker! You guys should come with me and shelter there until we can figure out who's hunting you! They're clearly well-armed and seem perfectly willing to blow shit up to get to you! They were even able to keep the incident off of law enforcement's radar. These guys are professional Assholes!"

I can see that Estee is not fond of leaving this bunker to shelter in another.

"I appreciate the offer Bernie, but we're okay here! I don't want to put you and your son at any more risk than you already placed yourself in by coming here!"

We can all see that Bernie doesn't like her answer, but he nods his head all the same.

"Well, if that's your choice Estee, there's something I should show you!"

Bernie walks to the kitchen and reaches down into the garbage disposal. We all hear two clicks before the wall on the far side of the living room opens up into a dark tunnel.

"What the hell is that Bernie?"

He seems to be embarrassed by what he has just revealed.

"Now don't be mad Estee, but this tunnel leads directly to a security door outside of my bunker. It goes on for a good three miles, thus the transport vehicle."

Estee shines a light on a small white golf cart parked a few feet into the tunnel.

"You never told me about this when you sold me this place Bernie!"

"I know. I should have told you, but you're so stubborn about your independence sometimes. I made a promise to your father to keep an eye on you after he died. I owe my life to that man, and I just wanted to have a way to help you if something went wrong!"

Burt peers down the dark tunnel and flicks a small switch. Tiny round lights appear hanging from the roof of the concrete tunnel. The small dots of light curve to the right before disappearing.

"I'll walk back and leave you the golf cart. Just in case you need to get out of here quickly! Don't underestimate the people hunting you Estee!"

We all watch as Bernie disappears down the tunnel.

Am I the only one who really likes this Bernie guy?

Kevin seems ecstatic about the developing situation. Estee walks into the kitchen and flips the switch attached to the garbage disposal in the sink. The wall slides sideways blocking the escape tunnel.

"Son of a Bitch had a master code to get in here! If that's not bad enough, he also had a tunnel between our bunkers this whole time? Now I know how you felt when you found out about Burt's Comic Book Series!"

I look over at Burt's face as Estee's comment hits home. He takes on a defiant tone while responding.

"I already said that I was sorry for that! Let it go already!"

I smile wide and nod towards Burt. He bows his head in my direction before sitting back down on the couch.

"Let's try and think this through calmly Estee! I know you feel betrayed, but at least that guy is looking out for you. Just like I think Burt was trying to look out for me. Even though he made a real mess out of it, I believe his intentions were mostly good!"

I turn and stare at Burt.

"But you better not think you're off the hook just yet dude! You still owe me bigtime!"

Burt shakes his head to agree to my terms of forgiveness. *If the Creator can find it within himself to forgive Gallus, I can find enough mercy in my heart to forgive Burt!*

We all spend the rest of the day combing the internet for information on the people hunting us. Burt and Kevin have gone full blown conspiracy theory and are wearing little hats made out of tin foil. If their paranoia wasn't so funny, I would probably be annoyed by their antics during such a dangerous time.

"I found it!"

Kevin sits in front of a laptop. His eyes scroll over the information that he has found about the organization hunting us.

"It says here... Cinatas Solutions is a multi-pronged enterprise serving the business world with first class security. They are based out of Fort Worth. Not too far from here. It says here that they are part of an umbrella corporation founded by former FBI officials in the 1990's. It lists their biggest clients here. Oh crap."

Kevin goes silent as Burt reads silently while looking over his shoulder.

"Their biggest client is Lockheed Martin! Are you getting alien vibes like I am right now?"

Kevin looks up at Burt and shakes his head. I think back to their time spent together in the Institute. Many a time I came across those two guys watching those "Aliens Are Out There" shows in the rec room.

"Take it easy guys! Lots of companies probably work for Lockheed Martin!"

Kevin turns to me and emphatically waves over the rest of us.

"Look at this freaking client list. The US Air Force, DOD, Boeing, Raytheon, Honeywell... The list goes on and on! And there are European defense contractors listed here as well!"

Burt reads much faster than Kevin, undistracted by every new piece of information combed through. He interrupts Kevin's tirade.

"Shut up for a second Crazy! They list all of these companies because they're supplying them with automated security systems! Cameras and motion sensors and the like. But I do see that they recruit former military personnel. We need to be really careful. As we saw up above, these guys don't mess around."

I interrupt the ongoing discovery session to present a new question for the group.

"But why are they just hunting me now? Nothing changed! I'm still a crippled boy in a wheelchair! I don't threaten anyone here on earth!"

Estee makes her opinion known.

"Maybe not here, but you do threaten the plans that Gallus has for Cyadonia. And with our two worlds so interconnected, he might have plans for this world too! His 'forces' have long been able to enter our world. They have been whispering from the shadows since the Creator made this place."

I can tell that even Burt is a little put off by the level of conspiracy Estee has suggested.

"Hold on... You think that Gallus wants to take over Earth?"

Estee shrugs her shoulders while responding.

"Why not Burt? If he conquers Cyadonia, what's to stop him from crossing over into our world like his warriors did at the Institute! Have you ever known a dictator throughout history to be content with what they have?"

I can see Burt access every piece of history he has ever learned about in his head. A couple of times he seems to want to speak before stopping himself and thinking harder.

"I can't think of a single one! But I think that might be a flaw in human nature. Most of us always want 'more.' Even the richest man on earth wants more money. I can eat ten 'Jack in the box' taco's and still want more!"

"Granted Burt... Greed is prevalent in human nature, but what makes you think that the beings of Cyadonia aren't infected with the same desires?"

"She makes some good points!"

Burt looks over at Kevin's disarming comment. His face shows the signs of relenting to Estee's argument.

"Okay, if you're right... And it's a big 'IF,' what do we do about it?"

I raise my voice to give my opinion. Fred and Ruth are now standing on either side of me. I like it when they take this positioning. It makes my words seem more powerful somehow.

"It's simple Burt. We fight him in every way we can! In both realms and anywhere else he plans on terrorizing. What's that phrase you told me about fighting evil?"

I stare at Burt while trying to remember the line that he fed me when I was like eleven years old about being a force for good. A conversation that took place after I had convinced Dr. Shade that Ms. Stella was purposefully terrorizing me by listening to Taylor Swift on repeat in the TV room.

"All it takes for evil to flourish, is for good people to stand by and do nothing!"

Burt nods his head while I say the words.

"I mean, you substituted a few of the words, but YES, that was the general premise of the philosophy! I actually like your version a little better than mine!"

"You can quote me then Burt, that lesson is free. For now we need to figure out how we are going to stay hidden here in the human realm, while me and Estee kick Gallus's ass in Cyadonia!"

CHAPTER 13

The Princess's breath smells of wine and cheese. Her eyes are closed when mine open to start the day in Cyadonia. She looks so peaceful that I don't want to wake her.

I feel Fred's soft touch on my shoulder. He can always sense when I arrive in Cyadonia from the real world.

"Come quickly Cameron, the King has requested that I bring you to the fortress gate when you wake. There will be a parlay with Gallus and his Commanders to see if terms can be reached!"

I slowly and deliberately roll to the edge of the bed before sliding my legs over. I hear a slight grumble from the slumbering princess.

"My first sleepover! In every sense of the word!"

My whispered excitement is understood by Fred. He gives me a solid head nod with the accompanying smile.

"I'm happy for you Cam!"

I stride carefully around a bevy of cats that have arrived during the night to shelter from the bombardment going on around the fortress. They hiss and complain as I push them off of my armor.

After getting dressed, I walk to the side of the bed that the Princess is laying on. I lean down and give her a light kiss on the cheek.

"I felt that Centurian!"

Her eyes snap open. I'm worried that I might have crossed

some sort of line or something. She smirks at me while sliding out from under a thick layer of bear pelts covering her.

"You should not dither here Cameron! My father will be waiting for you at the gates. Be well my Centurian! We shall see plenty of one another in the future if the Sky Gods wish it!"

I bow as gracefully as I can before leaving the room with a smile plastered on my face. Fred too seems amused by this morning's events.

"First Kiss?"

I turn and glance at my Guardian.

"I don't know... Does a cheek peck count as a real kiss?"

"Probably not Cam, but it's still something isn't it?"

"Sure was Fred, I can't wait for the real thing!"

We both exit the fortress within the greater castle and make our way in the direction of the main gate. The King is waiting there with his three Centurians, and a man that I haven't met yet. The man is tall and skinny. He wears a white cloak adorned with red stallions woven with thick yarn. His hands are covered in black tattoos.

"Come young Centurian! Gallus and his negotiators approach."

Fred and I climb the steps leading up to a raised defensive position overlooking the main path to the city. From down here I can look up at the cliff tops overlooking the approach to the fortress. There are archers and siege weapons overhead just waiting for the King's order to attack.

A small group approaches the gate. A large being is flanked on all four sides by men holding up a large red tent above him. *He walks in shadow both figuratively and literally.* Gallus is much more impressive to see in person than the way he has been described. He's similar in size and shape to Fendril, the Creator's servant that I woke in the Breathing Mountains.

The big difference between the two is in their skin tone. Gallus has skin that looks like the color of bruised flesh. I can trace his black veins underneath an assortment of fire brands lining his arms and legs. The symbols are burned into his flesh in the language of Gomorrah.

The mystery man standing next to the King has noticed my watchful gaze.

"They're incantations of power. Gallus had them seared into his flesh to increase his power! One must admire his commitment to cause!"

"What kind of power?"

"The kind of power that helps him maintain control over the western and northern Kingdoms. Those markings give him the ability to wield a magic that not even the Sky Gods dare try to harness."

"Quit being coy old man! What are these magic's that you speak of?"

"They are the magic's of dark energy… Of hate and malice, of jealousy and lies. Gallus has harnessed the magic of true Evil itself. Only he can wield its full power against the Creator and the Sky Gods!"

The King clears his throat after giving us a stern look to end the conversation. Gallus and three hulking Demon Commanders stand at the precipice of the mountain fortress. The Evil creatures glance at the defensive measures being taken for the parlay.

"I see that you do not trust my word to remain peaceful during these talks King Nero!"

"I do not trust the word of a being that enjoys the sound of lies coming from his own mouth Gallus!"

Gallus lets out a long guttural laughter. The sound of his confidence while clearly in danger is somehow unsettling. He shows no fear of the weapons aimed at him. I wish that I could feel as calm in the face of danger as he seems.

"Shall we get to the point then King Nero? You seem ill informed on your current station."

"We shall Gallus! I am willing to let you lead this army back over the Tigris river and back into your own lands. If you do not leave immediately, we will destroy all who remain! Those are my terms!"

I watch as the three Demon Commanders standing behind Gallus whisper among themselves. Their master is not pleased with the distraction and turns to give them a look. They all go silent without a word and hang their heads like small children after being chastised by a parent.

"I too have terms to lay before you great King! I require that you surrender this fortress immediately! If you do not, I will kill every man woman and child within its walls. After I'm done here, I will send my army into the Kingdom of Plenty and hunt down the rest of your people! All will be put to the sword, or burned on the prayer pyres that I will construct to celebrate my victory over you!"

The King scoffs at the suggestion he surrender. He begins to speak before being cut off.

"I'm not finished King Nero! I also require that you hand over the Centurian standing next to you."

The King looks sideways at the three Centurians dressed in black armor to his right.

"Not those worthless bags of bones. The one to your left. The young one they call Cameron. My priests have been calling him the 'Storm Sword'!"

At first I get caught up in the fact that the enemy has given me such a cool nickname. Then I realize that the King has not outwardly denied the request. I can feel Fred's posture change without looking at him. I too ready myself should the King decide to offer me up as a tribute to save himself and his people.

To my surprise the three Centurians standing to the right of the King draw their swords and move beside me. The King himself seems surprised at their movement. The tense moment is interrupted from below the gate.

"I see that your 'Loyal' Centurians might not be as loyal as you would hope Nero!"

The King's face turns red before he addresses his own Guardians.

"Stay your swords you idiots. I would never give up the boy! I have different things in mind for him."

Swords are sheathed, and the King refocuses his attention to the parlay with Gallus.

"You must know that this fortress cannot be taken by force Gallus. Not even your winged beasts will be able to overshadow the vantage point that my walls possess over your army."

"If you refuse me now, then we shall find out!"

Gallus turns to leave the Parlay. The King too turns his back and begins to climb the steps leading back to the ground. I call out to the back of the Enemy.

"I have a message for you Gallus!"

I watch as he turns and faces me. He moves closer to the gate than he had been standing while talking with the King.

"What message could you carry for me young Centurian?"

"The Creator asked me to speak with you when first we met. He says that he is still willing to forgive you for your betrayal. All you need to do is turn from your wicked ways, and ask his forgiveness, and it will be granted!"

Gallus lets out another guttural laugh. He points up at me while speaking. Two small stubs stick up from his shoulder blades where his wings were cut away. A punishment overseen by the Creator himself.

"You may still believe in the Creator and his 'goodness' Centurian! But I surely do not! You will soon realize that our Creator makes mistakes just like you and I, but unlike us, he never takes accountability for them. Have no fear though Storm Sword. We will have plenty of time to discuss these things once you have joined me in Gomorrah."

"I'll never join you!"

"We shall see. Many have said the same, only to become some of my most loyal servants. We shall see. Until then, I wish you good fortune in the battle to come."

Gallus bows to me before walking away in the shade of his moving canopy. I can see a look on the King's face that makes me regret passing the message so loudly.

"You offer him forgiveness? He deserves none! That foul creature tortured and killed my son not four years past. Tore him limb from limb. Burnt the body, so that I could not honor him in burial! Why do you offer such things to Evil beasts?"

I can tell that the King really feels betrayed by the message I passed on.

"It wasn't me who offered the message my King! I was tasked with relaying the Creator's words directly to Gallus. I feel as you feel! Evil like that deserves no mercy or forgiveness."

The King is relieved by my answer to his inquiry.

"I am glad to hear it Storm Sword!"

It feels really good to hear the King call me by that name. Burt is gonna eat this up when I tell him about it. I'm sure he'll break out his drawing pencils and get to work on a new comic book right away. This might be the best version yet!

"Come with me Centurian. We have a battle to prepare for!"

The sound of stone striking stone emanated on the outskirts of the fortress walls. The hordes of Demons below had begun their attack on the perimeter. Much like the night before, Their attacks did little to no damage on the thick walls protecting the people behind them.

We arrive in the King's Throne Room. Laid out on the table is a large map of the fortress. Small figurines of spearmen and archers are spread out covering portions of the map.

"Josephus, you will hold the front gate should any of the attackers make it through the 'Gauntlet'."

Joan, You shall be responsible for my daughter's safety. Lock down the hall of steel. Let nothing lay a finger on her."

"Armond, You will be responsible for Storm Sword's safety!"

"And you... I will need you on the highest tower. Your lightning magic will be most needed to stem the attack of the flying beasts. You will cover the wall defenders from aerial attack as best you can!"

I nod my head. Each one of us says a quick goodbye before heading towards our assigned defensive location. The tower is occupied with fifty archers and crossbowman when we arrive. I stand in the center of the tower next to the staircase leading down. Armond slams down a wooden hatch covering the stairway.

"No going back now! Or more importantly falling down!"

I begin breathing slowly in and out like Thoth has taught me. The clouds in the sky overhead begin turning black. I can feel the electrical energy pulsing through the air around me. Each hand is ready to unleash fury when the first sign of attack appears.

Tiny black dots appear through the dense black cloud layer. The screams of evil fall from above like auditory drops of rain. I spread my fingers wide and unleash on the diving creatures. The men around me fire their weapons as well. Dying creatures rain down on the battlements and ground all throughout the fortress. Some survive the fall. Those that survive are quickly dispatched with spear and sword.

Armond never leaves my side. Fred is flying a circular pattern around the tower just in case any of the enemy soldiers get through our defensive cloud of arrows and lightning. Suddenly a new threat emerges. Clutched in the talons of five armored flying beasts are Fallen Priests. Their fireballs strike all around me setting fire to the soldiers and arrow caches atop the tower.

I refocus my attention to them. I feel something that I have never felt before entering my chest. From above, a bright beam of light surrounds my body. The power and energy I feel is like nothing I could ever imagine existing.

I unleash a powerful bolt of lightning that arcs into five different fingers of blue energy. Each of the five priests are engulfed in a blue fire. The creatures holding them in hand release their cargo as the blue flames climb up to taloned fingers. Each falling man cries out in anguish before splattering on the stone defenses below.

I unleash one more attack before the winged creatures retreat back into the clouds. Fred gives chase before returning and letting us know that the enemy is in full retreat. I look down at the perimeter of the fortress and see small fires atop the walls. We have beaten back the first wave, but more are sure to come.

Armond opens the hatch leading down into the tower.

"Get down there and gather more ammunition!"

Ten men run down the stairs and return a few moments later hauling wooden barrels filled with arrows and bolts. Armond shuts the charred wooden hatch behind them after being satisfied with the amount of ordinance recovered from below. Fred lands beside me to rest during the lull in the action.

I stand next to Armond who points into the sky to the north. Two small black clouds of flying creatures approach on either side of the fortress. The enemy flyers skirt the perimeter of the mountain complex before converging on the southern approach. They are way too far away to attack with either bolt or magic.

"Those guys are getting swarmed down there! We should go and help them!"

Armond stares out at the battle unfolding above the gully leading to the main gate. There's smoke and ash rising from the well defended path. Attack after attack from the air begins to impact the ability of the defenders to fight back.

"You may be right Cameron!"

I look over at Fred.

"I know you can't fly me, but do you think you might be able to glide me down there?"

I can see that Armond and Fred are both against my insistence to join the fight below.

"Even if he could... The King has ordered us to defend this position! We must not abandon our post!"

I know that Armond is right, but something inside of me longs for action. The intense adrenaline rush of battle is intoxicating, and I have a deep craving for more action.

The peaceful moment is broken by a large crack followed by a fireball rising up out of the southern gully.

"They have deployed the 'Tar Cauldrons.' The entire gully will fill with fire now for hours. There must have been a massive force approaching for them to have released our precious 'Tar'."

Two horn blasts erupt into the air from the battlements above the southern approach. I can see that Armond knows what the horn signals.

"Two horn blasts signals the enemy is in retreat. We have won the day."

**

The smell of fresh roses fills my nostrils upon waking. The Queen's chambers are far nicer than the shrine I'm used to waking inside.

I get out of bed and dawn the set of freshly cleaned armor from the water closet in the room. The grip of my sword is dry so I gather some saliva and spit onto the leather overlapping a wooden handle. I squeeze my hand over the leather a few times before being satisfied by its condition.

I walk into the Throne Room. My eyes are shocked by what they find there. Lying on the floor is the body of Celeste. Her throat has been opened by a sharp blade. Beside her is a single word painted in blood. With her last act she continued to serve the Queen. "Taken." Beside the word is an arrow pointing towards the Celestial Door.

I hear screaming and the sounds of battle coming from the city below us. Demons and Foul Beasts run from home to home attacking the city inhabitants. I can see that the Queen's army is still fighting. Small lines of shields flank the lines of attacking Demons entering the city through an open gate. *Who opened the gate?*

The thought that any one of the Queen's men would betray her was preposterous. I hear footsteps coming from behind me. I pull my sword and prepare for battle. Marcus enters the Queen's Throne Room cautiously. His appearance matches the look he had when first arriving in the City of Light. A thin layer of smeared blood and black ash cover him from head to toe.

"Thank the Creator you're alive!"

I can hear a certain joy in the words. The Commander approaches me before kneeling."

"Where is the Queen?"

I point towards a small streak of blood leading towards the Celestial Door.

"Taken! They took her!"

"Who took her?"

"I have no idea! I woke up, and this is what I found! We need to find her!"

"I shall protect you Centurian. This city has fallen. The Queen's men fight on, but they do not stand a chance without the Queen's magic! We must get you out of here. Gallus will surely want you captured and brought before him!"

I pull my sword and look Marcus in the eyes.

"We will leave, If and only if I decide that it's necessary!"

I move to look out the window facing the main gate to the city. The Queen's men have formed a shield wall protecting the eastern approach to the castle gates. Within the inner gate to the castle complex are fifty mounted men.

"Your men below remain out of the fight! Why?"

"I ordered them to remain able to carry you and I to safety should we need it! We should be able to break through the siege lines now that the enemy forces are spread out within the city walls!"

My mind is racing. The city is covered in a thin layer of wispy smoke. There are small groups of mounted Knights riding between the pyramid shrines in the center of the city. Their war horses trample the enemy without mercy, and their lances spill the life force of the Demon hordes trying to resist them.

"Look down there! The Demons can't defend against the cavalry charges in the narrow streets of the city. We need to get down there!"

Marcus stands in the window looking at the scenes over my shoulder. He smells of sweat and soil. His deep breathing reflects the effort it took to get to the top of the tower through a series of stone staircases circling the outside of the Storm Tower.

"If you command it Centurian. With the Queen absent, you

have command!"

I can feel a pulsating force flow through my hands. I'm used to feeling a certain amount of magic flowing through them, but every feeling in my body seems amplified. A bright light from above surrounds my body. Marcus stumbles backwards, terrified by the light washing over my head. The light disappears leaving me with more internal power than I thought possible.

"We have work to do!"

I run down step after step. By the time we reach the bottom of the tower stairs, we're both out of breath. I mount a white horse being held by one of Marcus's Knights.

"Sure, take my horse!"

There is a certain amount of sarcasm in his voice.

"She will serve me just fine!"

He steps up gracefully into the stirrups of the massive black horse next to me.

"Be careful with my horse! She has been a most loyal companion to me since I was a boy!"

"She has, has she? What's her name?"

"Cleopatra! But I call her Patty for short!"

I reach down and pet the neck of the horse underneath me. I can feel the lifeforce flowing inside of her. I have always had a way with animals, but this is something different. I can hear her voice inside of my head. She's brave and ready for battle. I close my eyes and show her what the plan is. She rears back on her back legs and begins trotting towards the front gate of the castle grounds.

"Lower the drawbridge!"

The Queen's men manning the gate release the locks on either side of the drawbridge. There's a puff of dust and dirt as the bridge hits down on the other side of a deep moat. Marcus maneuver's his horse to stand next to me and Patty.

"Let us lead the charge Estee! We have some experience that you might not have. Stay close behind though. When we break through the Demon lines we will continue on until reaching the next group of savage beasts."

I can feel Patty flex her muscles between my legs. She is just as excited as I am. I ride two horses behind Marcus and his Black war horse. The man beside him blows a horn once. We charge forward three horses abreast. Our charging column fills the narrow streets between the city buildings. The horses instinctively break into a gallop after hearing three loud bursts of the horn.

We charge with lances down into a small group of Demons trying to break down the doors to buildings on either side of the road. They fall beneath hoof and lance like weak rooted trees in a windstorm. None can resist the power and force of the tight formations of flesh and steel running through and over them.

At the end of the street we turn left maintaining speed. In front of us are rows of Demon soldiers forming columns after coming through the main gate. Their attention is directed towards the Queen's men defending the walls above them. Small portions of the wall have been infiltrated using steep staircases leading to the battlements. We charge forward as the arrows from our allied soldiers rain down on the enemy.

The sound of breaking bone and splitting flesh fill the air around the cries of the fallen enemy. We ride right through them without stopping. At the end of the road we meet up with fifty more mounted men. Marcus stops for a moment to give orders to the Company of Lancers.

"Maintain your charges Sergeant! They can't resist the power of our horses, and their numbers will not last forever. Keep mowing down the Demons who try and enter the main gate.

We will clear the rest of the city! To the last man we defend!"

We ride past the Sergeant and his men towards the market. Patty is breathing heavily, but I can sense that she still has plenty of strength to keep fighting. It even seems as if she's enjoying the battle.

We charge past the 'Stew Shack' riding over a small group of foul creatures raiding the market stalls for food and loot. My eyes find the mangled body of a young man I recognize as the son of the "Stew Maker." My blood boils at the sight of all the innocent citizens lying in pools of blood. The Demon warriors are sparing no one.

After clearing the southern sections of the city, we return to the main road intersecting the city gate. The Queen's remaining defenders have fallen back. They form a wall of shields blocking the road leading south down the center of the city. There are fewer than three hundred remaining.

I can see that there is a frantic look on Marcus's face. He points his spear to the road to the west that runs parallel to the city walls. When we arrive at the wall the Sergeant and his men arrive as well. There are only twenty or so men still in his company. The rest have broken off and moved to chase down a group of Demons approaching the castle complex.

The Demon numbers are dwindled. We charge forward into the remaining enemy trying to push past the shield wall of the Queen's men. Hoof and steel knife through their ranks leaving a trail of dead enemies. We reach the end of the road and turn around to charge again.

The sound of a Demon horn cuts through the sounds of battle. We charge forward trampling the remaining Demon fighters inside of the gates. When we pass the front of the Shield Wall, the Queen's men bravely rush forward and form a new line at the city gate. Two loud clangs ring out as the metal gate closes.

The Queen's men climb the city steps and re-mount the

defensive walls before showering arrows upon the small groups of retreating Demon warriors. Their arrows reap the revenge that they all desire. Each one stands on the bodies of slain soldiers underfoot. After dismounting Patty and giving her a big kiss on the face, I climb the city wall and look out over the carnage filling the streets of the City of Light. The Queen's Commander's walk contains a heavy limp, and his face is bleeding above both brows.

"Centurian... Where is the Queen?"

I look the little warrior in the eyes.

"They took her. I failed to protect her during my slumber! It's my fault!"

"No Centurian, It is I who has failed! Someone withing the city walls facilitated the sabotage of the main gate. I failed to stop this plot. It is me who failed the Queen!"

"You fought bravely General! You and your men shall be remembered for all time for your bravery on this day!"

We are joined by Commander Brutus on the wall.

"My men are sweeping the city to root out any Demons or beasts that remain. Most of the citizens remained safe in their homes!"

"Where did they take the Queen?"

I don't know the answer to the question that the General has asked, and my frustration is almost at a boiling point. Not even the carnage of our cavalry charges have sated my lust for vengeance.

"I don't know... But I'm sure as hell going to find out! And nothing will quench my fury for those responsible for taking her! Mark my words Gentlemen. When I find the people responsible, they will rue the day they pledged their support to Gallus!"

CHAPTER 14

"They took the Queen?"

"What do you mean they 'Took' her? Who took her, where?"

Estee paces back and forth while explaining what she awoke to in Cyadonia during our last sleep cycle.

"I don't know who or where! I just know that her maid was dead on the floor. Her last act was to use her own spilt blood to leave me a clue. She drew an arrow towards the Celestial Door and scrawled 'taken' in blood!"

"How is that possible? She was supposed to lock the damn door after sending me through to Stonepass!"

I rack my mind for a reason that the Queen of Rain wouldn't have taken every precaution to protect the Storm Tower from being infiltrated again. As I run through a litany of scenarios in my head, Estee's continuing rant catches my attention.

"Wait, what do you mean they breached the walls?"

Estee kicks the rubber wheel of my chair before explaining exactly what happened during the battle inside of the City of Light.

"But the City is safe now… Right?"

"For now! I did my best to chase down the retreating Demon army. Commander Brutus is currently out hunting any remaining enemy forces with the remainder of his mounted Knights!"

Estee hangs her head for a second.

"What is it Estee?"

"Some of the 'Littles' were killed when the enemy breached the gate and walls. The 'Stew Maker's' son was torn apart by foul creatures, And many others were killed or wounded as well."

"Poor guy! He once told me that he was looking forward to retirement as soon as his son was able to master his recipe's and take over the Stew Shack!"

Burt clears his throat to let us know that he has been listening to the entire recap of our nightly adventure.

"Any chance you would be willing to let me make a Comic about this chapter of your adventure?"

I look over at Burt. In one hand he is holding a floppy sandwich, and in the other he is tightly gripping a bottle of light beer. I can tell he really wants to start drawing again. There isn't a single reason that I can think of to deny him the delight of retelling our stories in comic form.

"Go ahead Burt. But you will need to cut Estee in on the profits from now on too!"

Estee grins at me and rubs the top of my head with a flat hand.

"Thanks Cam! You still haven't told me how the battle went at Stonepass!"

I can still remember every moment in vivid detail. I speak the tale with as many colorful details as I can with words. Burt is practically drooling as I talk about the excitement of the battle, and the Hordes of flying Demon warriors surrounding the mountain fortress.

"Wait 'Storm Sword'... That's such a cool name!"

Burt's hands have not stopped taking notes since I started speaking. He flips over a sheet of paper before scrawling away at a frantic pace.

"Wait, slow down... You saw Gallus with your own eyes? Describe him to me. I've never told my readers what he actually looks like!"

I go into detail about the physical characteristics of our enemy before dropping another bomb on Burt.

"I talked to him too! He stood with three of his Demon Commanders below the gate to the fortress. The King and him had finished their parlay before I was able to relay a message that the Creator wanted me to deliver personally to Gallus!"

Kevin wanders into the kitchen at an inopportune time. Burt places his hand flat against Kevin's mouth to stop whatever smart ass comment is about to erupt, distracting me from the juicy part of the story. I finish recounting the battle for Burt and Estee. Kevin seems unfazed by all the information he just overheard.

"You need to wash your hands Burt! You smell like mustard and pickles. It's not a good combination dude!"

He closes the refrigerator door after grabbing a soda can. While leaving, Kevin glances back at me with a wink on his way back to the couch to watch the live security feeds with John.

Ruth enters the kitchen with a strange look on her face. She begins speaking, before we all realize that she is slowly becoming a shadow. She tries to talk before disappearing entirely.

"John! Ruth just freaking disappeared man! What happened?"

John leaps over the couch back to join us in the kitchen.

"What do you mean she 'Disappeared'? Like she walked away or something?"

Estee points at the spot in the kitchen that Ruth had just stood before vanishing like a fart in the wind.

"She was standing right there! Then she kind of went transparent before disappearing entirely!"

John walks to the spot and waves his hand around the area searching for his wife.

"What happened? Specifically what happened in Cyadonia last

night?"

Estee recounts the tale of the Queen's disappearance to the shocked face of John. He seems to be taking the information better than expected.

"I know this will sound weird, but Her disappearing kind of makes sense now. Ruth has a secret that she was hoping to tell you guys at some point."

We all look at each other in confusion.

"What secret? Tell us John!"

John leans against the counter and keeps his mouth shut for a second before explaining his reluctance to spill the beans.

"It's not my secret to tell! Ruth needs to tell you herself! But I can put everyone's mind at ease and reveal that she's not dead or anything!"

I sit in my wheelchair while staring at John's face for any hint that he will change his mind about telling us Ruth's secret. His lips are as solid as stone!

John looks relieved when Kevin starts making a scene in the living room.

"Get over here right now! There's two of those black helicopters doing circles over us!"

We all gather around the TV and watch as two shadows cover the ground moving in a circular pattern. Four black SUV's show up next before a dozen or so armed men exit and begin moving towards the bunker hatch.

Kevin seems more nervous than any of us. The tension in the room is cut in half by an unexpected voice coming from the bunker speakers.

"They came back for you Estee!"

We all recognize the gruff nature of Bernie's voice. Estee looks up at one of the speakers and lifts her arms into the air in a questioning fashion.

"What else haven't you told me about 'MY' bunker Bernie?"

There is a slight pause filled with anxiety before a new voice comes through the speakers.

"Hey Estee, Its Robbie! I've detected two helicopters over your position and there are at least five more vehicles blocking the interstate at the end of your driveway!"

"Hi Robbie! How do you know all this?"

"Because my dad and I have access to your security feeds and the communications terminals in your bunker... Sorry! It was only so that we could keep an eye on you for safety! Nothing creepy or stalkerish going on... I promise!"

"What should we do?"

Bernie's voice comes from the speakers next to the security monitor.

"It's not just the choppers and soldiers Estee! Robbie located a flight plan for a cargo plane on a direct trajectory over your property. He hacked 'Cinatas Solutions' network and located a supply request for a GBU-72 'Bunker Buster' bomb for research purposes! We think they are gonna drop the bomb on your bunker. You need to get out of there right now!"

The wall on the far side of the living room slides open revealing the golf cart sitting in the escape tunnel.

"Is that you too Bernie?"

"Yeah, Sorry Estee!"

Estee points at the golf cart.

"Everyone grab your stuff, we need to get out of here now!"

I watch as everyone frantically gathers their things. Estee is out of breath when she returns from the armory with a black duffle bag filled with guns and ammo. Kevin has loaded two cases of root beer into the back of the golf cart. Burt hops in the driver's seat. He waves his arms frantically for everyone to get on.

Kevin turns my chair around and sits on the back of the golf cart while holding the two handles of my wheelchair. Burt hits the accelerator almost dislodging Kevin from his seat in the bed of the cart. I roll along looking back at a long row of dim lights forming a curved line back to Estee's bunker.

A bright yellow light blinds me before a shockwave of fire and concussive energy hit me in the chest. The explosion is violent but short lived. The lights of the escape tunnel dim before I see the concrete lining of the tunnel behind us begin crumbling.

"We need to go faster Burt! Punch it man!"

There's a sharp pickup in the buzzing sound of the battery powered golf cart. I get a strong whiff of burning rubber. My wheelchair wasn't designed to maintain speed like this for long periods of time. I watch as the tunnel behind us collapses. The ceiling stops falling when it is only thirty feet away or so.

"Slow down Burt!"

One of my rubber wheels is about to fall off. Burt's voice is shrill and nervous when he yells back at me.

"What one is it Cam? Go fast? Or Go Slow!"

"It's okay Burt, you did great... But now that the sky isn't falling anymore we can take it a little slower. My chair wheels are about to fall off I think."

Burt stops the cart and gets out of the driver's seat. He gently lifts me out of my chair before placing me in Kevin's cradled arms. He then looks at Kevin and shakes his head.

"Next time put his chair in the cart and hold him Kevin! Wheelchairs don't grow on tree's you know!"

Kevin looks at me with a big grin spread across his face. I can tell that he still thinks his plan to drag me behind the golf cart was a good thing. He whispers into my ear for only me to hear.

"But that was really fun though… Right?"

I nod my head while smiling.

"Best ride I've had in years Kevin! But Burt's right. Next time maybe save my chair wheels some miles!"

I laugh out loud and turn my head to see where we are going. Burt drives forward behind the dull glow of two dusty headlights. The overhead lighting is no longer functioning so it comes as a surprise when we run into a closed gate in the middle of the tunnel. We can see that there is a long way to go behind the gate.

Burt honks the horn. We all look at him and the stupid look on his face before laughing. The sound of laughter filling the tunnel relieves some of the tension we all have been feeling the last few perilous moments.

A small round light above the gate blinks green before lifting up and clearing our path forward. After we pass by the gate closes, and three more gates close behind that one.

"Bernie really has this tunnel protected from unwanted guests!"

We arrive about a mile later at a complete dead end! John gets out of the cart and rubs his hand against a solid rock wall blocking our path. He jumps back in surprise as a ladder falls to the ground next to him.

Overhead a circular hatch is open and shining light down into the tunnel.

"Hurry up and get inside here! Those goons back there are still looking for you guys! That bomb collapsed half the damn escape tunnel. There's no knowing how the surface looks!"

Bernie reaches down and hands a makeshift harness made of climbing rope to John.

"Put the boy's legs and arms through this, and Me and my boy will pull him up here!"

John and Burt wrap the makeshift harness around my legs and arms before climbing the ladder underneath me. I arrive inside of the bunker being pulled up by Bernie and his son Robbie.

"Thanks for the lift Gentlemen!"

The rest of my companions climb up through the floor hatch leading to the escape tunnel. Estee is last through the hole after pushing her duffle bag of weapons through the hatch opening.

"You got a lot of explaining to do Bernie!"

She gives the man a hug before chastising him about his surveillance ability in her bunker.

"I want a refund Bernie! You sold me on the exclusive privacy of owning that bunker, and here I come to find out you and Robbie have been watching me the whole time?"

Bernie takes a sharp turn and hardens his posture.

"All sales are final! Besides, we have only been watching you since those guys attacked your cabin! We left you alone without a peep for years! Like I said Estee, I promised your father I'd look out for you if I had the chance. Forgive an old man his paranoia!"

"That doesn't excuse you dude!"

She turns and points her finger at the young man standing beside me. Robbie looks nervous. He puts his hands up in a surrendering posture before pointing at his father.

"He made me do it Estee! Don't hurt me!"

Estee stomps over to stand in front of Robbie. She reaches forward and grabs both of his cheeks in a tight pinch before hugging him tightly.

"Robbie and I used to play with the toys in my father's waiting room together. He is probably my oldest friend!"

Robbie smiles and waves in almost the same way his awkward father does. He's a tall dude. Must be about six foot four, and from the look of it he isn't a stranger to the gym. He has an interesting trident tattoo on his forearm. I recognize the symbol but can't put my finger on where from. His voice is stern and commanding, and I snap out of my daydream after he starts talking to us.

"You guys should be safe with us for the time being! This Bunker was built in an old top secret missile silo. We are a good five hundred feet below the surface, and I hacked into the DOD database to scrub the information about this place from the records. No one but the people who built it will know this place even exists."

I look down the halls of the bunker. The walls are painted a clean white color, and there are bushes and ferns lining the hallways to make the space feel less 'Confined.'

"This place is way nicer than your bunker Estee!"

She looks back at me and gives me the finger.

"My place had charm! This place feels like a bunker for rich people and politicians!"

"It is!"

Robbie's voice interrupts the conversation happening between us.

"This place was built in the sixties when the whole world was afraid of Nuclear War! It's way too big for just me and my dad, but the price was right, so we bought it and made it our own!"

"You guys live here by yourself?"

"Not exactly!"

Before I realize it my hand is being licked by two black and tan dogs. Each one is wearing some sort of harness with a short leash attached to a hoop on the spine.

"And who are these fine fella's?"

If I could pet them I would. I've always loved dogs, and they have always loved me back. It's just a shame that I have never been able to return their love while occupying this crippled body.

"These 'Ladies' are Peanut Butter and Jelly! Jelly is the one with the white dot on her neck and Peanut Butter has that small notch in her ear!"

Both dogs sit when Robbie gives them the command. He waves his arms and points down the hallway that everyone else has disappeared down while we speak.

"Go hump Dad's leg!"

The two dogs tear off down the hallway looking for Bernie. We hear a small commotion before a gruff voice echoes down the hallway.

"Down Girls! Off! Off I said!"

We all start laughing without seeing the outcome of Robbie's command.

"Took me like two days and a whole box of treats to teach them how to do that! Don't tell my dad though. He thinks they do it at random! Gotta keep things interesting when you spend most of your life in a doomsday bunker!"

"You need a girlfriend Robbie!"

He looks at Estee and slaps her on the back before responding.

"You have any friends that might be interested in an ex-Navy Seal who lives in a secret bunker underground with his deranged and paranoid father? If you do, I'd be more than happy to meet her!"

Robbie moves behind me and begins pushing my chair down the brightly lit hallway. He glances down at the wobbly rubber on the right wheel and lifts that side of the chair slightly while still pushing. He's strong enough to levitate me and my chair down the hallway without breaking a sweat.

"Don't worry kid, I can get you a new chair from the medical wing!"

"Medical wing? How big is this place?"

We arrive at a window that looks out into the center of the facility. There is a large open space that runs a couple hundred feet vertically in either direction. In the middle of the space is a rocket painted red, white, and blue. In black letters are spelled out "USAF' down the side of the massive rocket.

"Holy crap! Does that thing work?"

Robbie looks out over the rocket housed in the center of his father's bunker.

"They took the nuclear warheads out of these things in like 1991. But the DOD decided it was too expensive to remove the rockets entirely. So they just sealed the silo's, and left everything here after the Soviet Union fell! There're probably a hundred more of these things spread out across the country! The Airforce has bigger and better weapons now, so in true government fashion this place was abandoned and lost to history!"

I look at Estee's face. She seems as awe struck as I am.

"That might be the coolest thing I've ever seen up close!"

"Yeah, this place rocks! Let me show you where we spend most of our time!"

Robbie pushes me through a set of double doors that opens automatically as we approach. Inside is an array of TV monitors behind a line of twenty or so laptops. Each computer is controlling a different security measure inside and outside of the silo.

"This one monitors the motion sensor around your property and ours!"

Estee looks at an overhead image that seems to be live.

"How are you watching everything from above?"

"I hacked into one of the Navy's satellite monitoring stations. The guys they have monitoring them will never detect my spyware. So we can see almost anything in the world in real time! Pretty handy wouldn't you say?"

There is a large smoking crater where Estee's bunker used to sit. Tiny black helicopters circle the area, and the men from the SUV's are fanned out searching the crater for something.

"Those idiots don't actually think they'll be able to find a body after that blast do they?"

Robbie looks at us and grins.

"Never underestimate the potential stupidity of a man who blows stuff up first, then want's to ask questions later!"

On the far side of the room is a door leading out of the command center. A small blue sign glows over the door jamb, "Dormitory A."

"Head down that hallway Estee!"

Robbie pushes me down a hallway lined with closed doors. Over each door is an illuminated sign depicting the room's intended usage. I see many things, bathroom, intel, theatre, kitchen, showers, recreation, bunks, and pool.

"Theres a freaking swimming pool down here?"

"Dang right there's a pool down here! Gotta get my laps in before breakfast every morning! This body didn't build itself!"

"This one did!"

I look up at Robbie and see a wry smile cross his face! I'm glad that he gets my self-deprecating humor. I hate it when people act like they feel sorry for me all the time.

"When you wake up tomorrow, maybe I'll take you for a swim, or float, or whatever that bag of bones you're rocking does in the water!"

I laugh out loud and make sure he knows I'm not offended by

his comment.

"It's a deal Robbie! Has Estee ever told you about the dream world?"

I see a look of pure fear run across her lips as my words reach Robbie's ears.

"What's that now? What about her dreams?"

"I haven't told them Cam! I didn't want them to think I'm a freak or crazy or something!"

"I'm the one who was in the literal 'Looney Bin' Estee. Tell them! They need to know the danger that they're in for harboring us."

We move into the Kitchen and find Bernie who is giving the rest of my friends the tour. Estee gets Bernie's attention and begins telling him and his son the reason that we are being hunted. Both men seem to be getting emotional as the different elements of our journey are retold. After Estee finishes telling Bernie and Robbie everything, there's a short moment of silence as Bernie wipes away his tears.

"You all need to follow me."

Bernie leaves the room, to his side Robbie walks with his arm around his father's shoulder. We all follow nervously until we arrive back at the makeshift command center. Bernie unlocks a drawer with a small silver key. He reaches into the drawer and pulls out a folded piece of paper.

"You never met my wife Estee. She died when Robbie was just a young child before my battle with the Cancer!"

Robbie moves to stand next to his father. He seems to know exactly where his dad is going with the coming tale.

"She was a deeply kind woman, and she was a woman of faith. She used to tell me that she sometimes heard voices telling her to do this and that. I always brushed off her stories out of pure ignorance. I found her lying on the floor one day after getting home from work. The doctors said she had one of them brain aneurysms or something…"

Robbie's eyes go blank for a second before he snaps out of the memory of watching his mother collapse onto the kitchen floor. He was too young to know what to do, so he sat by her side stroking her hair until his father arrived.

"She left a note on the Kitchen Counter… Like she knew that something was about to happen."

Bernie carefully unfolds the piece of paper in his hand. A short message is written in messy handwriting.

"Dear Bernie:"

He begins to read the note as tears roll down his cheeks.

Dear Bernie:

I need you to know that I love you and Robbie more than anything. Something is coming that you need to prepare for. Someone soon will need you to protect them from the coming darkness. I know that you don't always share the faith that I possess, but you must believe the 'Dreamers.' Be well my love, and tell Robbie that I wish I could have watched him grow up and become the man I have seen him become in my dreams!

Love Mary

P.S. I'll be watching you…

He finishes reading the letter before gently folding it up and placing it back into the drawer for safe keeping.

"So you see… I've been waiting for you all to come into our lives for the better part of twenty years! Welcome 'Dreamers"!"

I can see that Estee is shook by the words in the letter. I too feel a deep sense of gratitude for a woman that I never knew.

"I've been waiting for you to tell me your secret ever since your father helped me beat the Cancer. He once mentioned that you had a vivid imagination, and had begun recounting tales of a 'dream land' to him. It was a real tragedy when he lost his own battle with the same disease he saved me from!"

I begin to understand the cryptic parts of Estee's words in the Cave of Lost Travelers. I remember a specific conversation about the things that Gallus tempts us with. I look over at my fellow Centurian to get her attention. She is fighting off the urge to cry.

"Gallus offered to save your father's life didn't he? That's what you refused to sacrifice in order to serve the light... Isn't it?"

The tears falling from Estee's eyes increase. Robbie grabs her and pulls her into a tight embrace before Kevin has the chance to. I glance at Kevin who seems a bit disappointed in his own slow reaction time.

"It isn't your fault he died Estee! Gallus is a liar! He offered to make me whole in this world if I would just serve him... He finds the things that we care most about, then he twists them to manipulate our hearts to serve his cause. Who knows... That Asshat probably gave your father the Cancer in the first place!"

I see a flash of anger in the eyes of my fellow Centurian. She wipes away the tears from her eyes before thanking Robbie for his kind gesture.

"You're probably right Cam... Welp, now that we are all on the same page, what are we going to do about him?"

I look around the room at the hodgepodge army we are slowly assembling to survive in the real world. Robbie breaks the silence.

"I have a couple ideas how we can hit back at these 'Cinatas Solutions' people!"

He glances toward his father and displays a tight grin. There is a secret conversation going on that only they seem to understand. Bernie nods his head.

"I think you're right son. It's time for operation 'Wild Stallion'!"

CHAPTER 15

"He did say that the keys are hidden underneath a tin can next to a big pile of discarded truck tires, right?"

John looks out over a junkyard of discarded truck parts. He kicks a rusting truck hood off of a small pile of metal rims sitting next to a concrete garage. The titanium locks securing the structure dangles in the sunlight like a big middle finger.

"Robbie said they would be hidden under a rusty coffee can next to the truck tires!"

Kevin aimlessly wanders around a big stack of discarded tires while kicking every aluminum can in the area. Suddenly he yells out.

"I found them!"

The young boy runs over to the garage and slips under the camouflage netting covering the entire structure. He slides a small silver key into the pad lock and twists. The lock comes free to the sound of a long exhale from both of the onlooking faces.

"It's about time! We've been up here sifting through garbage for like fifteen minutes!"

The doors slide open revealing a neatly maintained car.

"Holy crap! Is it a freaking Corvette? Robbie didn't say that he drove a hot rod like this!"

Kevin maneuvers towards the driver's seat before being shoved unceremoniously out of the way.

"Not a chance in hell Kevin. You're not old enough to drive this thing!"

"Maybe not... But you come from a land that doesn't even have cars! You guys still ride around on horses, and live in castles and stuff!"

John gives Kevin a look that sends the boy dragging his feet towards the passenger seat. The engine starts at the push of the button that Robbie had mentioned. John pushes the gas pedal sending a cloud of dust into the air behind the car. Kevin glances over and begins to make a smart ass comment before being thrown into the back of his seat.

"Gallop on speedy steed!"

John lets out a loud howl as the black Corvette fly's out of the garage and begins speeding down a long asphalt driveway leading to the highway. They reach the end of the road and wait for a second before entering the highway leading south.

"Have you ever been to Fort Worth?"

"What do you think? I've been locked up in an insane asylum for years. Haven't really gotten the opportunity to travel much!"

John glances over at Kevin before punching him in the shoulder.

"If we're gonna work together, I need you to be a little less sarcastic kid. Take it down like three notches!"

"Take it easy old man! I hear you. I'll try not to be too annoying. My dad used to hit my shins with grandpa's old cane when I annoyed him... That's before..."

Kevin stops talking while staring out his window, captured inside a quiet trance. John punches Kevin again in the thigh.

"Snap out of it kid! I know you probably got some ghosts hanging around in that head of yours... But I need you to focus right now. Robbie gave us a job to do! And I sure as hell plan on getting it done. You with me?"

Kevin nods his head in resolve.

"I'm with you John. Let's go get this done!"

The car drives past a large green sign labeling the approaching cities and towns.

"Only ninety four miles left to Fort Worth! What's our plan when we get there?"

John keeps his eyes on the road while walking Kevin through the plan. The teenage boy takes in the instructions while trying to visualize his part in the upcoming operation.

"And Robbie said that this code will get us through the lobby door for sure?"

"That's what he said! He seems to know his stuff."

Kevin nods his head while looking into the side mirror of the vehicle.

"Yeah, I trust him. I get a really good feeling when I stand next to him and Bernie. They seem like pretty good dudes! Maybe they'll consider letting me live with them in the bunker after all this is over with. I'm sure as hell never going back to the Institute!"

"Who knows Kevin? Maybe you'll grow on me so much that I'll be forced to find a way to take you back to Cyadonia with me!"

Kevin looks over at John with a weird look on his face.

"I'm not sure I want to live in a place that doesn't have HBO, or wireless internet! Or pretty much anything I like to spend my time doing!"

John begins laughing while trying to picture Kevin living the rest of his life in the City of Light.

"Maybe you're right Kevin, but don't knock it till you try it! Things may be a lot different in Cyadonia, but that doesn't mean it's worse than this world. At least people there seem to care for one another. Even a stranger in Cyadonia is treated with kindness and respect. From the little of this world I've seen, humans in this realm are selfish and full of lies. Not just for other people, but they lie to themselves to convince themselves that the wrong that they do doesn't matter! There's no personal accountability in this realm."

Kevin rolls down the window and places his forehead out into the wind.

"You might be right John, but I could never have the feeling of the wind in my hair like this in your world!"

John makes a sour face and glances for a brief moment at his little buddy riding shotgun.

"Think again Kevin. In Cyadonia I could pick you up in my arms and fly you anywhere you could want to go! I have freaking wings there! And if the Queen likes you enough, she might give you a pair too!"

Kevins face morphs into deep thought.

"Do you think that I would be able to use magic in Cyadonia like Cam and Estee? Could I become a Centurian like they are?"

The boy's face lights up with a look of hope and longing.

"I don't know Kevin. Besides, we are getting a little ahead of ourselves here! I don't even know if it's possible to get you there. We would definitely need the favor of the Sky Gods, and I haven't seen you say any prayers since meeting you!"

John grins at Kevin before briefly tapping in the brakes to avoid slamming into a yellow sedan merging onto the highway. Kevin glances over at the driver in the sedan. A woman with glasses so thick that she could serve sushi on the lenses, looks over to make eye contact with the car that she cut off. Her middle finger separates from the others on her left hand before waving back and forth in front of Kevin's gaze. Her scowling face and aggressive gesture make both Kevin and John begin laughing.

The engine growls as John places his foot on the accelerator. The yellow car disappears into the distance behind them. Keven reaches forward and activates the radio in the car. It seems that Robbie has an affinity for vintage music players and eighties rock and roll. John begins nodding his head as the sweet melodies of Van Halen fill the car with good vibes.

"You sure as heck don't have Van Halen in Cyadonia!"

"I plan on teaching "Country Road' to the Queen's music assembly. It won't be quite the same, but it might be cool to hear it in lute and harp!"

Kevin shakes his head and begins smiling while picturing some of his favorite rock songs being played with medieval instruments. He pictures monks with shaved heads singing 'Runnin with the Devil' in the Queen's castle. The vision then shifts to the song being played in Gallus's Throne Room before he can't contain his amusement anymore.

"I take it all back. I'd give my left nut to see Gallus bobbing his head to some rock songs! It just seems like it would be more appropriate in his halls!"

John shakes his head to correct Kevin's assumption.

"Not exactly. From what I've heard he's more into angry chanting and jazz ensembles!"

Kevin breaks out laughing while thinking about the Master of Gomorrah rocking his head to saxophone melodies!"

"Fifty seven more miles, then we can stick it to those bastards at 'Cinatas Solutions'!"

"That's the spirit kid!"

**

"I still think you should have gone with them Robbie!"

Bernie leans forward while looking over his son's busy fingers stroking the keyboard.

"They'll be fine dad! Estee said that they're good people, and I can't help but see a young 'Me' in that Kevin kid! He has a certain 'edge' about him!"

"Yeah, I wasn't going to say anything, but I thought the same thing. Although you were never quite as jaded as he seems to be!"

Robbie finishes typing in a command sequence before slapping down the enter key and leaning back. He folds his fingers together behind his head and leans back to look at his father.

"I had you to constantly remind me that the world is not a perfect place. And you gave me a hug every birthday! That poor kid has been living in a looney bin, being pumped full of drugs that he doesn't need, and being told by adults that he's crazy. The only crazy thing about him is that he managed to survive all of that, and still be able to trust."

Bernie points at the computer screen displaying his son's ongoing work.

"You convinced me Robbie! You can keep him if you like!"

"He's not a lost puppy dad! No kid his age would want to live his life in a bunker with two suspect adult men! I'm not even sure I want to!"

Both men look at each other while smiling about the strange conditions of which they have chosen to live in.

"I told you a long time ago Robbie... You should go out more! Meet a woman, have some kids! I'll be fine down here by myself! Your mother gave me this mission, not you!"

Robbie twists his mouth into an awkward form.

"Sure she did dad!"

The sarcasm in his voice is thick!

"We've talked about this ad nauseum 'ABBA'! You would be lost without me! You don't even know how to work that vintage VCR out in the den! Besides, the men of the Adler family stick together! We aren't the type of people that abandon each other for the promise of a cushy life. Our people walked the deserts with Moses for forty years searching for the holy land! We'll get there too dad! I got another twelve years to get us there by my count! We're ahead of schedule!"

Bernie slaps his son on the shoulder. Robbie rocks forward in his chair and pulls up the active locator on his Corvette.

"They better not get a scratch on my baby!"

Bernie points at the dot on the map parked two city blocks away from the target building.

"You sure we can trust those Aberman brothers? I know you like them, but they never seem to take anything seriously!"

Robbie looks up at his father and clicks his tongue making a snapping sound of annoyance.

"I trust them dad! They may not act like you want them to all the time, but we can rely on them to accomplish their task, or die trying. They know the stakes at play. You know what happened to their parents!"

Bernie taps his son on the shoulder and nods his head to show his support for Robbie's judgement.

"If you trust them, then say no more son! I knew their father well. He was a good and honest man. It seems that our people are reminded of the evil that exists in this world on a regular basis!"

Robbie places his hand in the air to pause the ongoing conversation.

"They arrived at the meet up location. I'm gonna zoom in the overhead image."

**

Kevin approaches the van in front of him. He moves to the passenger side of the vehicle before cautiously tapping on the window. Small squeaks fill the air as the man riding shotgun manually rolls down the window.

"You Robbie's guy?"

Kevin nods his head.

"Prove it kid! What lies beneath the mattress?"

Kevin closes his eyes and tries hard to remember the second part of the phrase that Robbie told him.

"The fortune of our father's!"

The man in the van smiles before opening the door.

"Names Abraham kid, the ugly guy over there is my brother Issac. What do we call you?"

"I'm Kevin, and the guy in the car is John. You guys got the stuff?"

Abraham walks to the back of the van and swings open the doors. Inside are two janitorial outfits hanging on a metal rod. Beside the disguises are two rolling janitorial carts.

"Hop in and get dressed. We will drive you to the building!"

Abraham waves his hands at John.

"Come my friend! We are on the same team brother!"

John exits the car before clicking the locking mechanism on the Corvette. He shakes the hand extended in his direction before climbing into the back of the van. Both doors are slammed shut before Abraham jogs forward and gets back into the passenger seat. The van puffs black smoke as it pulls forward.

In the back Kevin and John zip up the black and grey jumpsuits displaying the logo of 'Cinatas Solutions.'

"How did you guys get ahold of these uniforms?"

"Our Uncle Avner owns the dry cleaners that contracts with Cinatas. He had to give them a hefty discount to win the contract! All part of the great plan though!"

The van pulls up to the front of a tall high rise in the center of the financial district. At the top of the building are large illuminated red letters spelling out "Cinatas Solutions.'

"Here we are boys! Just remember... You belong here as far as anyone will think! Good luck!"

John hops out of the back of the van and helps Kevin lower the janitorial carts onto the ground. He slams the back doors and knocks twice. The van pulls away leaving a small cloud of black smoke. Kevin waves away the smoke while coughing.

"Here we go kid!"

Kevin can't help but display a big grin. He is enjoying the cloak and dagger of the operation. It's like every spy movie he has ever seen, and in this movie he is the main character.

John pushes forward his cleaning cart while whistling an unfamiliar tune. He reaches the front door and pulls out the security card that Robbie has provided. The door reader beeps twice. John then types in the six digit code assigned to the replicated keycard. A swoosh of air escapes from the building as the doors open into the lobby!

As Kevin and John enter the building, two large men in red and black camouflage move to intercept them.

"Where we headed today fella's?"

John pauses for just long enough for Kevin to take charge.

"Headed up to the sixth floor to do a deep clean! Someone made a mess up there and called us in to clean up after them. My dad brought me along to show me the ropes! Not exactly my idea of a good Saturday though!"

One of the security guards nods his head and smiles while doing a short visual search of our cleaning supplies.

"Probably those damn accountants again. Those heathens had a bunch of pizza and beer delivered last night while they were finalizing the quarterly reports. You guys are good to go.

Hopefully, you don't have to clean up any vomit this time! Goodluck kid. It's nice to see a young man like yourself willing to get his hands dirty!"

Kevin glances at John and nods his head towards the elevator. Both men push their carts inside of a gold paneled elevator car.

"Wow, this place is nice!"

"Thanks for picking up the slack back there! I froze when I realized that they might think I speak funny. I just froze up!"

"No worries John. Did you happen to see their eyes?"

"Not really. Why?"

"The quiet guard had ember eyes John! We are definitely in the right place!" The elevator stops on the sixth floor. The doors open and reveal a room full of cubicles. On the outside of the room are individual offices with closed doors made of glass.

Kevin points at the actual target they need to penetrate. Behind a thick pane of black glass are the computer servers controlling the whole building.

"Hand me the caulking gun!"

Kevin reaches into the bottom of his garbage bin and pulls out a caulking gun. He hands it to John before pulling out a long round container.

"Don't get any of that stuff on your skin. Robbie said it will eat through flesh and metal alike."

Kevin hands the tube of Hydrofluoric acid to John, who places it in the caulking gun. He cuts off the tip of the plastic tube before squeezing out a thick liquid onto the glass. The clear liquid coats the glass blocking our path and begins eating away the surface. Before long Robbie's "Super Sauce" as he called it, eats completely through the glass.

Kevin reaches forward and plugs a small device into the closest server's USB port. The device is shaped like a small Mustang. Drawn on the side of the device are the words "Wild Stallion."

Kevin nods his head and points at the USB drive.

"That's why they called this operation 'Wild Stallion'!"

John nods his head before placing the caulking gun into a plastic bin sitting on his cart. He snaps on the lid and places the bin at the bottom of his garbage bin.

"Job is done Kevin. We should get out of here!"

Kevin leads the way back to the elevator. He clicks the button for the building loading dock where their escape vehicle should be waiting. The doors of the elevator open. Before they can walk forward a security guard appears in between the doors. A large muscular man with ember eyes stands in between them and the elevator.

"I was sent to investigate a silent alarm on this floor. Is it just you two up here?"

Kevin takes the lead.

"Just us up here!"

The possessed man looks carefully at both of the janitors standing in front of him before speaking.

"That is bad news for you then!"

He kicks the cart in front of Kevin sending him tumbling to the floor in pain. John lunges forward and grabs hold of the arms of the security guard. He is nowhere near strong enough to hold the man back. He too is thrown to the floor. The camouflaged man marches forward and lifts the sole of his boot into the air.

John rolls just out of the boot strike destined for his face. He sees a human blur fly into the air. Kevin is now hanging from the security guards neck while rabbit punching him in the back of the head. He's dislodged rather easily and tossed against the wall. A pained shriek leaves his lips as his body tumbles to the ground.

John gets back up to his feet and tries to punch the guard

while he is distracted by Kevin's haphazard assault. He misses the target and is thrown back down. The guard climbs on top of John before wrapping both of his meaty hands around his neck. He Squeezes while wearing an open mouth smile.

John's eyes roll back before a small snapping sound rings out into the air. From behind a tube of clear liquid is forced into the guards mouth. Kevin squeezes both of his hands around the Acid tube sending a wave of deadly fluid down the Guard's throat. The massive man rises to his feet and begins coughing up blood while staggering in the direction that Kevin is retreating.

Kevin's eyes lock onto the dead gaze of his partner lying on the floor ten paces away. The Guard falls to his knees and crashes to the ground in front of the elevator doors before drowning in his own blood.

"You okay John?"

Kevin crawls forward to check on John. John doesn't move. He lays there next to a toppled janitorial cart staring at the ceiling.

"John, you okay?"

Kevin leans down and listens for signs of life. He hears one last shallow breath of air leave the lungs of his partner as a single tear falls from his eyes.

"Damnit!"

Kevin gets back up to his feet as John's body explodes into a ball of light and disappears. The look on the young boys face runs through a myriad of emotions.

"I'll see you on the other side old man!"

The ride down to the loading dock is quick. Kevin rolls his cart onto the dock before grabbing the handles of the van door and ripping them open. He hops inside and closes the doors behind him.

Abraham looks back from the passenger seat.

"Where's your buddy?"

"He's not coming! Let's get out of here!"

The van pulls out of the loading dock and heads in the direction of the parked Corvette half a mile away.

'What happened in there? Did you guys get to the servers?"

"Yeah, we got the job done! But one of those ember eyed assholes caught us and snapped John's neck. Dude had superhuman strength!"

"They saw your faces then?"

"Yeah, but he won't be telling anyone about us. I ended his pathetic life!"

The driver of the van pulls over behind the parked Corvette.

"This is your stop kid! You gonna be okay?"

Kevin looks at Abraham's face while responding.

"Not the first Demon I've killed! And not the first person I've lost! Thanks for the ride guys!"

Kevin jumps out of the van and closes the back doors. Abraham joins him outside the vehicle and hands him a set of keys to the Corvette.

"You might need these! Goodluck kid! I hope we see you again! The 'Cause' can always use another soldier! Look us up if you get lonely out there!"

Kevin crawls into the Corvette and replays the messy fight that he has just experienced. He can hear the sound of John's snapping neck echoing in his ears on repeat over and over again. He pulls out of the parking spot and cranks the tunes in the car to drown out the memory of his friend dying.

He drives the speed limit on the way back to the bunker to avoid any trouble with the law. Unfortunately, he fails to use his turn signal to exit the highway. A state trooper pulls up behind him and turns on the red and blue lights.

"What the hell man!"

Keving pulls over the car and begins to formulate a story that a police officer might believe. After the day he's had, everything he can think of sounds ridiculous. Two taps on the driver side window snap him out of his daydream.

"Roll it down son!"

The window slides down with the sound of expending battery power.

"Go ahead and turn the car off kid. Is this your car?"

Kevin pushes the start button of the car. The engine goes silent. The trooper's hands grip the driver's side window frame.

"You with me here kid? I asked if this is your vehicle?"

"No sir! It's my Uncle's car. He asked me to change the oil, and I was just taking a quick test drive to make sure I filled the oil reservoir to the right level."

Kevin points at an oil gauge on the dash of the vehicle.

"That's what a 'dipstick' is for son! You happen to have your driver's license on you?"

"No Sir, I left my wallet back at the garage!"

The trooper activates the radio attached to his shoulder.

"You got me caught in quite a pickle then kid. I'm gonna have to take you down to the station until your Uncle can come down and confirm your story."

Kevin exhales loudly before slapping his hands on the steering wheel. The trooper opens the car door and grabs hold of the young boys arm. He places the kid in the back of his patrol car. The man then locks the Corvette and uses a grease pen to label the back window with a green check mark.

"Don't worry kid. If your story checks out you won't be in any trouble. I'm not out here trying to make trouble for normal folks, but I also can't have unlicensed kids out on the road. It's just not safe!"

The trooper pulls off the side of the road and drives away leaving the abandoned Corvette sitting on the side of the highway. Kevin looks back at the car as it disappears into the distance. He whispers to himself.

"Robbie is gonna be pissed!"

CHAPTER 16

"I got it handled dad! Just keep the channel clear! I'm meeting up with the Aberman boys just off the highway. We'll figure out a plan and get Kevin back!"

"Alright Robbie, but you make sure to slither back to the cave without a tail, you hear!"

"Roger that! I'll make sure no one finds our 'Fortress of Solitude' old man! OVER AND OUT!"

I place the CB radio back down onto the dash of an old 1976 Chevy Scottsdale. After a quick U turn, I pull over slowly and park behind my trusted steed. As I exit the truck and walk forward I can see a large green check mark in the back window! *Gonna have to switch the registration in the DMV database again!*

Other than the green grease mark on the window, everything seems to be exactly how I left it when I last parked my precious car in the camouflaged garage outside the silo entrance.

"Thank the lord you're alright my sweet little thing!"

I reach into my pocket and pull out the spare key fob I brought along before unlocking my "Black Beauty." After sliding into her warm embrace, I gently run my hand over the supple leather of her steering wheel.

"That's right baby, daddy is back! He won't let anything bad happen to you!"

The engine cranks over and fires without a hiccup.

Two men approach from behind after exiting a beat up van.

"That you Robbie?"

"Yup, It's me boys! I hate to ask, but that kid I sent to the city got picked up by a Sherriff on his way back to basecamp!"

Abraham and Isacc both nod their heads at the statement of fact.

"We know, heard it over the police scanner! They don't know what they got yet though. We swung by the station to get a feel for the place. It's a pretty small operation maybe three or four sheriffs on duty inside. Limited security. I'm thinking we go with the old 'Barny Fife' play!"

I get out of the Corvette and stand facing my two oldest friends. The brothers and I go way back. All the way back to the good old days when we were still innocent to the world around us.

"You guys didn't happen to bring any 'Special' uniforms with you, did you?"

Issac spits on the ground before pointing at the van parked behind my truck.

"Sure did. Swung over to the shop before heading out here to meet up! We figured you would be onboard with a little stealth operation."

As kids the three of us pulled many heists at varying success rates. No matter what though, we never sold one another out if one of us was caught during the caper. Many a priest lost their Kippah. Only to find it later in the priests office or below the Brasen Alter. The point was never to steal anything. The thrill of the chase was what we were after.

That same thrill seeking attitude led me to join the Navy. After figuring out the toughest job in the force, I was submitted and accepted for SEAL training. I can't tell you how many times I thought about quitting during those first few weeks of hell. Something inside of me kept me warm and resolved to persevere. No matter how cold the water was in that damn ocean, I always had a spark of warmth in my chest.

My moment of reminiscing is interrupted by the horn of a passing semi-truck.

I point at Abraham and toss him the keys to my dad's truck.

"You guys follow me. We need to go fishing!"

Issac and Abraham pull onto the highway behind me. I take it slow to make sure that the van they were driving doesn't break down or something. We pull into the first Starbucks parking lot I see. I get out and go into the shop to order a coffee as my accomplices wait for me to set the bait.

After avoiding the watchful gaze of the security camera, I go into the bathroom and pull out a long range radio.

"This is unit 41 requesting backup for a 10-96. We got a crazy homeless guy in a Starbucks swinging around a pickleball paddle, OVER!"

"Unit 63 responding! Five minutes out, OVER!"

"Copy that Unit 63, Unit 41 will isolate the individual and protect the civilians, OVER AND OUT!

I imagine my partners in crime are concocting a couple roofies for the cops on their way to assist me with the fake radio call. I toss the radio into the garbage can after wiping down any fingerprints that might exist. I then pull out a fake mustache and apply it to my upper lip. *Burt Selleck would be proud of this baby!*

I walk out into the lobby making sure to keep my head facing away from the camera's on the other side of the shop. After walking out the front doors into the hot sun, I get back into my car and close the door.

The cops arrive within three minutes and approach the front doors of the building. I can tell that they're looking for the other cop who called for backup. Issac and Abraham covertly slide out of their vehicles and gain entry to the idling police car parked beside them. In the center console are two bottles of water. They squeeze some sleepy juice in each one before sealing the caps. Abraham turns the heater to max and cuts the activator to the air conditioning controller. Both brothers then quietly close the doors to the cruiser and enter the Starbucks like nothing has happened.

After realizing that there's nothing wrong, the two cops exit the store and look around for anything out of the ordinary. After scanning the scene, they seem to decide that everything looks normal. Both men get back into their cruiser. All four windows immediately roll down as a small argument breaks out between the two men.

Each one blames the other for leaving the heat on full blast when they left the vehicle. After realizing that the heat will not turn off, both men reach to the center console and grab a bottle of water before getting out of the vehicle.

"I told you Virgil… I told you like ten times that the buttons on this car are sensitive. Now we are gonna sweat our asses off all the way back down to the Motor Pool!"

"I didn't touch a damn thing! I'm telling you Jacob, I didn't touch the air buttons! Maybe my knight stick hit it when I was getting out or something?"

Both men drink deeply from the water bottles in hand. The brothers exit the Starbucks just in time to catch the two officers before they fall to the ground. Each man is stuffed into the back of the windowless van Issac arrived in. I look around to make sure that nobody saw what went down. We seem to be in the clear. I watch as Abraham gets into the driver's seat of the cruiser and fixes the alteration he made to the vent controls.

In only a few seconds he's sitting in front of a stream of cold air while wearing one of the Officer's pairs of aviator sunglasses. We leave the van behind with the drugged Cops inside. They'll wake up confused and disoriented hours from now. Long after we've hopefully fulfilled our mission and ditched their cruiser.

We all meet up and pull into an abandoned 'Halloween Costume' parking lot to get ready. The uniform they brought for me is really tight. Abraham notices as well.

"You been working out big guy? I used to know your uniform size before you disappeared into that bunker!"

"I think your uncle probably shrunk this poor dude's shirt! Is he skimping on cleaning chemicals again to make a profit?"

Issac smiles wide while buttoning up his borrowed cop uniform.

"Probably! But no refunds!"

We all laugh while imagining Uncle Avner's most recognizable phrasing. As kids we would sit in whatever shop he owned at the time and listen to him argue with unhappy customers. Every dispute always ended the same way. "No Refunds!"

I hop back into my Corvette and follow Issac and Abraham while they drive the police cruiser. When we get to the sheriff's office the two brothers enter the parking lot and purposefully crash into a line of police motorcycles parked next to the entrance.

Every Sheriff in the building comes outside to investigate the ongoing distraction. I park on the side of the building and enter through a side door. The flat brim of my trooper hat blocks the camera angles overhead, and my mustache and sunglasses will do the rest to conceal my identity.

I can hear Abraham and Issac yelling at each other about who was at fault for causing the crash.

"I told you not to touch the radio! It's your fault this happened!"

The Sheriffs from the station do their best to separate the two fighting officers. I take a sharp right and give a thumbs up to the camera overhead the locked door blocking my path forward. There's a loud buzz before the door clicks open. I push through and see a line of empty cells on my left and right. There is a Sheriff's deputy at the end of the lockdown corridor reading a thin comic book.

"Howdy partner! I'm here to pick up that kid! You know, the John Doe you picked up on the Highway outside Fort Worth! Someone downtown flagged his description for an ongoing investigation!"

Without looking at me, the Deputy reaches into the drawer in the desk under his feet and tosses me the keys.

"He's in C-6, Knock yourself out. Save me some paperwork!"

When I open the door Kevin is attempting and failing to do a pullup. There are three other men in the cell with him. He gives them all fist bumps and tells them good luck before walking out the door.

"You making friends in here or something?"

"Nothing quite brings people together like hating the cops! How the heck did you find me?"

"Never mind that right now. Just hang your head down."

I put a pair of plastic handcuffs on Kevin's wrists just in case someone is watching me through the cameras.

"Did you seriously just put a pair of toy cuffs on me?"

"Just go with it kid. Keep your eyes down."

I pull the hood of Kevin's sweatshirt over his head. I then toss the keys onto the Deputy's desk. He doesn't look up once. I can see Kevin's eyes light up after seeing what the officer is reading. *NO WAY, It's Burts series, Dream Warrior!*

"Thanks a lot buddy!"

The man nods his head without breaking his reading stride. I notice that there is a pile of comics on the desk in front of him.

I get Kevin outside just as the Sheriffs from the station have broken up the fight happening between Issac and Abraham. I give them a covert nod to indicate that they can go to phase two of the operation. I then pull apart Kevin's wrists breaking the plastic cuffs and placing him in the passenger seat of the car.

As I drive away from the station, Kevin once again questions how I was able to find him so quickly.

"You actually think I'm gonna loan the 'Black Beauty' out to people I barely know and not track her? You're crazy kid! Now tell me what happened to John!"

**

"Robbie and his idiot friends got him back! I told him not to come back right away just in case this whole thing is a trap to find us!"

Estee leans back in the computer chair under her butt and tosses a white baseball up and down while listening to Bernie. I can't help but feel a rush of relief that Kevin is safe again with Robbie. Part of me is kind of jealous that Kevin got to go on a secret mission in the first place.

"I think you might be a bit paranoid Bernie. Why would someone be tracking Kevin? Robbie's virus would have wiped the surveillance video of the infiltration at Cinatas Solutions!"

"My boy is pretty damn smart. It's true! But he also doesn't have a suspicious enough mind for my liking. He takes after his mother! She was always saying "Don't worry about it." Her philosophy never took root in my head though."

Estee stands up after noticing that the Corvette is now parked in front of Angelo's BBQ.

"Those guys better bring me back some brisket. Can we call them and put in an order for takeout?"

Bernie waves away Estee's question as nonsense.

"This isn't a game Estee! "Wild Stallion" will really piss these guys off. If we thought they were dangerous before, they will be even more frantic to find you guys now! And now I've hitched my wagon to you two. So no! We're not going to call them and provide the opportunity for someone smarter than both of us to trace the call!"

I can see that Estee is disappointed by Bernie's emphatic denial of her BBQ craving.

"Fine, but Angelo's is the best BBQ you will ever taste! If I was on death row, I'd order one of every kind of their meats and every side they offer, then I'd die happy with a full belly!"

Bernie stands up from his chair causing a squeaking sound to fill the room over the sound of buzzing computer monitors. After tossing a package of Saltine Crackers into Estee's lap, he points down the hall.

"I need to show you two something! Its time you guys see the 'Panic Room'!"

Bernie pushes my chair down the hallway towards the main dormitory. Before we pass the bathroom sign, he stops my chair and reaches under a small silver drinking fountain attached to the wall. He pushes what looks like a rusty bolt head.

Beside me a thin hallway opens up revealing a brightly lit room. Inside is a bed and a small sitting area. Next to the bed is a mini fridge filled with bottled water. A small cabinet next to the sitting area contains a month's worth of MRE meal packages.

"What is this place?"

Estee runs her hand along the back of the couch.

"A bunker inside of a bunker? Your paranoia has a case of its own paranoia Bernie!"

"You won't be thinking that if the bad guys ever find this bunker! I think it would be wise if you two sleep in here while you go to the other place!"

"You mean Cyadonia?"

"Yeah, the other place!"

"Why do you want us to sleep in here? We're already inside a secret bunker underground!"

Bernie shrugs his shoulders.

"I'm just thinking that without Robbie to protect us all, we can't be too careful! Don't worry, I'll be in here with you as well."

Bernie and Estee spend the better part of the next two hours trying to connect the VCR to the vintage TV in the sitting area of the Panic Room. They eventually figure it out and begin watching a movie called Jaws. I've heard of it before, but never had a chance to watch it. For a movie made in the Seventies, it's still pretty scary.

It's a good thing that I'm not planning on going for a swim in the ocean anytime soon. Cause this movie probably just ruined swimming in open water for me for the rest of my life!

After the movie ends, Estee looks at her watch and decides that it is time for us to head back to Cyadonia. She tucks me into bed beside her and fluffs my pillow one last time before laying her own head back. Bernie is watching a new movie, and I recognize the sound of it immediately. I feel a deep sense of irony while thinking that 'Old Man Bernie' is watching Star Wars. He reminds me of a paranoid version of Obi-Wan for sure! I close my eyes and wait for sleep to take me.

**

I wake and hear the telltale sounds of the ongoing siege outside. Fred is sitting on the bed next to me. It takes me a moment to realize that his wings are gone, and he looks painfully human to my eyes.

"What happened to you?"

Fred looks miserable. He rolls off the side of the bed and

begins dressing in a borrowed armor set baring the sigil of the "Dueling Stallions."

"I have no idea. I felt a pain engulf my chest before I transformed back into human shape! It hurt like hell if your curious?"

I put on my own set of Centurian armor before inquiring further about Fred's status.

"Has this ever happened before?"

Fred thinks carefully before responding.

"Not that I can remember. Ever since my father cast the 'Guardian' spells over me, I've assumed the bird form in Cyadonia like him! Something weird is going on!"

I wiggle my sword to make sure it is loose enough to pull if I need to access its sharp blade.

"Is this gonna be a problem Fred?"

I watch as my Guardian flexes his fingers and concentrates. Two balls of ice form in his fists.

"Holy cow! I've never been able to form two at the same time! Either I'm a late bloomer, or whatever shifted me into this human form, also gave me a magic upgrade!"

Fred reaches his hand towards the fireplace at the far end of the room and contains its flames within a dome of ice. The fire is extinguished to the delight of my oldest friend.

"I've never been able to do that before!"

"I'm happy for you buddy! But maybe don't kill our fire next time. I can almost see my breath again!"

I focus my fire magic and light the roaring flames that Fred has just extinguished.

"My bad! At least we know that I can still defend you!"

We both walk down a long winding set of stone stairs until we reach the King's Throne Room. Inside are hundreds of

Knights feasting and drinking. The overnight watch is on half strength, and the King's men deserve a rest after the resounding victory of the day before.

"The Demon siege weapons continued throughout the night young Centurian! But our lookouts say that the bulk of their force has pulled back out of range of our counter attacks. They are surely licking their wounds from yesterday's defeat!"

I sit down next to the King before tearing off a piece of spiced bread from a loaf sitting on the table. I wash it down with a glass of Honey Wine. The wine soaks into my blood stream and relieves some of the anxiety filling my thoughts.

"A great victory my King, but without the Tar Cauldrons overlooking the Gully, how will you turn back the next attack?"

"A good question young Centurian. I can see that you have a mind for warfare! If it was up to you, how would you repel a large attack at the gates?"

I think back to the limited information I know of the defenses overlooking the gully approach to the fortress.

"I guess that I would line the overlooking cliffs with stones and archers. When the enemy approaches I would first drop the stones on their heads. When the shields they carry are destroyed by the stones, I would rain arrows tipped with fire onto their heads. Once the first few Demon's in line fall, they will form a wall of flesh stopping the others from marching forward."

The King shakes his head and smiles. He then snaps his fingers.

"A good plan Centurian! But you have overlooked one small detail."

I rack my brain and try and find the flaw in my strategy while gulping down another cup of Honey Wine.

"You forget that the Demon Warriors explode into light and dust when they are killed!"

I nod my head after realizing the truth in the King's words. He slaps the top of my armored shoulder and grunts the next few words.

"All the same your plan will work!"

I cock my head to the side trying to figure out what the King is talking about.

"The stones we drop will serve two purposes! They will shatter the shields of the enemy, and If concentrated will naturally build a wall blocking the rest of the attackers. I shall order my men to gather and position piles of stone above the narrowest places in the gully!"

"And where will you station me for the battle to come?"

The King smiles.

"You and the rest of my Centurians will be stationed at the main gate, and overlooks at the front of the fortress. You shall guard my forces from the flying beasts as you so successfully did from the central tower yesterday. If our strategy fails to halt the enemy advance through the Gully, we will need your magic to defend the gatehouse. You must not let the enemy Priests infiltrate the fortress and allow the Demon Hordes on our side of the defenses. They outnumber us ten to one! From the top of our walls we can repel their attack. But if they get inside, we will be forced to fall back to the main castle keep. From there it will only be a matter of time before Gallus's forces can cut our supply of water and food and starve us to death!"

I can see that Fred is nervous after listening to the King's plan. They make eye contact.

"It's good to see that you came to your senses and took the form of a man! My men will now be able to identify you more easily as an ally in the battle to come!"

I can't disagree with the King's logic. I too was worried that some disoriented archer might take a shot at Fred while he protected me. We both bow to the king after standing up.

"We shall prepare for battle my lord!"

The King points at his three Centurians leaning against the stone wall of the Throne Room.

"Take them with you. It seems their true loyalty lies with you anyways!"

The look on the King's face as he points at his Centurians leaves a bad taste in my mouth. My gut tells me that King Nero holds a deep grudge against my fellow Centurians who rallied to my defense during the Parlay with Gallus.

I wave my arms in the air to get the attention of my black armored allies. They all fall into line and follow me and Fred through the gatehouse leading outside. We all walk in a small group before climbing the steps leading to the defensive structures overlooking the Gully approach. When we arrive, the King's men are already creating large stacks of basketball sized stones on the edge of the cliff side.

I walk to the far edge of the battlements atop the side of the Gully and look out over a vast field of small campfires below. The enemy is just starting to form small groups to move into position to attack. The winged beasts from the day before are nowhere to be seen. Not knowing where they are makes me nervous.

I glance up into a cloudless sky. The sun is almost ready to poke its head over the mountain peaks to the east of Stonepass. I will feel better once the light of day arrives. We all prepare in our own ways. The three armor clad Centurians drop to their knees and pray in the direction of the rising sun. I recognize some of the prayer. Thoth used to pray like that when I was a young boy.

Fred charges and releases his magical talents over and over again like he is a sprinter stretching his legs before a race. The King's men filter out of the Throne Room and begin taking their places along the battlements. I say a quick prayer to the Creator. Fred see's my lips moving and smiles at me.

"I see that you're asking the Sky Gods for their blessing!"

I feel the immediate need to correct Fred's assumption.

"Not the Sky Gods! I'm bypassing the middlemen and going straight to the Creator. He's the only one who has a reason to talk back!"

The formations of Demon warriors form large lines two abreast. The enemy soldiers in the front of the miles long line hold massive wooden shields overhead as they march forward into the Gully. We wait until the front of the attacking line reaches a tight space in the fortress approach. At Joan's command the King's Knights begin tossing stones over the edge of the overlooking cliffs. The enemy below cries out in pain. Sharp bursts of bright light fill the Gully as the stones begin to inhibit the forward movement of the attacking columns.

The rock piles overlooking the Gully dwindle as the piles of Demon weapons and armor grow. The battle is going well, and the enemy is suffering greatly when a large explosion from below knocks me off of my feet. After regaining consciousness, I crawl carefully to the edge of the cliff and look down. Two Dark Priests are powering a spell aimed at the only stone pile still blocking the enemies approach.

A second explosion fills the Gully sending the stones of the pile flying towards the main gate of the fortress complex. The men standing atop the wall above the gate are crushed by the flying stones. Arrows and bolts rain down on the charging Demons in the Gully.

"We need to get down there and guard the gate!"

Fred drops two more ice balls over the edge of the Gully before following me. They nearly hit the top of the Priests, drawing their attention to us. We run down the stone stairs leading to the top of the wall guarding the main gate. The King has sent reinforcements to the gate, and a hundred men are lobbing arrows, bolts, and small clay jars filled with lamp oil onto the approaching swarm of enemy soldiers.

I power my fire magic and light the accumulation of oil covering the ground below the enemy's feet. My spell is countered by the two Dark Priests marching with the Demon Hordes. My fire is extinguished and the Demons march forward.

"I got something for them!"

Fred charges his magic and focuses his hands towards the ground sloping away from the main gate. A thick layer of ice covers the ground causing the charging enemy to slip and slide back into the Demons following them. Like bowling pins, the enemy soldiers topple after sliding into one another. I high five Fred while watching the Dark Priests struggle to maintain their footing as well. Each one is slipping and sliding backwards as my lightning bolt hits them in the chest. Two bright balls of light fill the air.

"Nice shot Cam!"

Fred gives me a firm slap on the back as we duck behind the wall to avoid a cloud of Demon arrows striking all around. I poke my head up above a blackened parapet to see what else is coming our way. Puff after puff of bright light fills the Gully. The arrows from the King's archers are holding the enemy back from approaching the Gate.

Over and over again Fred covers the ground outside the gate with ice. Once the enemy is consolidated in a large pile I blow them away with a lightning bolt. Fewer enemies seem to be approaching until the remaining attackers turn tail and run. We hoot and holler from the top of the gatehouse wall. Each one of us is breathing heavy, and the King's men seem relieved that the main assault has fallen back.

A multitude of Demon horn blasts fill the air with a melody of unknown commands. We climb the stone stairs leading to the top of the Gully defenses and look out over the retreating enemy forces. I'm astounded by what I see. There are two long black lines leading from the mountains to the west into the Enemies battle camp. For as many as we have slain on the day, ten more are marching to replace them. I sense a feeling of despair overtaking the joy of victory I just experienced.

The King arrives beside me in his spotless armor and pats the top of my shoulder.

"Well done Centurian! The enemy has probed our defenses. They now know that we will not be defeated without great loss. Let's hope that this realization causes Gallus to turn around and head back to the lands of Gomorrah! If not we shall beat back every attack they levy against us. We shall eventually win the war of attrition. Not even Gallus has unlimited minions to throw against our thick walls!"

We stand side by side while looking out at the enemy replenishing their ranks. Behind me stands Fred. He whispers into my ear.

"Seems to me the enemy keeps getting re-enforcements. I think it might be us who will lose a war of attrition!"

CHAPTER 17

I wake up with Ruth's smiling face hovering six inches from my lips. I should be startled, but instead I feel a rush of relief that she's alive and well.

"You've got some explaining to do Ruth!"

My eyes comb over the woman's appearance standing over the Queen's bed. Ruth is dressed from head to toe in a shiny blue and black armor. Each scale of metal has the same look and feel as the stones making up the Storm Tower. She glimmers in electrical energy, and there's a confidence about her that didn't exist in the Human Realm.

I roll out of bed and throw my arms through my own set of armor.

"Start talking woman!"

"That's no way to address your Queen!"

Ruth's smile erodes the startling nature of the revelation.

"What do you mean? You're the Queen now?"

Ruth spreads her fingers apart and bounces small pops of lightning back and forth between her hands.

"I was always meant to be Queen. When I was a much younger woman I chose to let my younger sister assume the throne so that I could follow my heart!"

I nod my head as the details begin to come into focus.

"Keep going!"

My hands swirl in a tight circle in the air as I shove my foot into a plated riding boot.

"I fell in love when I was very young with a handsome Guardian in training. You know him as John! When the Sky Gods learned of our attachment, they decreed that I must choose. John, or my future Queenship. I chose love over power!"

Ruth reaches out her hand and helps me up off the bed.

"Before my sister was taken from the Storm Tower against her will, she managed to cast a spell of recall on my soul. I was brought back to my rightful place in this realm, and the power of the Queenship engulfed my body."

I glance down at the powerful electricity pulsing in her palms.

"I can see that..."

"Do I still call you Ruth? I serve at your pleasure My Queen!"

Ruth's soft smile alleviates the feeling of nervousness inside me.

"Stand up child! Nothing shall change between us! My sister did well to choose you as her Centurian! I'm sure you will serve me as well with the same vigor and loyalty! At least until we can figure out who took her, and rescue her!"

"I Will!"

"Good, onto bigger and more important things! We need to get word to Cameron at Stonepass! The King is foolish in his belief that he can hold the Demon Army back indefinitely without help. I have a plan to break the siege at his gates. I need you to talk to someone for me!"

"I'll go wherever you send me..."

Ruth smiles before pointing towards the Celestial Door on the other side of the Throne Room.

"When it's just us you should call me Ruth, but when others are around we must keep up appearances. The people are rightfully calling me the Queen of Storms!"

I nod my head. It's a pretty cool name, and I'm happy to be serving under Ruth's command. The stone door begins to glow as the Queen presses her magical chanting into its surface. I see the glyphs surrounding the stone cutout begin to pulsate with colorful light.

"Listen carefully Estee! You too can command the Celestial Door. Say the words I've just spoken, and send your most powerful magic into the stone door. You try it!"

Ruth closes the Celestial Door and then waits for me to try my hand at activating it. I say the words, and point my healing magic towards the stone door. Bright lights fill the glyphs and activate the door. The Queen claps twice before pointing at the portal and pushing me forward!

"You're a natural Estee! When you get there... This is the message!"

The Queen explains her plan before laying out the finer details of her request.

"Do you understand?"

I nod my head and check one last time to make sure that my sword is seated properly in its sheath before moving forward.

I push through the stone wall slowly. My feet adorn the top of a pathway made of shooting stars and colorful constellations. The door at the end of the Celestial Hallway glows with the light of a burning sun. When I push through it, there is a light brighter than I can handle with open eyes.

A large hand grasps my shoulder startling me. The voice I hear is familiar, and I pull my hand away from the sword that I instinctually grabbed for.

"Fendril? Is that you?"

"Welcome Centurian. The Creator is very eager to hear the message that the Queen of Storms has sent to him. She has always been in his favor."

Fendril leads me up a ridiculously long staircase leading towards some sort of floating Throne Room. When we reach the top of the stairs I look back down, aware that at some point I will need to climb back down every step.

Fendril bows before the Creator. He glances sideways at me and points his eyes toward the floor. I hesitate to bow before a god that I have never known, but something in the way the room itself feels makes me drop to one knee.

"I can see that I will need to earn your trust Centurian. This is good! I often question the loyalty of a person when that same loyalty is not earned properly."

I raise my head and block my eyes from the bright light emanating off of the God sitting atop a throne made of firelight.

"I have been sent…"

The Creator cuts off my sentence.

"I know why you are here Young Lady! I see and hear everything in the kingdoms that I have created! I am most eager to speak with you if you would allow me?"

I'm slightly caught off guard by the Creator asking permission to speak with me.

"You're a God right? You don't need my permission to speak to me! Just like you didn't need permission to give my dad Cancer!"

Out of the corner of my eye, I see Fendril shoot me a look that suggests that he is displeased with my accusation.

"You did give him Cancer didn't you? Or at the very least you allowed it to kill him! Just like you let babies starve to death, and evil men take liberty's with innocent children. You have a lot of explaining to do if you want to earn my 'Loyalty' buddy!"

The Creator's response is not what I expect. Not that I really knew what I was expecting. I never planned on letting my anger boil over like this!

"You are passionate about many things Estee! In this way we are very much alike. I too feel the pain of loss when each of my Creations decide to serve the darkness! Every bad thing that happens in the world is of my making simply by the fact that I have given Free Will to all of my Creations!"

I listen to the words coming from a light too bright to look at. There is some logic in the responses to my accusations, but my anger is so strong that I start to talk myself into remaining angry, even though there is a warm feeling actively trying to take it away from my heart.

"Even now you choose to feel the pain of loss in your life. I can wipe it away should you desire Estee, but even now you are gripping that pain and anger even tighter. It seems to be a part of you now. Just like the pain of betrayal has become a part of me!"

"My pain is the only way that I can remember him! If it goes away, his memory fades with it!"

The Creator lowers his voice.

"It is true Estee that much of your ability to channel the magic of this world comes from the pain you hold onto in both realms. But I tell you now, If you would choose to join me, and let go of your anger and pain, I shall fill you with a power that would rival that of Gallus himself."

I feel a small trickle of tears roll down my cheek. Though the Creator's words bring a sort of comfort, I am not yet ready to release the anger I've held onto for many years.

"You say no! I can feel your anger still. My offer will continue to exist until the last breath of your life young Centurian. Go now and fulfil the other requests of your Queen!"

I stand up and try to speak. It's as if the Creator can read my mind. *Hell, he probably can!*

"I have already heard the words of your Queen when she spoke them to you from the Storm Tower. I will contemplate her request. Go now! I shall send Fendril to help you keep The Storm Sword safe from the coming evil that hunts him!"

Fendril bows deeply and growls in my direction. He then points back to the top of the stairs leading back to the Celestial Door.

"I had thought you to be a Wise Human for your age Estee, but I see now that you are just as foolish as those around you!"

I snap my head sideways to respond to the slight.

"I speak the truth, even to the God who made me Fendril. You just grovel and bow to an entity that you fear!"

"It is true young Centurian. I do fear the Creator, but I also serve him at my own pleasure. He is not the one responsible for the horrors of the human world, or the atrocities committed by Gallus and his minions in this world. Every choice leads to consequences. Something that you humans seem to think doesn't apply to you!"

I hear the truth in his words while looking over the edge of the massive staircase. His strong arms grasp onto my shoulders before shoving me over the side. We coast to a stop just in front of the Celestial Door! After activating the portal with a small prayer, Fendril follows me through the opening.

"Why did the Creator send you to help me defend Cameron?"

"It is not for me to know the plans of the Creator. But I suspect that Cameron is a pretty important boy for the plan the Creator has concocted. His desire is to return this realm to peace!"

The door to my left glows yellow after Fendril touches it.

"This door leads to the castle at Stonepass. We should be wise to expect a hostile greeting. Stay your hand from your sword. The King's men are not always the brightest, and I don't want to be forced to kill any of them!"

We enter the portal and arrive in a dark room. There's a violent crescendo of sound upon arrival that makes my eyes squint and my body instinctively search for safety.

"The siege is in full swing now! Follow behind me Estee, we can't be sure the walls haven't been breached. The enemy could be around every corner!"

"I thought you said not to draw my sword?"

"I would like to amend my statement! Kill anything that looks at us funny! We need to find Cameron and get him out of here before this place falls!"

I look at Fendril. There is something that he knows that he isn't sharing. I formulate a probing response to gauge his reaction.

"But the Queen of Storms, she said that she has a plan to win the ongoing battle!"

Fendril looks down a long corridor lit on both sides by torches protruding from the stone walls at a slight angle. He points his sword at two glowing sets of Demon eyes sticking out among the darkness of the space.

"Prepare yourself Centurian! We will bathe in the stench of our enemy's demise!"

Fendril charges forward without offering an explanation for anything. I power a ball of fire light in my right palm and throw it ahead of my charging ally. It strikes the wall behind what is more than two Demon Warriors.

His movements are quick and graceful. For a being that size I guess I just thought he wouldn't be as flexible and skilled in combat. I half expected him to lower his head like a goat and try and head butt the enemy Demons. Alas, there is an elegance to the way his shoulders and feet move with each sword thrust. His body spins and ducks to avoid the enemy attacks before slashing and stabbing in response.

I stand there in total awe of the prowess of Fendril with a sword. I know very little about the Arch Servants of the

Creator. My wise Teacher never 'taught' me anything about them, but it is quickly becoming clear that this day will be filled with carnage.

Pop after pop of light signifies Fendril's strikes. I watch with mouth open as he easily cuts down the last of the Demons blocking the hallway. He spins after the strike and lowers his body to a knee facing me. There is a massive smile on his soot covered face. His eyes shine like bright green balls of light. There is a sense of pleasure in his appearance.

"It has been many an age since the Creator has seen fit to unleash me upon his enemies! The lifetimes spent stuck in the 'Stone Spell' made me slow."

He looks down at his arm before wiping a small trail of blood coming from a small gash above his elbow.

"You see…"

He points at the small wound before looking me in the eye and shaking his head from side to side in disappointment.

"In my prime I would have smite these Demons without taking a scratch!"

There is a power radiating off of him. I feel like I might be able to draw some of that power for use myself. I step carefully over the piles of strewn ash containing Demon armor. On the way down a winding staircase Fendril stops and puts a finger to his ear.

"Do you hear it Centurian?"

I listen to the pattering of footsteps echoing up the chamber containing the spiral staircase.

"Someone is coming!"

He nods his chin before rocking his head from side to side. He is preparing himself for combat when we hear human voices accompanying the footsteps.

"Back up to the last landing!"

We climb back up ten stairs and make our way into a large alcove containing window slits designed for firing arrows at enemy attackers in the courtyard below. I stand beside Fendril with sword in hand. A man dressed in black armor bearing the sigil of the Kingdom of Plenty arrives at the alcove with ten men in tow.

I can see the eyes of the man in charge through a small slit in his helmet visor.

"Estee?"

There is a great familiarity in the voice, but it is a voice that should not be speaking to me in Cyadonia. The Knight lifts his helmet visor.

"What the hell is that thing?"

Fendril flares his wings in a show of dominance before crouching his shoulders in attack stance. I raise my hand up and place it against his chest to calm his posture.

"Easy Fendril! This is Cameron's Guardian, Fred!"

I look Fred up and down. The description that I had been given of his form in Cyadonia was completely different than the plain muscular man standing in front of me.

"I thought you had wings and the face of a lion here dude? What gives?"

Fred pulls off the helmet entirely before telling his men to go back down to the battlements where he took them from.

"No Idea why, but when I woke up this morning, I had transformed into the shape of my 'Real World' body! It's kinda inconvenient to say the least! I miss my wings already."

"I bet you do!"

Fendril ruffles his own feathers before making a show of having a set of wings himself.

"Why have you abandoned your 'charge' Guardian? Your only

job is to protect him!"

"Cam sent me to defend the Celestial Door. We might need to retreat! The battle took a turn about an hour ago. You're not going to believe this!"

Fred points back the way he came from.

"Gallus has the support of one of the Sky Gods! A creature that quite frankly looks a lot like you is giving the King's Centurians and Cameron all they can handle at the front gate! The King himself has fallen back to defend the keep. The enemy is sending small groups of Demon Warriors over the perimeter walls to attack the castle, but the main defenses are still holding."

Fendril's eyes change color from green to yellow. His respiration picks up and I can see his hand squeeze the grip of his sword.

"It was only a matter of time before one of my siblings saw the advantages of aiding Gallus against the Creator! Take me to him! I shall look upon his face before I remove his wings and take his head!"

"You go do that I guess? I have to guard the Celestial Door remember! But he's easy to find… The bastard is throwing magic at the front gate. Goodluck!"

Fred glances back at me while climbing the stairs leading to the Celestial Door tower.

"Give em hell Estee!"

His voice echoes all the way down the stairs until I reach the Throne Room. There are armored men laying all over the floor and table. Women and healers in black robes do their best to aid the wounded soldiers. A singular man in a white robe covered in blood is using magic to heal some of the men. Each man that is healed returns to his feet before marching out the large double doors to reengage the enemy.

Fendril stops for a quick moment to listen to the screams of dying men!

"You stay here Centurian! Heal the ones you can, and wait for Cameron. When he arrives take him through the portal to the Storm Tower. Wait there for my return. If you do not see me again... I wish you good luck in the future battles!"

He runs out the door leaving behind the soft fragrance of sweat and wine. I kneel beside the first man I come upon. His belly has been opened by a well-placed arrow. The wound is filled with black sludge and there's a foul odor coming from somewhere. I place my palm over his wound and focus on mending the flesh below it. The man's open flesh seals before the air is cleansed of the rotten smell coming from the wound.

The Knight's scowling face twists into a soft smile. His eyes say thank you before his mouth can accomplish the task. I move onto the next man, and the next man. There's an unending flow of pain and anguish coming through the doors of the Throne Room. I can feel a warm energy on the top of my head. I look up and am almost blinded by the beam of light encompassing me.

**

Fendril charges out into the courtyard. His sandaled feet leave small puffs of dust behind each footfall. Arrows rain down from the sky everywhere except the front gate. Someone is powering a defensive spell to protect the King's men there! The Creator's Arch Servant arrives below the protective spell before climbing the stone steps leading to the battlements overlooking the Gully of Stonepass.

Cameron is startled by his sudden appearance. The other soldiers pivot to defend themselves from the surprise guest that looks a lot like the creature attacking the gate.

"Stand down men of the Kingdom of Plenty! I am Fendril, servant to the Creator! I shall do you no harm!"

"He's a good guy! Don't stab him!"

Each man atop the wall has reason to suspect the new arrival's motivation. In the Gully, a Fallen Servant stands a hundred feet from the gate. His feet are spread wide and both of his hands are extended towards the defenders. There is a swirling cloud of black mist surrounding him. His magic is strong. Each spell he casts rips chunks of stone from the defensive wall next to the steel gate.

Behind him stands two columns of Demon Warriors waiting for the wall to come down before they charge forward.

"I did not expect to see you here Brother! Has the Creator finally decided to take an interest in his creations? How long has it been since we have spoken Fendril?"

The Fallen Servant ceases his attacks while addressing Fendril.

"We have not spoken since you came to this realm and convinced the people here that you represent the Creator's will! You tell me how long it has been Thadius! I have been away for quite some time!"

The Fallen Servant laughs to himself before unfurling a set of golden wings. The Demons behind him seem bothered by the light reflecting off of them. He quickly folds them back behind his back.

"For you, I'm sure it seems just like yesterday you were clipping the wings of our 'Fallen Brethren' and casting them into the Valley of Purgatory! For those of us who were not turned to stone, It has been many generations. In that time the people of Cyadonia have turned to me and my sisters to guide them!"

Fendril unfurls his wings and hops over the edge of the wall. He glides to the ground and lands in front of the steel gatehouse. Two groups of Demons standing behind Thadius charge forward to attack. Fendril stands his ground and braces for the coming onslaught. Before the Demons reach his position, a bolt of lightning strikes the closest enemy before arching through the chests of all those following it!

Fendril looks up at Cameron and winks. He then turns his gaze back to the real threat.

"I have a message for you Thadius! One from the Creator himself. Unlike you, he has seen what will happen here before it has happened."

Thadius unleashes a black stream of smoking fluid towards Fendril. The spell fades without impacting its target. A bright light emanates from the sky onto the top of Fendril's head. A second light shines down on Cameron's head before two bright lights streak out of the clouds and land on either side of Thadius.

Two female Sky Gods compress to one knee upon landing before standing up. Each one holds a long spear covered in plated gold and fire.

"Welcome Sisters! I see that you too have made a choice to defy the Creator?"

Each Fallen Sister hisses at the accusation. Thadius addresses the comment.

"The Creator chose first when he denied our requests to intervene in the decimation of moral values in his creations! Lucia and Lilith chose like I did to do what we felt was right!"

Fendril see's movement behind the three Fallen Servants. Gallus approaches the Gatehouse and makes an announcement to all the men guarding it.

"Defy your King and Surrender! I will spare any man who lays down their weapon and kneels before me! Do it now, or live to hear the screams of death from the lips of everyone you know!"

He looks toward the three winged beings standing behind him. Fendril speaks one last time while raising his sword point towards Gallus.

"This is your last warning! The Creator offers you a pardon

from your evil deeds! Refuse this olive branch at your own peril!"

Gallus turns his back on the coming fight and slowly walks between the two columns of Demon Warriors filling the Gully. Each of his warriors are pressed firmly against the stone walls of the tight space as he pushes through them to escape the front lines of the coming battle.

"Can you now see the character of the one you have allied yourselves with? Not even now does he stay and fight beside you! Gallus is a coward! He uses others to fight his battles, and then he betrays them once they have won the day for him. Surely you can see this?"

The look on the Sky God's face named Lucia shifts after taking in the words of her brother. She turns and says something to Thadius before disappearing into a bright light and lifting off into the sky. Thadius yells into the air behind the trail of light carrying her away.

"How dare you defy me Lucia! You shall pay for this betrayal sister!"

There is a tense moment while Thadius stares at Lilith to make sure she doesn't try and retreat as well.

"Stop staring at me brother! You know my heart! I do not fight this battle for Gallus. I fight to restore balance and morality to this world! To change the hearts of men, we must first rule over them with complete control! We shall smite Gallus and take power once his minions subjugate the people of this realm!"

Thadius nods his head before drawing a long sword from a silver sheath at his hip.

"What say you brother? Shall we get this fight started? The sooner I send you crawling back to the Creator, the sooner I can restore morality to this world in the way in which I choose!"

Fendril bows in respect to his two siblings squaring off in front of him. The Demon Hordes standing ready to attack, wait nervously for an opportunity to rush forward.

"Storm Sword... Hold back the enemy Horde while I dispatch my brother and sister."

Thadius and Lilith charge forward. A spear thrust slides just under Fendril's armpit before he extends his foot and kicks his sister in the chest. Her body flies through the air and knocks over the first ten Demon Soldiers moving forward. Thadius swings his sword with speed and strength. Each slash and thrust is turned aside with precision.

Cameron points his fingers towards the opening in the Gully. The light shining down on him provides a power unlike anything he has ever had access to. Two bolts of lightning stream through the air and burst through the chests of twenty Demon Warriors charging towards the gate. Arrows rain down in the gully. Overhead, the flying beasts serving Gallus dive down at the wall defenders manning the defenses above the main gate. Armored bodies crash down from the heights above. Flying beast fall as well. The area in front of the gate fills with carnage.

Fendril battles one on one with his brother as Lilith uses her magic to shield the Demons in the Gully from the human arrows and stones falling from above. She takes to flight and lands on the ridge overhead. Screams of dying men fill the air before bodies begin raining down on the Demon Hordes. Each falling body becomes a projectile of its own.

Thadius picks up a discarded sword from one of the fallen Knights from the walls above. The human longsword looks like a small dagger in his hand. He attacks over and over again striking the shining armor and blade of his foe. The battle seems evenly matched before Fendril fanes a retreat. He steps back before spinning away from a stabbing attack. His hand grasps onto his foes sword hand before slashing down with his own blade.

Thadius screams in the air as his sword hand falls to the

ground still clutching a golden Celestial Blade. He falls to his knees and braces himself with the small human sword. Fendril kicks the blade from hand while grasping his enemy by the neck. The screaming intensifies as each wing is sawed away from the bone spurs holding them in place. With a final stroke Thadius's head hits the ground.

Fendril roars in the air and points his sword towards Lilith. She watched the final sword stroke while shrieking like a battle eagle. Her hands extend towards the Gatehouse and send a massive firebolt. Everyone standing on the wall and parapets by the gate are thrown to the ground. Cameron dusts himself off while assessing the damage to the gate.

Where once a steel gate stood, a melted pile of rubble exists. Fendril's voice echoes in the air for all to hear.

"Go Storm Sword! Fall back to the Celestial Door and tell the Queen of Storms what you have seen here. Leave this rabble to me!"

Cameron shakes his head to clear the cobwebs formed by the recent magical blast. He looks back one last time to see an unending line of Demon Warriors charging through the breach in the wall. Knights and Archers retreat into the keep before raising the drawbridge. Cameron is dragged away from the drawbridge by a familiar face. Estee grabs his shoulders and hugs him tight for a brief moment.

"Come on Cam! We need to do what Fendril said! Trust me! We can always use the Celestial Door to come back once things play out here!"

**

I usher Cam up the stairs towards the tower containing the Celestial Door. He seems reluctant to leave the battle.

"We can't just leave Fendril out there by himself Estee!"

I look him in the eyes and nod my head incredulously.

"Yes we can! He can handle himself. The dude has freaking wings and magical powers! I think he knows what he's doing!"

Cam looks at me before explaining his logic.

"You didn't see what happened out there! The Sky Gods are helping Gallus! Fendril killed one of them. Chopped off his wings then cut off his head. There's another Sky god out there with a long ass spear who blew up the entire gatehouse with a flick of her wrist! He needs our help!"

I keep shoving him up the stairs. When we reach the top chamber containing the Celestial Door, there are piles of foul creatures lying dead inside of the tower. Fred is kneeling beside a wounded woman.

"Get over here Estee! The Princess is hurt!"

I run forward and place my hand over a large blood stain covering the Princess's stomach. Her breath is shallow, but I can feel my magic restoring her wound. Each pulse of healing magic that flows from my hand weaves torn muscle and flesh back together.

"Adrianna, can you hear me?"

Her eyes open before she winces in pain and grabs a wound that I hadn't seen on the back of her head. I place my palm over the wound and close the gash on her skull. Her hair is matted in dried blood when I finish.

"You need to come with us!"

We are interrupted by the King entering the tower with his three Centurians in tow. He doesn't even take the time to check on his daughter before insisting that I open the Celestial Door.

"Open the door! The battle is lost! The King must not perish here!"

Cameron makes a sarcastic joke that makes the Princess smile as I cradle her head.

"Dude's talking in third person now... That's probably not

good!"

The King's voice is raised and nervous. Before I can object, The Celestial Door opens without my doing anything. A man dressed in black armor bearing the crest of the Storm Tower walks through with two other Knights dressed similarly.

I can't help but feel nervous as Commander Brutus glances in my direction.

"I see that you have changed your sigil Commander?"

He smiles at the statement.

"I have seen fit to serve the Queen of Storms! She is kind and just, and she puts the wellbeing of her people above her own safety!"

The King scoffs at the statement!

"Get out of the way Commander! The day is lost. We must retreat to the Storm Tower!"

Marcus Brutus stares at the man that he once called King. A man that if the rumors were true, was his father!

"Go then King Nero. I shall stay here and defend the keep! The enemy surely surrounds this fortress, and hope might be fading, but I will stand and fight with the men who remain!"

It's hard to believe the words that I'm hearing. I feel a sudden wave of selfishness fill my words.

"But you serve the Queen now! How can you serve her if you die here!"

Marcus smiles wide before pointing behind him. Through the Celestial door a line of marching Shield Bearers stream through and down the stairs towards the battlements overlooking the Demon army filling the courtyards below. As they march they all hum a song that I vaguely recognize. Each one is holding spear and shield close to their chest.

"The Queen has ordered me to hold this fortress even if the

King decides to flee!"

He glances in the direction of King Nero waiting for his turn to use the Celestial Door. The King and his former Commander make eye contact before more words are spoken.

"Seems the Queen knows the content of the King's true character!"

King Nero scowls at the comment.

"You are a fool to remain Commander Brutus! The battle is lost. None can stand against the magic of Gallus and his allies. Even the Sky Gods have taken his side during this battle!"

Marcus spits on the ground in front of the King before looking at his Centurians.

"Will you three stay and help me defend the keep?"

Each one nods their head and moves away from the King's side.

"Traitors! You swore to protect the rightful King of the Kingdom of Plenty! I should have you all put to the sword when next we meet!"

Joan looks at the King before speaking.

"No true King would abandon his people to save himself. You are no True King, and I will not serve a man who would not risk death to protect his people!"

The King spits in the direction of his once protectors before walking alone through the Celestial Door. I say one last goodbye to Marcus just in case this is the last time we see one another.

"Goodluck Marcus! I hope we see each other again!"

I stand on my tippy toes to reach higher. We share a quick but passion filled kiss. Cameron's face breaks into a wide grin. Even Fred seems taken back by my action. I look back one last time before walking through the glowing stone surface of the magic portal. I then do something I haven't done since before my

father died. I ask the Creator to protect my handsome friend!

CHAPTER 18

The Queen is waiting anxiously on the other side of the Celestial Door leading back into the Storm Tower. King Nero is standing by the doorway, yelling accusations and claims of abandonment into the side of Ruth's face.

"Hold your tongue for a moment King Nero!"

The Queen shoots the angry man a sharp look before approaching Estee and I. Her eyes show surprise upon identifying Fred in his human form walking behind us.

The Queen looks distressed. Her eyes are shiny as if she is holding back a wave of tears. She only says one word.

"John…"

We all stand confused as the Queen of Storms clenches her fists and screams into the air. Fred rushes forward to console his mother. At the touch of her hand he is thrown backwards by a rush of energy. Every bird surrounding the City of Light instantly takes to flight forming a storm of black and yellow.

The Queen closes her eyes as if she is speaking to them all at once. I can see that Estee understands what Ruth is doing. She turns to me to explain.

"She's asking the friendly creatures to search for her husband in this realm."

I still don't quite understand why all of this is happening. The sun will be going down soon, and although we are safe in the Storm Tower, I can't help but fixate on Fendril's fate outside the gates of Stonepass. Those thoughts are quickly dissipated when the Queen lets out a terrified shriek.

Estee grasps her in one arm while grabbing my hand. I can feel the pulsating energy of Ruth's Lightning about to explode out of her body. I take the magical waves of energy and dissolve them as they occur. I can see that Estee is also feeling pain during the wailing of the Queen of Storms. She whispers into the distraught Queen's ear.

"Tell me Ruth, what's wrong? We're right here to help you through whatever is happening!"

The Queen snaps her pained gaze from the ceiling to me and Estee. Her eyes are as bright and captivating as the Northern Lights in the Real World. I tilt my eyes down to escape the pain and rage I feel when looking into them.

"He's gone! John is no more!"

Estee turns to me with a terrified look on her face as a small bird chirps from the window.

"John's statue was in pieces at your shrine! I forgot to tell you! He was killed in Fort Worth! I didn't think anything of it because Kevin told us he burst into a ball of light like Fred did. We all assumed he would just show up back here in Guardian form like your son did! The birds just found his statue destroyed beside your alter!"

I think back to the last time that I saw John. There was something different in his eyes when he last spoke to me.

"You don't need me anymore Cam! You got people around you now that are far more powerful than I am. I'll be seeing you soon kid!"

He said the words just before leaving with Kevin to sabotage some computer server. At the time I brushed it off as him being worried about going on a mission with Kevin. Now I can't help but wonder if he knew something, but was afraid to tell me."

The Queen eases her assault on the senses before releasing the grip of her fingers on her own flesh and moving to speak with her son.

"Your father is gone Fred! It is just you and I now who must protect the boy!"

Fred seems to take the news in stride. He nods his head while gripping his mother tightly and staring out the window behind her.

"I felt something when I changed back into this form mother. A warmth unlike anything I've ever felt! Was that the moment my father left us?"

The Queen nods her head while grasping onto each cheek of her grown son and looking him in the eyes.

"It was his lifeforce that maintained your Guardian form in this realm. When he passed, the spell of protection that he cast over you as a child was removed. At last I can look upon my son's face as it should be."

The Queen does her best to smile through the pain of her loss. Her eyes shift away from us and come to rest on King Nero. His daughter stands beside him while gripping tightly onto his arm.

"You must not fear me Adrianna, I have kept tabs on you ever since you were born Princess."

Adrianna bows in respect before stepping to the side of her father and releasing the grip that she had on his arm.

"I am thankful that you have allowed us to enjoy the safety of your Tower my Queen!"

King Nero physically pushes past the grateful words of his daughter. He is angry. My instincts take over and I quickly step between the King's angry words and Ruth. He is taken back by my action.

"You presume to lay your hands on me Centurian? Move aside boy and let the rulers of this Realm speak to each other!"

I stand my ground taking a step toward the King. My hand reaches down for my sword handle. King Nero steps back while looking at my hand.

"How dare you bare steel against me Centurian! You are Sworn!..."

I cut off the statement that everyone in the room can see is coming.

"I serve the Queen, not you King Nero! With respect, you have proven to me over the last few days that you are not worthy of loyalty."

I see the Princess's eyes on me and lower the intensity of the accusations of cowardice I would very much like to scream at him. Her gaze lessens the anger in my words, and I decide to stay my tongue and let the Queen handle the rest of the encounter.

The Queen taps me on the shoulder. I turn and see a small grin on Ruth's face. She leans forward and whispers into my ear.

"I'm your protecter kiddo, not the other way around. Don't worry, I can split this man in half with a flick of my wrist."

I suddenly remember that Ruth is nothing like her sister. She is a warrior first and foremost.

"You are welcome to shelter with us here in the Storm Tower King Nero! You will be treated with respect and dignity by all my people moving forward."

Ruth turns her face and gives me a stern look. I nod my head and take two steps back arriving beside Estee and Fred. Fred gives me a covert pat on the back while his mother continues to speak to the King.

"Furthermore, as you have already seen with your own eyes... I have dispatched every fighting man at my command to defend Stonepass..."

She pauses and changes her tone.

"To help Commander Brutus hold the keep at Stonepass!"

The King scoffs at the words.

"They will not be able to hold the keep against the hordes of Gallus. The battle is lost, and like you just said… You have now dispatched the remainder of your fighting men into a death trap. This is folly Queen of Storms!"

The Queen shakes her head and places her hand on the King's shoulder. She turns his body and begins guiding him towards the window looking out over her city. His eyes brighten when he looks upon what is below. The city is safe, and the damage done during the Siege has disappeared. Small groups of people are training with shield and spear.

"I have asked my people for volunteers to replenish the soldiers lost during the siege. There were too many to count. Even the women of this city volunteered to fight against the coming darkness. Do you wish me to believe that the people of the Kingdom of Plenty would be unwilling to take up arms to save themselves?"

The King shakes his head.

"The men that serve me are all stuck in Stonepass! How should we spread the word to the people of my Kingdom? There is only one man that could rally the people! But we are not on good terms! He has spread false propaganda to the people in his territory about me! He calls me a 'Coward'!"

The Queen looks back at me and Estee before speaking to the King at a volume that we can't hear. Whatever she says to him changes his entire attitude.

"Truly? Is that even possible?"

The Queen points to the west while clarifying her plan. King Nero begins shaking his head up and down while listening to the soft words coming out of Ruth's mouth. He nods his head and bows one last time before leaving the room. His daughter smiles in my direction while following behind her father and a small entourage.

Fred joins his mother at the window overlooking the City of Light.

"If father isn't here... Where is he?"

Ruth points towards the sky.

"He was a good man. His heart was pure, and he always held faith that the Creator would receive him in the Kingdom of Light when his life expired. I too believe he is there!"

"I've been there mother! Can I go and speak to him there? Cameron can guide me through the door!"

Fred looks over at me with hope in his eyes.

"Or maybe I can just bring him back through the Celestial door?"

The Queen raises her hand up to stop the unfiltered words spewing from her son's mouth.

"The residents of the Creator's Kingdom cannot leave. They are forbidden from interfering within the Realms of the Creator, lest they be cast down like the 'Fallen,' but not to the Realms of man... Those who have gained residence in the Kingdom of light, and choose to break the rules, are cast into the nest of despair! A place created by Gallus himself. Those who enter that place are tortured by their own regret and failures for eternity."

I can see from across the room that Fred is still trying to think of a way to bring back his father.

"You must let it go Fred!"

The young man's facial features harden upon hearing his mother's words.

"Not until I know that he's okay!"

Fred's eyes lock onto mine.

"Will you take me there Cam?"

I nod my head and point towards the Celestial Door. Before

speaking, I decide to pull out the gold coin and flip it end over end, catching it in my palm.

"Whenever you want buddy! Say the word!"

The Queen steps in between me and her son before speaking to both of us.

"You shall see your father again, but not now Fred! I forbid you from leaving the Storm Tower without my permission! That goes for all of you standing in this room. Except you Simeon!"

A Little man folding the Queen's laundry looks to his ruler expressing a posture filled with surprise. He then points back at his own chest while realizing that the Queen was actually speaking to him..

"That's good my Queen! My wife would not like me to be absent from our home overnight! She is a jealous woman, and the Queen… You… Are most beautiful!"

He smiles and bows before grabbing a bucket and mop on his way out of the Throne Room.

"Estee, take Cameron into the Queen's chamber and prepare him for the long sleep! The sun will soon disappear behind the Breathing Mountains! I will watch over you tonight so that my son can be well rested for tomorrow's journey!"

I glance over at Fred. His eyes haven't stopped venturing in the direction of the Celestial Door since finding out his father might be in the land of the Creator.

"Snap out of it Dude! I promise to take you there as soon as your mother…"

I stop and readjust my words.

"The Queen… Decides to let us go!"

Fred nods his head at me and begins to move in the same direction that Estee is now dragging me. We all remove the soot covered armor from our bodies. Simeon enters the Queen's bedchamber and places each set of dirty armor inside of a closet beside the entryway.

I turn my back so that Estee can put on a pair of silken pajamas folded and placed for her on the bed. I can see the reflection of her womanly shape dancing in the shadows being cast onto the floor. I pull on a set of pinstriped pajama pants as a breeze coming through the window reminds me of the coming cold season in Cydonia.

Fred is shameless in his naked appearance. I avoid staring directly at his dangle before commenting.

"Dude, cover your twig and berries! There's a lady present!"

Fred suddenly realizes that Estee has a full view of him while changing. He yanks up a black pair of shorts before raising his hands in the air and apologizing to the room.

"My bad guys! I forgot I wasn't wearing underwear!"

Estee turns her body and shakes her head at Fred while admiring his muscular body.

"You seriously don't work out?"

She smiles wide while tracing the lines of his stomach muscles up and down.

"I don't buy it! Your one of those dudes who wakes up before everyone else and does like a thousand sit ups, then goes back to sleep so that he can say he doesn't work out! Right?"

Fred grabs a folded blanket from the edge of the bed and lays it on the floor in front of an empty fireplace. A neat set of logs is placed in the center of the firebox.

"You want me to give it a light Fred-O?"

He turns and looks at me with a sullen face.

"You know I hate that name Cameron!"

I walk over towards the stone fireplace. A small ball of fire covers my fingers before streaming into and around the dry wood in the firebox. The evident crackle sound of burning wood fills the Queen's chamber. Fred leaves the room before reappearing with a fur bear rug. He replaces the blanket on the floor and lays down on his back. His head rests on the snarling head of a massive brown bear. A smile creeps onto his face.

"You think your pretty clever for finding a rug with a built in pillow, aren't you Fred!"

He glances over at me and smiles even wider.

"I thought you might like that!"

I toss aside a thick fluffy comforter to the protest of Estee who is already warming up underneath it.

"Hurry up Cam! You're letting all the warm air out!"

I lay down and tuck the edge of the comforter under my right side and buttocks. I then charge my fire magic at the lowest level I can muster. The air under the blanket warms as the gap in Estee's lips split into a smile.

"That feels good! Just try not to light the blankets on fire Cam!"

The light coming through the tower windows dims one last time, replaced by total darkness. Estee is snoring loudly for a good ten minutes before I feel tired enough to close my eyes and fall asleep. I take one last look at Fred sleeping beside the fireplace. While I watch his chest rise and fall with each breath, a deep voice whispers in my ears.

**

When I wake in the Real World, Estee is no longer in the Panic Room bed beside me. Bernie is also missing, and the lights of the room are flickering in and out. I yell out after two failed attempts to sit up by myself.

"Not cool guys! You forgot the crippled boy in the Panic Room!"

Estee appears in the short hallway with a piece of toast clasped in between her teeth.

"Chill out! I was starving. You didn't wake up for a while! What were you doing in Cyadonia?"

I try to remember why it took me so long to fall asleep in the Dream World.

"I don't know.."

I think hard before remembering a small voice inside of my head. A voice that began speaking to me while I watched firelight dance over the resting body of Fred.

"I can't really explain it! But I heard a voice in my head. It said that I needed to stay close to the ones I trust…"

I see the expression on Estee's face shift. She has a nervous look about her before revealing her own secret.

"I think I heard a voice in my head too!"

I can see that Estee is contemplating if she wants to tell me her secret.

"Just freaking tell me! I already told you about the voice I heard… If you can't trust me, who the hell are you ever going to be able to trust?"

I can see the struggle going on behind her eyes. The debate rages internally before a victor is crowned.

"Fine… I did something that I haven't done in a long time! I prayed!"

From what I know about Estee, this is a big deal.

"Okay… give me the details. Who, what, when…"

She looks at me and slides her hands under my frail body. My butt cheeks find the familiar feel of their rightful place on top of the wheelchair pad. Estee moves to the back of my rolling chair.

"Keep talking Estee! Walk and Talk! Who, what, when…"

Estee pushes my wheelchair through the narrow hallway leading back to the main concourse of the bunker complex.

"Fine, I asked the Creator to protect 'Someone'... And after I said the words I felt a warmth rush over me, and a small light came from my fingertips..."

I listen as Estee explains her experience before leaving the battle at Stonepass. I have a million questions. As if she can read my mind, Estee speaks up in a controlling tone.

"I'll give you two questions Cam. Use them wisely!"

I think carefully about how to use my two questions.

"Who did you ask the Creator to protect?"

"Commander Brutus! Last question kid!"

I begin smiling. I wish that I could turn my head and show Estee the joy that her embarrassment is bringing me.

"The 'Dreamy' Commander huh? He looked like a total 'Badass' walking through the Celestial Door in his black armor and unshaven face. And then all those soldiers marched through humming a battle song. Shivers, I got shivers down my whole body watching it! Dude is a hero of mine now! Sure made King Nero look like a real 'Pansy Ass'...!"

I wish that I could see the look on Estee's face. I imagine she is reliving the moment herself, and I would have been able to gauge her affection for the Commander by watching how high her lips curled up when I described his arrival at Stonepass.

"One more question Cam, better make it good!"

I purse my lips while thinking about what I want to ask.

"What did the Creator say back... After you asked him to protect your 'Boyfriend'?"

"He's not my Boyfriend! And I'm not sure I want to tell you that!"

I immediately remind her of the deal!

"You said two questions! You never said some questions were off limits! Now tell me what he said!"

There is silence while Estee pushes me down the hallway lined with ferns and other potted plants. She stops pushing before we reach the kitchen and walks in front of my chair to look at me.

"He said that only I can decide the fate of the Commander. Then his voice got really serious... You've met him!"

"Yeah, I've spoken with him. I have some reservations about the way he runs things, but I got a really profound sense of 'Goodness' when he spoke in that deep voice of his."

"Exactly! Well, his voice deepened before he said that the fate of both realms will rest in the decisions that you and I make. Then he said that the choice to serve the light is one that we must make every day... I can't explain it, but I think I had a vision or something while he was talking to me."

I'm intrigued by the end of her statement.

"You mean like... The future?"

Estee moves back behind me and begins pushing the wheelchair again.

"Oh come on! You can't leave me hanging like that! What did you see Estee? Did it seem real?"

"I sure hope not Cam. It was a pretty dark vision, and you already used up your two questions."

I wish with every fiber of my body that I could turn my head and flash my manipulative puppy dog eyes. I really want to know what she saw! Her gaze is distant, and I'm pretty sure she is reliving the vision as we roll down the hallway.

Estee looks down the hallway as she pushes the wheelchair, but her mind is on other things. She is reliving the vision. On either side of her the hallway is covered in a deep lightless mist. Black shadows in the shape of humans appear and disappear in the moving fog.

Fred and Cameron are dressed in battle attire. Each one is

holding a sword covered in blue flame. They're running away from something until a creature unlike any Demon I have ever seen blocks their path. The beast is ten feet tall with ember eyes. Its horns hook in three full circles and its feet are made of cloven hoof. It holds a large club in one hand and a thin whip in the other.

Its armor is blacker than the night sky, and its exposed skin looks wet to the touch. Small rounded scales cover its body, but its face and head are covered in a featureless black mist.

Cam and Fred fight tooth and nail to defeat the creature. The Demon is covered in wounds before it finally falls to the ground. Out of breath, Fred slices off the monster's head before taking a knee. Cameron too seems out of energy, and for some reason he wasn't using his magic to fight off the evil creature. They both remain still as a group of chasing enemy Demon Warriors surround them with blades in hand.

The vision fades before her eyes clear and the black mist is no longer lining the hallway. This is the first time that Estee has ever felt such a vivid vision in the Real World. She pushes the chair faster, trying to get the vision out of her mind. The thought that Cam and Fred were alone and surrounded by Demon blades, makes her stomach cramp in anxiety.

"You still with me back there?"

"Yeah, I'm here! It's probably not the future or anything. I've never seen anything in Cyadonia or the Real World like the environment the vision takes place in! Either way. I don't want you to be worrying about something that's probably just my overreaching imagination..."

"Fine, but we should make a pact to tell each other everything! I think that the Creator is talking to us for a reason! You and I are a team Estee! You need to start acting like it!"

When we reach the command space, Bernie is using one finger to type a command into one of Robbie's computers. A small red light in the center of the room is flashing. Estee inquires as to the purpose of the warning light.

"What's that all about?"

Bernie is startled for a moment before responding.

"Geesh... You guys rolled up on me all silent, and scared me! I need to put a bell on you or something!"

Estee slaps the old man on the back before asking her question again.

"Anything we should be worried about? Should I be grabbing a rifle or something Bernie?"

"Nope, no need to fret. Robbie and the weird kid tripped the motion sensors near the highway. They've been driving around all night long to make sure that nobody is following them back to basecamp!"

The red light is deactivated by whatever command Bernie just finger poked into the computer. His inability to type using multiple fingers brings a smile to my face. I can see that Estee is amused with his lack of technical abilities as well.

One poke at a time, he deliberately enters what seems like a fifty digit security code to open the surface ladder hatch.

"They'll be down here in a few minutes! Robbie always likes to wipe down that stupid black car of his after every trip! Waste of time if you ask me, but he never does!"

Estee leaves the room before returning with a bagel smeared with cream cheese. She feeds me small chunks of the bread and chive and onion spread before placing a straw to my mouth. I suck in a long gulp of milk and swallow hard. Whatever magical fix she has made to my throat seems to be permanent.

I thank her after she wipes my lips and face with a wet towel. We can all hear a commotion coming from somewhere in the bunker. Two voices are arguing over trivial matters in a volume that suggests there is no lack of passion coming from either debater.

"There's no way you think 'Return of the Jedi" is better than 'Empire' Dude!"

Kevin's voice picks up to explain his reasoning.

"Sure I do! It's like this Robbie... I always think that the last movie in a series is the best one, because the story gets wrapped up and I get to feel a sense of closure. Whenever I'm watching one of the middle movies in a long series, I'm always sitting there nervous that it's going to end. Then it does, and none of the plot points have played out. I hate that feeling of wondering what's coming next!"

We all hear a loud scoffing of the explanation at the tip of Robbie's lips. They both enter the control room to greet us.

"Hey guys! What did we miss?"

Robbie crashes down on a swivel chair and does a full circle with his head laying back before responding to my question.

"Not a whole lot... You know just an average day. Had to break this one out of jail, then drive around all night so that my dad will trust that I know how to spot a 'Follow' car! What's new with you guys? How was the Dream Land? Did you guys get to see your Guardian? Kevin saw him go up in a puff of bright light and go back to the other place!"

Estee looks over at Robbie and shakes her head.

"No, he didn't exactly show up there. Unfortunately, his Stone Form was destroyed during the siege of the City of Light. There was no body waiting for him when his soul returned to Cyadonia."

I can see the look on Kevin's face shift from emotionless fatigue into real concern.

"Wait... If he isn't there, where did he go?"

"Ruth thinks he went to the Creator's Kingdom."

Kevin squints his eyes before coming to a conclusion in his head.

"But that would mean that he's dead! Wouldn't it?"

Estee steps forward to explain the full situation. She tells the story of the developments in Cyadonia from her perspective. It feels weird to look around the room and realize that none of my Guardians are present to hear the morning update. I listen to every detail of her story while trying to remember where I was at and what I was doing during each part of her journey.

When she's done talking, I tell my side of the story. The two tales interweave at the end, and I decide that Estee's retelling was sufficient.

"And here we are now! Other than the whole John thing... How did the mission go? Did you get what we needed?"

I look over at Robbie. He's still deep in his own thoughts processing the information divulged by Estee.

"Did you get what you needed Robbie? Earth to Robbie!"

He snaps out of the daydream after shaking his head.

"Yeah, let me pull up the worm program Kevin and John installed in the "Cinatas Solutions" mainframe!"

Robbie sets his feet against the table in front of his chair and pushes off. He glides on shaky wheels until crashing into the counter holding twenty laptops. His nimble fingers send a symphony of clicking into my ears. I look over at Bernie and imagine how long it would take him to enter the commands that his son just completed in the blink of an eye.

His eyes move from each dialog box popping up with every tagline search he is running in the Cinatas mainframe.

"Holy crap! These guys are into everything! They're running guns and ammo all over the globe. They're even sending anti-drone weaponry to Ukraine, while also providing military drones to Russia at the same time! Talk about playing both sides!"

I decide to focus Robbie's attention to any relevant facts about our current situation.

"Anything in there about Estee or Me? Or anything about Cyadonia or Gallus?"

Robbie leans forward while typing in a myriad of search functions.

"Nothing about you guys specifically, but there is a ton of security functions protecting a file called 'Celestial Doorway, Operation Coming Storm'... You said something about a Celestial Door when you were talking about the other place!"

He looks at Estee before displaying the file folder on the main screen. I look up and stare at a picture of a temple somewhere on earth called Puma Punku. At the bottom of the screen is a tagline that reads ' Puma Punku, Bolivia. The picture displays a stone doorway very similar in size and shape to the ones that Estee and I have seen while traveling the Celestial Road in Cyadonia. Even the markings surrounding the stone door look familiar.

I look at Robbie one last time before shifting my gaze to Estee. We both recognize what we are all looking at. Estee nods her head at me as if she's giving me permission to make a big reveal. Her lips are spread into a wide smile as I begin to speak. Burt enters the room rubbing his eyes. Clutched tightly in one hand is his sketch book with a charcoal pencil trapped in the binding. I say a quick hello before redirecting everyone's attention to the information on the screen.

"You guys aren't going to believe this, but I think that doorway could lead us to Cyadonia!"

CHAPTER 19

We all sit around scouring the internet for more information about the Ancient Ruins that were documented in Cinatas Solutions' secure files. There isn't much more to find though. Keven at one point just abandoned the search and began doing a deep dive into short video clips taken from a history channel show about aliens. He seems convinced that there is some truth to the stories contained within the show's storytelling.

Robbie makes fun of Kevin for the better part of two hours. Those two seem to have bonded during their time spent running from the long arm of the law. Bernie has fallen asleep in his chair. Estee and Burt are sitting across from him trying to throw pieces of microwave popcorn into his mouth without waking him. Every giggle I hear precedes a tally mark on the white board under one of their names.

Bernie doesn't notice. He even started chewing the popcorn and swallowing in his sleep. He must be having a pretty weird dream right now.

"If he chokes on that damn popcorn, and wakes up, I'm gonna rat you two out faster than you can run away."

Robbie points at Estee. She doesn't seem deterred by his warning. Burt on the other hand swivels his computer chair and goes back to the drawing he started working on this morning. He gave me a few peeks at the scenery in the newest edition of "Dream Warrior." Looks like he is going to be introducing a new hero into the story. Estee is finally going to make her first appearance in the series.

"Hey Burt, I'm gonna need to approve all visual depictions in that episode! I don't want you making my butt and chest all cartoonishly big like most of you graphic artists seem prone to do!"

"I don't do that... I like the look of the real female form Estee! And of course you can take a look! Come check out what I got so far!"

Estee puts a handful of popcorn back into a plastic bowl before sliding her chair next to Burt.

"Wow, Burt, this looks really good man! I can't wait to spend the money we make from this thing. I got my eye on a really nice Armored Personnel Vehicle. Some Russian Ex Pat is selling one just outside Dallas. I've had my eye on that baby for two years now!"

Burt grins while shading in the background of a battle scene in which Estee and Commander Brutus are riding down entire formations of Demon warriors inside of the City of Light.

"Don't spend the money before you get it! Wait till it burns a hole in your pocket at least!"

"What the heck is that supposed to mean? You sound like an old man!"

Burt hardens the outline surrounding the Commander's chin line in the battle scene. His hard pencil stroke makes the Commander's facial features look fierce.

"Sorry, I always forget that you kids these days don't get all the parables and folksy 'Sayings' that my grandpa and my dad used to throw at me when I was your age."

"How old are you Burt?"

Burt stops drawing. He seems to be counting in his head.

"Damn, I'm forty three now! Forty three and all on my own!"

He fakes a sad face while looking at Estee. She seems to understand the sarcasm in his statement. He then smiles wide.

"I'm alone with all my MONEY!"

Burt begins laughing maniacally like a supervillain. He rubs his palms together and leans back in his chair. Estee lifts her foot with a sullen look on her face. Burt starts falling backwards before she reaches out with lightning fast reflexes and pushes his feet back down towards the floor.

The supervillain grin on Burt's face is now replaced with a look of panic. Estee has her own giggle while enjoying the new look on the Artist's face. He sticks his tongue out before exchanging the pencil in his hand for a different one. Laying on the table is a pouch filled with close to twenty different pencils. Each one is slightly different. Some have flat edges for shading, while others have angled points at varying degrees.

There are various shades of charcoal as well, and at least two or three of the pencils look to be white.

"What are the white ones for?"

Estee points at a stack of three white pencils.

"I like to use those to blend different shades of charcoal. They make it easier to make it look like there's depth to a certain part of my scenery. Like making a cloud look dimensional, or topping a rolling wave to look like there is frothy foam on the surface."

Burt reaches into a bag beside him. His hand reveals a vintage lunch box. Embossed on the aluminum top is the picture of the Teenage Mutant Ninja Turtles. The box is worn, and I suspect that it contains some sort of sentimental value.

He swings up the lid and places the box below Estee's eyes. Inside are about a hundred colored pencils and pens. Each one looks old. The label along the cylinder of each pen has been rubbed almost entirely away by frequent skin contact. He closes the box and places the tin back into his backpack. I can tell from feet away that Estee wants to ask more questions, but the look on Burt's face suggests that he is done with show and tell.

Estee looks over at me and points down at her watch.

"What do you think Cam? We still got enough 'Sleepy Juice' to take a long trip to Cyadonia tonight. We might need it with what Ruth is sending us to do!"

Bernie wakes himself up after snorting loudly and rocking forward in his chair.

"What did I miss?"

Estee rotates my wheelchair and speaks in Bernie's direction.

"We're gonna go and lay down now! I need you to inject us with the last of the 'Sleepy Juice' that Ruth took from the 'Loony Bin'!"

The old man shakes his head while trying to shake the cobwebs of sleep from his mind.

"Not a chance! I hate needles! Robbie… You're up kid!"

Robbie types a command into his laptop before jumping up and slamming down the screen of his machine.

"I'm right behind you!"

Estee grabs the backpack that Kevin has been carrying around with us since leaving the Institute. Inside is the last vial of sedatives we plan on using to dream through the afternoon and through the night. We have lots to do in Cyadonia.

**

When we wake in Cyadonia Fred is still snoring on the floor. The flames in the fireplace are gone, replaced with red hot coals dying with each passing second. Estee arrives a couple minutes after I do. We both quietly crawl out of bed and walk towards the closet containing our armor. To our surprise the closet is empty.

We both look at one another.

"Someone took our armor?"

After Estee asks the obvious question, we both notice a weird sound coming from the Throne Room. The Queen's servant is dragging two heavy sacks behind him as he moves in our direction.

"Simeon? Is that you?"

"Oh thank the Sky Gods! I didn't know how much farther I could drag these things!"

I rush forward and pick up one of the large burlap bags. It isn't as heavy as the little man made it out to be.

"That one is for you Storm Sword! Compliments of the Queen! The other one is yours Estee!"

We both open the burlap bags to find matte black sets of armor. Adorning the breastplate of each set of magical armor is the sigil of the Queen of Storms. The emblem consists of a black tower surrounded by storm clouds and blue mist.

We both help each other clasp the armor locks running down our rib cage. The rest we can clasp on our own. Estee looks at me and nods her head in approval. She too looks fierce in her new armor. After getting fully dressed and making a small amount of noise, Fred begins to stir from his slumber. He finally gives in to the need to wake up, before rolling over onto his side facing the fireplace.

"What time is it?"

I stroll over in his direction and stand in the moonlight coming from a window in the Queen's chamber.

"It's still late! Robbie gave us the last of the injectable sedative so that we can have more time in Cyadonia today."

Fred groans before sitting up and looking for his armor. Simeon enters the room dragging one more sack of armor.

"This one is for you Prince Fred! The Queen of Rain ordered me to make for her Centurians new magical armor before she was taken. I saw fit to change the Sigil for our new Queen! May the old return one day as well!"

We all smirk after hearing the word Prince in front of Fred. He seems unsure of the title himself, but by all accounts he is now a Prince in his own right. Part of me is starting to wonder who's... Who's "Guardian" now.

Simeon's voice breaks through the cloud of thought that my mind is trapped inside.

"If you will all follow me... The Queen of Storms has asked that I provide you with the swords that she has blessed."

We walk into the Throne Room behind Simeon. His strides are short, so it's easy to keep up. He points towards the wooden table at the far side of the room. On top of the surface are three swords of similar design. One is longer than the others. Obviously meant for Fred since he's a good foot taller than either me or Estee.

"Pick them up and feel the balance and power within your new weapons of war!"

I reach forward after Estee nods her head at the sword in the middle. The handle is wrapped in a black leather material. The blade is made from a metal that contains small waves of black and silver. The edge of the blade is shiny and sharp to the touch. I lick away the blood that comes to the tip of my finger after testing the sharpness.

There's something else about the weapon that feels different from my former blade. I channel a small amount of my lightning magic into the sword handle. The edges of the blade begin to glow blue with a fire like quality. Estee seems disturbed by the glowing edge of my sword blade. Fred's blade edge also lights up at his command. It seems to be a strange development.

It makes sense that my blade would channel my electrical magic, but I have never known Fred to possess the ability to control lightning. My mind races. I guess that the concerned look on Estee's face is in response to Fred's newly realized power. *He is the Prince of Storms now! Makes sense he might get a few magical perks with the title change!*

When Estee grips her blackened sword, the edges begin to glow with intense green fire.

"Whoa, why is yours different?"

Fred points at the green flames lining the edge of Estee's sword blade.

"Her most potent magic ability is that of healing. The green fire signifies the balance of nature and growth! Hey Estee... have you ever tried to grow something? Like a bush or a tree?"

Estee stares at the dancing green flames of the sword she is holding.

"Yeah! My wise master used to bring me strawberry plants and make me grow breakfast berries every morning for practice!"

"Figures! She can control not just the regeneration of human flesh and bone... She can also control nature itself! It's a very rare gift! I have only heard of one other person in Cyadonia ever having that particular ability. You knew him as Thoth!"

I immediately recoil after hearing the name. Ever since he was taken I have often wondered about his fate. *Is he dead? Is he a prisoner?* The questions only make me feel anger.

"Thoth? He never told me that!"

I feel a small amount of betrayal rush through my chest. *My own "Wise Master" didn't tell me the one singular thing about himself that I might be able to relate to!*

We all stop talking as the stone surrounding the Celestial Door lights up in bright blue light. The Queen of Storms strolls through the surface of the door with a big smile on her face.

"Where were you?"

Fred steps in front of me to speak directly with his mother.

She strolls right past him and slumps down upon the throne. Her legs stick strait out from the fur lined chair as if she is exhausted.

"I was having a visit with the Creator! Man has like a thousand stairs leading to his Throne! He seriously needs to consider getting an elevator or something!"

Estee looks at me and smiles. We both have experienced that climb. Fred too nods his head at the Queen's words.

"Was he there?"

The Queen kicks off a pair of white shoes before rubbing the arches of each foot with ring adorned fingers.

"Yes Fred, your father is there! The Creator has enlisted John into his Corps of Servants. His new set of wings is far superior to his old set here in Cyadonia."

Fred smiles wide while thinking about his father alive and well.

"Will the Creator let him come back down to Cyadonia and live with us?"

The Queen gives her son a tart look.

"That's not how it works Fred. He's in the Service of the Creator now! He will have to do as he's told, not what he wants! But I trained him well! He will feel right at home taking orders from a superior being!"

The Queen breaks the tension in the conversation with her comment before pointing down at the sword dangling from my hip.

"I see that Simeon has presented you all with my gifts! See that you hold onto those. If they fall into the hands of the enemy... Who knows what kind of weapons Gallus could replicate using the magic template I created within them. Each blade will amplify the magic you channel through them!"

I glance down at the handle of my new blade before the Queen changes the subject.

"In any case... I have fresh horses waiting for each of you at the city gates. You had better get a move on if you are going to reach the Valley by the end of the day. Be careful Young Centurians!"

We all bow before leaving the Throne Room. After floating down a wind filled shaft, we reach the ground with a collective sigh!

"It seemed way safer when the Queen of Rain used to transport me up and down that thing. There is just something about being lifted and lowered with wind. It's really scary!"

We all agree with a sharp head nod. Fred breaks away and runs off towards the temples located in the middle of the city.

"I'll be right back. I just want to grab something from Cam's Shrine! Meet you guys at the gates."

Estee and I continue towards the main gate to the city. By the time we get there, Fred can be seen a hundred meters away running in our direction. Estee climbs up on a white horse with small black handprints lining its wide body in some sort of black paint. I mount the grey and black horse beside hers.

Estee leans forward and begins whispering into the ear of her horse before petting its neck and scratching behind its ears.

"What did you say to him?"

Estee gives me a look before sitting up and thrusting her heels deep into the stirrups attached to the saddle.

"Not much, Just getting to know him. He says that I'm much lighter than his last rider! He is very thankful for that!"

I look down at the back of my horse's neck. After leaning forward I say hello to the majestic creature that I sit upon. The horse clasps her lips and lets out a deep whinny! I look over at Estee who has a smile on her face.

"What did she say?"

Estee chuckles before answering me.

"She says that you are far too small to be a warrior. And she said that you remind her of the princess's servant who used to ride her through the gardens of Stonepass!"

I lean back in the saddle after realizing that my horse is making fun of me.

"Well, you can tell her that I'm a kick ass warrior! And that she smells like goat crap!"

The horse beneath me rears back, sending me tumbling to the ground. I land in a pile of animal dung as Fred approaches and hops up on the black stallion standing beside Estee's horse.

"Great, now we both smell like goat crap!"

The Horse Whinny's one more time before bending her front leg and bowing. I can tell she is mocking me. I decide to end the argument in the only way I know how. After reaching into my satchel, I reveal a large green apple that I had planned on eating on our journey to the Valley of Purgatory. A journey that would be much more comfortable atop a horse that isn't mad at me.

I reach forward with the apple. She seems interested in the deal being struck. Her massive teeth cut the apple in half in one swift biting motion. I quickly imagine the pain that would have come if I had still been holding the apple.

"Are we good now?"

The grey horse trots in place before glancing over at Estee.

"She says that she will try not to throw you off anymore, but that you are so light that she can't really even tell when you are on top of her!"

I look at my horse and scratch the flat spot between her eyes. I can see that she likes the gentle motion of my fingers. Her head moves forward with a soft pressure to receive my affection.

Fred seems confused by the whole interaction.

"What the hell are you guys doing anyways?"

I glance up at the Prince of Storms and point at Estee.

"Apparently she can speak with animals or something!"

Fred looks over.

"Really?"

He moves his horse closer to whisper out of my hearing range.

"Are you just messing with Cam? I will totally go with it if you are!"

"No, I have always been able to talk to and hear the thoughts of some animals here in Cyadonia."

I climb back up onto my horse.

"Her name is Paige if you were wondering Cam!"

I reach down and whisper that it is nice to meet her. Apparently Paige is the leader of this particular group of horses. She bolts away from the front gate. I can barely hold on after the suddenness of her movement. Estee and Fred catch up eventually and the three of us make good time to the first barrier protecting the Breathing Mountains to the west.

Paige instinctually stops before entering each veil of protected space. At each checkpoint Fred dismounts and speaks certain words and magical phrases into the stones indicating the protective magic ahead. Each time he pulls out a small piece of paper that the Queen handed him before we departed.

We travel this way for hours. In just the short time since we were last here, the weather has warmed significantly. It seems that this time around we will not be forced to shelter inside of the Cave of Lost Travelers to escape the cold.

We arrive at a place that feels familiar. Looking down into the Valley brings and uneasiness to my chest. My horse takes the lead again and begins slowly walking down a narrow pathway lined with stone warriors in different states of battle. Some are engaged with foes, while others are ready to throw spears. The same style spear that I watched the Fallen Sky Gods do battle with against Fendril.

We all dismount. Fred points at a singular stone figure pointing his sword in the direction of a wingless statue!

"We should try and wake up a few of the ones with wings! The Queen says that the ones without wings are bad guys! We should be safe if we only wake the good guys to help us!"

I place my hand on the arm of the winged statue. Warm shivers run up my spine as a power flows through my fingers. The warrior wakes in a frenzied way. We all step back and try to make ourselves look small and less threatening.

Before we can speak with the Creator's Servant, he shoots up into the sky in a massive ball of light. I look at Estee and Fred for some sort of explanation.

"What the hell? He didn't even say a thing. Just flew off like nothing happened."

I can't help but smile at the awkwardness of the events of the last few moments.

Fred points at another winged statue while trying not to laugh.

"Maybe that guy will stick around and hear us out?"

I try my luck again. This time I touch the chest of the statue before stepping back and kneeling in front of it. We are all shocked when the warrior kicks me in the chest out of pure reflex. I fly backwards. The flight is shortened when I smash into another stone warrior. My hands grasp the ankle of the stone statue as the Creator's warrior disappears into a ball of light like the last one.

I stand up and gather my wits after watching our potential ally disappear into the cloudy sky. That's when Estee gasps. I turn slowly and look into the ember eyes waking from a deep slumber. The statue I crashed into begins to move. Its hands grasp a long sword before moving to massage the stumps where a set of wings used to exist. Fred jumps in front of me after drawing his sword. I fall backwards and crash into another statue.

Estee quickly helps me back up to my feet. We both look up at the secondary stone warrior that I have just accidentally awakened. Her eyes are red like the lava inside a volcano.

"Quit touching things Cam!"

Fred's voice is shaky and frightened.

"How have I come to be alive again human?"

I raise my hand and point to my palm.

"Yeah, that's probably my fault. I accidentally woke you!"

The Fallen Servant behind us moves to stand next to her brother.

"What should we do with these tiny fleshlings brother?"

Her spear is now pointing at Fred's chest. Estee and I take a step forward and draw our swords. Colored fire dances along each of our blades. I charge a lightning ball in my free hand and wait for the enemy to make a move.

The first attack is devastating. A spearpoint strikes Fred in the chest sending him flying backwards into a clump of yellow flowers. I charge forward beside Estee. Both of the Fallen Servants are smiling as we swing wildly. Each attack is thwarted. It's clear to both of us that we are greatly outmatched.

I put all my strength into a lightning bolt and throw it into the chest of the Fallen Sister. She absorbs the spell like it was Child's Play, and points the tip of her spear at my face. Before her spearpoint splits my nose in half, a strong hand stops the forward movement of the weapon. A bright light accompanies the ally that the creator has sent to aid us.

Fred jumps back into the fight before getting a good look at our savior's face.

"Dad?"

The Winged Warrior attacks with a fervor that inspires me to move forward. Estee and I unleash every ounce of magic we can muster. Our attacks only slightly distract the Fallen warriors, but they are just enough for John to take advantage of the small gaps in their defenses. He slashes through the chest plate of the Fallen Brother before he catches the Sister's spear point and snaps her weapon in half.

I charge forward beside Estee and Fred. We all hack at the armor of our foe. She takes a wound from one of our blades before John thrusts her own captured spearpoint through her neck. A few words exit her mouth sounding more like gurgles than any language I can understand. She lets out one last gurgle before exploding into a ball of light. Her brother also takes his last breath before disappearing.

The smile on John's face is replaced by a look of pure pain. He contorts his body as the wings attached to his back turn into black mist.

"Worth it"

Fred reaches out to hold his father's hand. Before their fingers touch, John's body explodes into a ball of black light. All that remains where he once stood is a pile of armor and black soot.

Fred looks up into the sky and places both of his hands out to his side. The look on his face is one of confusion and pain. His tormented gaze is meant for the Creator himself.

CHAPTER 20

I hear a deep voice in my ears. I glance around the cave to make sure that none of the Shadow People lingering in the dark spaces away from the fire have moved closer. There is nothing next to me. I glance to my side and see that both Estee and Fred are curled up by the fire.

I close my eyes and focus on picturing the Throne Room of the Creator. When I open my eyes I'm suddenly standing in front of a bright light sitting atop a throne.

"Welcome back Cameron! I am glad that you have reached out to me with your heart!"

I look behind me hoping to see John or Fendril. Neither is standing by the long descending staircase.

"Where is John?"

The light surrounding the Creator's body dims slightly, allowing me to squint through the displeasure of looking upon his feet.

"He is no longer in this Realm! He made a choice, and that choice led to his banishment to the 'Shadow Realm'."

I replay the sight of John bursting into a ball of black light.

"But he was just trying to save us? Why would you send him there? He was your Servant, and my Protector! He's on YOUR side!"

The Creator pauses for a brief moment before answering.

"There are rules here Cameron! He chose to interfere in the affairs of men and shadows. I warned him that he must not interfere. The consequences of his choice played out just as I had warned."

The last words that John spoke begin to make sense now. "Worth it."

I stand from the position of kneeling that I had instinctively taken when arriving in front of the Creator.

"But you sent Fendril to fight at Stonepass! You seem to play pretty "Willy Nilly" with your own rules… Don't you? Where I come from, we call that a Hypocrite!"

A slight vibration shakes the ground beneath my feet as a crescendo of thunder fills the air. The Creator's tone shifts as the conversation continues.

"Hold your tongue young man. There are things that you fail to understand about the law of nature surrounding the Realms of Man and Shadow."

I struggle to hold my tongue. I have a million questions, and all I ever seem to get from these conversations with the man with answers, is more questions.

"I'm sorry I called you a 'Hypocrite'… John served the Light his entire existence. He served you and the ones that we thought were the voice relaying your instructions to the people of Cyadonia. How can you be okay with him being in the Shadow Realm?"

"There are many in the Shadow Realm that I wish were here by my side young man, but actions have consequences. For example, you recently woke two of my Loyal Servants from the Valley of Purgatory. Now the gates of Stonepass are being guarded by three of my Arch Servants! The army of Gallus has fallen back to the fortress of Knifespike, and the Demon warriors and Dark priests serving the darkness are afraid!"

I nod my head and smile at the thought of Fendril and two other Celestial warriors kicking butt in front of the tumbled gates of Stonepass.

"Mission accomplished then. That was my intent the entire time before one of those jerks I woke up kicked me into one of the Fallen Servant statues! If you think about it, it was his action that caused the fight that John had to save us from! And if you think about it that way... That dude was definitely on your team... So in turn you were partly responsible for John needing to break the rules!"

I hear a slight rumble in the Creator's throat. *Is he laughing at me?*

"Nice try kid! Though your plan to resurrect my Servants in the Valley was a good one... That choice was yours, and yours alone. But fear not young man. There is a way for you to rescue John!"

I perk up after feeling a ray of hope enter my body.

"Quit speaking in riddles dude! Just tell me how!"

"I can't tell you Cameron, but the answer is close at hand."

I feel a small vibration in my pocket. The small golden coin appears in my palm with the pyramid and snake emblem facing up. For the first time in this conversation I feel a rush of warmth fill my chest while thinking about what I hold.

"So your trying to tell me..."

Before I can finish the question the light in front of me disappears, replaced by the ember glow of the dying campfire. Fred stirs from his nap and wakes in a sudden panic.

"I fell asleep?"

He wipes crusted tear marks away from the corners of his eyes. Watching his father disappear into the Shadow Realm had sapped his strength.

"Don't worry about it dude! Just try and stay awake now. I think I found a way to save your dad from the Shadow Realm!"

The light in Fred's eyes return. He stands up and draws his sword.

"I hope you're right Cam. I don't know if I can live with the thought that he's in that place. You know what they say about the Shadow Realm don't you?"

I nod my head while lowering my eyes.

"Yeah Fred, I know what they say about it! We won't let him stay down there for a moment longer than it takes us to rescue him. I promise!"

As I lay my head down to fall asleep I feel the presence of the Shadow People in the cave gather around my body. Fred powers his sword and steps beside me.

"Stay back!"

The misty figures move back into the depths of the cave as his words echo against the stone walls. I can feel the slight warmth of campfire flames touch my cheeks. My eyes close, destined to open in another place.

**

When I wake up my body is bouncing up and down in the arms of Robbie. Loud noises are echoing down the halls of the bunker. I pick up the distinct sound of shotgun blasts behind us.

Estee is running beside Robbie. In each hand she is holding one of the pistols that normally rest in the holsters on either side of her legs. She looks like the Freaking Tomb Raider!

"What's happening?"

Robbie kicks open a door under a large illuminated sign with a red cross in the center. He rushes into the room and places my body into a wheelchair!

"No time to talk kid! They found us!"

My mind races as Estee begins pushing me down a long darkened hallway leading away from the sounds of battle.

"Where is everyone else?"

"Holding the bad guys back! Anymore dumb questions you'd like to ask?"

When we come to the end of the hallway, Robbie lets go of the rifle in his hand. It dangles from a short strap attached at his shoulder to a black vest. He then begins tapping on a small keypad while whispering a sequence of letters and numbers.

A small door hidden in the wall slides open beside a picture of George Bush Senior. Robbie kisses his palm and places it against the face adorning the mural on his way past. Estee pushes me forward. The door closes behind us. Robbie leads the way with a long green glowstick in hand.

I hold my tongue for as long as I can bear before needing more information.

"Someone tell me what the hell just happened!"

Estee leans forward and begins telling me what happened in the half an hour or so between when she woke up, and when I finally woke up.

"They found us somehow! Robbie thinks that Cinatas Solutions might have followed him and Kevin with a satellite, or Drone, or something that he couldn't see. Bernie is holding off the assault teams with Kevin and Burt so that we can escape!"

"But what about those guys? I never wanted anyone to die for me!"

Robbie looks back at my face.

"Who said anything about dying. My dad knows how to handle himself! He will get Kevin and Burt out to the secondary escape tunnel. We'll all be drinking coffee and eating pancakes together in like two days!"

All of the sound coming from behind us is gone now. Nothing but the sound of dripping water and splashing feet fill my ear canals. We go on this way for a couple of hours before Robbie stops and cracks open a second glow stick. He places the new glow stick against a spot on the tunnel wall before reaching his hand into a hole that I hadn't seen before.

Three loud cracking sounds fill the space before a dirt covered ramp opens up leading the way to the surface.

"They used to drive supplies for the bunker down this tunnel. We are about three miles west of the main entrance to the bunker."

After reaching the surface Estee turns my chair to look back in the direction we came from. Small lines of smoke rise up from the surface. Above the smoldering wreckage of the bunker are no less than five black helicopters flying a circular pattern. Robbie stands beside me looking back at his former home.

"That's a real shame! I was just starting to get comfortable in that place!"

Estee leans against his shoulder.

"The real shame is the fact that your dad will never trust you to lose a 'Tail' ever again!"

Robbie nods after hearing Estee's comment.

"You're right about that! He is never going to let me live this one down!"

As we all watch the fingers of smoke rise into the air I feel a sudden wave of pressure hit my chest. A large fireball rises up into the sky engulfing the circling helicopters. I'm thrown backwards into the dirt. When I recover from the fall, my eyes are locked onto the confused face of Robbie. He shakes his head while sitting back up.

Estee dusts me off after flipping my chair upright and placing me back atop it.

"Dad must have activated 'Zombie' protocol! He detonated the rocket!"

Estee looks over at Robbie.

"I thought you said that the government removed the warhead from that thing?"

"They did! But they didn't remove the fuel! I rigged that think up with enough 'Det Cord' to ignite a gas station!"

Estee begins slow clapping while watching the fireball and smoke cloud rise into the cloudy sky.

"I sure hope they got out of there before that thing went off!"

"I'm sure they did! The detonator pad is at the end of the secondary escape tunnel!"

Robbie begins walking towards a large clump of shrubs. He begins moving chunks of dead branches revealing a tan tarp. Underneath the tarp is a wood paneled station wagon from the 1970's.

"Does that thing even run?"

Estee leaves me behind before inspecting the transportation available. The hood pops open revealing a squeaky clean engine underneath.

"Don't let her skin fool you! I built this baby myself! I left her visible surfaces alone to fool anyone who might be looking for a more reliable getaway car, but underneath the wood paneling she's brand new!"

Robbie slams down the hood of the car before picking me up and placing me in the backseat of the station wagon. I hear the trunk close after my chair is placed inside. The engine roars to life. Robbie wasn't joking. The throaty sound of the purring engine fills me with confidence.

A small trail of dust follows behind the car until we come to the end of a dirt road blocked by a yellow metal bar. On either side of the road are green trees and tall grass. Robbie gets out of the driver's seat. He walks forward and unlocks the padlock holding the gate in place.

Estee begins to say something to me before my eyes see Robbie get hit with something. His body shakes violently before collapsing into the dirt. Two men in camouflage approach holding weapons in hand attached to four silver wires leading to Robbie's chest. Estee tries to get out of the car before the driver's side window shatters. A can of smoke pops after landing on the floor beneath her feet.

I can taste and smell something funny. The yellow substance coming out of the smoke grenade isn't smoke at all. I fight with every ounce of consciousness within me to stay awake, but the effort is all in vain.

**

I wake in a bright white room. I can't remember where or how I went to sleep, but something feels wrong. My memory is fuzzy, and when I try to talk, the words won't come out! My chest feels tight and an anxiety fills my stomach and head.

A familiar woman walks into my room and pulls away the covers. Nurse Bridgette. I know her name, and I can remember that she has been kind to me in the past. She lifts my frail body into the power chair next to the bed and smiles.

"Welcome back Cameron! We missed you while you were away!"

I blink my eyes and rotate my focus across the reader of the voice modulator attached to the chair. Something about the robotic voice that comes from the speaker is alarming.

"What happened? How did I get here?"

The Nurse points towards the door before responding to me. Gentle sunlight fills the room and hallway outside of my door.

"You have an appointment with Dr. Shade and the medical team in ten minutes… It's probably better if they answer any questions you might have."

I activate the power chair controls with my eyes and follow Nurse Bridgette out of the room. She walks forward down the hallway and says hello to some of the other 'Patients' coming out of their rooms for free time. At the end of the dormitory hallway I see a flash of memory. The flash of remembrance is quick, and I only get a short glimpse of a broken pool stick.

I power through the doorway after shaking off the image coming to mind. My eyes make contact with Ms. Stella standing on the far side of the Rec Room. She watches me the entire journey through the room and into the medical hallway leading to Dr. Shade's office. Bridget opens the door and ushers me inside before closing the door behind me. I stop in front of the familiar desk of a man I have known for years.

Beside Dr. Shade are two men dressed in lab coats. Each one has a nametag and credentials associated with some sort of research lab. I can't quite make out the names of the men or the name of the lab printed on their badges.

"Hey Cameron, It's good to see you again! How are you settling back in?"

I'm confused on every level. I have very distinct memories of this place, but nothing about it seems welcoming. It's as if my entire being wants to leave as soon as possible, but I can't remember why. I trace my eyes over the voice modulator.

"Where am I, How did I get here?"

Doctor shade looks at the two men standing next to him before jotting something down on his notepad. He then begins speaking into a voice recorder sitting in between us.

"Patient, Fifteen years old, Suffering from acute memory lapse and Psychotic delusion… Patient seemed disoriented after a medication change. Patient spent two weeks recovering from the chemical imbalance before being transferred back into my care!"

I'm annoyed that the doctor is spending more time speaking into his recorder instead of answering my questions. He seems to see the shift in my eyes.

belly before every medication pass. A voice in my head tells me every time to spit out the oblong pills being placed on my tongue. Nurse Bridgette is very thorough though. She checks my mouth after every pill I swallow to make sure that it's no longer visible.

Time becomes a string of highs and lows. I have many memories of a place that feels almost more real than the place I'm sitting in right now, but the evidence that I'm crazy is too much to ignore. *Maybe I am crazy? Maybe I made up everything about Cyadonia and my friends there because I'm lonely and sad about being stuck in this chair?*

The words of Dr. Shade play over and over again in my head in the couple of hours of clarity I have between medication pass times. "Theres no such thing as Demons Cameron."

Everything he says to me during our daily meeting makes sense, and the medications are making it easier to accept the reality of my situation. *I'm just a crippled boy who needs to think there's something more to life!*

I move my power chair down the hallway. A small line of other kids in wheelchairs roll past me on their way to the gardens outside. I bump into the wall on accident next to the door leading to the Rec Room. A small chunk of paint falls to the floor. A black steak of dried sludge appears on the wall under the missing paint.

Scenes of a battle in this very hallway fill my head for a split second before Ms. Stella sees what I've done and begins yelling at me.

"Now look what you've done you little brat! You think the grounds crew wants to keep painting the walls every time you run into them? Keep it up and I'll be forced to speak to Doctor Shade about revoking your driving privileges."

I turn my eyes up to look at the face spitting the hateful words at me. For only a split second a see a flash of ember inside of each of her eyes. The flash is so short that I can't help but question whether I saw it or not. Before I can make a decision if I'm seeing things or not, I smell the distinct scent of freshly mown grass enter my nostrils.

I power past Ms. Stella after apologizing for hitting the wall. My path is direct. The automatic doors leading to the gardens open in front of me. I breathe in deeply while looking out over the lawn of the Institute grounds. The grass is tall and hasn't been mowed for a good week or so. I drive around the entire perimeter of the building looking for a reason that I smelled what I smelled.

I find nothing in sight to explain what I experienced in the last ten minutes. The air even smells slightly stale and crisp outside. My eyes then find something strange sitting in the parking lot. Something sparks inside of me when seeing two idle black SUV's. My memory flashes back to a scene that must not be real.

As I roll back into the Institute Rec Room, I hear a deep voice inside of my head.

"Follow your heart Young Centurian!"

After hearing the voice, I spot two men in black suits pretending not to be watching me. There is something off about them. Each man has a curly white cord coming out of their ear. I pretend that I don't notice and wheel past them. I go straight to Dr. Shades office. The foot pedals of my chair slam into the bottom of his door. If I could knock like a normal person I would.

The Doctor opens the door and greets me.

"Hey Cameron, is everything okay buddy?"

I roll forward while trying to formulate a response.

"I'm fine, but there are some weird guys outside in black suits that were watching me! I felt really scared when I saw them. Who are they? And why are they watching me?"

Dr. Shade pulls down the sunscreen covering his window.

"I don't see any guys in black suits Cameron! Where were they?"

I ram my chair against the window.

"Over there by the garden entrance!"

The place where the two men were watching me from is empty. Dr. Shade lowers the window screen to block the sun and walks back behind his desk.

"Is this the first time you've seen these 'Men' that are watching you?"

The tone in the Doctor's voice shifts as he sits down and tells me to explain. It becomes apparently clear to me that he doesn't believe me.

"They were out there! You have to believe me!"

The Doctor pushes a button on his desk.

"I believe that... You... Believe that you saw them Cameron. I don't want this setback to worry you kid. I'll adjust your meds to try and find the sweet spot where you stop seeing things that aren't there!"

Ms. Stella enters the office before glaring at me.

"I'm sorry that Cameron decided to disturb you Doctor Shade! I'll take care of this immediately!"

She follows me all the way back to the Rec Room where two men in orderly uniforms wait for us. They lift me out of my Power Chair and place me in a good old fashion wheelchair.

"I told you that I would have to take away your driving privileges if you didn't act right Cameron! The Doctor is not to be disturbed outside of your daily meetings. Do you understand?"

I sit there and stare at her mouth unable to respond. One of the Orderly's rolls me in front of the TV next to the boy that sits on the rug to watch his shows every day. A lump of depression settles in my stomach while watching the show. The little boy looks up at me and smiles every few moments. His eyes are bright blue, and remind me of something I can't put my finger on.

After the show ends, I feel a presence behind me. A set of hands grab onto the handles of my wheelchair and roll me over to the medication counter. The Orderly collects my medication and rolls me over to the door leading out into the Garden. When we arrive, I open my mouth to take the first pill.

The man chuckles before tossing a cup full of white and yellow pills into the frog pond. Something in the man's eyes are familiar.

"What do you say kid... Should we get out of here?"

My mind races to try and recognize the bearded man now pushing my wheelchair towards the parking lot. When we roll off the sidewalk and begin racing through the lawn, I see the two men in black I saw before chasing after us.

"Bernie! His name is Bernie!"

The two men in black suits chasing us both carry a pistol in hand. Bernie isn't nearly fast enough and the men begin shouting for him to 'freeze.' Each man points his pistol at Bernie. We stop rolling forward before Bernie stands in front of my chair with his hands in the air. The situation seems dire, but a very distinct wink from the man standing in front of me sets my mind at ease. *He has a plan!*

The two men are speaking to someone on the other end of their ear devices as they circle to stand in front of me. Out of the corner of my eye I see a green bush begin to rustle. Two shots ring out from the direction of the movement. Each of the armed men falls to the ground before bursting into clouds of black dust.

A boy about my age begins running in our direction with a

smile on his face and a shotgun in his hand.

"What are we waiting for Bernie? Burt is waiting in the car! Let's get going!"

Bernie pushes me as fast as he can towards the parking lot while Kevin runs beside me pointing his shotgun in every direction he see's movement.

Two more men in black try to stop us. They stand and point their pistols directly at Kevin and Bernie.

"That's as far as you get!"

Kevin lowers his shotgun and begins to get down on his knees to signal his surrender. A loud squealing sound rings out. Both approaching men are crushed underneath the nose of a speeding black sedan. The car comes to a stop overtop a cloud of black soot.

"Get in!"

I recognize Burt's nervous face immediately. He keeps looking behind the car as Bernie and Kevin load me into the back seat. We speed away from the parking lot with a nervous sense of relief.

Before we get too far, Burt seems to recognize that we have a tail. Two Black SUV's gain ground while speeding up behind us. We swerve back and forth through traffic trying to outmaneuver the people following us.

A radio in the front seat squeaks before Kevin responds to the message.

"We are moving now! Two minutes out, and we are not alone! Two black SUV's are chasing us!"

I can't make out the exact words that come back over the radio, but as we drive under an overpass, I notice a rusty white van parked overhead. Kevin also identifies the van and points up to alert Burt to the development. Beside the van two men are pointing rocket launchers directly at us. Two lines of smoke shoot out from the top of the overpass. Each missile streaks past the black sedan and hits one of the trailing black SUV's.

"Nice shot guys!"

The excitement in Kevin's voice is impossible to miss. I try to speak before remembering that I can't. But there is a weird tingling feeling developing in my throat. I gurgle out the closest thing to speech I can muster.

Kevin turns around from the front seat and looks at me.

"Take it easy dude... Those Dickheads have been dosing you with a paralytic drug so that you can't speak. Give it a couple more hours and you're gonna feel like your old self again! Once all the drugs are flushed out of your system, you're gonna feel so much better!"

We drive down a highway flanked on all sides by random travelers just trying to get to and from wherever they are going. I'm almost jealous at the simplicity of their lives. At that exact moment, a revelation of thought and hope fill my mind.

"I'm not CRAZY! The Dream World is real!"

Stay tuned for the followup book- Lucid, Flat tires and big fires... comming soon. You can follow my Author page and get automatic updates sent to you when each of the books in the series releases.

Made in the USA
Middletown, DE
29 July 2024